·GLINT·

ANN COBURN

An Imprint of HarperCollins*Publishers*

Eos is an imprint of HarperCollins Publishers.

Glint
Copyright © 2005 by Ann Coburn
For information address HarperCollins Children's Books,
a division of HarperCollins Publishers,
1350 Avenue of the Americas, New York, NY 10019.
www.harpercollinschildrens.com
Library of Congress Cataloging-in-Publication Data is available.
ISBN-10: 0-06-084723-9 (trade bdg.)
ISBN-13: 978-0-06-084723-4 (trade bdg.)
ISBN-10: 0-06-084724-7 (lib. bdg.)
ISBN-13: 978-0-06-084724-1 (lib. bdg.)
Typography by Christopher Stengel
1 2 3 4 5 6 7 8 9 10
❖
First U.S. Edition, HarperCollins Publishers, 2007

Originally published in 2005 in Great Britain by Red Fox,
an imprint of Random House Children's Books

For my sisters, Hazel and Heather,
and my brothers, Trevor and Mike,
who listened to my stories

ACKNOWLEDGMENTS

Glint came out of a yearlong writing residency, based in my hometown of Berwick-upon-Tweed. My thanks go to Seven Stories, the Newcastle-based center for children's books, for organizing the residency with such dedicated enthusiasm.

Thanks also to the staff and students of Berwick and Tweedmouth Middle Schools, particularly the talented young writers who shared with me the names of their favorite meeting places. These place names appear throughout *Glint*, transformed into locations in Argent's world.

The students, in alphabetical order, were:

From Berwick Middle School: Roan Forrester, Lillie Fraser, Sarah Henderson, Scott Jeffrey, Stuart Laverty, Inga McDougall, George Reavley, Greig Sharp, Lydia Smith, Scott Taylor, Devon Vogel, Sean Wales.

From Tweedmouth Middle School: Ryan Barrack, Melissa Bloomfield, Rianne Bruce, Gemma Chalmers, Kyle Dickson, Cheryl Dixon, Danny Easton, Martin Goodlet, Alex Hume, Graeme Steele, Karl Strachan, James Virtue.

Thanks also to teachers Susan Straughan and Dougal Moir for their help in organizing the writing workshops.

Finally, my grateful thanks go to New Writing North and Arts Council, England, for their financial support during the writing of *Glint*.

CONTENTS

THE MAKING OF MAPS

To pierce the skin, they used a sliver of broken glass. It was shaped like a dagger and came to a needle-sharp point. Danny had pulled it from the slew of loose stones and pebbles at the cave mouth. He had folded an empty crisp packet around the widest part of the sliver so that he could grip it without the sharp edge slicing into his palm. Ellie swallowed nervously as she studied the makeshift tool resting in her brother's hand. He had used it on himself first. Now it was her turn.

"Ready?" asked Danny.

Ellie nodded.

"Give me your foot, then." He held out his other hand, palm upward, creating a cup for her heel to rest in.

Ellie hesitated. "Umm . . ." They were sitting cross-legged on the rough ground outside the cave entrance, facing each other knee to knee. They were both barefoot. Their summer sandals rested in the pebbly dirt beside them. Ellie glanced at Danny's heel and saw the glistening trails of blood there. She swallowed, turned her head away, and looked down at her own foot instead. The hollow place beneath her anklebone was smooth and unbroken. She thought of the dagger point puncturing the soft skin and a shudder ran all the way from the base of her spine to the top of her skull. Quickly she disguised the shudder with one of her habitual head flicks. Her long, dark hair lifted from her shoulders, swinging back to form one shining length that fell nearly to her waist.

"Does it hurt?" she asked casually, tucking a few stray hairs behind her ears.

Danny looked at her with his clear gray eyes full of a weary patience. "Ye-es," he said.

Ellie had to smile in spite of her nerves. Danny was only six years old to her ten, but he was the boss. As far as Ellie could remember, he had been born that way.

"Ready?" repeated Danny.

Ellie stopped smiling and bit her lip as she returned to studying the glass dagger. Danny had washed it clean with water from his bottle, and the sliver gleamed brightly in his hand. She grimaced in an agony of indecision. "Umm . . ."

She turned to look down at the housing on the lower slopes of the hillside. Their new house was on the outer edge of the development, in a raw-edged road that still had a building site at the end of it. Ellie counted along the rooftops until she reached the house where her mum and dad were trying to hack a garden out of the compacted square of earth the builders had left behind. *Mum's going to kill me,* she thought, gazing down at the little house. *I'm supposed to be the one in charge.*

"Ell-iiee!" said Danny, out of patience now.

Ellie jumped and swung back to face him again. She took a deep breath, uncrossed her legs, and stuck out her bare foot.

"Go on, then."

Danny gripped her heel and turned it so that her foot was resting in his lap with the inside of her ankle facing upward. He balanced the glass sliver on his thigh next to her foot and picked up a broken pen that was leaning against a large stone. Black ink dripped from the pen when he tilted it over her foot, pooling in the hollow below her anklebone. Danny discarded the pen, picked up the sliver of glass, and brought the pointed end into position.

Suddenly Ellie could not bear to look. Instead, she stared intently at her brother's face, taking in every detail. The top layer of his thick, fair hair had been bleached nearly white by the sun but, underneath, it was dark with sweat. His eyebrows were drawn together in a slight frown of concentration. The tanned skin covering his broad cheekbones was speckled with freckles, and there was a smudge of dirt across the bridge of his nose. As he leaned over her foot, his lips parted and the tip of his tongue poked through the gap where one of his first teeth had come out.

Argent wouldn't flinch, thought Ellie wildly as a panicky pulse began to flutter at the base of her throat. *Argent would be brave. She wouldn't make a sound. . . .*

The first jab burned into her ankle. "Oww! O-o-www!" she cried, but Danny did not stop.

"I'll be quick," he murmured, punching through her skin again and again and creating a spiral of fiery pinpoints. "Hold on."

Ellie clenched her fists and held on. She held on for the sake of the extraordinary summer they had just spent together; a summer that had begun with a move to a new part of the country at the start of the school holidays. While their parents had sorted out the house and settled into their new jobs, she and Danny had spent the long, hot days exploring the town, the wild coastline, and the sheltering hills. At first they had felt lost and unreal in their strange new surroundings. They had no history there, and the place felt as hollow to them as a film set; a facade with nothing behind it. So they had created a history of their own. They had acted out the story of a girl called Argent, who loved to visit the dragon cave on the hillside above her village. The story had grown stronger with each passing day until, finally, Argent and her village felt as real to them as the modern town where they lived—and an alternative landscape lay just under the surface of the hills like a tattoo under the skin.

"All done," said Danny, dropping the shard. He unscrewed the top of his water bottle and dribbled cold water over Ellie's ankle. Black streaks of ink and red streaks of blood were washed away in the flow. Danny grabbed a handful of the front of his T-shirt and wiped her foot dry.

"There," he said, leaning back to study his handiwork.

Ellie stared at her foot. A tiny black spiral tattoo now nestled below her anklebone. Danny slid his foot forward to rest against hers. He had an identical tattoo on his ankle.

Ellie peered down at the paired tattoos. The pattern reminded her of the spiraling descent of the dragons in Argent's world, when they had to leave their home high above the clouds to come down to earth. "What are they?"

Danny frowned at the tattoos. "Not sure. I think—maps."

"Maps?"

"Sort of," said Danny. "So we remember."

Ellie looked at him. "So we remember what?"

Danny lifted his head. His gray eyes were flat and unfocused. Ellie felt a chill climb her spine. "Danny? So we remember what? Where we've been?"

"No," said Danny, his voice strangely off-key. "So we remember where we have to go."

Ellie sat up straight and stared at her brother with wide eyes. "Stop it. You're scaring me."

Danny blinked. When he looked at her again, his gray eyes were clear. He pulled his eyebrows down into a puzzled frown. "What?"

"You were . . ."

"What?"

"Danny, you were talking funny."

"Was not!"

"You were."

"Well, you look funny," retorted Danny.

"Do not."

Danny picked up his bottle of water and poured it over her head. "Do now."

"Oh! You!" gasped Ellie, yanking her cold, wet T-shirt away from her back.

Danny jumped up and ran, leaving his high laugh floating in the air behind him. Ellie struggled to her feet and cleared the water from her eyes. Danny was already halfway down the hillside, leaping barefoot over the tufty grass with his sandals clutched in his hand. Ellie set off in pursuit and, by the time she caught up with him at the bottom of the hill, they had both forgotten the strange incident outside the dragon cave.

Once they were back home, they had to endure their mother's fury over the tattoos and take a painful and humiliating trip to the emergency room for anti-tetanus jabs. The sting of the jabs subsided more quickly than their mother's anger, but even she finally forgot about the little tattoos and then. . . . Well, then the garden grew over the raw clay and they both settled into the town, starting school and finding friends. Life moved on, and the years went by. *So we remember*, Danny had said, but little by little he and Ellie both forgot everything about that summer. They had no need to remember.

Until five years later, when Danny reached his eleventh birthday.

· ONE ·

MISSING

The birthday cake was a rectangular slab, encased in white icing. It was so big it took up half the kitchen bench. Ellie leaned against the fridge, looked down at the cake, and frowned. There was something about the shape and color of the slab that made the skin of her arms roughen into goose bumps. It reminded her of something else. Something disturbing . . .

Ellie straightened up, rubbed the goose bumps away, and made herself concentrate on the immediate problem. What to do with the cake? To make it fit into any of their storage tins, she would have to cut it into quarters and, somehow, that felt wrong. Danny was the only one who should be cutting this cake.

Ellie reached out and gently traced her finger over the words that were piped across the top of the cake in blue icing: "Happy Eleventh Birthday, Danny!" Arranged below the slightly wobbly writing were a miniature chocolate fishing rod and a marzipan trout that bore a more than passing resemblance to a large, brown, speckled slug. Ellie smiled and felt the breath catch in her throat both at the same time. Less than twenty-four hours earlier, she had been trying to mold that same lump of marzipan into a lithe, fishlike shape when Danny had burst into the kitchen.

"Whoa! Slug alert!" he had yelled. "Big slug! On my cake!"

"It's not a slug, stupid. It's a fish."

"Really?" Danny had hitched his new fishing tackle higher onto his shoulder and opened the back door. "Must be a new species. Or a mutation."

"Go away. Go—fish."

" 'Scientists admitted today that they were baffled by the horrific slug creature found on Danny Brody's birthday cake—' "

She had picked up a wooden spoon and sent it flying across the kitchen, but Danny had dodged behind the back door.

"Missed," he had crowed, sticking his head back into the kitchen to grin at her.

"I hope you drown!" she had yelled, and Danny's high laugh had been cut in half as the back door closed behind him. That was the last time she had seen him. Her brother had gone fishing on the morning of his eleventh birthday and he had not come home again. Now, a day and a night later, Danny was officially missing.

Ellie felt her eyes sting with tears as she stared down at the cake. *I hope you drown!* Those were the last words she had said to him. "I didn't mean it, Danny," she whispered. "I didn't mean—" The words choked in her throat and her eyes widened with horror as she suddenly realized what the cake reminded her of. The white slab with "Danny" written across the top looked horribly like a marble tombstone.

"No!" The word came out in a fierce hiss. "He's not dead!" Blinking away tears, she opened a drawer and yanked out a clean tablecloth. She threw the cloth over the cake and turned her back on it.

Picking up a plate of toast and honey, she left the kitchen and walked down the hallway, passing the closed door to the living room where her dad was talking to two police officers. She climbed the stairs and edged into Danny's room, stepping over the mushroom piles of clothes that were growing all over the carpet. Mrs. Brody was sitting on Danny's unmade bed, clutching his pillow to her face.

"Mum. . . ? I've brought you something to eat."

Mrs. Brody nodded.

"And I've cleared all the party stuff away. I

threw out the sandwiches. Everything else is in the fridge. Except the cake."

Mrs. Brody nodded again, then, with her face still buried in Danny's pillow, she took a deep, shuddering breath and wailed until her lungs were empty.

Watching her mother slump down onto Danny's bed, Ellie felt a lonely terror prickle up her spine. Danny was missing. Really missing. This was the sort of nightmare that only happened to other families. She looked around Danny's bedroom. A bowl of soggy cereal was sitting on his desk, and his Xbox game had been left on pause. She turned to the door, half expecting him to come hurtling in, grab the handset, and continue his game. The doorway was empty. Suddenly desperate for something to do, Ellie put the plate of toast on Danny's desk and bent to pick up his clothes.

"Leave them!"

Ellie jumped. Her mother was glaring at her from red-rimmed eyes.

"Sorry." She dropped the clothes, and her mother slumped back onto the pillow. Ellie stood for a few seconds, at a loss. It was as though two members of her family had gone missing. First Danny had disappeared and then, overnight, her mother had been replaced with this strange, wild woman who howled and snapped and refused to come out of the den she had made.

Downstairs, the front door slammed. For one second, two, there was silence, and Ellie held her breath. When quick, light footsteps started up the stairs toward them, she and her mother both turned to the doorway with identical expressions of hope.

"Danny?" called Mrs. Brody, hastily putting the pillow back in its place and smoothing out the creases. "Is that you?"

"Only me. Sorry." Lisa appeared in the bedroom doorway, smiling sympathetically. Ellie tried to return the smile but only managed a disappointed grimace. Mrs. Brody groaned and hid her face in the pillow again. Lisa did not seem to mind at all. Ellie supposed that she must have learned to cope with all kinds of behavior in her job.

Lisa was one of the two police officers who had been talking to Mr. Brody downstairs. She specialized in family liaison work and she did not wear a uniform. Instead, she was dressed in creamy linen trousers and a pink, fluffy sweater. Her hair was soft and fluffy too. She was slim and pretty, with a smooth, round face and big blue eyes. When Ellie had answered the door to her earlier that morning, she had presumed the well-groomed blonde standing on the doorstep was there to sell cosmetics, but to her surprise Lisa had produced a police ID card and stepped across the threshold with a sympathetic smile.

Lisa and her sympathetic smile had been there

ever since, making pots of strong tea and giving regular updates on the police search. Before her arrival, Mrs. Brody had been almost demented, but she was much calmer now, and had already come to rely on Lisa's reassuring presence. Ellie had to admit that the liaison officer was good at her job, but there was something about that Mary Poppins smile that was beginning to grate on her.

"I heard the front door slam," said Ellie. "Who came in?"

"No one came in," Lisa replied. "That was your dad going out."

Ellie frowned. Her dad never left the house without shouting a good-bye, even when he was only nipping down to the postbox at the end of the road. All through the desperate hours of the previous night, when he had lurched between sitting statuelike in his chair and rushing out to search the dark streets again, he had always let them know when he was leaving the house. Why not this time?

"Was he upset?" she asked.

Lisa turned to look at Ellie, and suddenly there was nothing soft and fluffy about her at all. "Upset?" she asked, her eyes as sharp as tacks.

"You know. After the interview . . ."

"Why would your dad be upset about having a chat with us, Ellie? He wants to help us find Danny, doesn't he?"

"'Course he does," mumbled Ellie. Lisa's piercing gaze was making her uncomfortable. She found herself looking down at her feet, even though she had nothing to feel guilty about. With an effort, she raised her head again. Lisa was still staring at her, waiting for her to say something else. Ellie kept her mouth shut for five long, silent seconds before the soft, fluffy version of Lisa appeared again.

"I'm sure you're right, Ellie," she said, smiling sweetly. "My colleague Sergeant Donaldson would like to talk to you now. If you're feeling up to it, of course."

"Of course," said Ellie.

"Don't worry," said Lisa, turning to Mrs. Brody and giving her a mother-to-mother sort of look. "I'll sit in with her—make sure she's all right."

Ellie wondered whether Lisa actually had any children of her own.

Mrs. Brody nodded dully. "Thank you."

Lisa smiled and headed downstairs again, but Ellie hesitated in the doorway.

"Mum?"

With a great effort, Mrs. Brody lowered the pillow and gave Ellie a wobbly smile that nearly broke her heart. In two strides she was at the bed and hugging her mother close. Under the sour, metallic, wild-woman smell of stale sweat and fear, the familiar mother scent was still there. Ellie took a deep breath, then pulled away as tears threatened to overwhelm her.

"Drink that tea while it's hot," she ordered, backing out of Danny's room. She blundered downstairs and stumbled into the living room after Lisa. Still blinded by tears, she made her way over to the sofa and sank into the saggy cushions. Lisa sat down beside her and Ellie realized that, despite her earlier irritation, she was grateful to have her there. At least she knew Lisa a little. She had been in the kitchen when Sergeant Donaldson arrived, and all she had seen of him was a dark silhouette through the frosted glass of the front door and then a glimpse of a broad, uniformed back as her dad had shown him into the living room.

Sergeant Donaldson had not spoken, but Ellie knew he was somewhere in the room with her now. She could smell boot polish and an unfamiliar after-shave. She swallowed, suddenly nervous, and clasped her hands together to stop them from trembling. The armchair in the bay window creaked as someone levered themselves out of it. Ellie looked up, but her eyes were still blurred by tears and, as Sergeant Donaldson moved across the carpet toward her with a heavy tread, all she could see was a dark shape large enough to block out most of the light from the window.

"Here," said a deep voice with a strong Borders accent.

Something white floated in front of her face. It was a tissue. Ellie took it gratefully, and Sergeant

Donaldson waited while she wiped the tears from her eyes and blew her nose. When she raised her head again, her vision was clear, and she got her first good look at him. He was tall, with a square, open face and thick, dark hair. Ellie guessed him to be in his mid-thirties. He was carrying a bit too much weight, but there was plenty of solid muscle, too—enough to make the Saturday night drinkers think twice about causing any trouble. In contrast to Lisa's perma-smile, his expression was stern as he studied her, but his brown eyes were surprisingly gentle.

"All right?" he asked. "Just let me know when you're ready to start."

Ellie nodded, and Sergeant Donaldson returned the nod before tramping back to his chair.

"Good girl," cooed Lisa, patting her knee. Ellie grimaced. She was fifteen and, after the last twenty-four hours, felt closer to ninety, yet Lisa was treating her like an eight-year-old. Ellie sat up as straight as she could on the saggy sofa and looked over at Sergeant Donaldson.

"I—I'm ready, Constable."

"You can call him David, if you like," said Lisa. "Then we're all on first-name terms."

Sergeant Donaldson shifted uncomfortably in his chair, and Ellie guessed that he would very much prefer it if she did not call him David. He cleared his throat and held up an official-looking form. "This is the standard next-of-kin question-naire we use in Missing Persons inquiries," he explained. "We try to go through it with all members of the immediate family, but . . ." He hesitated.

"But what?" asked Ellie.

"But some people find it quite—difficult."

"Why?"

"These questions are designed to help us build up a profile of the missing per— of Danny. Some of them are quite personal. If at any point you need to stop, just let us know and we'll have a break."

"And a nice cup of tea," added Lisa.

Ellie felt the bile rise in her throat at the thought of swallowing one more mouthful of Lisa's thick, brown tea, and suddenly all the hours of helpless waiting rose up inside her too, in a great surge of frustration. She wanted to scream at them to get on with it. Danny was out there somewhere and they were all sitting around, drinking tea and doing absolutely nothing. She wanted to, but she didn't. Instead, she kept her head down and gave her usual timid performance.

"Please . . . Please just . . . I'll be all right."

Sergeant Donaldson nodded and got straight into it. "Tell us about the last time you saw Danny."

"Yesterday morning, just after nine. He was going fishing, and he came through the kitchen on his way out."

"What was he wearing?"

"Jeans. A white T-shirt. And a green padded jacket—the sort with loads of pockets and stuff. He was carrying his new fishing gear and a pair of waders, but he was wearing trainers for the walk down to the river."

"What brand?"

"Um, Nike, I think."

"You think?"

"I'm sure. Nike."

"And the style?"

"Style?" Ellie screwed up her face as she tried to remember. "Is it important?"

"If we know the brand and style, we can identify the sole print. It might help in the riverbank search."

Ellie thought hard but eventually had to shake her head. "Sorry. I don't know."

"No problem. How was Danny?"

"How was he?" Ellie remembered his high laugh, cut off when the back door closed behind him. "Happy. He was happy. He loves fishing. And he was looking forward to his birthday evening."

"So you had no reason to think he wouldn't come home?"

"No. Six of his friends were coming round to tea and they were all going out to a movie afterward."

"Did all his friends arrive?"

"Yes. Everyone. Except Danny."

Ellie looked over at the stack of brightly wrapped presents in the corner, remembering how the six boys had sat waiting for Danny. The day had darkened and the streetlight outside the house had flickered on, but still Danny had not come home, and the tension had grown as the minutes ticked by. Finally the boys had looked at one another and then risen to their feet together, muttering apologies. They had headed for the front door in silence, despite Mrs. Brody's shrill offers of sandwiches and promises that Danny would be along any minute.

"Does Danny have many friends?" asked Sergeant Donaldson, breaking into her thoughts.

"Loads," said Ellie. "You should try going into town with him. He knows everyone!" She smiled. Whenever she walked through the town center with Danny, it took twice as long as walking through on her own. He was on first-name terms with the most unlikely people. The last time they were in town together, Danny had stopped to chat with the local fishmonger, the street cleaners, and two American tourists he had never met before. He had even called out a greeting to the crazy old bag lady who spent her days pulling a cart around and around town on the same circular route.

"What about enemies?"

Ellie shook her head. "Everyone likes Danny."

"Would he tell you if he was being bullied?"

"I think so," said Ellie.

"Would you say you're close?"

"Close?" Ellie had girlfriends at school who hated their younger brothers. Sometimes she played along with their moaning, pretending she hated Danny, too, but the truth was, she loved him. She had loved him ever since she was first introduced to him, a tiny baby lying in a plastic crib next to her mother's hospital bed. She had taken one look and her love for him had uncurled in her chest and had been growing there ever since. Ellie swallowed hard, forcing back the sob that threatened to leap from her throat. "Yes," she said simply. "We're close."

"How did your last conversation go?"

Ellie blinked.

I hope you drown!

"Um . . ."

I hope—

"Ellie?" Sergeant Donaldson was watching her closely.

"Fine. It went fine."

—you drown!

"It . . . We . . . we were just, you know, joking about. He was laughing when he left the house."

Sergeant Donaldson watched her for a second or two, then looked down at his checklist and made a mark with his pen. "Moving on. Did Danny have any distinguishing marks?"

Ellie frowned. "Like what?"

"Birthmarks, for instance. Or moles. That sort of thing."

"No. He gets freckles in the summer. That's all."

"Or scars," suggested Sergeant Donaldson. "Has Danny had any operations? Any accidents?"

Ellie thought hard, picturing her brother and working her way down from his head to his feet. She could not think of a single scar. He had never had any operations, and the only injury she could remember was a cracked rib, sustained when he had cannoned into a tree on his sled two winters ago. It seemed that Danny had led a charmed life. Until now. "No," she said. "No scars."

Sergeant Donaldson made two more marks on his checklist. "I'm guessing no tattoos in Danny's case," he muttered, almost to himself. He was already making another mark on his checklist, when Ellie's sharp intake of breath made him look up again.

"But he does!" whispered Ellie, staring at Sergeant Donaldson, her eyes wide. "It was just over five years ago—I'd forgotten all about it!"

"Danny had a tattoo done when he was six years old?" asked Sergeant Donaldson, his eyebrows rising in disbelief.

"He did it himself," explained Ellie.

"Oh. I see. Can you describe it for me?"

Ellie bent, rolled up her trouser leg, and pulled

down her sock. There it was, the tiny black spiral tattoo, nestled below her anklebone. "It's just like this one," she said, sticking out her foot. "In the same place and everything."

As Sergeant Donaldson and Lisa both leaned forward to study the little tattoo, Ellie gazed over their bent heads, her eyes unfocused. Suddenly she was back on the hillside five years earlier, sitting at the entrance to the dragon cave, knee to knee with Danny. The fresh tattoo on her ankle had been stinging more than the worst nettle rash, but she had momentarily forgotten all about the pain because her brother had just said something in a strange, flat voice that had sent a chill climbing up her spine.

Ellie shivered on the sofa as she remembered that strange moment. What was it he had said? *The tattoos are maps of where we have to go.* That was it. Ellie frowned down at the little tattoo in the hollow of her ankle. How could that simple black spiral be a map?

·TWO·

DRAGON

Danny tried to open his eyes. A bright disk of light blazed into his face, and he squeezed them shut again. His head was spinning, and a deep, slow voice was booming in his ears. He tried to understand what the voice was saying, but the words all ran together like molasses. He was drifting away again when he felt a hand grab his jaw and then squeeze, so that his mouth popped open. His head was tilted back, and water gushed in over his tongue.

Danny gasped, choked, swallowed, and choked some more. His first thought was that he had fallen into the river and was drowning. He tried to move his arms and legs in a swimming action, but his trainers scrabbled uselessly on a rough surface and his hands were anchored together in his lap. Danny continued to struggle weakly for a time until his brain woke up enough to tell him it was pointless.

The water stopped pouring into his mouth, and the grip on his jaw was loosened. Danny choked and spluttered, trying to cough up the water that he had breathed into his lungs. Consciousness was flooding back now, and he tensed with fear as he realized that he was in a dark, cold place and his ankles and wrists were tied. He opened his eyes again and squinted at the bright disk of light. It was a flashlight beam. A dark shape crouched behind the beam and Danny peered at it, trying to make out what was there. At that instant the shape lunged forward and Danny winced as something sharp was rammed into the muscle of his thigh.

Danny tried to yell, but his voice was weak and hoarse. He thought he had been stabbed. Seconds later a strange warmth spread through his body and his head seemed to swell until it felt as light as a balloon. *Syringe*, thought Danny, as the flashlight beam turned into a tunnel of light. *It was a syringe.* For a second he was very afraid, but then he spiraled into the tunnel of light and, suddenly, he wasn't frightened anymore. A story was about to unfold, and he had to make sure it was properly told. His life depended on it. Danny took a deep breath and began. Once upon a time . . .

——————

. . . A dragon's egg rolled from the dark cave and into the sunshine. It came to a stop in the center of a scorched circle of bare earth in front of the cave, where it rocked back and forth for a few seconds before settling into the dirt. It looked wrinkled and dull, just like a giant-sized version of the old, cracked pig bladder the village boys liked to kick around for sport, but Argent gazed at it intently, with her dark eyes full of anticipation.

Glint.

Suddenly one final pulse of golden light came from the center of the egg and, just for an instant, the leathery shell was transformed into glowing amber. Argent grinned, flipped over onto her back in the undergrowth, and stared up through the branches of the bush that sheltered her. She scanned the sky, looking for an answering flash of light.

Glint.

There it was! A tiny glint of gold, high above the earth. As Argent watched, the glint began to spiral lazily downward and a strange, wild call, like the rush of wind in a chimney, came winging down with it.

Argent hugged herself with excitement and flipped back onto her belly to watch the egg. As she twisted, her foot caught in the hem of her skirts and there was an ominous ripping sound. Argent groaned, imagining what her mother would have to say about the torn skirt. Then she shrugged. What was one more thunderclap in the storm of trouble that was already waiting for her at home?

Argent sighed as she looked down at the little girl lying beside her. Morgana was the daughter of the village cowherd, and Argent had been given the chore of minding her while the cowherd's wife gave birth to her sixth baby. She and Morgana were supposed to have gone blackberry picking but, instead, Argent had dragged the little girl up the hill with her to try to catch another sort of birth. Autumn was the hatching season for dragons and, each year, Argent always tried to watch at least one baby emerge from the egg. This year she had not seen a single hatching, although she had been slipping away from her chores whenever she could in the hope of being outside the cave at the right time. Now, finally, she had struck lucky, but Morgana was being a problem. They had been lying in the under-growth at the edge of the scorched patch of earth for most of the morning, and the little girl's patience had worn thin.

"Nowt's happening," she whined, fidgeting in the long grass beside Argent.

"Wait just a little longer," whispered Argent. "It will."

They both stared at the egg in silence for a while.

"Nowt's happening!" insisted Morgana.

"Be quiet!" hissed Argent, narrowing her eyes and glaring at the little girl. With her sleek, black hair and her face as thin and pale as a nail clipping, Argent could look very menacing when she wanted to. Morgana's lip began to tremble.

"Want to go home," she quavered.

"No you don't," whispered Argent hastily. "You just watch. That baby dragon is fighting to get out of the egg. Come on, little one!"

As though in response to her call, the egg gave a quiver, then a jump. A small tear appeared in the leathery skin, and a feeble wisp of smoke twisted out.

"See?" breathed Argent. Morgana's lip stopped quivering, and she gazed at the egg. Argent whispered on, using her voice to weave a spell and keep the little girl interested. "That tiny dragon is going through one of the most dangerous times of his life."

"Why?"

"Well, dragons live high in the sky—"

"I know that!"

"Clever girl. Do you know why?"

Morgana shook her head.

"They feed off the sun."

"I thought they fed off our cattle?"

Argent tutted impatiently. "'Course they don't! Even if they wanted to, they couldn't get down as far as our lower pastures. And I don't think they eat cattle anyway. That's just an old wives' tale."

"But Old Crocus went missing down by the bog—"

"Because she fell in! She's at the bottom of the bog, not in a dragon's belly!"

Morgana's lip began to quiver again. Old Crocus had been her favorite cow. Hastily, Argent moved on. "Dragons don't even have bellies. At least, I don't think they do. I think they use their wings to feed. They spread them out, thin as gossamer, and the wings soak up the sunshine."

"Don't they get all hot and tired, being so high?" asked Morgana.

"Oh, they like being hot. And it doesn't tire them. They're as light as anything. They're built to float on air, see? They find it hard to come down to earth. It must be like us trying to swim down to the bottom of the ocean. That's why they only come down to lay their eggs. In our cave," she added with a swelling of pride.

"Why?" asked Morgana.

"They have to anchor the eggs, see? Otherwise the eggs would float right up into the stars. This dragon's mother filled his egg full of energy from the sun for him to feed on. Then she came down to earth and lodged her egg safely inside the cave. The egg stays safe and warm because it can only float up as far as the roof of the cave, see?"

"Have you been in the cave?" asked Morgana,

looking up at Argent with wide eyes.

"Oh, yes." Argent nodded. "Once. It's very hot in there, because of the eggs, but I wrapped myself up in some wet sacking before I went in." She smiled, remembering the magical moment when she had squinted up through a gap in the sacking to see at least twenty eggs floating above her head like miniature suns. At the blazing center of each one, Argent had glimpsed the dark, shifting shadow of a baby dragon. She had peered into the glare for as long as she dared, watching the little creatures twist and coil inside the eggs. At that stage, there had been plenty of room for the baby dragons to move around. The eggs were so large that Tillie, her father's sheepdog, could have curled up comfortably inside any one of them.

Argent turned to look again at the dull, wrinkled egg lying on the ground outside the cave. The skin of the egg had shriveled as the growing dragon had absorbed the sun energy within, and now there was no room left to move at all. The sheltering egg had become a prison from which the baby had to break free.

"And is there a big pile of gold in the egg cave?" Morgana asked.

Argent gave a disdainful snort. "No! That's another old wives' tale. Dragons aren't interested in gold. What would they do with it? It's the eggs that glow, see? They glow with a golden light, but they're not gold."

"That one isn't glowing," said Morgana, pointing to the dull, leathery egg in front of the cave.

"Well, the sun energy in that egg is all used up now. That's why it fell to the floor of the cave and rolled out. The little dragon has to fight his way out of the shell before he grows too tired to get free."

"But once he's out, he'll be all right?" asked Morgana, watching the rip in the leathery surface of the skin grow larger.

"No, he has to spread out his wings and soak up some more energy from the sun before he can float up out of harm's way. Something could get him while he's on the ground. That's why his mother is coming down to help him on his way."

Morgana peered up into the sky. The glint of gold was larger now, but it was still very high. They watched the spiraling glimmer for a while.

"Why doesn't she come down faster?" asked Morgana.

"I told you. It's really hard for them to come down to earth. The lower they get, the more the air presses down on them. That's why they have to spiral down slowly, so they can adjust."

"Look!" yelled the little girl, pointing at the egg. A long, thin muzzle had appeared, poking out through the tear.

"Shhh!" hissed Argent. "You'll scare him." The muzzle jerked farther out of the shell and a golden eye appeared. The eye swiveled back and forth, checking for danger. Then, with a convulsive shudder, the whole head emerged and immediately swung toward the sun like a compass needle finding north. The baby dragon opened its jaws and sounded a high, birdlike call. Argent looked up as an answering call came from above. The glint in the sky was much lower now. She could see the shape of the mother dragon outlined against the sun. The great ribbed wings were stretched taut like the curved sails of some huge ship, and the sinuous tail acted like a rudder, guiding the dragon's flight.

"Here he comes!" whispered Argent, pointing to the egg, where two bony hooks had pushed out on either side of the head. She was so excited, she hardly noticed a furtive rustle in the undergrowth over to her right. They watched as the hooks tore through the skin of the egg, splitting it open. Then the baby dragon tumbled out in a wreath of smoke and lay panting on the stony ground. The rustling came again. Argent turned her head and saw a large bush near the cave mouth shiver as though an invisible wind had blown through it. She raised her head slightly to take a closer look, but collapsed to the ground again with a grunt of pain when Morgana dug an elbow into her side.

"What?" she hissed.

"I said, it ain't got no legs," said Morgana, staring at the golden, snakelike body of the dragon.

"How's it going to move?"

"Watch," whispered Argent.

Almost immediately two large, ribbed wings unfolded, one from each side of the dragon. Their combined span dwarfed the tiny body between them. The two hooks that had ripped through the skin of the egg were protruding from the first joint of each wing, and now the little dragon drove them into the ground, using them as anchors. The hooks held the wings steady at the best angle for the sun to reach every inch of their membranous surface and, within seconds, the little creature had absorbed enough energy to rise a full inch above the stony ground. The hooks continued to hold it in place, and the flattened paddle at the end of its tail spread out, making minute adjustments to keep the dragon on an even keel.

Argent shook her head in admiration. The little creature had only just hatched, and already it was ready to fly. The dragon tilted its narrow head and turned its golden eye to the sky. Argent glanced up too, then hastily scrambled into a crouch. "Come on," she whispered, tapping Morgana on the shoulder. "Time for us to leave."

"Why?" demanded Morgana. "I want to see it fly away."

At that instant the baby dragon opened its jaws and sent out another high call. The answering shriek from the mother dragon was loud enough to make Morgana flinch and stuff her fingers into her ears. Argent hauled the little girl to her feet and hurried her away down the hillside. As they ran, a huge, dark shape raced across the grass toward them, plunging them into shadow for an instant before skimming away again. The shadow was cast by the mother dragon. She was circling directly overhead now, much closer to earth and getting lower with every turn. Soon she was close enough for Argent to hear the creak of her great wings as they cut through the air.

Morgana began to whimper with fear as they headed for the shelter of a small copse of trees. "Is it going to eat us?"

"I told you! Dragons don't feed on meat!" snapped Argent. "Oh, what's the use!" She had explained this to others in the village many times, but they kept on blaming the dragons for every missing sheep or cow. Superstition was a powerful force. She sighed and squeezed Morgana's hand. "It's all right," she soothed. "If we don't bother her, she won't bother us. I promise."

But then something dreadful happened. Just as the mother dragon reached the outer edge of her spiraling flight path, the baby dragon let out a piping scream that was abruptly cut off. Instantly the mother banked and dived toward the cave. Argent bundled Morgana into the trees and turned in time to see the dragon hit the ground. A plume of dust and smoke rose into the air and the dragon rose with it, turning her narrow head this way and that as she scanned the hillside.

Argent ran back up the slope, dodging from bush to bush all the way. The mother dragon was swooping overhead and letting out screams of rage, but Argent had to see whether she could do anything to help the baby. She reached the scorched ground outside the cave, but the little dragon was nowhere to be seen. Argent remembered the rustling she had heard from the bush beside the cave mouth. She hurried across the patch of bare earth, picking up the discarded egg casing as she passed, as though she might find the baby dragon hiding underneath. When she reached the bush, Argent bent to peer under the lowest branches. There was a man-sized patch of flattened grass. Argent laid her hand on the grass and scowled as she felt the faintest warmth. Someone had been lying in wait, intending to steal the baby dragon. She and Morgana must have been an unforeseen complication but, once they had left the scene, the thief had taken his chance.

Argent cursed and stood up, scanning the hillside. There were any number of bushes, shrubs, and trees the thief could be using for cover, and he probably had a horse waiting for him in one of the bigger copses. As Argent hesitated, wondering what to do next, the mother dragon slammed down onto the earth directly in front of her. Instantly Argent felt the skin on her face begin to tighten from the intense heat that radiated from the body of the huge beast. She flung an arm up in front of her face and stumbled backward. The dragon's wing hooks raked the earth perilously close to Argent's feet as it attempted to keep itself anchored to the ground, then it lunged for her, opening its jaws.

Argent screamed, turned, and threw herself down the slope. The jaws snapped shut inches from the back of her neck. A furnace blast of heat singed her jerkin and set her cap ribbons alight, then the dragon lost its hold on the earth and floated up into the sky, screaming with rage. Argent ran down the hillside with huge strides, desperately batting out the flames that were turning her cap ribbons to ash. She knew she had been very lucky to survive. The great beast had used a lot of energy in its slow descent to the earth, and the heat coming off it was not as fierce as it could have been. Even so, Argent was not keen on risking another encounter. If she could reach the cover of the trees where Morgana was hiding, she might be safe.

Above her, the dragon gathered its strength, folded its wings against its body, and went into another dive. Argent had no time to look up as the dragon arrowed toward her, but she knew it was coming: she could hear the air whistling past the plummeting body. With a sobbing gasp, Argent hitched up her skirts and careered down the slope at breakneck speed. She flung herself into the trees and slammed up against the trunk of a large oak a second before the dragon hit the ground outside the copse.

Argent grabbed Morgana's hand and dragged her into the center of the copse, away from the hair-crinkling heat that radiated from the dragon.

"I want to go home!" Morgana bawled.

"We will." Argent panted, looking over her shoulder. "We just have to wait until the dragon's gone. She thinks we have her baby."

"I want to go home!" howled Morgana, her face red and wet.

"Soon," soothed Argent. "She won't be able to stay down here long. She'll have to rise again soon."

"I want to go h-home!" cried Morgana for the third time, and Argent squashed down a surge of irritation with the little girl. She was understandably terrified. Argent reached out, intending to give Morgana a reassuring hug. The little girl shrank away from her, and Argent realized that she was still clutching the discarded skin of the dragon's egg in one hand. Quickly she rolled it up and stuffed it into her belt pouch, marveling at how the tough, thin skin could fold down into such a small parcel. As soon as the egg skin was out of sight, Morgana relaxed a little and allowed Argent to hug her close.

"Don't worry," Argent promised. "We're safe

here. She's too big to get through the trees." Argent coughed as a streamer of acrid woodsmoke curled around her head. She turned to see where the smoke was coming from and realized with a sinking heart that they were not at all safe. It was true that the dragon could not get into the heart of the copse, but the heat radiating from her body had set fire to all the outermost trees on that side of the slope. After a long, hot summer, the copse was bone dry, and fire was already jumping from tree to tree with frightening speed. The smoke thickened, and flakes of ash began to fall around them like gray snow.

"It's trying to burn us up!" wailed Morgana, the tears on her face turning to black streaks.

"She doesn't mean to," Argent said. "It's just that she's soaked up a lot of energy from the sun, so she's really hot. Come on." She took Morgana by the hand and hurried her to the other side of the copse, away from the worst of the heat. Cautiously she peered out through the trees, checking the lower slopes of the hill for the best escape route. There was very little cover. Most of the trees nearer the village had been felled over the years, and only a few bushes had escaped being chopped up for fire-wood. There were haystacks in the harvested fields at the base of the hill, but Argent quickly dismissed them. A pile of tinder-dry hay was not the best place to hide from a dragon.

"Want to go home." Morgana coughed, pointing to their village nestling at the foot of the hill.

"Me too," said Argent, staring down at the little cluster of cottages and barns surrounded by cultivated fields. If they could reach home, they would be safe. Their village was known as Haven's Edge because it sat just below the Boundary Cairn: a pile of stones that had been built on the hillside to mark the lowest point any dragon had ever managed to reach. Argent stared at the Boundary Cairn. Once they were beyond that pile of stones, they would be safe. The trouble was, there was a swathe of bare hillside between the copse and the cairn. That was a lot of distance to cover, especially with a little girl who was almost too frightened to run.

Argent looked back through the copse, wondering whether it might be better to stay hidden in the trees and hope that the dragon would be forced to rise before the fire reached them. Through the swirling smoke, she could see that the dragon was showing no sign of leaving. It had sunk its wing hooks deep into the ground at the far edge of the copse and was lashing its tail against the burning trees. As Argent watched, two of the trees suddenly toppled, sending gouts of flame blasting through the copse toward them.

Argent pushed Morgana to the ground and

flung herself across the little girl's sprawled body an instant before a fireball roared overhead and engulfed the tree trunk they had just been standing beside. It took only seconds for the fireball to burn itself out, but Argent winced when she saw the damage it had done to the tree. At head height, the trunk was charred and smoking. If she had remained standing, she would not have survived. Behind her another burning tree creaked ominously, and Argent realized that there was no option. They could not stay in the burning copse any longer. It was time to run for their lives.

She clambered to her feet, pulled Morgana up, and gripped her hand firmly. "Can you run for me, Morgana? As fast as you can?"

The little girl stared at the blackened tree with wide eyes and then nodded vigorously.

"Then let's go home."

Argent broke cover and ran hard, keeping as low to the ground as she could. Morgana bounced alongside, half running, half flying as her short legs struggled to keep up with Argent's long strides. Behind them, the dragon shrieked.

"Is it coming after us?" screamed Morgana, her voice shrill with panic.

"Keep running," panted Argent. All the skin on her back seemed to be trying to shrink upward and hide under her cap, but she resisted the desire to look behind her. She knew that even a glance over her shoulder would slow them down, and every second counted in this race.

They were on the gentler slopes at the base of the hill and had nearly reached the Boundary Cairn when another unearthly shriek echoed down the hillside.

"Don't look!" screamed Argent. "Keep running!"

But Morgana was too frightened not to look. She turned her head, lost her footing, and somersaulted down the slope before coming to a halt in a winded heap. Argent reached Morgana in ten strides and tried to set her on her feet again, but the terrified little girl could not, or would not, stand up. Frantically Argent scanned the hillside above them. The whole copse was in flames now. A thick smudge of black smoke rose into the blue sky and, rising with it, came the dragon. As Argent watched, the dragon angled its wings and allowed itself to soar up into the sky. Had it given up the struggle to stay so low, or was it simply gaining height before it turned in the air, folded its wings against its body, and prepared to dive deeper than any dragon had gone before?

Argent did not wait to find out. She hoisted Morgana under her arm and staggered down toward the Boundary Cairn. A few seconds later she had reached the pile of stones, but something kept her stumbling on down the slope and into the first of the cultivated fields that edged the village. No dragon had ever been lower than the Boundary Cairn, but this dragon was desperate, and Argent wanted to be sure they were safe.

The field had been harvested but not yet ploughed, and the rough stubble was difficult to walk across. Argent was near the end of her strength, and Morgana was a dead weight in her arms, but she kept putting one foot in front of the other. As she stumbled on, following the line of haystacks that ran across the middle of the field, Argent looked for help, but without much hope. Most of the men of the village, including her own father, had gone to the Corn Exchange in the nearby town of Scremerston to negotiate a price for their surplus grain. The women and older children would be busy in the threshing barns or grazing their cattle down by the river.

Argent had passed three of the haystacks and was beginning to think that they were safe when she heard an ominous whistling overhead. A second later the dragon came in low over the field, skimming the haystacks. Instantly all the haystacks behind Argent exploded into enormous torches of flame. With a sobbing gasp, she hoisted Morgana over her shoulder and tried to run, but the dragon swooped around in front of her and came in to land, causing three of the haystacks ahead of Argent to burst into flame too.

The dragon dug its wing hooks deep into the ground. The heat from its body ignited the stubble, and a widening circle of flame spread around it. Argent put Morgana down and moved in front of her, trying to protect her from the worst of the heat. They were surrounded with blazing haystacks and the stubble fire was closing in on them, but the worst blast of heat was coming from the dragon itself. Argent squinted through the wavering heat haze and saw that the dragon was suffering too. The great beast was struggling to stay earthbound at a depth far beyond its normal limits. Its huge wings were threatening to crumple under the pressure and the dragon was quivering with the effort of keeping them rigid, but still it clung to the earth and its golden eyes glared at her.

Argent felt a sudden surge of sympathy. The mother dragon wanted her baby. That was all. Argent took a step forward, spread her arms, and slowly turned around, showing the mother that she did not have the little dragon. For a few more seconds, the mother dragon clung to the earth, but then its wing hooks tore free of the ground and it soared up into the sky, shrieking as it went. Argent had no idea whether the dragon had understood what she had been trying to convey, or whether it had simply been unable to stay earthbound any longer. Whatever the reason, the result was the same: the dragon was gone and they were safe.

Weeping with relief, Argent took Morgana's hand and began to pick a path through the flames and smoke, heading for home.

· THREE ·

DOA

Ellie frowned as she stared at the little spiral tattoo on her ankle. What was that story she and Danny had spent the whole summer creating? Was it something about a girl named Silver? No. Her name meant silver. Argent. That was it. Her name was Argent, and she was the mirror image of Ellie: the same age, with the same dark hair and pale skin. But a mirror reverses as well as reflects an image and, in many ways, Argent was the opposite of Ellie. She was as outspoken as Ellie was quiet, as confident as Ellie was shy, and as headstrong as Ellie was indecisive. Ellie had loved playing the role of Argent, and she had loved Danny for letting her. Usually he was the lead in the games they had played when they were younger, but not that summer. Ellie tried to remember more about her mirror image, but only the name stayed, floating behind her eyes. *Argent . . .*

Ellie shook her head and forced herself to concentrate on what Sergeant Donaldson and Lisa were saying. They were still crouched together over her ankle, talking in low voices. She tuned in to the conversation and realized that they were discussing who should be informed about the tattoo on Danny's ankle.

"The divers, of course," said Sergeant Donaldson. "And all the land search teams."

"I'll put out the word to the hospitals," said Lisa. "Get them to check their unidentified DOAs for a spiral tattoo."

"DOAs?" asked Ellie. "What does that mean?"

Sergeant Donaldson and Lisa exchanged an uncomfortable glance.

"Just police talk." Lisa smiled, but Ellie had seen her share of police and hospital dramas on the television. Suddenly she realized she did not need an explanation. She knew what DOA meant. The initials stood for "dead on arrival."

"He's not dead!" She gasped, surging to her feet.

"Ellie," said Lisa. "We have to accept that it is a possibility—"

"No! He's not dead. If Danny was dead, I would know. I would know!"

"Okay, let's move on," said Sergeant Donaldson calmly.

Ellie looked from him to Lisa. DOA. Dead on arrival. The words were still sending surges of adrenalin through her body. She was breathing hard and shaking with a combination of fear and fury.

"Ellie?" Lisa patted the sofa cushion beside her. "Why don't you sit down?"

Ellie remained on her feet. She wanted to tell Lisa to get out of her house. Instead, she hung her head and muttered, "Just so long as you know . . ."

"Know what, Ellie?"

"Danny's not, you know . . . He isn't!"

Lisa shook her head and began to say something, but Sergeant Donaldson interrupted her. "We understand, Ellie. Now, shall we move on?"

Reluctantly Ellie sat down beside Lisa again.

"Can you tell us what happened after Danny's friends left last night?" asked Sergeant Donaldson. He spoke in the same carefully neutral tone he had used throughout the interview, but Ellie felt Lisa shift on the sofa beside her. She glanced sideways and saw that the family liaison officer had turned and was watching her with bright-eyed interest as though this was what she had been waiting for. The trailers were over, and the main feature was about to start. Ellie felt as though she was missing something, but she could not work out what it was. She shifted her gaze back to Sergeant Donaldson, but he only nodded encouragingly with that same unreadable expression on his face.

Ellie took a deep breath and started her account of the events of the previous evening. "After Danny's friends left, Mum tried his mobile again, but it was still turned off."

"Is that unusual?"

"Not when he's fishing. He says he doesn't want it to ring in case it scares the fish. Mum tells him to set it to silent mode, but he never does. I think he just doesn't want anything to disturb the bubble."

"The bubble?"

"I asked Danny once what the deal was with fishing. What was so good about standing around in the cold all day, waiting for a bite? He said it was like stepping inside a bubble and leaving the rest of the world on the outside."

"Sort of like meditation?" asked Sergeant Donaldson.

"Yeah. Sort of. Fishing is Danny's downtime."

"So. His mobile was still turned off. What next?"

"We phoned around, looking for Danny."

"Who did you call?" asked Sergeant Donaldson.

"Everyone we could think of," said Ellie. "But none of them had seen him."

"Can you give me their names?" Sergeant Donaldson persisted, flicking through the pages of his notebook until he came to a particular page. Ellie could just make out a handwritten list of names there. Sergeant Donaldson must have asked her dad the same question, and now he was checking her answers against his list.

Ellie reeled off the names of all Danny's school friends, ticking them off on her fingers as Sergeant Donaldson ticked them off on his list.

"Who else?"

"My boyfriend, Ross." As she said his name, Ellie caught her breath, suddenly longing to see him again, but she was not expecting him to show up before midday. She had texted him earlier that morning to say that there was no news and he should catch up on some sleep. The previous night, when she had called to ask whether he had seen Danny, he had insisted on coming over. He had stayed until three in the morning, sitting with her mum or going out with her dad to search the dark streets. Ellie was sure Ross would have stayed with them all night if her dad had not insisted on driving him home after he fell asleep over a cup of coffee.

"Ross Avery?" asked Sergeant Donaldson, looking down at his list.

"Yes."

Sergeant Donaldson put a tick against the list and then looked up at Ellie expectantly. She pushed Ross to the back of her mind and concentrated on remembering the rest of the names.

"Um, well. Then we called the Swan Rescue Center. Danny often helps out there. He feels he owes it to them, since a lot of the swans' injuries or problems are due to getting tangled in fishing line or swallowing fishing weights. Not that he ever leaves anything like that lying about on the river-bank. Danny's always very careful about—"

"Ellie."

Ellie looked up, and Sergeant Donaldson twisted his face into something between a smile and a grimace. She realized she had been gabbling and ducked her head in embarrassment.

"Who answered the phone at the Swan Rescue Center?"

"I don't know. I'm not even sure it was still open. Mum made that call."

Sergeant Donaldson and Lisa shared a look. Ellie knew what they were thinking. Her mother was in no state to be answering questions right now.

"They have a duty roster for all the volunteers," Ellie offered. "It would be easy to check."

"Thanks. That's a good idea." Sergeant Donaldson smiled as though he had not already thought of it himself.

"And then we phoned all of the regular fisher-men, the ones who know Danny. Some of them had been on the river yesterday, but none of them had seen Danny."

"And their names?"

Ellie sighed, and dutifully went through the names of all the fishermen they had called. Sergeant Donaldson checked his list one last time and then nodded in satisfaction and closed his notebook. "What happened next?"

"It was getting really dark by then. Dad said Danny had probably lost track of the time, and he would drive down to the river and fetch him back. Mum stayed at the house in case Danny came home or phoned to say where he was. I went with Dad—"

"Did he ask you to go?" asked Lisa, speaking for the first time in the interview.

"No." Ellie glanced at Lisa and then away again, unnerved by the sharp intensity of her gaze. "I—I said I would go with him. I wanted to get out of the house."

"Why?"

"Mum was sort of pretending everything was still all right, but she wasn't doing a very good job of it. She was making me nervous. I wasn't too sure about leaving her, but I knew she wouldn't be on her own for long. Ross was on his way over, and they get on together really well. I knew he'd look after her."

"And how was your dad acting?" asked Lisa.

"Worried. We drove down to the river, to the bridge by Chuggie's Pool—"

"How did your dad know where to go?" interrupted Lisa.

"He didn't. But he knows all of Danny's favorite places, and he took a guess at Chuggie's Pool. Dad parked the car by the bridge, and we walked along the footpath calling Danny's name." Ellie paused, remembering how their voices had sounded loud in the still night air, carrying across the water and sending a flurry of startled waterfowl flapping from the reed beds. "We called and called, but there was no answer. Then we reached Chuggie's Pool—and that's when we found . . ."

"Found what, Ellie?"

"All his stuff. But no Danny. He just—wasn't there."

Ellie covered her face with her hands, suddenly overcome as she remembered the fear that had flooded through them both when they saw Danny's brand-new fishing tackle, waders, and rucksack lined up neatly on the riverbank. It was top-of-the-line gear, the most expensive birthday present Danny had ever received. He would never wander off and leave it lying unattended.

"What did you do then?" asked Sergeant Donaldson. "Can you tell us?"

What had they done? They had both panicked. She had stood by Danny's abandoned fishing tackle, shaking uncontrollably, while her dad had blundered back and forth through the dark undergrowth at the side of the footpath, calling for his son in a hoarse, scared voice. When he had drawn a blank in the undergrowth, he had jumped into the river and floundered around in the shallows at the edge, trying to push the black water aside with his arms. Finally he had climbed out onto the bank with his hair plastered to his head and his clothes heavy with river water. Together they had gathered up Danny's fishing gear and stumbled back to the car, where she had left her mobile phone.

"We searched," whispered Ellie. "Then we called home, but he still wasn't there. So we called the police."

"Well done, Ellie," said Sergeant Donaldson quietly. "We'll take a break now."

He started to lever himself out of the chair, but Lisa had not finished. "Why did you move Danny's fishing gear?" she asked.

"Why? We didn't want to leave it there—"

"Did it not occur to your father that it would be best to leave the evidence at the scene?"

"'Scene'?" said Ellie, turning to look at Lisa. "What do you mean, 'scene'? Crime scene? Are you saying there's been a crime? Do you think someone attacked Danny?"

There was a short silence as the two police officers exchanged glances.

"Was Danny happy at home?" countered Lisa.

"Of course he was. Is! He is."

"Has your father ever hit you or Danny?"

Ellie felt the words jolt through her like an electric shock. "Oh! No. No, never. What are you trying to . . . Please, what are you saying?"

Sergeant Donaldson got to his feet. "All right. Let's just take a break here—"

"Who puts Danny to bed?" interrupted Lisa.

"No one puts him to bed," said Ellie. "He's eleven years old. He puts himself to bed."

"Used to, then. Who used to put Danny to bed? Your father?"

Ellie half stood up, then sat down again and looked at her hands. She flexed her fingers, imagining how it would feel to grip Lisa by the shoulders, haul her to her feet, and march her to the front door. She took a deep breath. "I'm not saying another word until you tell me . . . Please, can you tell me why you're asking these things?"

Lisa smiled at Ellie and patted her knee. "Police business. Don't worry about it. Now, shall we continue?" She looked up at Sergeant Donaldson pointedly, and he sighed and plodded back to his chair. Lisa returned her attention to Ellie. "What I can tell you is that my colleagues have examined the scene. There is no sign of a struggle, and the grass at the edge of the bank shows no sign of damage, such as might have occurred with a slip or accidental fall into the river."

"But that's good, isn't it?" asked Ellie, looking at Sergeant Donaldson.

"Also," continued Lisa. "You and your father both say that Danny's fishing gear was laid out neatly on the bank. Arranged rather than dropped."

"So?"

"So your brother could have tried to stage an accident to cover up the fact that he has run away from home."

"That's ridiculous! I—I mean, I don't think . . ."

"It's a likely scenario," said Lisa.

"Did Danny have any money with him when he left yesterday morning?" asked Sergeant Donaldson.

"I don't know. I wouldn't've thought so. He was carrying everything he needed with him. Sandwiches. A flask. And"—she added, turning to look at Lisa triumphantly—"it was all still there on the bank. So he can't have run away, otherwise he would have taken it with him."

"Not if he was trying to make it look as though he'd had an accident," said Lisa.

"Danny wouldn't do that," muttered Ellie, pushing down a rising feeling of panic.

"Another scenario we're looking at is that Danny could have jumped into the river deliberately."

Ellie swallowed down a hysterical giggle. This conversation was becoming more ridiculous by the second. "Um. Why would he do that?"

"That's what we're trying to find out," said Lisa.

"I think you mean . . . Do you mean suicide?" She glanced at Lisa then back down at her hands. "Um, Danny wouldn't . . . I don't think he would do that. He was happy. I mean is! He is happy. Besides—you've searched the house, and you didn't find a note, did you?"

"That's true." Sergeant Donaldson nodded. "I'm sure you're right, Ellie. Thank you. I think we've asked you enough questions for now." He looked at Lisa, and she nodded her agreement. Gratefully Ellie stood up and headed for the door, but stopped short as a thought hit her.

"Yes?" asked Lisa. "Was there something else?"

"Um. I just wanted to know . . . Can you tell me, did you ask my dad these questions? Did you ask him about hurting Danny and stuff?"

Again Lisa and Sergeant Donaldson exchanged glances. That was answer enough for Ellie. She turned and walked out of the room. No wonder her dad had rushed out of the house without saying good-bye! She hurried into the hallway and headed for the front door, shrugging on her jacket and shoving her bare feet into trainers on the way.

"Where are you going, Ellie?" asked Lisa from the living room doorway.

To find my dad and let him know I don't believe a single word that comes out of your stupid mouth, thought Ellie as she turned to look at Lisa. "Um, just for a walk. Is—is that all right?"

"Take your mobile and keep in touch. We don't want your mum worrying about you, too, do we now?"

"No." Ellie smiled at Lisa through gritted teeth as she picked up her mobile from the hall table and slipped it into her jacket pocket. "We don't."

She closed the front door gently behind her and made a face at the frosted glass before hurrying away down the garden path. The house did not feel like home anymore. Danny was not there and, in some weird and intrusive way, Lisa had taken over from her mother. Ellie glanced up at Danny's bedroom window as she closed the front gate. Her mother was standing there, and Ellie half raised a hand before she realized that Mrs. Brody was not looking at her, but staring off down the street. She was watching for Danny coming home.

Ellie felt stupid. She used her raised hand to tuck some stray strands of hair behind her ear instead and shifted her gaze away from Danny's window to the hillside behind the house.

Glint.

A tiny flash of gold caught her eye. Ellie blinked and scanned the hillside, trying to work out what she had seen.

Glint.

There it was again. Ellie marked the place. She was looking at a rock outcrop near the summit of the hill. There was a little cave in the outcrop that had been one of their favorite places to play five summers ago, but she and Danny had not been there for years.

Glint.

Ellie frowned. Something up there was catching the sun. She thought about climbing up to investigate, but rain clouds were drifting in over the shoulder of the hill like coils of black smoke. Ellie had no waterproof jacket and she really did not want to go back into the house to collect one if it meant facing Lisa again. She decided to stick to her original plan of walking down to the river to find her dad. The way to the river was through town, and there would be plenty of places to shelter if it began to rain. Ellie turned her back on the hill and set off down the street, heading for the river and Chuggie's Pool.

· FOUR ·

HAVEN'S EDGE

The door of the Dragonsbane Inn opened, and the mayor led the village elders into the square. They walked solemnly through the crowd, heading for the five chairs that had been set out for them in the shade of the chestnut tree. The people of Haven's Edge fell silent. It had been years since an emergency meeting of the elders had been called, and everyone was eager to hear what had been decided. Everyone except Argent. She was dreading it. She scrambled to her feet and made an attempt at brushing down her torn and blackened skirts as the elders approached.

"Step forward, girl!" ordered the mayor, lowering himself into the central chair and straightening his chain of office. Argent hurried to stand in front of the elders. She bowed her head and tried to look suitably respectful, but her face refused to cooperate. The elders might look impressive in their fur-lined robes, but Argent knew the people inside those robes, and there was not one she would give two pins for.

The mayor was Florian, the publican of the Dragonsbane Inn. He was a round, red-faced man with a self-important manner and a reputation for stinginess. The Dragonsbane Inn served watered-down ale and pies filled with gravy and gristle, but it was the only hostelry in the village, and so locals and travelers alike had to put up with Florian's mean ways.

On Florian's left sat Abel, a wasted stick of a man with a face like a funeral. He taught the village children their letters and was also the church choir-master. Somehow he managed to leach every scrap of joy out of both activities and Argent, who loved stories and singing, hated him for it.

Next to Abel was Marion, the wife of the wealthiest farmer in the district. She was a solid slab of a woman with an overshot lower jaw that made her look like a large pike. She was as sly as a pike, too, with the same ravenous appetite. She was brushing crumbs from the front of her robes as she settled into her chair, and her little eyes moved left and right, missing nothing.

On Florian's right, Will the pigman was trying to hide his mucky work boots under his robes. Will was not too bright. Argent suspected that some of his pigs had more brains than he did. His only role as an elder was to agree with everything Florian said.

Finally there was Margaret. Margaret liked to help. She had helped Jenny, the miller's daughter, by letting her know that her beloved Robert was seeing another girl. Margaret insisted it was hardly her fault that Jenny had subsequently been dragged from the millrace, barely alive. Margaret had also helped Ishmael out of his cottage and into the poorhouse, claiming that the old man could no longer fend for himself. When Ishmael did not survive a winter in the poorhouse, Margaret said that his death simply proved her point. Now Margaret's son and daughter-in-law were living in Ishmael's cottage.

"Order! Let's have some order!" called Florian unnecessarily, glaring around at the already silent villagers. "This is a black day for Haven's Edge. For the first time in living memory, a dragon has come below the Boundary Cairn."

"Black day. Aye," echoed Will, nodding his head vigorously.

"And you, my girl," barked Florian, focusing his glare on Argent. "You brought this trouble upon us."

Argent opened her mouth to protest, but then closed it again. She had promised her mother that she would stand quietly and take whatever punishment the elders meted out.

"Trade will suffer when this gets out," said Florian, casting a glance toward his inn. "Folk won't come near Haven's Edge for fear of a dragon attack."

"Not to mention half a dozen of my haystacks razed to the ground!" hissed Marion, whose field was still smoking several hours after the fires had burned out. "How will local folk feed their cattle this winter?"

"How?" said Argent, lifting her head. "They'll buy hay elsewhere for a lot less than you charge them. That's how."

Marion reeled back in her seat with a gasp of outrage, and a chuckle rippled through the crowd. Argent began to grin, but then caught her mother's warning glance and looked down at her feet again.

"Proof!" said Abel, pointing a skeletal finger at Argent. "Undeniable proof of what I was saying not twenty minutes ago! This girl is as wild as a fox. I blame the mother."

Argent's head snapped up again, this time to see what her mother thought of Abel's last remark. Her mother was glaring at Abel, and Argent could see that now she was the one struggling to stay silent.

"Of course, she was wild too," continued Abel, with a sly glance at Argent's mother. "When she was young."

"Still angry with me for slapping you down all

those years ago, Abel?"

Another chuckle rippled through the crowd, and Argent raised her singed eyebrows at her mother. So much for keeping quiet and letting the elders talk. Her mother gave her a shamefaced look and an embarrassed shrug.

"Order!" yelled Florian. "Argent, you are charged with bringing a dragon down upon us and putting young Morgana into danger."

Argent glanced over at Morgana and felt a spasm of guilt. She had tried her best to protect the little girl up on the hillside, but Morgana had caught a blast of heat from the dragon. One half of her face was as red as a boiled lobster, and the hair on that side had a shriveled, crispy look to it.

"The elders have decided that you must repay Morgana and her family for the trouble you have caused them. Every day for a month, you will take care of Morgana while her mother regains her strength."

"For a month. Aye," echoed Will faithfully.

"While you have Morgana in your care, you will keep to the village, the cattle meadows, and the cultivated fields. If you stray beyond these boundaries, you will be severely punished."

Argent looked from Morgana to the little girl's mother, who was sitting holding her new baby and drooping with exhaustion. She had to admit that the elders had come up with a fair ruling this time, even though she knew it would be a hard month for her. The mere thought of being confined to the village made her shoulder muscles tighten, and she had never been good with young children, but Morgana's mother really needed the help. Argent gritted her teeth, turned back to the elders, and nodded her agreement.

"And now to the second part of our decision," said Margaret, giving Argent a toothy smile. "Once the month is up, we have a much more pleasant task for you, one that I am sure will help you to find your place in our little community."

Argent froze, watching the elders warily. She had a feeling that she was not going to like Margaret's helpful idea.

"As you know, a girl does not usually become eligible to marry before she is sixteen but, in your case, we have decided to make an exception. Instead of waiting until next summer to become Thomas's wife, you will be allowed to marry at the end of the month!"

Argent cast a horrified glance over at Thomas. She had always accepted that she and Thomas would marry one day—their family fields bordered one another and their parents were good friends—but that day had always seemed a long way off. Now, all of a sudden, it was very close, and Argent felt despair flood through her at the thought of being tied to Thomas for the rest of her life. He was likeable enough, but he was also as dull as a puddle. Thomas was gazing at her with the same expression of horror on his face and Argent realized that she must look a sorry sight, standing in front of the elders in her ruined clothes. Her cap had protected her hair from the worst of the heat on the hillside, but the skin across her nose and cheekbones was tight and sore, and she guessed that her face must be as red as Morgana's.

Argent looked to her mother, hoping that she would disapprove of Margaret's interference in their family business, but her mother was nodding in reluctant agreement. Argent felt her heart sink. The trap was set, and there was nothing she could do about it. When Florian dismissed her, she trudged over to join her mother with a heavy step.

"And now to the problem of the dragon," said Florian.

The village square grew silent as everyone looked up into the sky. The mother dragon was still circling high above the hill, and her forlorn calls drifted down to them on the breeze.

"Abel?" continued Florian. "Would you like to tell the folk here what you told us?"

Abel cleared his throat and steepled his fingers. "I have some small knowledge of animal behavior," he said. "Enough to make me believe that this dragon is highly dangerous."

Argent had been slowly sinking into a pool of

her own misery, but she sat up sharply when she heard what Abel was saying.

"Let us dwell for a moment on the fox that takes a chicken from the coop. That fox learns that there is good eating to be had for little effort, and it will then return to the coop again and again. Until it is stopped."

The crowd murmured their agreement, and Abel warmed to his subject. "Or perhaps we should consider the wolves that roam in Unthank Forest. We know that once a wolf ventures from the forest to take a domestic animal such as a sheep or a calf, it will never again be satisfied with venison or hare. That wolf becomes a rogue hunter. Until it is stopped."

"Now just a minute," began Argent, seeing where Abel was going.

"In the same way," continued Abel, ignoring her interruption, "this dragon has discovered that it can fly as low as our upper pastures, maybe even lower. If we are to learn from the behavior of the fox and the wolf, then we must reluctantly conclude that, from this day forth, our cattle, our sheep, even our children will not be safe from that dragon. The beast must be stopped."

"No! You don't understand!" shouted Argent, desperately trying to make her voice heard over the growing rumble of agreement from the crowd. "She only came down below the Boundary Cairn because she thought I had taken her baby. I saw how hard it was for her to stoop so low. It nearly killed her. Now she knows her baby isn't here, she won't come this far down again. I'm sure of it."

Marion gave a disbelieving snort. "Tell that to my prize cattle. They're out in the far pasture right now!"

"She won't touch your cattle," Argent insisted. "Dragons don't eat cattle. They feed off the sun."

"Aye. And my pigs dine on ale and oysters every night." Will guffawed.

The crowd laughed with Will, and one or two shook their heads at Argent's silliness. Across the square, Thomas bowed his head and covered his eyes with his hand.

"Argent!" hissed her mother, behind her.

"Please listen!" continued Argent, ignoring her mother's warning. "I have studied the behavior of dragons, just as Abel has studied the behavior of other creatures. I'm sure dragons don't eat in the same way that we do. I—I have notes and drawings at home. Let me get them. Then I can explain all my ideas more clearly to you—"

"You? Explain to us?" sneered Abel. "Explain this, girl. If dragons are not interested in our livestock, then why is that murderous creature continuing to circle over our land?"

"I told you!" yelled Argent. "She's looking for her baby! Someone stole it—"

"Ah, the mystery dragon thief." Margaret smiled. "Why would anyone want to steal such a creature?"

"Because—well . . ." Argent stumbled to a halt. She had no answer.

"Order!" shouted Florian. "Sit down, Argent. We've finished with you. The elders have decided that the dragon must be killed."

"No!"

"I said sit down, girl!" Florian glared at Argent until she flung herself onto the grass. "Now, as I was trying to explain, we have decided to send a representative to the duke. Our representative will carry a petition from the people of Haven's Edge, asking the duke to help us. My good friend William has offered to take the petition for us."

Will the pigman swelled with pride. "Aye. I'll tek it."

Argent sat up again. They were sending Will the pigman? It would take him days to reach Goldstone Castle. He would stop at every inn along the road and, once he had a jug of ale in his fist, he would not be able to resist pulling the petition from his pack and telling the whole room about his important business. Argent felt a flicker of hope, and her eyes grew distant as a plan began to form in her mind.

"What will the duke do?" called a voice from the crowd.

"He'll send us a troop of his soldiers, along with one of their big crossbow devices. Once they're in position, the soldiers only have to wait for the dragon to fly low enough and—"

"And then they blast the long-tailed devil out of the sky!" finished Marion, rubbing her fat hands together.

As the crowd cheered, Argent took the opportunity to jump to her feet and storm out of the square as though in a furious temper.

"Let her go." Florian chuckled, settling back in his chair. He could afford to be generous. Everything had gone just the way he wanted. A troop of soldiers in the village would be very good for business. They would need food and lodging, and Dragonsbane Inn was the only hostelry. And, now he thought of it, perhaps he should spread the word about the dragon killing. Folk would come for miles to see such a spectacle and, once they arrived in Haven's Edge, they would need food and lodging, too. Florian smiled smugly as he watched Argent march away. Yes, he could afford to be generous.

Argent was smiling too as she hurried home, but her smile was one of grim determination. The meeting in the square would begin to break up soon, and she only had a short time to put her plan into action. She had decided to go to Goldstone to see the duke. If she cut across country rather than following the roads, she was sure she could reach the castle before Will the pigman. True, he would be on horseback and she would be on foot, but then she was not planning to stop for several jugs of ale at every inn she came across. And if she managed to pick up the trail of the dragon thief along the way, then so much the better.

Once she reached Goldstone, Argent was sure she could convince the duke not to harm the dragon. By all accounts, he was an intelligent, educated man who always listened to reason, whatever the source. Argent slowed and looked each way before stepping into a lane on the outer edge of the village. From where she stood, the cottage at the far end of the lane looked quiet and dark, but she padded toward it cautiously. Her father should still be in Scremerston, having a well-earned mug of ale in one of the inns and boasting about the price his grain had fetched, but Argent was not taking any chances. If the bidding had gone badly at the Corn Exchange, he could have decided to travel straight home. He could be sitting in the warm darkness in front of their banked-up fire, brooding on how they were to get through the winter.

Argent reached the front of the cottage, but she did not go in. Instead, she ducked below window level and scuttled along to the adjoining stable. There she opened the rough wooden door, stuck her head inside, and clicked her tongue. No answering whinny came from the warm, hay-smelling darkness, and Argent relaxed. If their horse Sam was not in his stall, then her father was not yet home.

Inside the cottage Argent lit a candle and set to work. She climbed the ladder to the loft where she slept, pulled the blanket from her straw pallet, and spread it on the floor. Opening the wooden chest beside the pallet, she lifted out her best skirt, blouse, and shawl and laid them in the center of the blanket. The only other thing in the box was a sheaf of parchment scraps, tied up with a strip of soft leather. Argent untied the leather strip and unrolled the crackling parchments. There, scribbled on the back of old church notices, tradesmen's bills, and any other scraps of parchment she had been able to scrounge, were her dragon notes and diagrams.

Argent's hands trembled suddenly, and she bit her lip as she stared down at her notes. Was she really planning to show these scrappy bits of parchment to the most important man in the county? And what about the journey she was planning to undertake? If she traveled to Goldstone by the most direct route, she would have to walk, on her own, through Unthank Forest and, if the stories were to be believed, there were worse things than wolves living there.

Argent threw back her head and groaned as her courage began to drain away. She stared out through the skylight window above her pallet. It was getting dark outside. The sun had already set behind the hill, and soon the moon would rise. Argent had always loved lying in bed, warm under her blankets, waiting for the moment when the moon reached the skylight and a silvery glow flooded into her sleeping loft. It would be easy to climb into bed now and forget all about traveling to Goldstone. She would see the moon rise from the safety of her sleeping loft rather than on a lonely road to Unthank Forest.

Argent rolled up the parchments and was about to put them back into the chest when the call of the mother dragon drifted down to her. Her jaw tightened with determination. There was no way she was going to lie on her pallet every night for the next week, listening to those forlorn cries and waiting for the soldiers to arrive. Argent slapped her parchments down onto the blanket instead and rolled the whole thing up into a cylinder with quick, deft movements. She secured the blanket roll with a length of twine and then swung herself down the ladder.

Downstairs Argent wrapped a loaf of bread and some cheese in a muslin cloth and filled her water bottle. She tucked her provisions into the top end of the blanket roll, slung it across her back, and was heading for the door when she remembered her ruined clothes. She came to a halt and stared down at her scorched top and ripped skirt with dismay.

They would not last more than a day of hard traveling, but the only other clothes she owned were stowed away in her blanket roll, ready for her audience with the duke.

For a few seconds Argent stood at a loss, but then a smile spread across her face. She hurried over to the chest next to her parents' alcove bed, stripping off her ruined outer clothes as she went. The only thing she kept hold of was her belt pouch, containing the folded, leathery skin of the dragon's egg. Opening the chest, she pulled out her father's oldest work trousers, a thick flannel shirt, a leather jerkin, and a woolen cap. Swiftly she dressed in the unfamiliar clothes, smiling at the strangeness of it all. She had strapped on her belt pouch again and was tucking her hair up into the woolen cap when a sudden draft set the candle flame dancing. A second later the draft curled coldly across the back of her neck.

Argent froze in place. The draft was coming through the open door of the cottage. She turned. Her mother was standing at the table, looking down at the blanket roll. She had her hands clutched together at her throat, and her face was ugly with grief. Argent took a step forward, but her mother put out her hands to fend her off.

"Mother," pleaded Argent, "I'm not running away. Once I've talked to the duke about the dragon, I'll come home again." Even as she said the words, she wondered how true they were. Would she really return to marry Thomas and live out her whole life in the village? Argent shook the thought away. "I must try to save the dragon."

Her mother nodded sharply, then marched over to the mantel shelf. When she returned to the table, she was carrying a knife in a sheath and a handful of small coins. She slammed down the money and the knife next to the blanket roll and then glared across at Argent. A tear trickled down each cheek, but her face was set like stone.

"Mother. What about Morgana?" pleaded Argent, feeling a twist of guilt as she thought about the exhausted face of the little girl's mother. "I promised I would take care of her for a month."

Argent's mother scowled at her. "You want me to keep your promise for you? Is that it? Very well. She can come here to me. I won't miss you so much with Morgana to keep me company."

"I'll miss you too—" began Argent.

"Don't." Argent's mother shook her head a few times. "You've made your choice, just as I made mine once. You are braver than I was. I chose to stay. Argent, I would ask one thing of you. If you decide not to come back—"

Argent began to protest, but her mother held up a hand to stop her.

"If that is what you decide, then send me a message when you can, to let me know you are safe and well." Argent's mother stopped, clamping her mouth shut as her voice began to quiver. Picking up the blanket roll, she threw it over to her daughter.

Argent slung the roll across her back and pocketed the knife and coins while her mother stood silently, arms wrapped tightly across her chest as though they were all that was holding her together.

"Bye," whispered Argent.

She took a step toward the door of the cottage, but her mother caught her up in a fierce, short hug, then, just as fiercely, pushed her away. Argent stumbled out into the darkening lane, and the cold evening air chilled the tears on her cheeks. She took one look back at the candlelit windows, wondering whether she would ever see her home again, then she turned her back on the cottage and began her journey.

· FIVE ·

CHUGGIE'S POOL

Chuggie's Pool had been transformed from a quiet fishing spot into a macabre circus. A whole stretch of the riverside footpath from the bridge to well beyond the pool had been cordoned off with streamers of striped police incident tape that snapped and fluttered in the wind. An audience lined the ramparts of the bridge and, in the river below, police divers in gleaming black wet suits bobbed and ducked like a troupe of performing seals. On the bank a chorus line of white-suited police inched forward in unison, stepping and bowing together in a synchronized search pattern that covered every tuft of grass on the riverbank.

Ellie was up on the bridge with the rest of the onlookers. She had come to find her dad but, if he was in the crowd, she had been unable to spot him. She had squeezed her way through to the ramparts of the bridge to check out the riverbank, but when she saw what was down here, she had forgotten all about her dad. Instead, she had gazed at the scene below the bridge with a mixture of shock and disbelief. She counted at least twenty officers—and she knew there were more of them talking to Danny's friends and making door-to-door inquiries. That was an awful lot of police time and money for one missing boy. They were taking the search for Danny very seriously, which made Ellie's worst fears suddenly seem more real.

Her stomach lurched with panic, then lurched again as she looked at the people around her. She was beginning to feel sickened by the atmosphere on the bridge. There was something disgusting about the way the onlookers craned their necks expectantly every time a police diver surfaced. They were turning the search for Danny into a spectator sport. Ellie spotted one group in particular who seemed to have made themselves very comfortable. They had staked out a prime viewing position in front of the police barrier at the footpath end of the bridge. Cups of coffee were being poured from thermos flasks, and some of them had even brought folding stools. As Ellie stared at this strange group of sightseers, she saw that at least half of them had cameras with telephoto lenses strung around their necks. They were photographers and reporters, waiting for breaking news.

Ellie decided it was time for her to leave. She leaned over the ramparts to check out the riverbank one last time, and that was when she saw her father. He was standing on the footpath, watching the progress of the search from the shadow of the bridge. The police must have allowed him to step under the tape into the search area. He had his back to the crowd and his coat collar turned up. For a moment Ellie wondered why he had not gone farther along the footpath, away from the crowd, but then she saw that the arch of the bridge was hiding him from the reporters above.

She took a deep breath and prepared to force her way through the crowd to get to her father but, at that moment, two police divers emerged from the central channel of the river and swam toward the bank, dragging something between them. Suddenly all the photographers at the end of the bridge were on their feet. For a few seconds the murmuring of the crowd stopped and, in the silence, Ellie could hear the press cameras clicking and whirring. Then the call went up, passed from onlooker to onlooker.

"They've got something!"

"The divers, look!"

"They've found something!"

The crowd surged forward, crushing Ellie

against the ramparts. They were trying to get a glimpse of the object the divers were dragging between them, but it was still hidden under the water. The two divers reached the shallows and waded out onto the bank, dragging a tangled mass of salmon netting behind them. There was something caught in the netting: something too heavy for the divers to lift out on their own. Other officers went to help them and together they managed to drag the object up onto the bank.

Ellie was breathing so fast, she thought she might pass out. She tried to catch a glimpse of what had been pulled from the river, but her view was blocked by the huddle of police officers as they bent over the netting. A second later they all reeled backward with their hands over their noses, and Ellie gripped the stonework of the bridge as the object in the netting came into view. At first Ellie could not make sense of the mottled gray and white shape lying on the riverbank, then the heavy stench of decaying flesh came drifting across the water to the bridge. Ellie's fingertips grated convulsively against the rough stone as she realized that she was looking at a grossly bloated corpse.

"Oh, my . . . that smell!

"It's a body. They've found a body."

The crowd surged forward again, pressing Ellie even harder against the ramparts as everyone tried to get a better look. Her mouth opened wide, gasping for breath, but the beginnings of a terrible grief had paralyzed her throat and no air would pass. A high-pitched whining filled her head, and sparks of white light began to explode in front of her eyes. She closed them, but the sparks only grew brighter. Around her the onlookers were still talking and exclaiming. Ellie tried to listen, but their voices echoed hollowly, as though they were shouting from the other end of a long tunnel, and she found it hard to understand what they were saying. Then, just as she was about to pass out, the man right next to her spat out three words in a tone of deep disappointment.

"Only a seal!"

A seal? Ellie's eyes snapped open, and air poured into her lungs as her throat relaxed. She leaned against the wall, weak with relief. Below her the divers pushed at the bloated body of the dead seal until it flopped over, rolled down the bank, and sank into the water, leaving a greasy scum behind it on the surface.

Ellie turned her head away and caught sight of her father. He had taken a few steps out from under the shadow of the bridge and his face in the sunshine was chalk white. Ellie put her head down and bulldozed her way through the crowd until she was at the police barrier at the footpath end of the bridge. The young constable on duty there was looking the same way as everyone else, toward the divers on the bank. Quickly Ellie ducked under the tape, dodged past the constable, and ran down the slope to the footpath, calling out to her father.

"Dad! It's not him! It's only a seal!"

Her father turned when he heard her voice. "It's all right, Ellie," he called back. "It wasn't Danny! It's only a seal!"

"I know." Ellie smiled, coming to a stop on the footpath in front of him. "That's what I came to tell you."

"You saw the divers pulling it out of the water?" asked Mr. Brody.

Ellie nodded, losing her smile.

"You shouldn't be down here," said her dad, shaking his head.

"I'm tougher—"

"Than you look. I know. But you shouldn't have to see this."

"Hoy!"

Ellie turned. The young constable was hurrying down the slope toward her.

"It's all right, Officer," called Mr. Brody. "This is my daughter."

The press cameras all turned their way and began clicking. Mr. Brody moved in front of Ellie, placing himself between her and the telephoto lenses.

"Then perhaps you would like to take her home, sir," said the constable huffily as he trudged back up the slope. "This isn't the place for her."

"See?" said Mr. Brody. "He agrees with me. Why on earth did you come down here, Ellie?"

"I had my interview with Lisa and Sergeant Donaldson," explained Ellie. "Lisa asked me some stupid things, like—" Ellie hesitated and looked up at her father. His broad, normally expressive face had become as impenetrable as a slab of granite. "You know . . . stupid things."

"Like, they think he might be a runaway?"

Ellie nodded. "I told her, Danny wouldn't run away."

"Anything else?" asked Mr. Brody.

Ellie swallowed and looked down at her feet. "Yes. But I told her they were wrong. Then I came to find you, to tell you the same thing."

"You haven't said anything about this to your mum, have you?" asked Mr. Brody.

"Of course not! She's upset enough as it is, without having to listen to all this nonsense. The police have got it wrong, Dad. I know that." She looked up at her father again. He nodded, but she could see that he wasn't really listening. He was reliving the interview. "Dad? Lisa asked you the same questions, didn't she? That's why you left the house without saying good-bye."

"She asked if Danny was happy at home. She wanted to know—" A quake of fury shivered across her father's face and he stopped.

"I know, Dad. Shhh. It's all right."

"They wanted to know if I . . . hit him. They wanted to know . . . who put him to bed at night." Mr. Brody's face reddened with shame and, suddenly, Ellie wanted him to stop talking. She reached out and hugged him tight. Normally Mr. Brody would have returned her hug, but this time he kept his arms at his sides. After a few seconds he gently broke her grip and eased her away from him. Ellie looked up and caught her father sending a wary glance toward the police officers farther along the footpath. Her father was afraid to give her a hug.

"See what she's done?" said Ellie bitterly, wanting to run home and punch the smug face of the family liaison officer. "How dare she?"

Mr. Brody's shoulders slumped, and he looked down at Ellie with his face full of sorrow. Tears sprang to her eyes. "Dad. Let's both go home—" she began.

"Hoy!" shouted the constable at the top of the slope. "You can't go down there!"

Ellie and Mr. Brody both looked around to see Ross hurrying toward them. The constable was marching after him, and the crowd was watching this development with great interest, but Ross was ignoring the young policeman. Instead, he was looking at Ellie as though they were the only two people on the riverbank. Sometimes Ellie found it hard to believe that she and Ross were nearly the same age. He was sixteen, only a year older than her, but he had a way of treating adults as though they were his equals. Or even his inferiors.

When he reached Ellie, Ross folded her into his arms and gave her the hug she realized she had been needing. Ellie let herself sink against his chest and breathed in the familiar smell of his soft leather jacket.

"Hoy, you!" repeated the constable, coming up behind Ross. "I said, this is a restricted area."

Ross did not even turn round. "I'm family," he said.

Ellie stiffened in his arms as she heard the lie. She glanced over at her dad and gave a small wince of embarrassment when she saw him frown. Ross was not family, but he had told the lie with such confidence, it sounded like the truth. Ellie cringed, waiting for the constable to grab Ross by the collar and frog-march him back behind the police tape, but the young policeman faltered and looked questioningly at Mr. Brody. Ellie looked too, and saw her dad hesitate for a second before he gave the constable a nod of confirmation.

"Sir! . . ."

"I know, Constable. I know. I'll get them both out of here," promised Mr. Brody.

The constable sighed and looked at the sky. "And it's going to rain," he announced sourly to no one in particular, before tramping back up the slope to his post.

Ellie broke away from Ross and looked up. The rain clouds she had seen curling round the brow of the hill earlier that afternoon had solidified and unrolled over the town like a huge gray carpet. The sun was still shining over the sea, but the cloud carpet was continuing to unroll, slowly obliterating any remaining blue sky.

Ellie looked over at the white-suited police officers. They had returned to their search, working in a disciplined line across the whole width of the riverbank, but they were glancing uneasily at the darkening sky. Rain was bad news. It would wash away scraps of evidence and turn any footprints into puddles of mud. The river turned iron gray as the clouds moved in. A cold wind began to blow, and the first, heavy drops of rain splatted down onto the footpath.

"Come on, Dad," said Ellie. "Let's go."

Mr. Brody shook his head. "No. I'm staying a bit longer."

"But it's going to pour," protested Ellie.

"I can shelter under there," said Mr. Brody, nodding toward the bridge. "Ross? Will you take Ellie home?"

"Sure thing, Mr. B. I'll look after her."

Mr. Brody clasped Ross by the shoulder. "Thanks, son," he said, his voice suddenly rough with emotion. "And thanks for last night, too. I don't know what we would've done without you."

Ross beamed with pride. "We'll find him," he said. "Don't you worry."

Mr. Brody nodded his gratitude, then turned and trudged tiredly away, heading for the shelter of the bridge arch. He looked so lonely that Ellie wanted to go after him and insist that either he came home or she stayed there with him. She wanted to do that, but she could not make herself move. The truth was, Ellie could not face staying at Chuggie's Pool a minute longer, but she did not want to go back home, either. The silence in the house only emphasized Danny's absence and, with nothing to do but wait for news, she felt particularly useless there.

"Ready?" asked Ross.

Ellie shook her head. "I don't want to go back just yet. I'm a bit of a spare part at home. There's this family liaison officer—Lisa—she's taken over a bit."

"Want to come back to my place?" asked Ross.

Ellie shot him a grateful look but shook her head. Ross lived with his parents in a detached stone-built house half a mile farther inland on the far side of the river. It was a beautiful house, but Ellie was never comfortable there. Ross's father was a vet who spent most of his waking hours out on calls or at his surgery in town. Ross's mother worked at the surgery too, as a receptionist, and her spare time was filled with an endless round of board and committee meetings. As a result, the house was nearly always empty and, whenever they went there, Ellie felt as though she and Ross were rattling around in the huge, silent rooms like two pebbles in a jar. Usually Ellie much preferred the noisy warmth of her own house. But not today.

"Tell you what," said Ellie, seeing the hurt look on his face. "Let's go somewhere for a drink first."

"Sure." Ross smiled. "We can wait out the worst of this rain. And we can talk—or not. Whatever you want."

Ellie nodded, and Ross put an arm around her shoulders and guided her toward the slope.

The crowd on the bridge had started to thin out at the first sign of rain, but the reporters were still there, watching with interest as Ellie and Ross walked toward them. The noses of the cameras lifted and a busy clicking began, accompanied by an occasional starburst of light as automatic flashes compensated for the darkening sky. Ellie felt a flush spreading upward from her neck, and her feet became suddenly clumsy as she stumbled up the slope. She let her hair fall forward to block out the sight of the reporters, but she could not block out their voices as they talked amongst themselves.

"Is that the sister?"

"Yeah. Ellie Brody."

"Who's the boy? Another brother?"

"He said he was family."

"There is no other brother. I'm guessing boyfriend."

"Ross?" hissed Ellie. "Let's turn back. We can go the other way, under the bridge."

"What? Along the footpath to the railway steps?" Ross shook his head decisively. "We're not going the long way around just to avoid the press." He grabbed Ellie's hand and pulled her in behind him. "Just keep your head down. I'll deal with them."

He marched up the slope, nodding his thanks to the constable who was holding up the police tape for them. "No questions," he called as he ducked under the tape with Ellie following so closely, she was treading on his heels. "No questions, please."

The reporters ignored him. "Any news yet, Ellie?" called one.

"Do the police have any leads?" asked another.

"How's your family coping without Danny?"

"No comment," said Ross calmly, in answer to every question. He ploughed a way through the jostling reporters and, in no time at all, they were heading away from the bridge into town.

By the time they were safely inside their favorite café, the rain was getting serious. Ellie sat in a booth by the window, watching the gutters turn into rivers. The street outside was emptying quickly, and there were only a few stragglers left splashing along the pavement. Most of them had their heads down and were hurrying to reach somewhere dry, but there was one exception. The crazy old bag lady was plodding along in the middle of the road, pulling her cart behind her. She had her face upturned and she seemed to be shouting at the rain.

As Ellie watched, the bag lady stopped directly outside the window of the café to shake her fist at the sky, and Ellie realized that this was the closest she had ever been to the old woman. Crazy people frightened her, and she had always crossed over to the other side of the street when she saw the bag lady approaching. Danny never did. He always stopped for a chat. Ellie bit her lip as she wondered whether someone had finally taken advantage of her brother's friendly, trusting nature. She shook the thought away and turned back to the window.

Safely behind the glass barrier, Ellie took her first good look at the woman. She was bareheaded and her thin, gray hair hung in dripping tendrils with patches of startlingly white scalp showing through. From neck to ankle, she was encased in an old tweed coat. In better days it had been a good coat, but now the material was shiny with dirt, there were holes at the elbows, and all the buttons were missing. Poking out under the hem of the coat were a pair of oversized, army-style boots.

The bag lady finished shaking her fist at the rain and bent to check the black sack that sat in her little cart. She patted the sack fondly and then trudged away over the wet cobbles. She looked like some sort of windup toy, with her large boots appearing and disappearing under the hem of the coat and her little cart trundling along behind her. Ellie wondered whether the bag lady had somewhere dry to shelter, which brought her, as always, back to Danny. Where was he right now? Was he dry and warm, or was he outside somewhere in the cold, wet afternoon?

"Ellie?"

Ellie jumped and turned away from the window. Ross had come back from the counter and was sitting across the table from her. "Sorry," she said. "I was . . . You know."

"I got hot chocolate," said Ross, pushing a large white mug across the table to her. "Is that okay?"

"Anything except tea," muttered Ellie, wrapping her hands around the mug for warmth. "Thanks."

"Ellie, I'm so sorry," Ross said quietly. His face became serious as he leaned across the table and took her hand. "Danny's such a nice kid."

"Thank you," said Ellie dismally as her eyes filled up with stupid tears yet again. She was so tired of crying, but she could not seem to stop. Ross gently pushed her hair away from her face and handed her a paper napkin.

"It's on all the local news," he said. "Radio. TV.

The whole town's talking about it."

Ellie frowned and sat back in the booth. Had she detected a hint of eagerness in his voice? Ross thrived on drama, especially when he was somewhere at the center of it. She suspected that one of the reasons he went out with her was that she gave him no competition in that respect. Ellie always preferred to stay in the background.

"What?" asked Ross, noticing her suspicious look.

"Why were you down at the river just now?" she asked.

"I was on my way to see you," explained Ross. "I didn't want to phone or text first. You must be getting such a lot of calls and messages—and thinking it might be news about Danny every time."

"Every time," agreed Ellie.

"So I decided to walk over to your house. I was crossing the bridge and that's when I spotted you, down on the riverbank with your dad."

"So you weren't—"

"Rubbernecking? What do you think I am!" cried Ross, looking hurt.

"Sorry." Ellie sighed, leaning forward again and taking his hand. "I'm not thinking straight. It's been such a nightmare. They . . . they seem to think Dad might have . . . done something to Danny."

"I know," said Ross quietly. "A couple of police officers came to the house this morning to interview me. It was a bit embarrassing, actually. My parents were both out, and I was still in bed when they knocked. I had to stand there in my boxers answering their questions."

"What were they asking?" asked Ellie faintly.

"Stuff about Danny and your dad. Had I ever noticed anything strange about their relationship—"

"Oh! How could they?"

"They're just doing their job, Ellie. You know, if you look at the statistics for missing kids, there's often a family member at the root of it."

"Statistics!" snapped Ellie, a lot louder than she meant to. "That's just the sort of thing Lisa would say! But she doesn't know my dad. He wouldn't hurt us. He would die first!"

"I know," said Ross hastily. "And that's just what I told them."

Ellie subsided, once again blinking back tears.

"How are you doing?" asked Ross. "Want to talk about it?"

So she did. She talked, and Ross listened. All her fears and feelings for Danny came pouring out, and she only stopped when the streetlight outside the coffee shop flickered on, casting a dull red glow across the rain-washed street. Ellie blinked and faltered to a halt, suddenly aware of how dark it had become outside. She picked up her hot chocolate, but it was now a cold, congealed sludge. How long had she been talking? Hastily she put the mug down and looked at her watch instead. Two hours had passed in what seemed like minutes.

"Oh! I'd better get home. It was about this time yesterday that we realized Danny was missing. Mum might be needing me."

Ross looked at his own watch and let out a grunt of surprise.

"Is that the time? I should get back too. Homework."

Ellie looked blank.

"School tomorrow, remember?"

Ellie blinked with shock. It was frightening how quickly her normal life had disappeared. Just two days earlier, she had been walking home from school with her friends, carrying a bagful of books and looking forward to the weekend. Now "home-work" and "school" were like words in a foreign language; they meant nothing to her.

"No school for you, of course," amended Ross. "No one'll expect you to be there. Not with Danny missing."

"They'll probably find him before tomorrow," said Ellie quickly.

"That's right!" said Ross a little too brightly, and Ellie could see that he did not believe what he was saying. "Anyway," said Ross after an awkward pause. "I'll walk you home." He got to his feet, and Ellie began to get up too. "Hang on," said Ross, looking at the rain-splattered café window. "Just wait here a minute."

Before Ellie could say anything, Ross had ducked out of the door of the café and was sprinting across the street with his shoulders hunched against the driving rain. A few minutes later, he was back, shaking raindrops from his hair and waving a carrier bag triumphantly.

"Where've you been?" asked Ellie.

"Army Surplus Store." Ross grinned, producing two fluorescent orange hooded rain capes.

"You bought them?"

"Yeah," said Ross, pulling one of the capes over his head. "They were on sale."

"I'm not surprised," muttered Ellie, looking doubtfully at the bright orange plastic.

"Come on!" Ross laughed, helping her on with her cape. "At least we'll be dry."

"And easily seen," commented Ellie wryly as Ross pulled her hood up and fastened the Velcro tab under her chin.

"There. You look lovely."

"No I don't," said Ellie, imagining how her pale skin and swollen eyes must look framed by the orange hood. "I look like E.T."

Ross threw his head back and laughed. He looked good even in the cape, such was the power of his blue eyes, dark lashes, and white teeth. Ellie studied his face.

"What?" asked Ross.

Ellie shook her head. "Nothing. Just—thanks for listening." she whispered.

Ross leaned down and Ellie raised her head, expecting a kiss on the lips. Instead, Ross kissed her on the forehead. Ellie felt a small pang of loss. They had been going out together for eight months now. At the start of their relationship, Ross had been as keen to share kisses as she was, but then he had cooled off and now he was beginning to treat her more like a sister than a girlfriend. He was still around at her house as often as ever, but Ellie suspected that was more out of habit than passion. She sighed regretfully. She had seen the way Ross had started looking at Laura Jones, and she was expecting the old "let's just be friends" line from him any day now. *But not yet*, she wished silently, gazing up at Ross. *Wait until Danny's home again.*

"Ready?" asked Ross.

Ellie nodded and, together, they headed out into the rain.

· SIX ·

THE SHIELD

Danny frowned in his sleep. He was beginning to surface from his dreams, and he did not want to wake up. Being awake meant pain. Whatever he had been injected with had taken him into Argent's land, far away from the cold, dark place where his body lay. As long as he stayed there, he could not feel the cold floor beneath his back, or the chafing of the plastic strips that tied his hands and feet, but now the drug was wearing off and he was being dragged back into his world.

He groaned as a cramp bit into the back of his calf, twisting the muscle until he thought it would snap apart. Desperately he tried to sink back into his dreams, but he couldn't. The feeling was returning all over his body, and everywhere hurt. Danny took a sharp breath as another cramp wrapped around his thigh like a coil of barbed wire. The acrid smell of urine filled his nostrils, and he realized that he had lost control of his bladder while he was unconscious. He whimpered with shame, and then grew quiet as he detected another smell, almost hidden by the powerful stench of urine. Danny sniffed again. What was that smell? It was sweet and cloying, but with a bitter, chemical underlay. It made him think of the biology lab at school.

Formaldehyde. That was it. He could smell formaldehyde, the alcohol-based chemical used to preserve dead tissue. For some reason, that made him very afraid. Danny tried to open his eyes, but the lashes were gummy with sleep. He turned his head to one side as far as he could, lifted his shoulder, and scraped his face back and forth across the cloth of his jacket to clear the mucus away. Once he could open his eyes, Danny tried to see where he was, but the darkness was absolute.

A footstep crunched nearby. Panting with fear, Danny swiveled his head, homing in on the sound. *Click.* A flashlight was switched on, and the beam of white light hit him full in the face. Danny would have cried out in shock, but his throat and mouth were completely dry, and all that came out was a croak. His eyes watered with pain as the unaccustomed light burned into his retinas, but he continued to squint into the flashlight beam as it bobbed toward him. He was trying to get a glimpse of his captor, but whoever was carrying the flashlight kept the beam shining straight into his eyes.

"Please," whispered Danny.

"Shhh!"

The figure behind the flashlight lunged forward, and he caught a glimpse of a gloved hand holding a syringe. When the needle jabbed into his thigh, Danny almost welcomed it. The pain and fear in his world was too much to cope with right now, and he felt nothing but relief as the drug took hold again. He closed his eyes and let himself fall away from his body, spiraling back down into Argent's land where a perilous journey had begun. . . .

The moon was high in the sky by the time Argent had worked her way around the shoulder of the hill. The village, the cave, and the ceaselessly circling dragon were behind her now, on the other side of the hill and, spread out ahead of her, silver and black in the moonlight, were the unfamiliar depths of Unthank Forest. Argent swallowed as she looked down on the swaying, whispering treetops. There were village stories about Unthank Forest that were only told late at night, when little children were safely asleep.

Argent hesitated. Caution was screaming at her to wait until daylight before venturing into the forest, but time was of the essence on this journey, and the moon was bright and full. It seemed such a waste to stop and make camp. The way ahead was lit almost as clear as day, and she was buzzing with the energy that came at the start of a journey. She decided to keep going.

Adjusting the bedroll on her shoulder, Argent set off down the hill until she reached the head of a narrow gully. There, she sat on a large rock to catch her breath and check her surroundings. Over to her right, a fast-flowing stream emerged from the hillside and plunged down into the gully. Argent could hear water cascading over rocks far below. Every splash was magnified and echoed by the high walls.

On the left-hand side of the stream, there was a steep but walkable track. Argent knew that if she followed the track, it would take her all the way to the bottom, but she also knew how the track had been worn. It had been made by the feet of desperate folk. Only those with no options left followed the stream down to the bottom of the gully, folk whose loved ones were dying or who were desperate for a baby. They all came back pale and shaking, refusing to talk of what had happened there. The place was known locally as the Goodie Patchie because the small patch of land at the edge of the forest was the territory of the goodwife. A goodwife had always lived there, in a little wooden hut so covered with moss it could almost be mistaken for a small, grassy mound in the clearing. There were some in the village who claimed that the same goodwife had always lived there, but Argent refused to believe them. Nobody could live forever. Not even a goodwife.

Argent had never gone down into the Goodie Patchie before, but she knew it was the quickest way into the forest. If she did not follow the track into the gully, she would have to carry on around the shoulder of the hill until she reached the sea cliffs, and then follow the coastal path in a great loop that would take her miles out of her way. Argent pictured herself arriving at Goldstone just too late to stop a troop of hard-faced soldiers riding past her out of the gates and heading for Haven's Edge. She could not take that chance. Quickly she knelt by the stream and scooped a few handfuls of icy water into her dry mouth. Then, before she could change her mind, she stepped onto the steep track that would take her down to the Goodie Patchie.

At first, the going was fairly easy, but as Argent traveled deeper into the gully, she moved down into darkness. Above her the full moon still shone, but only the odd glimmer of light reached her. Argent stumbled on, feeling her way along the rocky path and hoping that the splashing of the stream was masking her footsteps. She did not want to attract the attention of anything that might be living in this damp, dark place. Her plan was to reach the bottom of the gully and then sneak silently across the Goodie Patchie into the forest, giving the goodwife's hut a wide berth.

When a stone rolled under her foot, it was all Argent could do to stay upright. As she struggled to find her balance, the stone dislodged itself and went clattering away down the track. Horrified, Argent froze in place with both hands clasped over her mouth as the clatter bounced off the high rock walls, creating a magnified echo that rolled around the enclosed space for what seemed like an age. She stayed motionless for ten long seconds after the final echo had died away, but nothing stirred in the dim recesses. Argent gave a deep sigh of relief and rolled her head back on her shoulders to ease the tension in her neck. Above her upturned face, the walls leaned inward until, at the top of the gully, the gap was barely more than the width of the stream below. Argent was staring longingly at the narrow strip of moonlit sky above her when something jumped across the gap.

All the hairs on the back of her neck stiffened as though an icy breeze had blown across them. She had only seen the thing for an instant, a black silhouette framed against the starlit sky. It had made a long, graceful shape when it jumped, like a pouncing cat, but much bigger. It had launched itself from the other side of the gully, jumping from right to left, which meant that it was now directly above her. Argent scanned the top of the gully, her eyes wide with sudden fear, but nothing moved up there. She told herself not to be stupid. The creature was probably already loping away across the hillside while she wasted precious time cowering in the darkness.

She checked one last time, then turned to continue on her way. That was when she did see a movement, but not at the top. It was halfway down, beneath a rock overhang. She stopped and stared at the place. There was definitely a patch of darker shadow there. Argent tensed. When the patch of shadow moved again, she nearly screamed. Whatever had jumped across the narrow gap high above was now climbing down a nearly vertical wall of rock toward her.

A shower of small stones pattered down the wall and fell at her feet. Argent bolted. She ran down the narrow track as fast as she could, not caring how much noise she made. By some miracle, she made it to the foot of the gully without falling in the dark. She burst out into the Goodie Patchie and raced full pelt across the rough grass, not daring to look behind her. The creature must be nearly on her now. There was no way she could outrun it for much longer.

The goodwife's little wooden hut was straight ahead, and Argent gave a sob of relief when she saw smoke rising from the chimney and the glow of a candle at the window. Any thought of sneaking past the hut unnoticed had disappeared from her mind.

"Help!" she cried hoarsely, running straight for the hut. "Help!"

The door of the hut creaked open and a figure peered out, then stood aside to let Argent through. Argent forced more speed from her aching legs and flew the last few yards to the hut. She flung herself through the door and fell onto the packed earth floor inside. Behind her, the door slammed shut and she heard a heavy wooden bar slot into place with a reassuringly solid thunk.

Argent scrambled on all fours to the far side of the room and turned to face the door with her back pressed against the wall. She was vaguely aware of a figure standing to one side of the frame, but all her attention was on the door itself. It looked very flimsy to her, even with the bar in place. She screwed up her eyes as she waited for the creature to thud against the other side of the door and smash it from its hinges, but the seconds ticked by and nothing happened. Argent slumped against the wall, nearly sobbing with relief. Her heart was pounding so hard and fast, it made the blood beat against her eardrums like the sea, and her rasping breaths were loud in the quiet hut. She wiped the sweat from her eyes, sat up, and took her first look around.

The corners of the room were in shadow, and

the rest was only dimly lit by one candle flame and the glow of a fire in the hearth. There were so many bunches of drying herbs hanging from the rafters, it was difficult to see the roof, and most of the walls were hidden behind rows and rows of earthenware jars that hung from pegs by leather straps. Something simmered in a large pot over the fire. To one side of the hearth, a drying rack was spread with rows of weirdly shaped fungi. The combined smell of herbs, woodsmoke, and cooking was almost overwhelming.

The hut was sparsely furnished. A neatly made bed with a shelf of books above fitted into the alcove by the hearth, a sturdy table stood under the window, and a stool and a straight-backed chair were set on either side of the fire. It did not take Argent long to finish her inspection. She turned back to the door, but the figure that had been standing to one side of the frame was no longer there.

"Hello?" ventured Argent, peering into the shadowy corners of the room. "Thank you for letting me in. Something was following me."

A soft voice came from the deepest pool of shadow, making Argent jump. "In this place, something always follows," said the voice. "The trick is to know whether it is a friend—or a foe. What are you?"

"What do you mean?" asked Argent, peering into the shadows.

"Friend or foe?" asked the soft voice, and Argent caught a long, silvery glint that could only be the blade of a knife.

"I am only a traveler," she began. "My name is"—Argent hesitated and looked down at the clothes she was dressed in—"Tom."

The glint of steel came again. "You are no boy," said the voice, this time with a hard edge to it that made Argent's spine prickle. "You had best tell me the truth."

"All right. I'm a girl," said Argent hastily. "My name is Argent, and I come from Haven's Edge. The traveler part is true, though."

The silence grew, and Argent peered warily at the blade glinting in the shadows. She was greatly relieved when she heard the knife being sheathed. The figure stepped out of the corner into the candlelight, and Argent got her first proper look at the goodwife. It was difficult to put an age to her. She moved like a young girl, but had streaks of gray in her dark hair. There were age lines on her hands, yet her body was slim and straight. Argent peered at the woman's face, trying to get a clear image, but it seemed to waver in the flickering candlelight. She rubbed at her eyes, lifted her head to take another look, and then let out a yelp of surprise. The woman had moved swiftly and silently across the room and was now squatting next to her holding out a wooden beaker.

"Here." The goodwife smiled. "Drink this."

Argent hesitated. The steam rising from the beaker smelled smoky and strange. "What is it?"

"It is good for shock," said the goodwife, moving to sit in the chair by the fire. "Of which you seem to have had several."

Argent clambered to her feet and took the stool opposite, balancing the steaming beaker on her knee and staring at it warily.

"It is not poison," said the goodwife, with a hint of impatience.

"How do I know that?" retorted Argent. "There are some in Haven's Edge who say you're a—"

"Witch?" The goodwife sighed. "That's original. The ones who call me a witch—would they be, by any chance, some of the folk I could not help?"

Argent thought about it and then had to give a reluctant nod of agreement.

"That is understandable. Their loved ones died, and I did nothing. They are bitter."

"Why did you do nothing?" asked Argent.

"Some people are beyond help. They will die whatever I try to do. Best just to make it as peaceful as possible. Most folk understand that, but a few come looking for miracles, and those I do not provide." The goodwife shook her head. "There is much ignorance in Haven's Edge."

"We're not that ignorant," said Argent stoutly.

"We let you stay here, don't we? Even the ones who call you a witch have not tried to drive you away."

"Only because the Goodie Patchie is no use for farming!" The goodwife laughed. "If this land could grow a crop, I would have been driven out years ago. It has everything I need, though. Fungi and lichens thrive in the gully—and many herbs and medicinal plants grow on the floor of Unthank Forest. That is where I collected the chamomile to make the tea you are drinking right now."

Argent snatched the beaker away from her lips, but it was already half empty. She had been taking sips of the comforting hot drink without realizing it. Argent shrugged and finished off the rest of the tea.

"So, Argent," said the goodwife, spooning dollops of stew from the hearth pot into two wooden bowls. "Where do you travel?" She handed one bowl and spoon to Argent and took the other back to her chair. "And why?"

The stew was excellent and, as she ate first one bowlful, then a second, Argent found herself telling the goodwife all about the dragon thief and the elders' plan to bring soldiers to Haven's Edge. "So I have to get to Goldstone before Will does," finished Argent, scraping her bowl clean. "Otherwise the soldiers will come and kill the mother dragon."

"This dragon thief," said the goodwife, moving

over to the ranks of hanging jars and hooking one down. "What did he look like?"

"I don't know," said Argent, watching as the goodwife scooped some salve from the jar. "He was hiding in the bushes. What's that?"

"For minor burns," said the goodwife, gently smearing the salve over Argent's face. Immediately a welcome coolness eased into the tight skin across her cheeks, nose, and forehead. Argent smiled and closed her eyes.

"That is good." She sighed, slumping back on the stool. A thought came to her, and she sat up straight again, reaching into her belt pouch and pulling out the handful of coins her mother had given her.

"Did I ask for payment?" asked the goodwife, frowning down at Argent's outstretched hand.

"Not for me," explained Argent hastily. "There is a young girl in the village. She was on the hillside with me. Her name is Morgana. Could you send a jar of salve to her, in Haven's Edge?"

The goodwife's face softened, and she took the coins with a gracious nod. "I will send some with the next traveler who passes through."

"Thank you," said Argent, letting her eyes slide shut again, the better to enjoy the soothing coolness of the salve.

"Speaking of travelers," said the goodwife, stoppering the jar and putting it back in its place, "I think I saw your dragon thief."

Argent's eyes snapped open. "Where? Where did you see him?"

"A red-haired man passed through the Goodie Patchie earlier today. A hunter, I think. His horse was a gray. He came down through the gully and stopped to wash in the stream before riding on into the forest. He had a large box strapped to one side of his saddle. The horse was skittish. I don't think it liked carrying the box."

"Because the baby dragon was in there?" whispered Argent.

"It's possible. I was out tending my vegetable plot, but the man did not stop to talk. He was in a great hurry. At the time I thought it was just that he wanted to get through the forest before dark."

"He must be heading for Goldstone. Maybe he has a buyer there. Oh! I have to go! There are ships leaving Goldstone port every day, sailing to all corners of the world. If he sells the baby dragon down in the harbor, it will be lost forever." Argent jumped to her feet and slung her bedroll over her shoulder. "Thank you for the food," she said as she hurried to the door. "And for letting me in . . ." Argent slowed to a stop and glanced apprehensively at the door as she remembered what had driven her into the goodwife's hut in the first place. "Will it still be out there?"

"I don't know," answered the goodwife truthfully. "But, I think if the creature had meant to catch you, it would have succeeded."

"Right," muttered Argent doubtfully.

"Not everything in Unthank is out to hurt you. If you tread carefully and treat the forest with respect, you will pass through it unharmed." The goodwife smiled. "There are more dangerous beasts in Goldstone City—and they all walk on two legs."

Argent grinned and looked down at her boots. "I don't know why folk are so afraid of you. Just then, you sounded exactly like my mother—"

A low, guttural growl came from the mouth of the goodwife. Argent jerked her head up and gasped. The woman's eyes had rolled right back in her head until only the whites were showing. Argent took a step back.

"Beware the man who offers his help!" screeched the goodwife, with bubbles of spit peppering her lips. Her voice sounded inhuman, as though something else had taken control.

"Th-thank you." whispered Argent, edging toward the door. "I'll remember that."

The goodwife turned and walked with jerky steps to a chest in the corner of the room. She pulled something from the chest and then, with her eyes still rolled back and the whites glistening in the sockets, she walked over to Argent. Argent shuddered. Her pupils were rolled right back in her head, but the goodwife was moving as though she could *see*. When the woman reached out and gripped Argent by the wrist without fumbling at all, it sent a cold chill all the way up her arm.

"Take this!" howled the goodwife. "You will have need of it!"

Argent prized her wrist from the woman's grip and took the object that was being thrust toward her. It was a small, round wooden shield with a disk of beaten and burnished metal on the front and a worn leather strap on the back. It was a simple, workmanlike shield. The only decoration was a spiral design etched into the metal disk. The instant Argent took hold of the shield, the goodwife's hand dropped to her side and her eyelids closed, covering the glistening whites. When she opened them again, she was gazing at Argent with a dazed expression.

"What. . . ?" She wiped her mouth on her sleeve and looked down at the shield that Argent held. "Did I give you that?"

"Y-yes."

"Ah." The goodwife gave a regretful sigh. "What a pity. It once belonged to someone who— loved me."

"You can have it back," said Argent, shakily, holding out the shield.

"No," said the goodwife. "If I gave it, you will need it. Keep it close." Argent nodded warily and slung the shield over her shoulder alongside her bedroll.

"If I frightened you, I am sorry," said the goodwife. Argent tried to smile, but could not quite manage it. When the goodwife suddenly stepped forward, Argent flinched. The goodwife shrugged. "Now you see why I live alone," she said bleakly, moving on past Argent to lift the bar from the door.

Argent could think of nothing to say, so she eased open the door and peered out. The Goodie Patchie was quiet and still in the moonlight. "Thank you," she said, glancing back at the goodwife one last time before stepping out into the night.

The goodwife stood in the doorway and watched until Argent had disappeared into the forest. "Good luck, child," she murmured, casting an uneasy glance at the full moon before stepping back into the hut and barring the door.

· SEVEN ·
ARGENT'S WAY

"**W**ould you look at that!" marveled Ross. "They get everywhere, don't they?"

Ellie lifted the hood of her rain cape and peered along the street. A white van was parked outside her house. There was a satellite dish on the roof, and the name and logo of a twenty-four-hour news channel was painted on the side. The back doors of the van were open, and the interior was dimly lit. They could see a huddle of people sitting inside. The man nearest the door had a camera across his knees, protected by a waterproof cover. Opposite him sat the soundman, with a boom microphone propped up beside him.

"Ready to go as soon as they spot something interesting," said Ross, with a note of disgust in his voice.

"Oh, no!" groaned Ellie. "How am I going to get past them?"

"You don't have to," said Ross. "You can go around the back. I'll deal with this lot."

Gratefully, Ellie went up on tiptoe and kissed Ross on the cheek. "Thanks."

"Listen," said Ross, "I'm on reception at the surgery for a couple of hours tomorrow. My mother has to go to—"

"A committee meeting," finished Ellie.

Ross grinned. "How did you guess? Anyway, I'll be heading to the surgery straight from school. Why don't you call in? Give me the latest news."

"They'll have found Danny by then," said Ellie, filling her voice with a confidence she did not really feel.

"Or he'll come back on his own," suggested Ross.

"Do you think he's run away, then?"

"Not so much run away. More likely seeing if he can survive in the wild. You know, all that 'Are you tough enough?' military stuff."

"Survival games? That sounds like Danny." Ellie nodded as though Ross had made a suggestion worth considering but, deep down, she knew that choosing to stay out overnight while his family and friends waited for him at home did not sound like Danny at all.

"He'll probably come home now it's raining,"

continued Ross, encouraged by her response. Ellie smiled and waved as she hurried toward the path that would take her around the back of the houses. She wanted so much to be convinced, but she was seeing Danny's brand-new fishing tackle laid out so neatly on the riverbank. Danny would never have gone off without it.

"See you tomorrow," called Ross as he strode off up the street toward the television van. Ellie waved again, then slipped into the narrow gap between the high garden fences. Immediately she felt calmer. She had always loved this quiet little tarmac path that ran along the back of the houses. It was a kind of border: a black line separating the neat, suburban estate from the wild freedom of the hillside. At night, she sometimes liked to walk along the path, looking through gaps in the back garden fences and into the sitting rooms of her neighbors. She wasn't spying. Not really. It was hard to explain, even to herself, but there was something thrilling about being outside looking in and feeling the contrast between the huge, dark bulk of the hill on one side and the warm, brightly lit little houses on the other.

Tonight as she hurried along the path, Ellie peered into the gaps between the fence slats and caught glimpses of people kissing, rocking their babies, eating beans on toast, and watching television, all completely oblivious to the rain-swept hill rising a few meters from their garden fences. It felt doubly strange to see other people carrying on with their normal lives when her family's life had so quickly fallen apart. She reached her own back fence and was about to open the garden gate when she saw her mother and Lisa standing in the kitchen. Her mother was crying on Lisa's shoulder while Lisa held her and patted her back.

Ellie stopped with her hand on the latch. She had come home because she thought her mother might need her, but it looked as though her mother was getting all the support she needed from Lisa. Ellie scowled and moved along the fence a little way until she could see the driveway at the side of the house. It was empty. Her dad must still be down at Chuggie's Pool, or driving around the streets looking for Danny. She reached into her pocket, pulled out her mobile phone, and bent her head to check the screen. No messages. No texts. No news about Danny. And no word from her mother, asking where she was. Ellie scowled. She knew she was being unfair. Her dad would have passed on the news that Ellie was with Ross, but still she felt like a bit of a spare part as she watched Lisa and her mum.

The house looked warm and inviting to Ellie as she stood in the dark with water dripping from the hood of her rain cape. She gripped the latch of the garden gate and prepared to go in, but the thought of spending a second evening with nothing to do but wait for the phone to ring was suddenly unbearable to her. She would rather be out in the rain, looking for Danny. But where could she start? Ellie became very still as she remembered the glint of gold she had seen up on the hillside that afternoon. The dragon cave! It had once been Danny's favorite place to play. That was where she would start.

Quickly she bent over her phone again and keyed in a text to her mother. "Still out wi Ross. C u L8r. Luv E." She sent the text and waited. A few seconds later Mrs. Brody pulled away from Lisa and lunged for her phone as the text alert sounded. While the two women huddled together over Mrs. Brody's phone, Ellie opened the gate as quietly as she could and slipped through into the back garden. She hurried over to the shed, eased open the door, and grabbed the flashlight that was always kept on the shelf. She was going to need it in the cave.

As she stepped out through the gate again, Ellie glanced back at the kitchen window. Her mother had just finished reading the text, and her face was crumpling into tears. Ellie understood. As she set off along the path to the hill, she felt a guilty relief to be out and looking for Danny, instead of sitting at home feeling her hopes rise and then die with every text and phone call. Her mum and dad wouldn't worry about her if they thought she was with Ross and, if there was any good news about Danny, it would reach her on her mobile.

The hill was a bigger, wilder place in the dark, and as she climbed, Ellie found it hard to keep her sense of direction. At first she used the flashlight but, although the beam lit the ground around her feet, it also made the surrounding hillside disappear into absolute darkness and, after a few minutes, she was completely lost. Ellie came to a halt, turned off the flashlight, and stood in the dark, waiting for her night vision to return. The rain drummed down on her cape and soaked into her trainers as she watched the silhouette of the hill gradually separate itself from the slightly lighter sky.

When she set off again, it was with the flashlight stowed in the front zip-pocket of her cape. The climbing was harder without the light to help her, and she often slipped on the rain-slick grass or stumbled over hidden stones, but she could see which part of the hillside she should be heading for and her sense of direction held true. Soon she was on the steeper slopes just below the cave and grabbing onto handfuls of tough hillside grass to stop herself from slipping backward.

The closer Ellie got to the cave, the more she became convinced that she would find Danny there. *So we remember where we have to go*, he had said on that day five summers ago as they sat together outside the cave with their newly tattooed ankles throbbing in unison. The cave had been very important to them back then. If, for some reason, Danny needed somewhere to hide now, he would head for the cave. Even if Ross was right and Danny was simply playing some sort of survival game, he would have remembered the cave and picked it out as a good place to sleep.

Ellie stopped to catch her breath and lifted her dripping hood to peer up the final slope. She could see the mouth of the cave now, a darker hole in the dark hillside, but there was no sign of a fire or a light. Her eyes widened. Perhaps Danny was hurt. Perhaps the glint she had seen in the cave mouth that afternoon had been a desperate signal for help. Ellie gasped. He could be lying in the cave right now, unable to light a fire or even reach into his pocket to turn on his mobile phone.

"I'm here, Danny!" she yelled, hauling herself up the last few meters of slope. "You're safe now!" She listened for a reply as she stumbled across the stony ground outside the cave, but the rain was drumming on her hood and her own panting breaths were loud in her ears.

Ellie pulled the hood from her head and rushed into the dark cave. She opened her mouth to call Danny's name again, but what came out instead was a shriek of pain and shock. Someone had grabbed her by the hair. Ellie's head jerked backward and she stumbled back on her heels, desperately trying to keep her balance. A big clump of hair on the top of her head felt as though it was about to part company with her scalp. If she fell over now, it surely would. For three agonizing seconds, Ellie teetered back on her heels, windmilling her arms until, finally, she rocked forward onto the balls of her feet.

"Please," begged Ellie, going up onto her toes to try to reduce the pull on her hair. "Let me go. . . ." Her hands went to the top of her head, but something soft and damp trailed across her fingers and she yanked them down again. "Let me go!" shrieked Ellie, kicking backward. Her foot sliced through thin air, and she nearly overbalanced again. Hastily she found her feet and returned to standing on her toes, swaying slightly as she hung from her hair in the darkness.

Ellie tried to ignore the burning pain in her scalp. Think! Her kick had failed to connect with anything behind her, so what was holding her by the hair? She twisted her head as far as she could manage and peered upward. It was too dark to see anything, and she did not want to reach up again without knowing what was there.

The flashlight! Frantically, Ellie fumbled it out of the front zip-pocket of her rain cape and flicked it on. In the bright beam of light, she could see what had caught her by the hair. A small tree branch had been wedged into a cleft in the rock above her head. Hanging from every twig was a spiral of gold foil, each one glittering with drops of rain that had been blown into the entrance of the cave. The golden spirals explained what she had seen glinting in the sunlight earlier that day—and it also explained the soft, damp tendril that had trailed across her hand a moment ago.

Wedging the flashlight in the front pocket of her cape with the beam pointing upward, Ellie set about untangling her hair from the tree branch. A few minutes later she was free. She stood back from the tree branch, rubbing her sore scalp and studying the golden spirals as they twisted in the wind. Spirals. Like their tattoos . . .

"Danny?" Ellie shone her flashlight into the cave. It was exactly as she remembered it, except that everything seemed to be smaller. The walls were of smooth, ridged stone, and the floor was covered with a dusty layer of packed earth. The shape was like a long, thin comma, curving into the hillside with the head of the comma hidden from view around a bend in the rock.

"Danny?" The flashlight beam flowed over the walls, throwing jerky shadows as she walked to the back of the cave. Taking a deep breath, Ellie shone the flashlight into the little round chamber beyond the bend in the rock. A figure was curled up on the floor. "Danny!" Ellie squeezed into the chamber and dropped to her knees. "Oh, Danny. It's okay. You'll be okay now."

He wasn't moving. She gripped his shoulder and gave it a gentle shake and he fell apart under her hand, collapsing gently into several pieces. Ellie swallowed a scream when she saw that it wasn't Danny at all. It was only a pile of old cushions some kids had brought to the cave with them to make a den. Ellie sat back on her heels and rested her sore head in her hands. She had been so sure she would find Danny up here.

"The spirals!" Her head came up again as she remembered the twists of foil hanging from the tree branch. Were they a message from Danny? She backed out of the chamber and hurried back to the cave mouth. Training the flashlight on the tree branch, she took her first good look at the spirals. They were hanging down on either side of a rough-edged cardboard disk that was spinning in the wind. There was a childlike drawing of a face on the disk and, underneath the face, some sort of crude writing. Ellie reached up and grabbed the disk, holding it steady while she deciphered the writing: LAUREN AND KIMS DEN PRIVIT KEPE OUT!!!

Ellie sent the disk spinning in the wind again and sat down on the floor at the mouth of the cave. The golden spirals were nothing to do with Danny. They were some kid's idea of hair, hanging from each side of a crudely drawn face on a cardboard disk. Her search had reached a dead end. Gloomily she shone the flashlight beam onto her ankle and stared at the little black spiral. She had been wrong. The tattoo had no significance at all, except as a—what had the police called it?—distinguishing mark. Ellie shuddered. Suddenly she did not want to look at the little spiral anymore. She switched off the flashlight and gazed out over the valley, blinking away tears and waiting for her night vision to return.

Below her the town was mapped out as points of light against a black background. She could see the white squares of windows; the dotted, yellow lines of streetlights; and the bright rectangles of flood-lights over at the speedway track. A sprinkling of red and green marked the railway bridge and, beyond the harbor, the lighthouse sent out a solid, wedge-shaped beam, filled with sea and rain. Ellie let her gaze drift idly over the town.

Glint.

She stopped as her eye was caught by the glint of a different sort of light. It was soft rather than bright: flickering rather than steady. It was also a light she had never noticed before. It was coming from the roof of the old swimming pool building.

Glint.

Ellie stood up to get a better look. The old swimming pool was near the river, in the narrow streets of the walled part of town. It was an impos-ing Victorian building, with an ornate glass dome set into the roof directly above the pool. When the pool first opened, it must have been the wonder of the town, with its great dome allowing the swimmers below to be bathed in sunlight while being hidden from the world outside. When Ellie and her family had first moved to the town, the old pool had still been in use and, every Friday morning, the whole of her class had walked down from the school in a long crocodile to have swimming lessons there. Now there was a new, glass-walled leisure center right next to the school, and the old pool building had been closed for years.

Glint.

So why was there a soft orange light glinting in the glass curves of the roof dome? Ellie realized that someone must be inside the boarded-up building. She watched the glinting light for a few more seconds and then shrugged and turned away, preparing to set off down the hill again. A break-in at the old swimming pool was not her problem. Let the police deal with it. But then how could the police deal with something they knew nothing about? She was probably the only one to have spotted the light in the dome because she was the only one high enough to see it.

Ellie hesitated. There was no reason to suppose that the glint of light in the old swimming pool had anything to do with Danny. There was also no reason for her to be standing halfway up the hillside on a dark, rainy Sunday evening, but if she had not followed a hunch and climbed the hill to check a glint of light coming from the cave mouth, then she would never have seen the glint of light inside the dome. Ellie felt a fizz of excitement in her chest as a crazy idea began to form. If the spiral tattoo represented a map of where she had to go, then maybe the way to find Danny was to let herself fall into that spiral? Ellie nodded. It all made a sort of crazy sense. The police search was following straight lines and logic because that was what the police did best. They had expertise, resources, and an enviable information network to back them up, but she had none of that. If she tried to use the same search methods as the police, she would never find Danny.

No, she had to fall into the spiral. And the dragon cave, where she and Danny had acted out the Argent stories together five summers ago, seemed a fitting place to start. She had to trust to instinct and chance and see where they took her. She had to be open to anything, just like Argent. Ellie pushed the flashlight into her rain cape pocket, pulled up her hood, and set off down the hill, heading for the old swimming pool building. It was time to be more like Argent. It was time to follow Argent's way.

· EIGHT ·

THE BECOMING

The solid thunk of the wooden bar slotting into place across the door of the goodwife's hut reached Argent as she stood among the trees, trying to decide which way to go. She turned and looked back at the Goodie Patchie. Part of her wanted to run to the little hut and beg the goodwife to let her stay the night. But if she did that, her only option would be to return meekly to Haven's Edge the next morning. Then the baby dragon would be lost, the mother dragon would be killed, and she would be married to Thomas within a month.

Argent shuddered at the thought and quickly chose one of the network of tracks that ran through the forest. She set off along the track, but after a few minutes it narrowed away into nothing. Argent found another track and tried again, but this time she ended up back where she had started.

"Stupid," hissed Argent, realizing that the tracks were not for human travelers. The winding paths had been made by the creatures of the forest, and they were not interested in journeying through it to the other side as fast and straight as they could. Why would they want to? The forest was their home. She would have to find her way by other means.

Argent looked up to the sky, picking out familiar constellations between the tree branches. From the position of the stars, she was able to work out which way was north. After that it was easy to point herself in the direction of Goldstone City and start walking. Sometimes she picked up a track going her way. At other times she was grateful for the sturdy cloth of her father's trousers, which offered her some protection as she pushed her way onward through the brambly undergrowth.

As she walked, Argent kept her eyes and ears open, constantly checking her surroundings. She was searching for the red-haired man and the box he carried, but she was also on the alert for the creature that had hunted her through the gully. There was no sign of either of them. Nothing moved on the network of tracks and, as Argent walked deeper into the forest, the only sounds she heard were the squeaks and rustles of smaller nocturnal animals going about their business. Argent began to relax. It seemed that the goodwife was right about Unthank Forest. Not everything in it was out to cause her harm.

After a time her journey developed a rhythm. She would walk until she came to a clearing, and there she would stop to check the stars. If she had begun drifting off course, she would alter her direction and then push on again until she reached the next clearing. The walking took on a dreamlike quality, and Argent began to feel in tune with the forest. Milky dapples of moonlight poured down through the leaf canopy, and the ground was soft under her boots. As she moved quietly through the trees, heading deeper into the forest, she wondered why she had ever been afraid of Unthank.

Two hours later Argent was beginning to stumble with tiredness. It was the middle of the night, and she had been up since early morning. If she were back home in Haven's Edge, she would be tucked up in her sleeping loft now, completely unaware of the high-riding moon or the ground mist that was rising as the air cooled. Argent wiped the sweat from her face and peered around at the coils of thickening mist curling around the tree roots. She was so tired, she was beginning to see things. At the edge of her vision, the mist coils seemed to take the shape of silvery gray beasts that slunk between the trees with their bellies low to the ground but, when she turned her head, there was nothing there.

She struggled to the top of a low rise and let out a sigh of relief when she spotted a small clearing just ahead. She was in the deepest part of the forest now, and the tree canopy was so dense, it blocked out most of the sky. Argent had not been able to take a reading from the stars for some time, and she had no idea whether she was still heading in the right direction. She was also beginning to find the endless lines of mist-wreathed tree trunks oppressive and was longing for some open space.

The clearing was small, but at least she could see the sky and feel a bit of a breeze on her face. Argent stood in the bracken in the middle of the open ground and gazed up at the stars. The air in the clearing seemed fresher than the dead, still air under the trees, and she breathed deeply as she worked out her position. As she thought, she had veered off course again. Argent turned on the spot until she was facing the right way, but she felt strangely reluctant to plunge straight back into the trees. Something about this part of the forest was making her uneasy, but she could not figure out what it was.

Argent reached over her shoulder and pulled her water bottle from the top of her bedroll. When she yanked at the stopper, it came out with a pop that echoed around the clearing. She lifted the bottle to her mouth, drank thirstily, and then stopped, embarrassed at the loud, gulping noises she was making. When she lowered the bottle again, she could clearly hear the water inside sloshing about. Argent frowned down at the bottle. Why was everything sounding so loud? That was when it struck her. Every noise she made was exaggerated because the forest around her was completely silent.

The bottle in her hand began to tremble. Argent stared down at it, listening to the silvery tinkle of the water inside. When had all the other noises stopped? Now she thought about it, it had been some time since she had been aware of any of the small rustles, squeaks, and patterings of a living forest, but she had failed to notice because she had been walking along in a sleepy stupor. Argent stoppered the bottle and slung it over her shoulder again, trying to move as quietly as possible.

Something gray moved on the edge of the clearing to her left. Argent glanced sideways, thinking that her tired eyes were playing tricks again. She expected to see a streamer of ground mist twisting lazily around a tree trunk. Instead, she saw a long, thin face with golden eyes hanging in the darkness beneath the trees like a Halloween mask.

Argent felt the breath stop in her throat. A distant voice in her head was screaming at her to run, but she was frozen with terror. She could not take her eyes from the face. The golden eyes that glared back at her through the swirling mist were sucking all the strength from her legs. Argent had listened to village stories about the evil spirits that haunted Unthank Forest, but she had never quite believed them. Now she was going to become one of those foolish travelers in the stories who disappeared in the forest never to be seen again. An evil spirit had found her, and she knew there would be no escape from it. Argent dropped her water bottle and slumped to her knees.

As soon as she was down, the face began to glide toward her. Argent started to tremble, and beads of cold sweat formed in her hairline and trickled down her forehead. The face moved farther into the clearing and, as it left the swirling mist under the trees, a gray, long-legged body materialized beneath it. Argent blinked the sweat from her eyes. For a moment she could not make sense of what she was seeing, but then she gave a gasp of relief. The thing moving across the clearing toward her was a wolf. Only a wolf.

The strength returned to her legs, and she scrambled to her feet. Immediately the wolf stopped. The golden eyes shifted from side to side, and the rangy gray body crouched lower to the ground. Argent pulled the knife her mother had given her from its sheath and slipped the goodwife's shield onto her arm. She was still trembling with fear, but she would rather face a wolf than a spirit any day. At least a wolf was made of blood and bone.

The wolf's long, thin muzzle wrinkled up into a snarl, exposing sharp white fangs and a bright red lolling tongue. It looked over its shoulder and gave two short, barking growls. Argent's heart lurched in her chest as six more of the creatures stepped from the darkness under the trees. They formed a curved line across the clearing and stood, tensed and ready, looking from Argent to the big male, who was obviously the leader of the pack.

Argent nearly despaired. With a lone wolf, she had a chance, but a whole pack would pull her down and rip her throat out however hard she fought. Retreat seemed her only choice. Slowly she eased one foot behind her and then shifted her weight back onto it. The pack took a step forward so that the distance between them remained the same. Argent swallowed and began to take another step back. The pack set up a growl that reverberated around the clearing, and the gray fur on their backs rose into ridges of hackles.

Hastily Argent stopped moving, and the wolves resumed their positions of tense readiness, looking from her to the big male, then back to her. Even through the fog of fear that surrounded her, Argent could see that they were unsure. Their body language was constantly changing. As she watched them, the whole pack went low to the ground with their teeth bared and their haunches tensed, ready to pounce. She took a firmer grip on her knife and prepared to go down fighting, but a second later the whole pack had straightened up again and were dancing nervously in place with their hackles raised and their ears flat to their heads.

What was going on? Suddenly Argent lost patience with the situation. She was tired and footsore, and she had experienced more scares in one day than anyone should have to endure. Before she realized what she was doing, Argent lifted her arms and took a giant step forward, yelling at the top of her voice. The pack took a startled step back, and two of the smaller wolves turned tail and headed for the trees until a fierce growl from the big male brought them back into line.

It was stalemate. Except that Argent was swaying on her feet, and the pack looked rested and alert. She knew that with every passing minute, the wolves would grow in confidence until, finally, they would take a step forward and then keep on going, moving in for the kill. Argent did not want to take her eyes off the pack, but she risked a few hasty glances at the trees edging the clearing until she spotted one with a sturdy branch at just above head height. She decided that, when the final rush came, she would run for that tree as fast as she could and swing herself up into it. And then . . . Well, she would work out her next move once she had made it into the tree. If she made it into the tree.

Just then the growling of the wolves developed a note of urgency, rising in pitch and volume. Argent went up on the balls of her feet and prepared to race for her chosen tree at the first sign of an attack, but the pack stayed where it was. She looked at the wolves, and a chill climbed her spine as she realized that they were no longer watching her. Instead, they were gazing intently at something over her left shoulder. The growling stopped as suddenly as it started and the whole pack, even the big male, began to back away from her, flattening their ears against their skulls and cowering in the bracken. In the space of a second, the wolves had been reduced to a state of terror. Argent began to tremble as she saw a black shadow lengthening across the space between her and the pack. Something big had stepped out of the forest behind her and was now moving toward the center of the clearing.

Argent did not want to see what could terrify a pack of wolves, so she did not turn around. Instead, she stayed perfectly still, listening to the bracken rustle behind her as something moved through it, coming closer and closer. When the creature stopped right beside her, Argent risked a quick sideways glance and found herself staring at the biggest wolf she had ever seen.

The creature towered over her, and Argent realized that it was standing on its hind legs like a man.

It was so big and so close to her that she could only take in one nightmarish detail at a time. As her gaze traveled upward, she saw claws as curved and sharp as scimitars and then a ruff of thick, coarse fur that did nothing to disguise the powerful shoulders beneath. She saw clouds of hot breath spurting from the open jaws and then, finally, she was staring up into a pair of fierce golden eyes and seeing her own frightened face reflected in the black pupils.

The wolf regarded her for a few seconds more before turning to face the pack. It opened its great jaws and sent a deep snarl rumbling around the clearing. The effect was instantaneous. All seven wolves fled howling into the mist with their tails between their legs, leaving Argent alone in the clearing with the creature. She dared not look at the beast again. Instead, she closed her eyes and waited for the claws to rip her apart. Nothing happened, but she knew it was still beside her. Her nostrils were full of a wild, musky smell, and she could hear it breathing.

Argent knew she could not outrun the beast, and her shield was no protection against those raking claws. Her only hope was to launch an unexpected attack. If she could drive her knife deep into one of its golden eyes, she might be able to kill it. At the very least, it would buy her enough time to escape into the forest. Argent opened her eyes, took a trembling breath, and gripped the knife more firmly. Instantly the creature was on her, crushing her wrist in a vicelike grip. Argent cried out in pain. She thought her arm must be caught in the creature's mouth, but when she looked down she saw something that made no sense to her at all. Her wrist was being held in the grip of a large but very human hand.

"Don't," growled a deep voice with a rough catch to it.

Argent stared stupidly at the hand. It was definitely human. Another hand came into view and eased the knife from her fingers. Only then was the grip on her wrist relaxed. Argent sprang sideways and then turned to face whatever had taken her knife from her. A tall young man was standing in the bracken, calmly slipping her knife through a rough leather belt that was tied around his waist.

"I'll keep this for now," he growled.

"I— There was a—" Argent stumbled to a halt and gazed at the young man. He was wearing a jerkin made from the pelt of a wolf, with the thickest fur covering his broad shoulders. His hair was long and dark, with two pennants of gray running back to a point from each temple. Argent looked into his eyes and flinched. They were long and narrow with an upward slant, but the most disturbing thing about them was their color. They were golden brown, with a black ring around the iris.

The young man saw her flinch, and his lips curved in a humorless smile, revealing unusually long canines that glinted in the light of the full moon.

"There was a what?" he asked.

"Did you see . . . I thought I saw a—wolf."

"Only one? I saw seven of them. They all ran away when I appeared."

"No. I mean"—Argent looked over her shoulder and then back to the young man—"I mean here. There was a big wolf standing right here beside me. . . ."

The young man shrugged. "Only me," he said.

"But—I saw it." Argent stopped. Had she seen a wolf, or had she only seen this wolflike man?

"That shield," he demanded, his rough-edged voice taking on a harsher edge. "Did you steal it?"

"Steal it?" repeated Argent, thrown by the sudden change of subject.

"From the goodwife," he snarled. "Did you steal it?"

"No! She gave it to me. I tried to give it back, but she said I would have need of it."

"Ah, I see." He gave Argent an assessing stare and then seemed to accept that she was telling the truth. "She is a kind woman. I would not have her harmed."

"How did you know I visited her?" asked Argent warily.

"I was watching."

Argent's eyes widened. "You! In the gully, it was you!"

"I meant you no harm. Unthank is not a place to walk alone at night—"

"I can protect myself," snapped Argent.

"With this?" he mocked, pulling her knife from his belt. It looked tiny, clasped in his big fist.

"I was keeping those wolves at bay with it," said Argent hotly.

"No you weren't," said the young man, shaking his head. "They were wary of your smell."

"I don't smell!"

"You do. You stink of dragon. They could smell it." His nostrils flared. "So can I. The dragon smell saved you, not your knife. The pack could not decide whether you were food or something to fear." The young man paused. He looked up at the night sky, and the light of the moon turned his eyes to silver disks. "All day the forest has been disturbed by the cries of a dragon. I can hear her still, on the other side of the hill, calling for her baby."

Argent strained her ears, but she could hear nothing except the rustling of the trees around her.

"What have you done with it?" snarled the young man, turning on her with a frightening swiftness. "Have you killed it?"

"Me? No, you don't understand. I didn't take the baby—" Argent halted with a gasp of pain as the young man gripped her by the shoulder. His hand was very strong, and she could feel his long, sharp nails digging into the side of her neck.

"Then why is the dragon smell so strong on you?"

Argent had no explanation. She tried to twist away from his hand, but he only gripped tighter until she thought his nails would pierce her skin. He moved closer, and his golden eyes glowed with anger. Argent stared up at him. Was he growing taller? The fur across his shoulders seemed to be rising into hackles, and the gray streaks in his hair were starting to look like two pointed ears. His lips wrinkled back from his teeth, and suddenly her nose was filled with the rank smell of wolf.

"No, wait a minute. . . ." Desperately Argent tried to think of an explanation, but fear was making her slow. Then, at last, the answer came to her. "Oh! I know what you can smell!" Argent reached for her belt pouch, giddy with relief, but a warning snarl stopped her. "It's a dragon's egg," she explained. "Not a whole egg. Only the skin. The baby had already hatched."

The young man released his grip on her shoulder, and Argent stepped back and rubbed at her sore neck.

"Let me see it," snarled the young man.

Hastily Argent pulled the parcel of leathery skin from her belt pouch, unfolded it, and hung it over her arm. The young man bent and sniffed at it. When he straightened up again, the anger had gone from his eyes, but he was still watching her suspiciously.

"Why do you have it?"

"I—just picked it up, after the baby dragon was taken," explained Argent, refolding the expanse of egg skin and stuffing it back into her pouch.

"Why?"

"I don't know why I picked it up. I just did." Her head was spinning with tiredness and the aftereffects of fear. She thought she might pass out, and that was the last thing she wanted to do in the presence of this strange young man. She turned and began to walk away from him. "I—I have to go. I must get to Goldstone, or the mother dragon will be killed. . . ." Argent stopped. The bracken under her feet seemed to be moving. Unsteadily she stumbled over to a mossy boulder and sat down, holding her spinning head in her hands.

After a moment the young man picked up her water bottle and squatted down beside her. "Here," he said, proffering the bottle. Argent took it gratefully and pulled out the stopper with shaking hands.

"My name is Lukos," he said quietly. "Tell me about the dragon."

For the second time that night, Argent found herself recounting the whole story, between reviving sips of cool water from her bottle. When she got to the bit about the red-haired hunter, Lukos made a noise of recognition.

"The man you describe traveled through the forest earlier today," he said. "He had a large box strapped to the saddle, but there was no dragon smell."

"The box would have to be sturdy and heat proof to hold a baby dragon," said Argent. "If the seal on the box was strong enough, the dragon's scent would be trapped inside, wouldn't it?" Her eyes widened as she remembered something else. "And the goodwife said he stopped to wash in the stream before he entered the forest! Why would a man in a hurry do that, except to get rid of any dragon scent?"

Lukos nodded. It was a logical explanation. He pulled Argent's knife from his belt and handed it back to her. "You should sleep before you go on," he said, watching Argent's weary movements as she tried to get her knife back into its sheath. "Just two hours. You'll be the stronger for it—and you'll save time in the long run."

Argent shook her head. "The wolves might come back."

"We'll stand guard," said Lukos.

"We?" asked Argent.

"My family," said Lukos.

"Where are they?" asked Argent.

"Here," said Lukos simply. He stood up, threw back his head, and gave a low, howling call. That was when the empty clearing slowly came to life.

Argent sat on the boulder openmouthed as she witnessed one of the strangest and most magical sights she had ever seen. The first movement she spotted was under the spreading branches of an old, gnarled oak tree. As she watched, a whole section of tree seemed to peel away from the trunk, but without leaving a scar on the bark. Argent stared first at the main trunk, with its unbroken covering of gray, mossy bark, then at the section that had peeled away. It seemed to shiver in front of her eyes, and what had been a branch became an arm. The arm bent at the elbow and ran its fingers through what she had thought was bark, but which was now obviously a head of long brown hair, streaked with gray.

"Oh!" breathed Argent as the section of tree turned and walked toward her. It wasn't a tree at all, but a woman with sleepy green eyes and a gentle smile.

"My mother," said Lukos. "And look—over there."

He pointed to a place where there was a lively disturbance in the bracken, and Argent thought she caught a glimpse of a small vixen as it sprang into view for a split second before plunging down beneath the vegetation again. When the bracken parted for a second time, a young girl with bushy red hair and a sharp little nose appeared and then jumped and bounced across the clearing toward them.

"My sister, Reya," said Lukos, and the girl gave Argent a cheeky smile that showed her small, slightly pointed teeth.

A loud flapping of wings made Argent spin around just in time to see a boy falling from the higher branches of a tree with his cloak fluttering out behind him. Argent gasped, but the boy landed lightly and safely. As he walked toward them, his thick, feathery brows were drawn in a frown over his hooked nose.

"Tawn, my brother," said Lukos. "He likes to make an entrance."

Tawn said nothing as he studied Argent intently, tilting his head from side to side.

"And finally, my father," said Lukos.

Argent looked around dazedly. "Where?"

Lukos leaned forward with an amused twinkle in his eye. "You're sitting on him," he whispered.

Argent gaped at him. "What?" An instant later the boulder moved beneath her, and she jumped to her feet with a small scream. In front of her astonished eyes, the boulder stretched, groaned, and became a gray-haired man slowly straightening up out of a crouch.

"Oh, I'm so sorry," said Argent. "I had no idea."

"Don't worry," said Lukos's father with a resigned smile. "It happens all the time. I take it as a compliment."

Within a few minutes, while Argent stood in shock in the middle of the clearing, Lukos's family had created a camp out of nothing. They cleared a space in the middle of the clearing and used the bracken they had collected to make a circle of comfortable beds. A pile of dead wood was collected, and soon a fire was glowing in the middle of the cleared space.

"How?" asked Argent once she had been persuaded to join them around the fire. "How did you do that?"

"Making camp is easy," said Reya. "We do it all the time."

"No, she means the becoming," said Lukos's mother.

"Oh, that." Tawn sighed in a bored tone. He tilted his head to one side in a swift, birdlike movement and stared into the darkness for a moment. "Mouse," he said, in answer to his mother's inquiring glance. "Under that bush."

"The becoming?" asked Argent, watching Tawn uneasily. She could not even see the bush, never mind the mouse.

"Explain it, Lukos," said his father, stretching out his feet to the fire and settling back on one of the soft bracken beds.

Argent turned to Lukos, who thought for a moment before starting to speak.

"There's nothing supernatural about it," he

said. "We are people, just like you, but long ago, when your people began to build shelters and farm the land, we chose to stay in the forest. We have been here ever since. Your people fear us. They call us were-creatures or shape-shifters, but once, long ago, your people knew the becoming too. You have forgotten it, that's all."

"That is not answering her question," began Reya, bouncing impatiently.

"All right!" said Lukos, reaching out and pushing her over into the bracken. Argent smiled. They were just like any ordinary brother and sister now, but only a short while ago she had seen, or thought she had seen, their other shapes.

"The becoming is something anyone can learn," said Lukos. "From when we are very young, we are trained to sit for hours, simply watching and listening. We learn how everything lives in the forest and, over time, each of us selects the thing most in tune with our own natures. For my mother it was the slow life of trees, for my father the endurance of rock. Tawn chose owl, Reya fox, and I found a connection to the wolf. Once we have chosen, then we learn how to become."

"But how?" insisted Argent.

Lukos grimaced as he tried to find the words to explain. "It is not a physical change. Not really. The becoming is in here," he said, tapping his temple. "It is to do with understanding the mind and the instincts of your chosen creature absolutely. It is to do with believing you can be that creature. When your belief is strong enough, you will become."

"An illusion, then?" asked Argent.

"If you wish." Lukos shrugged, leaning forward to snap a dead branch and place the two halves on the fire.

Argent yawned hugely and discovered that she could not sit up a minute longer. She curled onto her bed of bracken and gazed into the fire.

"Sleep now," said Lukos. "We will keep watch."

"Aren't you tired?" asked Argent.

Lukos smiled and pointed at the full moon riding high above the clearing. "Not tonight," he said, looking at her with his golden eyes full of a wild energy.

Argent yawned again. She was exhausted. Part of her could not believe she was about to fall asleep surrounded by this strange family of forest dwellers, but she felt no sense of threat. "Wake me at dawn," she mumbled. Her eyes closed, and she drifted off listening to the soft talk of Lukos and his family and the hiss and crackle of the fire.

·NINE·

THE KEY

The front doors of the old swimming pool building were chained together, and the chain was secured with a strong padlock. Ellie glanced up and down the street, checking for watchers, but it was deserted. The rain was pounding down as hard as ever, and most people were keeping to their houses. Ellie climbed the three steps up to the door, then reached out and gently tugged on the padlock. The chain rattled loudly, and Ellie could hear the sound echoing around the empty hallway behind the doors. Hastily she let go of the padlock and grabbed the chain instead, cupping it in her hands to stop the rattling. If there was anyone in the building, she had just sent a warning that she was trying to get in. When she was sure all movement had stopped, Ellie carefully let go of the chain and retreated down the steps onto the pavement. She was sweating under her rain cape, and her heart was beating in her head.

"Stupid, stupid," she muttered, checking the deserted street again before turning back to study the building. Whoever was in there could not have found a way in at the front. The tall arched windows on either side of the padlocked doors were well above head height, and they were boarded up for extra security. Ellie turned and walked to the corner, where she peered into the darkness of a narrow, cobbled alley. The alley ran along the sidewall of the building and then curved around to the back. Ellie prepared to step into the dark alley and then hesitated. Was she really going to break into a derelict building all alone? If her mum and dad knew what she was about to do, they would be frantic with worry. Their son was missing, and now their daughter was thoughtlessly planning to put herself in danger. Ellie thought about going home instead and telling Lisa about the light in the old swimming baths, but then she thought of Argent and her jaw tightened. That was not Argent's way.

Ellie checked the road at the front of the building one last time before slipping into the dark alleyway. The squelch of her sodden trainers and the hiss of the falling rain sounded loudly in the narrow space as she hurried through to the other end of the alleyway. There she paused, flattening herself against the wall and cautiously peering around the corner. The back of the building was much less grand. The windows were smaller and closer to the ground, and there were two doors, both opening directly onto the street. Ellie took a deep breath and ducked out of the alleyway. She did not look behind her. If she had, she would have seen a tall, dark shape silhouetted in the opening at the far end of the alley.

Ellie reached the back of the building and stood on the pavement looking for entry points. Every window was boarded, and both doors were blocked with a sheet of corrugated iron. There was no way in as far as she could see. She was just beginning to think she must have imagined the flickering light in the roof dome when she noticed that one of the iron sheets was bending outward slightly at the corner. Ellie moved in for a closer look. The bottom half of the sheet on one side was not attached to the doorframe. She lifted the sheet farther away and peered inside. The door behind the iron was slightly ajar. Ellie squeezed an arm through the gap and gave the door a push. It swung open onto complete and utter darkness.

Ellie straightened up and eased the corner of the sheet back into place. She stood motionless in the pouring rain for a few seconds, wondering whether to go any further. The sheet had lifted away from the door quite easily, and she thought it would be possible to make a gap big enough to squeeze through, as long as she kept her head low. Ellie hesitated. She did not like the idea of crawling into darkness with no idea of what might be waiting for her in there. *Be more like Argent!* she thought fiercely, grabbing the bottom corner of the corrugated iron sheet and giving it a decisive pull.

The metal screeched as it bent outward, and Ellie cringed at the noise. Quickly she ducked in under the sheet, holding it up with one hand until she had shuffled through far enough to be clear when it sprang back into place. The metal clanged down behind her, and Ellie was left kneeling in darkness. She pulled her hood down, held her breath, and listened hard, but the rain was drumming against the other side of the corrugated iron and drowning out any other sounds. Someone could be padding toward her and she would not hear. Someone could be standing over her right now and she would not see. Ellie gasped and scrabbled the flashlight from her rain cape pocket. It seemed to take an age to find the switch, and she began to panic as she crouched in darkness, imagining hands reaching out to grab her by the back of the neck.

By the time she managed to switch on the flashlight, Ellie was nearly sobbing with fear. Hastily she pointed it into the building, and the bright beam pierced the darkness. She was crouched at one end of a long corridor with three doors leading off on one side and a fourth door facing her at the far end. The corridor was empty.

With a trembling sigh of relief, Ellie stood up on wobbly legs. Rainwater dripped from her cape and pattered onto the dirty floor, where it made a circle of dark splashes. Ellie looked down at the splashes and then noticed other wet tracks in the dust. There were boot prints and a strange set of markings that she could not identify. Ellie placed her trainer over the top of one of the boot prints. The foot that had made that print was much larger than hers. It belonged to a big man. The boot prints went all the way to the other end of the corridor. Ellie stared at the far door. Whoever had made the boot prints had gone through that door, heading farther into the abandoned pool building.

Ellie drew back her foot and bit her lip as she stared along the corridor. Was she really thinking about following an unknown and possibly dangerous man into an abandoned building, on her own? As her conscious mind was occupied with fearful second thoughts, Ellie stared down at the strange markings, and another part of her brain suddenly identified what had caused them. They were drag marks. Something heavy had been dragged along this corridor and into the building. Something heavy like a body.

"Danny!"

Ellie was moving almost before she realized what she was doing. She hurried along to the far end of the corridor, then covered the flashlight beam with her hand and eased the door open. She stood absolutely still, listening until she had counted to ten, but she heard nothing. Either the dark space beyond the door was empty, or someone was waiting silently for her to step out of the corridor. Ellie lifted her hand away from the flashlight and stepped through the doorway.

The white beam of the flashlight wavered crazily around the grand entrance hall of the building, skittering over crumbling plasterwork, a marble staircase, and ornate oak banisters as Ellie tried to look everywhere at once. When her first frantic sweep revealed nothing, she checked the entrance hall more carefully a second time. Only when she was sure no one was there did she return to tracking the path of the wet drag marks. They were more difficult to spot on the marble floor, but she managed to follow them to the bottom of the staircase. She looked up to the landing at the top of the stairs and saw a faint flickering of orange light. Somebody was up there.

Slowly Ellie climbed the marble stairs. Her soaking trainers squelched loudly with every step, but she dared not take them off. If she had to make a run for it, she did not want to be racing barefoot through a dark and derelict building. She reached the top of the stairs and came to a halt on the landing. In front of her was a door with a window in the top half. The flickering orange light was coming from behind that window. Ellie remembered the layout of the place from her school swimming lessons, and she knew that the door opened directly onto the poolside.

The glass in the door was dirty, and it was difficult to see anything clearly through the grime. Ellie groaned softly. The prospect of opening a third door without knowing what was waiting behind it was too much for her dwindling store of courage. She turned away from the door and was heading back to the stairs when she was hit by a sense memory so strong, it stopped her breath. She caught the smell of chlorine and heard Danny's high laughter echoing around the high-roofed entrance hall, then she *saw* him, six years old and racing across the landing with his wet hair sticking up all over the place and his towel trailing behind him.

"Don't run; you might slip. . . ." whispered Ellie, but Danny had already faded into the darkness again. Ellie swallowed back tears, then lifted her chin and clicked off the flashlight. Gripping the handle of the door, she eased it open. A faint crackling noise seeped out onto the landing and with it came a strange smell: sweet and cloying but with an acrid edge to it and a sour undertone of decay. Ellie pushed the door open a little farther and edged sideways through the gap. She was tensed and ready to run at the slightest sign of danger, but what she saw on the other side of the door was so strange, she forgot all about keeping her escape route open. She stepped away from the door, and it sighed shut behind her as she stared down into the pool.

It had been drained of water, but it was not empty. At the deep end of the pool, a fire was burning on the blackened tiles. Acrid smoke curled up from the fire and formed a hazy layer below the high roof, before finding its way out through a broken pane in the glass dome. Beyond the fire, a small house sat on the pool bottom. Ellie blinked and then squinted through the smoke haze, thinking she might be seeing things. It was definitely a small, brightly colored house, about the size of a beach hut. Quickly Ellie checked around the sides of the pool, but they were empty, and there was no movement behind the glass wall of the gallery above the deep end. The only danger points that she could see were the openings that led to the changing rooms halfway down the side of the pool. Ellie studied them. Both openings were completely dark. If anyone was in the building, it would make no sense for them to be sitting in the unlit, cold changing rooms when there was warmth and light out here. That only left the strange little house at the deep end of the pool.

Ellie walked down the wide, curved steps into the shallow end of the pool and edged her way down the slope toward the deep end. The house reminded her of one of the fairy tales her dad used to read to them when they were younger. Ellie frowned, trying to remember. Hansel and Gretel, that was it! The witch's cottage in the woods had been made of gingerbread and marzipan and all kinds of brightly colored sweets to tempt little children. Ellie shuddered and came to a stop, staring at the house. The witch in that story had tried to kill and eat Hansel. But Hansel had been saved because his sister, Gretel, had used all her wits and courage to rescue him. Ellie straightened her shoulders and moved on down the slope.

The sweet smell of decay grew stronger as she walked down into the deep end. Ellie gagged at the thick, greasy stench coming from the house and covered her nose with her hand. A few steps farther on, she was close enough to identify what the house had been built with and, suddenly, she understood why it smelled so bad. The structure was made entirely of used fast-food containers. The bricks in the walls were interlayered polystyrene burger boxes, and the roof tiles were milkshake cartons that had all been opened out into fans and laced together with twisted drinking straws. The little square window in the front wall of the house was a patchwork of grease-soaked, translucent chip papers, and the door was a hanging curtain of plastic carton tops. It was an amazing piece of work. Ellie wondered how old it was. Outside, in the wind and the rain, it would not have lasted long, but here, in the dry, protected depths of the empty pool, it could have been standing for years.

As Ellie stared in astonishment at the little house, she heard a faint squeaking, scraping sound. She whirled, looking for the source of the noise. It was coming from the door of the house. All the plastic carton tops were moving very slightly and scraping together. Ellie felt her heart begin to pound as she gazed intently at the door curtain. Were the carton tops shivering in a breeze so faint she could not feel it, or was there someone behind the curtain, peering out at her right now?

Even though she had been half expecting it, Ellie screamed with shock when the curtain suddenly exploded outward and something came hurtling toward her. She stumbled backward and lost her balance. Her feet flew into the air, and she landed on her back on the hard tiles. All the breath was knocked out of her, and for a few seconds she lay gasping like a stranded fish, staring wide-eyed at the swirling smoke in the roof space and listening to heavy footsteps coming toward her. Still whooping for breath, Ellie turned over and slowly, painfully, pushed herself up onto her hands and knees.

Desperately she began to crawl out of the deep end, but the footsteps came to a stop right in front of her, and Ellie found herself staring down at a pair of large army-style boots. Trembling with fear, she pushed herself back on her heels and looked up into a lined and dirty face framed with lank twists of gray hair that hung down on either side. It was the bag lady, and she looked even more frightened than Ellie felt.

"Please, I didn't mean to scare you—" began Ellie.

"No ball games!" shrieked the bag lady, waving her arms in front of Ellie's face.

Ellie struggled to her feet. "I'm looking for my brother."

"No spitting!" continued the bag lady, flapping her old tweed coat at Ellie as though she were a chicken. "No diving!"

The bag lady's shooing motions became more frantic, and Ellie began to back away toward the shallow end. "I only want to ask you—"

"No running on the poolside!" screeched the bag lady, stamping her big boots down centimeters from Ellie's toes.

"Hey! You stop that!" yelled Ellie, stamping back.

The bag lady flinched away from her and then began to rock back and forth on the spot. Her face screwed up in anguish, and she began to cry. "No s-s-swimmers beyond this p-p-point!" she wailed, and the tears coursed down her face, making clean white tracks through the grime.

"Oh. Oh, dear. I'm sorry," said Ellie, reaching out a hand and then hastily pulling it back again as the bag lady's crying rose to a frightened scream. "I thought my brother might be here."

"The pool is closing now." The bag lady sobbed. "Please finish your swim and leave the water."

"His name is Danny," said Ellie, but the bag lady was now holding her hands in front of her face and waggling her fingers as though conducting a very small orchestra.

"Last swim, last swim," she crooned to herself.

"Oh, never mind," said Ellie, turning away and trudging despondently toward the shallow end.

"Danny. . . ?"

Ellie stopped and looked over her shoulder. The bag lady had lowered her hands and stopped rocking. "Danny?" she repeated, sending Ellie a shy glance from a pair of bright blue eyes.

"Yes, Danny," said Ellie. "He's my brother." She turned and walked back to the bag lady, taking care to move slowly and quietly and stopping when they were still a good distance apart.

"Danny Boy." The bag lady nodded. "Happy Chappie. Little Smiler." She gave Ellie a small smile of her own, which suddenly made her look much younger. Ellie realized with a little shock of surprise that the woman was probably only in her early fifties, despite the gray hair and the deep lines on her face.

"Happy Chappie. That sounds like Danny," she said, returning the smile. "I'm trying to find him. He's been missing since yesterday morning. Have you seen him?"

The bag lady shook her head.

"Is he here?"

"No! This is my place! My pool!" spat the bag lady, beginning to return to her earlier crazy behavior. "No ball games! No running—"

"Please! Please listen," begged Ellie. The bag lady stopped and glowered at her from under straggly brows. "My name is Ellie. I'm Danny's sister and I—I'm really worried about him," continued Ellie. "Especially now the rain's started."

"Rain!" hissed the bag lady, shaking her fist at the glass dome in exactly the same way as she had shaken her fist at the sky earlier that day. "Nasty cold, wet stuff." She shivered and then shuffled over to a stack of takeout bags near the fire. Each bag was tightly packed with folded cardboard and polystyrene fragments.

"Don't you like the rain?" asked Ellie, watching as the bag lady folded over the top of one of the bags and then stamped on it several times.

"Rain stops play!" snapped the bag lady, throwing the compressed wad of cardboard and polystyrene onto the fire. "No collecting when the raindrops fall. When the rain fall drops. When the fall drops rain—"

"Collecting?" Ellie interrupted. The bag lady frowned at her in confusion. "What do you collect?"

The bag lady's face brightened with pleasure. She hurried over to a pile of black sacks in one corner of the pool and pulled the nearest one open for Ellie to see inside. It was full of fast-food boxes and cartons. "All left for me out on the streets." The bag lady smiled proudly. "Just for me!"

Ellie looked at the black sack and realized that it must be the same one the bag lady had been pulling around in her cart earlier that day. It was still glistening wet from the rain and, suddenly, Ellie knew what had made the wet drag marks along the corridor downstairs. There was no way the bag lady could fit her cart through the gap between the back door and the corrugated metal sheet. She must have lifted the sack from the cart and then dragged it through the gap and along the floor, leaving the wet marks behind her. Ellie guessed that the cart must be hidden outside somewhere at the back of the pool building.

The bag lady suddenly gave a high squeal of pleasure, making Ellie jump. She had spotted a half-eaten burger in one of the polystyrene boxes. "All for me," she repeated, grabbing the burger and lifting it to her mouth.

Ellie felt her stomach heave. "Don't—" she said, before she could stop herself. The bag lady looked at her, then down at the half-eaten burger in her grimy hand. Reluctantly she held the burger out to Ellie.

"No thanks," said Ellie faintly. "I'm not hungry."

The bag lady gave a relieved sigh and snatched the burger back before Ellie could change her mind. "All mine to collect," she said, through a mouthful of burger. "But not in the rain. Rain makes them soggy, makes them saggy. Rain turns them into mush, into mash, into—"

"Do you know where Danny might have gone?" asked Ellie, stopping the bag lady in mid-flow. "Or—been taken?"

"Danny." The bag lady swallowed the last of the burger. "He helps me to collect. He's a good boy."

"Yes, I know, but have you seen— Oh, never mind," said Ellie, giving up. "Thank you. Excuse me. I have to go. I have to keep looking."

"All his friends," said the bag lady quietly, looking Ellie in the eye and suddenly sounding calm and sane. "We are all his friends."

Ellie nodded, feeling tears sting her eyes.

"We would not hurt Danny Boy," continued the bag lady. "If we knew where he was, we would bring him back to you."

Ellie nodded again, too choked up to speak. The bag lady patted her on the arm.

"You will need a key," she said decisively.

"A key?" echoed Ellie.

"Yes. To take with you on your search. Wait here." The bag lady shuffled over to the metal steps that descended into the deep end of the pool. From where she stood waiting, Ellie could see that lines of small objects had been carefully arranged along every tread, but she was too far away to work out what they were.

"A key to what?" she called.

"To open the right door when you need it," said the bag lady, running her finger along the front edge of each step like a librarian searching for a particular book. "Which one? Which one?" she muttered.

Ellie was intrigued. Perhaps it had been worth coming here after all. Perhaps, without knowing it, this crazy old woman had the answer to Danny's disappearance. Or at least a clue. Ellie took a step closer, but still could not see what the little objects were.

"Aha!" The bag lady grabbed one of the objects from the steps and hurried back to Ellie, cradling it against her chest. Ellie held out her hand, palm upward, and the bag lady dropped the object into it. "The key," she said solemnly.

Ellie looked down at her hand. "It's Bart," she

said stupidly, staring at the little plastic figure wearing blue shorts and riding a skateboard.

"No. That's Danny," explained the bag lady, pointing out the figure's yellow hair and wide smile. "See? And watch!" She scooped the plastic giveaway toy out of Ellie's hand and pressed a lever on Bart's back. His arms shot out sideways as though he was finding his balance on the board. The bag lady let out a high laugh and pressed the lever again. "Collect the whole set!" she crowed. "One free with every meal!"

Ellie closed her eyes. She could taste the bitter disappointment in her mouth.

"Take it," insisted the bag lady, pressing the little toy into her hand. "It is the key."

"Thank you," said Ellie, smiling as politely as she could.

Satisfied, the bag lady turned and shuffled off. As soon as her back was turned, Ellie stopped smiling. Wearily she stuffed the little toy into the front pocket of her rain cape and checked her phone. Nothing. Ellie trudged up to the shallow end of the pool, pulling her flashlight from her pocket. All she wanted to do now was to get home and curl up in her bed. She climbed up the steps to the poolside and opened the door onto the landing. When she looked back, the bag lady was nowhere to be seen. She must have ducked back into her little house. Ellie stared at the strange scene for a few seconds before slipping out onto the landing and letting the door swing shut behind her.

She was halfway down the marble staircase when she heard the screech of metal coming from somewhere in the building below. Ellie clutched at the banister rail and nearly dropped her flashlight. She recognized that metallic screech. Someone had just moved the corrugated iron screen over the back door. Ellie ran down the remaining steps, hurried over to the door that opened onto the corridor, and clicked off her flashlight. She had left the door slightly ajar on her way upstairs and now she put her ear to the gap and listened.

An instant later she flung herself away from the door and slammed against the wall behind it. She had heard someone padding up the corridor toward her. He was panting hard, as though he had been running and, as he walked, he was clicking his fingers. Ellie pressed herself against the wall and put a hand over her mouth to smother her frightened breathing. There was no time to find another hiding place. He would be opening the door any second now. Her only chance was to stay where she was and hope he would not see her.

Something knocked against the door and it swung open, but not far enough to completely hide her from view. Ellie squashed herself against the doorframe and raised the flashlight above her head. He might not look around but, if he did, at least she would have something to hit him with. The clicking had stopped, but she could still hear the panting breaths just on the other side of the door. Then the door was nudged again, and Ellie jumped as she caught a movement down by her feet. She looked down and her mouth fell open as a small brown mongrel padded out into the entrance hall with its claws clicking on the marble floor.

Ellie let out a relieved yelp of a laugh and then bent forward, hugging her stomach. She thought she was going to be sick. The mongrel turned and regarded her with friendly eyes before pushing its muzzle into her face and giving her a wet lick across the cheek. Hastily Ellie straightened up to avoid more of the same, but the mongrel did not take offense. It panted at her happily before trotting away toward the stairs. It seemed to know exactly where it was going, and Ellie guessed that this was not the first time the mongrel had called on the bag lady.

Ellie smiled tiredly as she left the entrance hall and set off toward the back door with her flashlight beam bobbing along the dark corridor ahead of her. She was glad that the bag lady had company. The old pool building must be a lonely place at times, especially when the rain was drumming on the glass roof dome and the darkness stretched out beyond the circle of firelight. She reached the outer door, turned off her flashlight, and put her hip to the corrugated iron sheet. It bent back with a groan, and she slipped through the gap and out into the rainy night.

Only when the metal sheet had clanged back into place did one of the doors in the side wall of the corridor ease open. A tall figure stepped out, made his way to the door, and followed Ellie out into the night. He tracked her through the alleyway, then stood with the rain soaking into his hair, watching Ellie hurry away up the street.

· *TEN* ·

TRUST

Danny had a plan. It was only a little plan, nothing like the with-one-bound-he-was-free sort of plan the hero always came up with in the movies. He did not have a knife hidden in his boot, or a piece of plastic explosive disguised as a stick of chewing gum. In fact, Danny had to admit that his plan would not change anything very much. He would still be a captive, lying in darkness and pain on a cold, damp floor. But at least he had *thought* of a plan. Despite the pain and the fear and the drugs clouding his brain, he, Danny Brody, had thought of a plan. And that gave him hope.

His plan was simple. The next time Jabber, his captor, returned to jab a needle into his thigh, Danny was planning to lie still, keep his eyes shut, and wait until the flashlight beam was shining full in his face. Then he was going to flip over onto his other side as fast as he could, turning his back on the flashlight. Instead of blinding him, the flashlight beam would then be lighting the darkness ahead, giving him his first glimpse of his prison. Danny was hoping that in the few seconds before Jabber reached him with the syringe, he would be able to identify the place where he was being held, or at least see something that could help him to escape the next time he surfaced.

The problem was, for Danny's plan to work he had to be capable of movement, but the drug Jabber was using on him seemed to split his mind from his body. In one way this was a good thing. It meant that while he was in Argent's world, he could not feel the cramps biting into his muscles, the pressure sores that were developing on his hip and shoulder, or the swellings at the injection sites in his thigh. Unfortunately it also meant that as the drug wore off, his mind always returned to consciousness before his body woke up. It felt as though his head was suspended in the air, slowly spinning, while his unresponsive body remained curled on the ground below.

Danny estimated that he had been struggling toward full consciousness for about twenty minutes now, and ever since he had been awake enough to think up his plan he had been trying to move, but his arms and legs were still as limp as pieces of wet string and time was running out. Jabber always seemed to know when the next dose of the drug was due and would be arriving any minute now to administer it. Danny gritted his teeth and tried to move again. This time his right leg twitched. Encouraged, Danny strained until beads of sweat popped out on his forehead, and he managed to curl both legs up to his chest.

After that things slowly improved. Danny worked on stretching and flexing his limbs until he heard Jabber's footsteps approaching. Then he took a deep, calming breath, closed his eyes, and lay still, curled on his side. He made his face go slack and tried to ignore the pain of the pressure sores on his hip and shoulder as he waited for the flashlight beam to find him. The light shone through his closed eyelids with a red glow as Jabber positioned the beam on his face. Danny tensed. His arms and legs were still weak, and he did not know whether he could manage to flip himself over when the moment came, but he had to try. As soon as Jabber started moving toward him again, Danny pushed against the floor with his joined hands and swung his knees up with all the strength he could muster. To his relief, he rolled right over onto his other side.

As soon as he was in position, Danny opened his eyes. In the blaze of the flashlight beam, he saw a rough brick wall and a rack of industrial shelving stacked with rows of large jars. Each jar was filled with a murky, pink-tinged liquid and there seemed to be things suspended in the liquid, half hidden in the murk. It took Danny a second to understand what he was looking at, then his eyes widened. One jar contained a thick, purple tongue. Another was full of eyeballs with filmed-over pupils and optic nerves dangling like balloon strings. There was a dull gray heart, a brain with a stump of spinal cord, and then something pale and delicately frilled that he could not identify.

Danny tried to scream, but his throat was parched and his tongue felt like a wad of cotton wool in his mouth. He stared at the horrors floating in the formaldehyde until Jabber grabbed his shoulder and pulled him onto his back. His jaw was squeezed open, and water poured in over his tongue and down his throat. He choked and swallowed, gagging on the liquid as he tried to turn his head to see who was there, but Jabber stayed hidden behind the flashlight beam. Danny was beside himself with terror. What was going to happen to him in this dreadful place? His only consolation was that Jabber was forcing water down his throat. That must mean that Jabber wanted him alive. For the time being. When the rush of water stopped and the needle was plunged into Danny's thigh, he welcomed the chance to spiral away from the jars on the shelves and back into Argent's world.

Argent opened her eyes. She was curled up on her side, warm and comfortable in her bed, but something was tickling her nose. Something green and feathery. Argent squinted at it, trying to work out what it was. A bracken frond came into focus and, suddenly, everything came flooding back. She was not in her bed at all, but lying in a clearing in Unthank Forest. Instantly Argent was fully awake and alert. It had been dark when she fell asleep, but now it was early morning. How could she have let herself sleep the night away surrounded by a family of were-creatures?

And where were they now?

Argent made herself stay still, moving only her eyes as she checked the forest clearing in front of her. It was deserted and quiet. Insects and dust motes floated in the slanting beams of low sunlight, and there was no sign of a camp or of the fire that had been burning when she went to sleep. The early sun had already burned off most of the mist, and she could see that the bracken all around her was whole and undisturbed.

Argent frowned. Had the meeting with the were-creatures really happened, or had she stumbled into the clearing, made up her own bracken bed, and then fallen into a night of disturbing dreams? She lay still for a moment longer, checking her surroundings. The meeting had seemed so real. She could remember their names, their soft voices, and the crackling heat of the fire, but the empty clearing was telling her it must have been a dream. Argent decided to go with the evidence in front of her eyes. She relaxed into the soft bracken and was about to give a relieved sigh when she heard a papery rustling right behind her.

Argent froze. The noise came again, and she recognized it as the sound of parchments rustling together. Someone, or something, was going through her things. Argent forced herself to stay still except for her hand, which began creeping toward the knife at her belt as slowly as cold molasses.

"Don't," said a soft voice behind her. Argent just managed to stop her body from jumping in shock. She recognized the voice. It was Lukos. She had not been dreaming, then. There really had been a fire in this clearing that now looked as though it had never been disturbed.

"If you're wondering where the camp has gone, we always leave as we find," said Lukos. "Before we set a fire, we dig up the bracken by the roots. Then we replant the bracken when the fire is cold."

Argent suppressed a shudder. How could he have known what she was thinking? Could he read her mind? She closed her eyes, lay still and frantically tried to work out what to do next.

"I know you're awake," said Lukos, with a touch of amusement in his voice. "You were snoring, and now you're not."

"I don't snore!" snapped Argent, sitting up and pushing aside the bracken that someone had piled over her in the night.

"Only little snores," said Lukos with a grin that revealed his sharp canine teeth. "You sounded like a cat purring."

Argent stared coldly at Lukos. He was squatting on his haunches with her blanket unrolled in front of him. Her clothes and meager provisions were scattered in the bracken, and he was holding her precious parchments in his hands. "What are you doing?" she demanded.

"These are interesting," said Lukos, ignoring her question. "I don't read, but the drawings are very clear. You have a kinship with dragons, I think. Perhaps this is the start of a becoming—"

"How dare you!" snapped Argent, scrambling to her feet and snatching the parchments from his hands. "I am not a were-creature!"

Lukos snarled and rose up to his full height in one smooth movement. Argent stared up into his amber eyes, then ducked her head and began to roll her parchments together.

"I told you," snarled Lukos. "We are people, just like you."

"Not like me," muttered Argent defiantly as she

gathered her possessions together and crouched to wrap them in her blanket.

"No. Not like you," he grated. "We do not put such store on ownership. In the forest nothing is owned, and everything is shared."

Argent did not reply. She could sense the anger radiating from him like heat from a fire, and her hands were shaking as she tied the twine around her blanket roll. From the corner of her eye, she saw his hands clenching and unclenching. Was she imagining it, or were his nails lengthening into yellow claws? Argent fumbled the knot and started again more slowly. She had to get away from him, but she must not let him see she was frightened.

By the time she had tied the twine and straightened up again, Lukos was calm. The amber light had faded slightly from his eyes, and his hands looked normal enough to Argent, but she could not forget what she had seen just a minute earlier.

"My family left before dawn," said Lukos formally. "I stayed to wake you, as you requested."

Or to go through my stuff, seeing what you could find, thought Argent. "Thank you," she said aloud, equally formally. "I must leave now if I am to reach the duke in time to save the dragon." She picked up the little wooden shield the goodwife had given her, slung it over her shoulder on top of the blanket roll, then turned and walked away across the clearing, but Lukos caught up and padded alongside her.

"Thank you," repeated Argent. "I'm going to Goldstone now."

"No you're not," said Lukos.

"Are you threatening me?"

"No. But you're not going to Goldstone. You're heading the wrong way."

Argent stopped, checked the position of the sun, altered her direction, and set off again without a word. She was stepping from the clearing into the trees when Lukos caught up with her again.

"I could guide you through the forest," he suggested, falling into step alongside her.

"I'll be fine."

"I could track the red-haired hunter," said Lukos, his nostrils flaring. "I know his scent. Let me help."

Argent felt the hairs prickle on the back of her neck. The goodwife had warned her to beware of the man who offered his help. "No thank you," she said, walking faster.

"But if we found him, we could save the baby dragon," persisted Lukos. "I would like to help."

There it was again. The offer of help. Argent stopped and looked him straight in the eye. "I don't need your help."

Lukos stopped smiling. "It is not you I wish to help, but the mother dragon and her baby."

"I can manage on my own," said Argent.

Lukos regarded her flatly for a few long seconds

and then gave her an ironic bow. This time when she started walking again, he did not follow. She hurried on through the trees. *Don't look back*, she told herself. *Don't look back*. But the skin on her neck grew tighter with every creaking branch and rustling leaf and, finally, she had to check over her shoulder. Lukos was still standing at the edge of the clearing, leaning against a tree and watching her. Argent pretended she had stopped to adjust her blanket roll and then hurried on. The next time she checked, the clearing and Lukos had both disappeared from sight.

Argent gave a sigh of relief and stopped to shrug the tightness out of her shoulders. She took a drink of water from her bottle and then tied the little wooden shield securely onto her blanket roll before resuming her journey. Her spirits lifted as she walked on, chewing the stale remains of yesterday's bread. She had managed to survive a night in Unthank Forest and now the sun was shining. If she set a good pace, she should reach Goldstone City by nightfall.

She walked all morning, stopping in every clearing to check the position of the sun and work out her direction from it. Gradually the clearings became less frequent and the forest became denser until at times the trees were so close together, Argent could not see the sun at all. She kept going, working out her direction from the pattern of moss growth on the tree trunks that surrounded her. She knew moss always grew thickest on the south side of a trunk and that seemed to hold true even in this deep forest, where only a pale, diffused sunlight filtered down to her through the leaf canopy.

Halfway through the morning, something else began to filter down through the leaves. Faintly at first, but growing louder by the second, the hoarse, breathy shriek of the mother dragon sounded over the forest. The great beast had widened her search. Argent knew she was hidden from sight under the dense tree canopy, but still she had to resist the urge to run every time the dragon passed overhead. The breathy roar of the beast was so loud, it seemed to make the ground shake, and its beating wings sent blasts of scorching air down through the trees, causing the topmost leaves to wilt instantly. Argent stumbled on, feeling her shoulders tighten into knots every time the dragon shrieked.

Then the terrain became more difficult, moving from level ground and gentle slopes into a succession of increasingly steep-sided gullies that sliced across her direction of travel. Argent carried on with grim determination, slipping and sliding down into a gully, splashing through an icy stream, then scrambling up the other side, but an hour later she was exhausted and she had hardly moved forward at all. As she leaned against a tree, staring down into the next gully, her chest was heaving and her legs were trembling with weariness. She had lost the sun completely, so she wiped the sweat from her eyes and peered at the tree she was leaning against in order to work out her direction. She was checking the pattern of moss growth, but in these damp, deep gullies the lush, green stuff seemed to be everywhere, including all over her. Her clothes were slimed with it, and more of it was packed under her nails.

As Argent swatted away a persistent mosquito, she began to feel, deep in her stomach, the first flutters of fear. Her early optimism about reaching Goldstone by nightfall was now beginning to seem ludicrous. She was bone weary, she had lost her sense of direction, and she was hardly making any headway. At this rate, the chances were she would still be in Unthank Forest when night fell.

A panicked moan escaped from her throat. She had to get out of this forest before dark. She could not face another night under the rustling trees.

When the dragon let out an earth-shaking roar directly above her, Argent's nerve snapped. She launched herself into the next gully at a run. As she slithered down the slope, digging her heels into the mud, she was grateful to see that at least this gully did not have a stream running through it. Her feet were still aching with cold from the last stream she had waded through.

She reached the bottom and set off across the

leaf-covered ground, sending panicked glances into the treetops. The high canopy was thick, but not thick enough to keep out a fully grown dragon. If the circling beast decided to dive now, the interwoven branches would splinter into kindling and Argent would have nowhere to hide. She was halfway across the gully, gazing upward and running blind, when the leaves gave way beneath her. Argent was too surprised to make a sound. An instant later she was up to her thighs in the freezing sludge that lay hidden beneath the crust of leaves. Argent gasped as the cold bit into her. She thrashed around, trying to find some solid ground, but her feet sank farther into a thick, sucking layer of mud and, suddenly, the sludge was up to her waist.

Argent became very still as she realized the trouble she was in. She had fallen into a hidden bog. The surface crust of leaves was rippling and bulging all around her as the sludge beneath slowly settled. Carefully Argent turned her head, checking how far the ripples were spreading. Fear gripped her as she saw that, in all directions, solid ground was too far away for her to reach. Her floundering had driven her right into the middle of the bog.

Desperately Argent looked around the gully for something, anything that might help her pull free. The only possibility was an overhanging tree branch just ahead of her. Slowly, carefully, Argent stretched her arms out to the branch. She could almost touch it with her fingertips, but it was just too far away to grasp. Argent attempted to push herself toward the branch and immediately sank another two inches. Hastily she lowered her arms and waited for the heaving sludge to subside. The cries of the mother dragon had faded into the distance as the great beast continued on her sweeping search and the gloopy, sucking noises of the mud and Argent's panicked breathing sounded loudly in the sudden quiet of the gully.

The branch was now unreachable, and she was sinking farther away from it with every passing second. Feverishly Argent looked around, searching for something that she could use to hook the branch down to her level, but there were only leaves floating on the surface of the mud. She looked again. Surely there must be something she could use? Her eyes widened as she remembered the blanket roll strung across her shoulders. She could swing that up over the branch and use it to pull herself free.

Carefully Argent eased the blanket roll from her shoulders. The little shield was still attached to it, and Argent debated whether to remove it first. She decided to leave it in place. The extra weight would help her to direct the throw. She gripped the shield with one hand and the twine strap with the other, and then she took a deep breath, judging distances and angles. She knew she would only have one chance to get this right. Argent lifted the blanket roll back over one shoulder and then flung it up at the tree. It flew through the air and landed sweetly over the top of the branch.

Argent gasped with relief, but the relief was short-lived. The sudden movement of her throw had disturbed the mud she was caught in, and she sank up to her chest. Argent still had the length of twine clutched in her hand, and she hung on until it felt as though her arm was about to be ripped out of its socket. Above her the tree branch creaked and groaned as it was bent downward by her weight. Her eyes filled with tears of pain and frustration as, slowly, the twine began to slip through her grasp, scraping the skin from her fingers as it went.

"No. . . ," gasped Argent, hooking her fingertips over the twine in a last, desperate attempt to hang on. An instant later the twine flew out of her hand, nearly taking her fingernails with it. The tree branch sprang upward, lifting the blanket roll far out of her reach. As Argent stared up at the dangling twine with a hopeless longing, she suddenly remembered what her father had told her to do if she was ever caught in the bog down by the river at Haven's Edge.

Don't try to walk out, he had told her. *That's what sheep and cattle do, but they're stupid, and that's why they die. You have to spread yourself out on the surface and then slowly swim your way to the edge.*

Argent groaned. It was too late to spread out on the surface. The bog was up to her neck. She had been stupid, and now she was going to pay for it. She was going to die alone, choking on mud just like Old Crocus, Morgana's favorite cow. It was becoming harder to fill her lungs with air as the bog pressed in on her chest, but Argent took as deep a breath as she could and sent out a desperate call for help. Her voice echoed around the gully, and a pair of startled wood pigeons rose into the air, clapping their wings.

Argent tried again. "Help! Somebody help me! He—"

Her last scream was choked off as leaves and slime poured into her open mouth. Argent coughed and retched, then lifted her chin out of the bog and attempted to clear her mouth. Mud oozed from her lips and the breath bubbled in her throat as she looked up at the leaf canopy high above her, trying to catch one last glimpse of sun. The mud flowed into her ears so that all she could hear was the wild beating of her own heart. Argent closed her eyes. She had run out of time. As she sank down into the bog and the cold mud blocked her nostrils, she wanted to scream and cry, but that would mean letting go of her last breath and she wanted to hold on to that for as long as she could.

Her lungs started to strain until the urge to take another breath was almost overwhelming. Argent knew that the last few seconds of her life were running out, and suddenly she wanted her mother so badly, it hurt. Red flashes exploded behind her eyelids, and a buzzing started in her head. Then something grabbed her hair by the roots and pulled until she thought her scalp would split.

Argent rose up out of the bog, took a whooping lungful of glorious air, and then screamed at the pain in her scalp. Her eyes flew open, and she stared straight into the straining, snarling face of Lukos. He was stretched full length along the tree branch, with one hand holding her by the hair. The muscles of his arm stood out like ropes, and he was shaking with the effort. Lukos hooked his legs around the branch, reached down with his other arm, and gripped her around the waist. The dreadful pain in her scalp eased as he let go of her hair, and Argent's scream subsided to a whimper. Her legs were still totally submerged in thick, sucking mud and she did not know how long Lukos could hold on to her, but just to be able to breathe again was all she cared about.

Blinking away mud, she looked up into Lukos's straining face again. His mouth was moving as he yelled at her, but her ears were full of mud and she could hear nothing. Argent was still struggling for breath, but she was becoming aware that she was still in great danger. Lukos could lose his grip at any moment, or the tree branch could break, plunging them both into the bog. She tried to concentrate on ways of helping Lukos, but a roaring was starting in her head and a red mist was clouding her vision. Argent tried to speak, but before she could form the words, she flopped forward over his arm and sank away into darkness.

· ELEVEN ·

SILVER AND RED

Ellie sat at the kitchen table watching the rain.
It was Monday morning, and there was still
no news of Danny. He had been missing for forty-
eight hours now, and for the last twenty of those
hours the rain had not stopped falling. Ellie felt her
stomach twist at the thought that Danny might be
out there somewhere, unprotected, while she sat in
a warm, dry house. She looked down at the slice of
buttered toast in front of her and then pushed the
plate away.

At this time on a Monday morning, the kitchen
was usually crowded and chaotic as all four of them
rushed around, eating toast on the run and getting
in one another's way. Today Ellie was alone, and the
kitchen was so quiet, she could hear the wall clock

ticking. Her father had left the house at eight o'clock, heading out for another day of searching, not long after Lisa had arrived. Ellie had the feeling that her dad disliked Lisa as much as she did, but they were both putting up with her for Mrs. Brody's sake. Her mother had not yet emerged from her den in Danny's bedroom, and Lisa was up there with her now, bringing her up-to-date on the police investigation.

The news was not good. Police inquiries had turned up two possible sightings of Danny. A bus driver thought he had seen a boy matching Danny's description hanging around the bus station on Saturday morning, but he had not seen which coach the boy had boarded. Lisa had looked particularly smug when she told Ellie and Mr. Brody about the bus station sighting. She did not say anything, but Ellie knew what she was thinking. The sighting supported Lisa's theory that Danny was a runaway.

More worryingly, a tourist had seen a boy of Danny's age getting into a red hatchback that had stopped on the bridge above Chuggie's Pool. The tourist remembered the incident because, as she passed the car, she had heard the boy protesting that he would rather walk. She also remembered that the red hatchback had stopped on the bridge at precisely five to two. She knew that because she had been taking her children to the cinema to see a two o'clock film, and they were rushing to make the start time. The only thing the tourist could not remember was what the person behind the wheel looked like. She had not looked into the car as she hurried past and could not provide a description of the driver.

Ellie had felt her stomach lurch with fear when she heard about the red hatchback. She and her dad had spent five minutes reassuring each other that Danny would never get into a stranger's car, but the fear had not gone away. It was still there now, lodged in the pit of her stomach like a stone. The only piece of good news that morning was that Ross had been true to his word. He had dealt with the television crew. The white van was no longer camped out in the front street.

Wearily Ellie now got to her feet, switched on the little television in the corner, and let the breakfast news drown out the ticking clock. She found it comforting to hear the babble of voices in the background while she cleared away the dishes. For a short while it made the day seem normal. Ellie was loading the dishwasher when she heard Ross outside. She hurried across the kitchen and opened the back door.

"You'll be late for school," she began, but Ross was not there. Ellie peered out, looking left and right. The back garden was empty. Ellie shut the door again with a puzzled frown. The lonely kitchen must be getting to her. She was hearing voices. She bent to shut the dishwasher door, and Ross spoke again.

"Of course, they're all devastated," he said. "Mrs. Brody rarely leaves Danny's bedroom, and Mr. Brody is out at all hours, helping with the search."

The dishwasher door slammed shut with a crockery-rattling crash as Ellie let go of the handle. She turned to face the little television on the kitchen bench. On the screen she saw Ross, standing in the rainy dark outside her house on Sunday night, giving an interview to the television crew from the white van. He had removed his fluorescent orange cape for the camera and was looking concerned and handsome in his leather jacket. The caption at the bottom of the screen described him as a "friend of the family."

Ellie stared at the screen in disbelief. She gasped. "What are you doing, Ross?"

"Can you tell us about Danny's sister?" asked the interviewer. "How is she coping?"

"Don't," pleaded Ellie, stepping closer to the television and shaking her head.

"Ellie is completely lost without Danny," said Ross, looking straight to camera. "She told me it was like having part of her own body cut away."

Ellie clapped her hands to her mouth and stepped away from the television, her eyes wide with shock and hurt. How could he?

"And what about the police search? Any progress?"

"Not according to Ellie," said Ross. "In fact, she's pretty upset with them."

"Really?" said the reporter, with a thrill of interest in his voice. "Why is that?"

"No, no, no," breathed Ellie, taking her hands from her mouth and holding them out to the screen, palm up, as though she could stop the pre-recorded interview. "Don't say it, Ross. Don't . . ."

"She doesn't like their line of questioning," said Ross. "Did her dad mistreat Danny? Was Danny happy at home? That sort of thing. It's almost as though the police are treating him as a suspect, and that's just ridiculous."

Ellie felt as though Ross had reached out of the screen and punched her in the stomach. Everything she had told him over hot chocolate in their favorite coffee shop had been private stuff, but he had blurted it all out to the camera without a hint of hesitation. Ellie knew exactly why he had done it. Ross loved being the center of attention: it was his great weakness. She could see him marching up to the white van, ready to tell the television crew to clear off, but then the reporter would have flattered and cajoled, talking about exclusives and breaking news, and Ross would not have been able to resist. He had dealt with the television crew by telling them everything they could possibly want to know.

Ellie glanced up at the kitchen clock. Ross would be at school now, walking down the corridor to his homeroom and lapping up the attention as kids called out to him from all sides. *Hey, Ross! Saw you on the news!* She imagined him going through the school day, repeating his story in every new lesson and making his involvement more central with each retelling.

"Stupid, stupid, stupid," muttered Ellie, turning off the television. She was talking about herself, not Ross. She knew what he was like, and she had still gone ahead and blurted everything out to him. But, if she was angry with herself, she was absolutely furious with Ross. How dare he! She had so needed someone to talk to, but he had betrayed her trust and her family for the chance to be on television. Well, if he thought he could carry on treating her house as a home away from home after this, he was very wrong.

Ellie grabbed her phone from the bench and prepared to send him a blistering text message. A second later the doorbell rang loudly in the quiet house. Ellie jumped and then backed away from the kitchen door until she fetched up against the table. She did not want to talk to any reporters. Lisa was the family liaison officer. Let her deal with them. Ellie waited until she heard Lisa's light footsteps hurrying down the stairs, then she edged back to the door and watched through the glass.

When Lisa opened the door, Ellie tensed, ready to slip out of sight at the first glimpse of a camera, but it was only Sergeant Donaldson standing on the doorstep. Lisa let him in, and the two police officers moved down the hallway, talking together in low voices. They were heading for the kitchen until Lisa spotted Ellie watching them through the kitchen door. Immediately Lisa diverted into the living room and Sergeant Donaldson stopped in surprise at her abrupt change of direction. He glanced up, saw Ellie, gave her one of his grave nods, and then followed Lisa into the living room, closing the door behind him.

Ellie frowned as she gazed after them. What was going on? She gave them a few minutes and then eased open the kitchen door and stepped silently into the hallway. She had decided to eavesdrop. If she was discovered, then she would throw Lisa's catchphrase back at her and innocently offer them a "nice cup of tea." But Ellie was pretty sure she would not be caught. She had the advantage. This was her house, and she knew every creaky floorboard and squeaky hinge. She knew the soft sigh the sofa made when somebody got up and the small tinkling sounds that came from her mum's glass ornament collection when someone walked across the living room. If the two police officers started to move, Ellie reckoned she would have enough warning to be back in the kitchen with the door shut while they were still halfway across the living room.

Ellie eased across the hallway and stood with her back against the wall. She could hear both voices through the closed living room door and, although it was difficult to make out the words in Sergeant Donaldson's low rumble, Lisa's high, girlish voice was very clear. Ellie settled down to listen.

"The interviews with Danny's friends," said Lisa, "did Danny confide anything to them about his dad?"

Rumble.

"Hmm. Pity. I was sure they'd turn something up. They've spoken to all of Danny's friends?"

Rumble.

"Bit short on leads, aren't we? The boyfriend checks out."

Ellie blinked with shock. They had even checked up on Ross. Was there anyone they didn't suspect?

"He was where he said he was on Saturday. At home with his parents early morning, then at the surgery with his dad, doing a shift on reception. In the afternoon he was back home, practicing with his band down in the cellar. The volunteers at the Swan Rescue Center check out, too. One of the fishermen we contacted could be our guy, though. A Mr. Lees? He's a single man living on his own up near the train station. It was a standard inquiry to start with. Was he fishing on Saturday? Had he seen Danny? The thing was, he was really jumpy when we talked to him, so we did a check and alarm bells started ringing. He moved up here from Birmingham six years ago, after two youngsters accused him of assault."

Ellie drew in her breath with a sharp hiss. Mr. Lees! She knew him by sight. The local kids called him Mr. Sleaze because he had an off-putting habit of staring for just a bit too long, but Ellie had always thought he was pretty harmless. Could he have taken Danny? She leaned toward the closed door of the living room, trying to catch what Lisa was saying.

"Nothing since the Birmingham incident, but it could just be that he hasn't been caught. We're bringing him in for questioning, and if he can't provide an alibi for Saturday, we'll see about a search warrant."

Rumble rumble rumble?

"Me? I've been having a look at the family computer," reported Lisa. "Checking out the Web sites and chat rooms they've been visiting. There's nothing obvious at the moment, but the father could be good at covering his tracks."

Out in the hallway, Ellie stiffened with shock. "Covering his tracks?" What was Lisa suggesting? The only sites her dad visited on the Net were online bathroom warehouses. Mr. Brody was a self-employed plumber, and he used the Net to order parts. Ellie scowled and moved nearer to the door to hear more clearly.

"Anyway, I've arranged for the techies to take the computer in and have a closer look," said Lisa. "If there's anything dodgy on there, the techies'll find it."

Rumble, rumble?

"The mum's given her permission. That's good enough for me. How have the door-to-doors been going? What do the neighbors say about Dad?"

Rumble. Rumble, rumble.

"Yeah, well he might seem like a decent man on the surface, but in these cases, once you start digging, you usually find dirt. There's something not right about him. You just need to look at the family dynamics. There's no connection between them, have you noticed? Mum is up in Danny's room all day, daughter is spending her time sobbing on boyfriend's shoulder, and Dad is out searching. At least, that's what he says, but I reckon he's just keeping out of our way. I think he's as guilty as hell, and as soon as I have some evidence, I'm pulling him in for questioning. His feet won't touch the ground."

Ellie stood in stunned silence, staring unseeingly at the opposite wall. How could Lisa say those things about her dad? It was true that the family had fallen apart since Danny had gone missing, but that was not because there was no connection between them. In fact, it was just the opposite.

They all loved Danny so much, they weren't sure how to function without him.

In the living room Sergeant Donaldson finished rumbling, and Lisa started talking again, her voice full of exasperation. "Oh, come on, David! The drowning theory is looking weaker by the hour. The divers and the coast guard have searched all the likely spots where a body might be washed up. So this is looking more and more like a runaway boy or an abduction. And you know the statistics as well as I do. If it's an abduction and they're not found within the first six hours, the chances are they're dead."

Ellie had heard enough. She stumbled back to the kitchen, closed the door, and then sank down onto the floor. All the strength had gone out of her legs. Lisa believed that Danny was dead and that her dad had killed him. Her dad. Her own dad. Ellie began to cry. Everything seemed hopeless. If Danny was still alive, the police were not going to find him. They were too busy trying to dig up evidence against Mr. Brody. What was she going to do? Ellie lifted her head and gazed around the kitchen as though she might find the answer written on the walls.

She caught sight of Danny's birthday cake, still sitting on the bench with a cloth thrown over it like a shroud. Ellie closed her eyes and began to turn her head away, but then her eyes flew open again. A shadow of an idea was forming at the back of her mind. Ellie concentrated on coaxing it forward. *All his friends* . . .

Ellie frowned up at the cake on the bench as she tried to work out why this phrase had come into her head. She had just heard Lisa use it, asking whether all Danny's friends had been interviewed by the police, but Ellie had heard that phrase somewhere else, too. *All his friends* . . .

Ellie clambered to her feet, walked over to the bench, and pulled the cloth away from the huge slab of sponge cake. Why had her mother made such a big cake? Because Danny had insisted on it. He had wanted a cake large enough to share out among all his friends. Not just the six boys coming to the birthday tea, or his other friends at school. All his friends. "We are all his friends," the bag lady had said. "All of us." So far, the police had only talked to his school friends, but he had many more friends than that. Everyone liked Danny.

"Of course!" Ellie suddenly realized what she had to do. She opened the cutlery drawer, pulled out the carving knife, and placed it next to the cake. Then she yanked their biggest storage container from its place under the bench and peeled back the plastic lid. Picking up the knife, she positioned it over the cake with the point just breaking the skin of the icing. "Make a wish," she muttered, gazing down at the writing on the cake. "Well, that's easy."

Ellie closed her eyes and stood perfectly still for a few seconds, then she plunged the point of the knife into the cake and began to carve slice after slice until she had filled the storage container.

A few minutes later Ellie was ready to leave. She was wearing the orange rain cape again, but had replaced her still-wet trainers with a pair of sturdy ankle boots. She had found a waterproof rucksack in the coat cupboard by the back door, and that was now slung over her shoulder with the storage container full of birthday cake wedged inside. In one hand she held a carrier bag containing a nearly full carton of orange juice and the entire contents of the kitchen fruit bowl.

Ellie put down the carrier bag and checked her pockets, making sure she had her mobile phone. There was an unfamiliar shape in the front pocket of her rain cape, and she pulled it out to see what it was. Bart Simpson grinned up at her from her open palm. Ellie smiled sadly as she looked at the little plastic giveaway toy. "You will need a key," the bag lady had said, and just for a moment Ellie had really believed she was being handed something important. She pressed the lever in Bart's back and watched his arms fly out from his sides to balance him on his skateboard and then she shook her head, walked over to the kitchen bin, and opened the lid. She was about to drop the little toy inside, but then she changed her mind and shoved it back into her rain cape pocket. It seemed wrong to throw away something that the bag lady had prized so highly. He could be her lucky charm. After all, it was not as though she did not need any luck. For this plan to work, Ellie was going to need all the luck she could get.

Ellie was heading for the back door again when she noticed a small pile of photographs on the table. They were all recent photographs of Danny. Lisa and Mrs. Brody had been going through them to select the best one for the police to use. They had opted for his most recent school photograph, but that was not Ellie's favorite. She leaned across and picked out an unposed snapshot. It had been taken two months back, on a hot, bright day at the local beach. Danny had just careered all the way down from the top of the highest dune on the little plastic sled they used for sand surfing. Her dad had clicked the camera and caught Danny jumping up from the toboggan at the bottom of the slope. Danny's face was so bright with laughter and exhilaration, it was impossible to look at the photograph without smiling. Ellie was smiling now as she studied his wide grin and crazy, salt-stiffened hair. Quickly she stored the photograph in her rain cape before picking up her carrier bag and heading out into the pouring rain.

When she reached the rain-swept street at the front of the old swimming pool building, it was deserted. Ellie checked both ways before slipping into the alley and splashing her way around to the back of the building. She checked again before she pulled the corrugated iron sheet back and squeezed through into the dark corridor. Hurrying into the main part of the building, Ellie remembered how scared she had been the last time she had crept through the silent hallway and up the stairs.

"Hello?" she called, pushing open the door that lead to the pool. "It's only me. I've brought you something."

A rustling came from the little house in the deep end, but there was no other reply. Ellie hesitated. She discovered that she did not want to step down into the pool itself without being invited. The pool was the bag lady's territory, surrounding the little house like some sort of a weird, white-tiled garden.

"I have fresh orange juice," called Ellie, removing the carton from her carrier bag and placing it on the side of the pool. She looked across at the little house, but the curtain of milkshake lids remained in place. There was no fire today. The place was cold and damp. Rain dripped from cracked panes in the roof, and the only illumination was a gray, watery daylight that filtered down through the glass dome. Ellie guessed that the bag lady had been sleeping, curled up inside her house as she waited for the rain to stop.

"I have red grapes," continued Ellie, lifting the

grapes from the bag and arranging them next to the orange juice. "Some lovely apples—and a bunch of ripe bananas." Still there was no response. Ellie thought the bag lady would have welcomed some good fresh fruit to supplement her diet of half-eaten burgers and milkshake dregs, but it seemed that she could take it or leave it.

Ellie opened her rucksack and pulled out the storage container. "Or . . . what about a big slice of birthday cake?" she asked, peeling back the plastic lid and lifting out a chunk.

The milkshake lid curtain quivered. "Cake?"

"With icing and everything."

"Cake?" repeated the bag lady, emerging from her house with her hair sticking up all over the place. "Cake?"

She scurried across the bottom of the pool, grabbed the cake from Ellie's outstretched hand, and began stuffing it into her mouth.

"It's Danny's cake," explained Ellie.

"Danny Boy." The bag lady smiled, sending sprays of cake crumbs everywhere.

"He wanted all his friends to have a slice. So I'm delivering it for him."

"Very nice," said the bag lady politely, dabbing at her mouth. She eyed the storage container. Ellie lifted the lid and handed over another slice.

"Some for each of his friends," said Ellie. "The trouble is, I'm not sure I know all of them.

Who else should get a piece?"

"Hmm." The bag lady gave the question serious thought while she finished off her second slice. "Meat man."

"The butcher, yes. Who else?"

"The other collectors. They have a bigger cart, but they always share."

"You mean the street cleaners? Okay. Anyone else?"

"The gut people."

Ellie blinked. "I'm sorry. Who?"

"The gut people. Fishy fingers. Slow talkers. Silver and red!" snapped the bag lady, becoming annoyed at Ellie's lack of understanding. "Silver and red! In the harbor!"

"Silver and red. In the harbor. I see," said Ellie. "Thank you."

The bag lady subsided. "Secret, though," she muttered. "Secret gut people."

Secret? Ellie opened her mouth and then shut it again. It was probably best not to ask the bag lady any more questions. At least she had a location and, once she reached the harbor, she could start asking around. That was what Argent would do, and she was supposed to be following Argent's way, wasn't she? Ellie pushed the storage container back into her rucksack and stood up. The bag lady watched hungrily as she swung the rucksack full of cake onto her shoulder.

"Um, I brought you some fruit, too," said Ellie, pointing to the arrangement on the poolside.

"Pah!" spat the bag lady, glaring at the fruit. "Pah! Pah!" she repeated for emphasis, stalking back to her house at the deep end of the pool and disappearing behind the milkshake lid curtain.

"It's good for you," ventured Ellie, but there was no reply. The bag lady had retreated to her bed again.

As Ellie headed down the marble staircase and hurried along the corridor, she decided to try the harbor first. The secret gut people, whoever they were, might know something about Danny's disappearance. After all, Danny had vanished from Chuggie's Pool on the river, and the harbor was on the river too. She leaned against the corrugated iron sheet, squeezed through the gap, and came to a sudden halt, halfway out. There was someone standing on the other side of the back lane. He was leaning against the wall with his arms folded, watching her.

Ellie froze. He was a young man, just a few years older than she was. His hat and jacket were both dark with rain, but he seemed not to notice the downpour. All his attention was on her. There was no surprise on his broad, dark face at the sight of a girl in a bright orange cape squeezing her way out of a derelict building, so he must have been expecting her, and he did not look too happy about it.

The dark eyes above his prominent cheekbones were like two black stones as he glared at her with open hostility.

Ellie thought about retreating back behind the corrugated sheet, but quickly decided against it. This door was the only way in or out of the building. If he came after her, she would be trapped. Quickly Ellie pushed against the sheet and stepped out into the rain. The watcher straightened up and took a step toward her. Ellie gasped and broke into a run. She sprinted down the narrow alleyway that ran along the side of the building and burst out onto the front street. When she looked behind her, he was striding down the alleyway toward her.

Ellie turned left and ran down the hill toward the archway that would take her under the fortified walls of the old town and out onto the quayside. As soon as she skidded out of the other side of the archway onto the slippery expanse of cobbles, Ellie realized she had made a mistake. This part of the quayside was normally a popular route for walkers, but nobody was interested in a quayside stroll on a rainy Monday morning. The whole area was completely empty.

In front of her was the river, brown with mud and running swift and high after all the rain. Behind her were the high, fortified walls of the old town. The only way to escape from the empty stretch of quayside was to retrace her steps through the archway under the walls. Once she was through, she would be able to head up the hill into the center of town, but was there time? Ellie began to sprint back to the archway, but she had only run a few steps when her pursuer stepped out onto the quayside in front of her.

· TWELVE ·

GOLDSTONE

Snick-snack, snick-snack. Argent came around to the sound of steel on stone. Somewhere very close to her, a knife was being sharpened. She tried to open her eyes, but the mud she was plastered in had dried, sticking her lashes together. Argent sat up with a panicked gasp and clawed at her eyelids until the mud cracked and fell away. The first thing she saw was Lukos. He was sitting on a fallen tree, with a stone in one hand and a wicked-looking hunting knife in the other.

"What's that for?" demanded Argent, rising to her knees and spitting out flakes of dried mud. Her own voice sounded strangely loud in her ears.

"The knife?" asked Lukos in a muffled voice. "I've been skinning a rabbit." Lukos jerked the knife toward her and Argent flinched, but he was only pointing out a fire with a roasting rabbit carcass suspended above it on a spit. "Can't you smell it?" he asked.

Argent realized with a shock that she could not smell anything. She raised a shaking hand to her nose and discovered that both nostrils were blocked with plugs of dried mud. She checked her ears and found that they were plugged too. That explained why she sounded so loud and he sounded so faint. Argent staggered to her feet, with chunks and flakes of drying mud pattering to the ground all around her. Lukos ducked his head but did not quite manage to hide a smile.

Argent drew herself up to her full height. "Thank you for pulling me from the bog," she said with as much dignity as she could muster.

"You are shouting," said Lukos.

"Pardon?"

"I said, you are shouting."

"Oh." Argent scraped some of the mud from her ears and then looked Lukos straight in the eye. "Now, if you could kindly set me on the right track to Goldstone, I'll be on my way."

"You can't go anywhere like that." Lukos grinned. "You look like a very large cowpat." He sniffed. "Smell like one too."

"Oh, no!" Argent looked down at herself, suddenly realizing the implications of her mud-covered state. She could not present herself at Goldstone Castle looking like this. "What am I to do?"

"There's a pool in the dip behind you," said Lukos. "You can wash there."

"But—I have nothing to change into."

"Your other clothes are laid out beside the pool."

"My—?" Argent spun around. Her blanket was spread out at the bottom of a gentle slope and her best skirt, blouse, and jerkin were laid out on top of it. One edge of the blanket was wearing a frill of brown mud, but the rest of the blanket and the clothes upon it looked clean and dry. Argent sighed with relief, but then realized that there was no sign of her roll of parchments. She turned on Lukos again. "Where are my dragon drawings?"

"Oh, those," replied Lukos. "I used them to light the fire."

"You *what*!" shouted Argent, but Lukos was grinning and picking something up from the fallen tree beside him. "Safe and dry," he said, holding up the parchment roll. "Your shield is here too," he added, pointing to the little wooden shield resting against the tree trunk. "Your pack seems to have survived the bog very well. Which is more than I can say for you. Go and wash."

Argent hesitated, looking down into the dip where a pool had formed from the slow-running stream. "Is it deep?"

"Waist deep at most. It is cold, but safe to bathe. That is why I brought you here."

"You brought me? How?" asked Argent.

"I carried you," said Lukos.

"Carried me?" squawked Argent, looking about her and realizing that they were in a completely different part of the forest. The trees were more widely spaced, and the late-afternoon sun shone down through the leaves and danced on the surface of the pool. "Where are we?"

"The northern boundary of the forest is over that rise, and Goldstone City is just over an hour's walk away."

Argent blinked. "You carried me all the way here?"

"It was not difficult. You are very light. Even when plastered in mud. Speaking of which, go and wash. Go on! I won't look."

Lukos moved over to the fire and squatted there with his back to the pool, turning the rabbit carcass and tending to a strangely shaped container with something bubbling away inside it. Argent hesitated, shifting from foot to foot, but she could see no other option. She hurried down the slope and waded into the pool, still fully clothed and gasping at the icy water. Once she reached the middle of the pool, Argent took a deep breath and let herself sink backward into the water. She floated under the surface and her long, dark hair fanned out around her.

She ran her fingers through it, easing the mud away from her scalp until she ran out of breath. When she rose to the surface again and cleared the water from her eyes, she saw a widening trail of mud flowing away downstream. Argent stayed on her back with her head raised, paddling to keep herself in place and batting at her clothes with her hands. By the time the mud trail in the water had thinned out to nothing, her teeth were chattering with cold.

Argent waded back to the bank and checked to make sure Lukos was still out of sight before picking up the blanket and draping it over her like a tent. Under cover of the blanket, she peeled off her wet clothes and rubbed herself dry. She had no change of footwear, so she left her soaking boots on her feet. At least they were clean now. Finally she pulled on her dry skirt and blouse and wrapped the blanket around her hair, squeezing as much water out of it as she could before gathering up her wet clothes and heading back up the slope to the fire.

The rich smell of roasting rabbit made Argent's stomach rumble with hunger as she squelched over to the fallen tree. Lukos was still crouched over the fire, sprinkling freshly torn herbs into the strangely shaped pot.

"You smell better," he said, without turning around.

Argent chose not to reply. Instead, she busied herself with wringing the water from her clothes and spreading them out on the fallen tree to dry. She felt awkward and clumsy in her skirt after wearing her father's work trousers. There seemed to be way too much material, and she kept having to lift it out of the way of her feet.

"Why do you wear such an awkward thing?" asked Lukos. "It seems willfully stupid to restrict your movements like that."

Argent stiffened and turned to face Lukos. He was standing gazing at her skirt with his arms folded and a puzzled look on his face. Argent felt offended by his criticism, even though she had just been thinking exactly the same thing herself. "It is our way," she said tightly.

Lukos shrugged. "Not ours," he said, still staring critically at her skirt. Argent remembered that there had not been a long skirt in sight during her strange meeting with his family in the clearing. His sister, Reya, had been wearing a simple, short shift, and his mother had been wearing soft leggings. She felt a twinge of envy for the freedom of their forest lifestyle. "That is because you don't know how to act in a civilized manner," she snapped, and instantly regretted it.

Lukos let his arms drop to his sides. His amber eyes turned cold, and he looked her up and down as though she were an irritating insect. "Hmm. Maybe not a dragon after all. Let me see. What has black fur, a narrow white face, a foul temper, and likes to walk at night? A badger. Yes, you would make an excellent badger." Lukos hunched his shoulders, put a scowl on his face, and gave an uncannily accurate imitation of the rolling gait of a badger.

Argent laughed, despite herself. Lukos glanced up at her in surprise and came out of his crouch with a slow smile spreading across his face in response.

"I'm sorry," said Argent quickly. "You are right about my skirt. It is awkward and clumsy, but I must wear it if I am to be allowed an audience with the duke. It is the only way to save the dragon."

There was a short silence as they both remembered the importance of Argent's journey, then Lukos nodded and looked up at the sky. The mother dragon was still circling above the forest. She was far over to the west, and the low sun was glinting on her wings. The sun was heading toward the horizon now. In less than two hours, it would be dusk. "Let us eat," he said simply.

Argent sat on the fallen tree with her boots out to the fire, watching hungrily as Lukos cut chunks of cooked rabbit meat and dropped them into the strangely shaped pot that was hanging over the fire. Her mouth watered at the smell.

"What's in there?" she asked.

"A stew of herbs and roots from the forest," said Lukos, lifting the pot from the fire and carrying it over to the fallen tree.

"Oh. That's clever," marveled Argent, studying the strangely shaped pot as Lukos sat down beside her and placed the food between them on the tree trunk. "How did you make it?"

"From a single strip of birch bark," said Lukos. "The inner layer is very flexible. I folded up the corners and pegged them with split sticks, see?"

"And it doesn't catch fire?" Argent asked.

Lukos shook his head. "Not if it hangs above the flames rather than in them. Useful stuff, birch bark," he added, patting the pouch at his belt.

They ate in a companionable silence, using their knives to spear chunks of stew from the pot and transfer it to their mouths. It was hot and good, and Argent felt her energy returning with every bite she took. Her boots steamed in the heat from the fire. With luck, they would be dry by the time she had to move on. Finally, when the bark bowl was empty, Argent clambered to her feet. With her belly full, her hair freshly washed, and her best clothes on, she felt ready for the task ahead.

"Again. Thank you," she said, pulling on her jerkin and tying the parchment roll to her belt.

"I will show you to the edge of the forest," said Lukos, sheathing his knife. "But no farther. I am not—comfortable—outside Unthank."

Argent nodded her agreement. She realized that she would be sorry to say good-bye to Lukos. She was growing to like him despite her deep suspicion of his were-creature nature, but always at the back of her mind was the goodwife's warning: "Beware the man who offers his help." On balance, she thought it would be best for them to part.

While Argent rolled her nearly dry clothes into her blanket and filled her water bottle at the stream, Lukos buried the remains of the rabbit carcass, doused the fire, and covered it with earth. By the time Argent returned to the glade with her bedroll and shield slung over her shoulder, all signs of their presence there had vanished.

Together they set out to climb the final rise that would take them to the edge of the forest. "Oh, look!" Argent said, gasping, a few moments later as they reached the tree line. "Isn't it beautiful?" Beyond the trees the land sloped away in a gentle curve of pasture and farmland, dipping down into a broad valley. A wide river ran through the valley to the sea, opening out into a natural harbor when it reached the coast. Built around that harbor and climbing up the far valley side was the great fortified city of Goldstone. The duke's castle stood on a mound in the northwestern corner of the city, and the castle's Bell Tower rose into the sky, at least three times higher than any of the buildings that surrounded it. The local sandstone of the houses glowed gold in the early evening sun, showing how the city had earned its name.

Argent had only been to Goldstone twice in her life, but she remembered every detail of her visits. "See the bridge across the river?" she asked Lukos, pointing to the graceful stone arches striding across the water. "That's the only way into the city. There's a gate in the walls at the other end of the bridge, and the guards check everyone going in or out. They close the gate at night, when the Bell Tower bell tolls. That's the Bell Tower, right at the top of the castle. See it?"

Argent pointed out the Bell Tower and looked around for Lukos. He was not there. He had been standing beside her a few seconds ago, but now he had vanished. She looked behind her into the forest, but the space under the trees was quiet and empty. It seemed that Lukos had been as good as his word. He had taken her to the edge of the forest and left her there without even a good-bye. Argent felt a tug of loss. "Lukos?" she called. The name felt strange in her mouth, and Argent suddenly realized two things. This was the first time she had said his name and, perhaps because of her lingering mistrust of him, she had never told him her name. In her village they believed that the telling of a name gave power over the owner. It was not polite to ask the name of a stranger, but to wait until it was freely given.

"Good-bye, Lukos," called Argent, gazing into the quiet forest. She hesitated and then softly made him a gift of her name. "I am called Argent." There was no reply. Argent sighed, squared her shoulders, and set off down the slope toward the road that wound through the fields to the river. When Lukos came running up the slope toward her with a snarl on his face and a golden light in his eyes, Argent nearly screamed.

"Argent," growled Lukos, "I have found it."

"I thought you had returned to the forest," faltered Argent, backing away.

"No. I have found the trail of the red-haired hunter. The dragon thief! I picked up his scent at the edge of the forest, and I followed it down the slope. He is heading for the Goldstone road."

Argent groaned. "As I thought. He must have a buyer there. Can you tell how old the trail is?"

Lukos nodded grimly. "A day old."

"But this is dreadful! The baby dragon could already be sold. It could be anywhere." She shaded her eyes with her hand, watching a tall-masted ship leaving Goldstone harbor on the outgoing tide. "It could be on that ship right now! What am I to do? I cannot beg an audience with the duke and search for the dragon thief both at the same time. . . ."

She stopped and gazed at Lukos, who seemed to be going through some sort of struggle with himself. For a long moment he stared longingly into the forest, and then he looked down at his soft, leather boots. Finally he lifted his head with a sigh and looked at Argent. "I will help," he growled. "You must see the duke. So I will follow the trail of the dragon thief."

Argent bit her lip, shifting from foot to foot as she debated with herself. "Beware the man who offers his help," the goodwife had said. On the other hand, Lukos had saved her life. Twice. And, for most of her time with him so far, she had been asleep or unconscious. Surely if he meant to harm her, he would have done it by now? Logic told her she should trust him, but superstition made her wary of his were-creature nature. Argent hesitated, but she could see no option but to accept Lukos's offer. Lukos noticed her hesitation, and his face hardened. "Well?" he demanded.

"Thank you," said Argent reluctantly.

Lukos glowered at her before turning and setting off down the slope with long strides. Argent hurried to catch up, and they traveled on in silence, together but apart. Lukos grew edgier with every step away from Unthank Forest, and Argent could swear that his features were becoming more wolflike as his agitation grew. He kept stooping to check the dragon thief's trail, and every time he rose to his feet again, his shoulders seemed broader and more hunched, his eyes more slanted, and his canines more prominent. Argent shuddered and glanced frequently at the low sun. She had to reach Goldstone City before nightfall. The full moon was already hanging in the sky like a pale ghost, and Argent did not want to be alone in the dark with Lukos.

They reached the dry, packed-earth road and marched on toward Goldstone, walking so fast they left a long banner of dust floating in the air behind them. The closer they came to Goldstone, the more agitated Lukos became. It did not help matters that, at every farm they passed, the dogs went wild as soon as they scented him. Without fail they would come charging down the farm track, barking savagely all the way. The first time it happened, Argent hastily found a stout stick in the hedgerow, but she never needed to use it. Each group of dogs made a lot of noise, but they were too frightened of Lukos to launch an outright attack. Instead, they harried him, snarling at his heels until he turned on them, when they would simply fall back a few paces, dancing on the spot with their ears laid flat until he turned away again.

As they drew closer to Goldstone, the farms became more closely clustered together, and then the road began to pass through tiny villages dotted along the route. Soon Argent and Lukos were walking along the road with a permanent escort of enraged dogs of one sort or another. The constant barking began to shred Argent's nerves, and Lukos was stomping along with a face that could have been carved out of stone, apart from a muscle twitching in his jaw.

A horse-drawn cart came alongside them and slowed to walking pace. "Them dogs don't like you, do 'em?" said a friendly voice, shouting to be heard above the barking.

Argent looked up at the smiling farmer and bit back a tart reply. "No," she said dismally.

"You headed for Goldstone?"

"Yes."

"Hop up, then," said the farmer, leaning down from his seat and holding his hand out to her. "There's room for you and your friend there. I'm going to Goldstone, and I could do with the company."

Argent gave the farmer a grateful smile. She was just about to grab his hand when Lukos turned to face the cart. Immediately the horses shied away from him, showing the whites of their eyes and whinnying with fear. The farmer took one look at Lukos and quickly withdrew his hand. "Gid up," he called, clicking his tongue and twitching his whip. The horses needed no encouragement, and the cart set off down the road at a smart pace, leaving Argent and Lukos choking in a cloud of dust.

"When we get to Goldstone," growled Lukos, after a pause. "You must pretend we are not together. Otherwise you will never be allowed through the city gate."

"But how will you get in?" asked Argent.

"I will find a way," snarled Lukos.

The sun was dipping behind the western hills when they reached the bridge that would take them across the river to Goldstone. They had left the last of the farm dogs behind about a mile back, but still Lukos was as tense as a drawn bowstring as they neared Goldstone. There were other stragglers hurrying to get into the city before nightfall, and soon Argent and Lukos became part of a crowd of people moving across the bridge toward the gates. Lukos had managed to follow the dragon thief's trail as far as the bridge, but now there were too many people and too many different smells for him to track it any farther. He was grim faced, darting glances all around and glaring at anyone who came too close to him, but the other travelers were intent on their own business, already planning which inn to head for once they were inside the gates, and no one paid much attention to the strange youth striding among them.

Up ahead the two soldiers on duty were ushering people through the gate with little more than a weary glance and a wave of the arm. Argent began to hope that they would get through after all, but then she saw that one of the guards had a large hound with him. Her heart sank. The hound was lying at the guard's feet with its head on its huge paws. It was half asleep, opening one eye every now and then to check on the passing throng, but Argent knew that as soon as it scented Lukos, there was going to be trouble. She looked across at Lukos. He was still trying to pick up the dragon thief's scent, and he had not noticed what lay ahead. Argent nudged him in the side and pointed to the dog. Lukos stiffened.

"You go on ahead," whispered Argent. "If you can't get through, we'll have to fall back and think of a different plan."

"No." Lukos shook his head. "You must go into the city to see the duke, whatever happens to me. The life of the mother dragon is in your hands."

Lukos was right. Argent gave him a sideways glance and then bowed her head in agreement. "If we get separated, we'll meet back here on the bridge tomorrow morning," she whispered.

Lukos nodded and then quickened his pace and moved smoothly away from her, disappearing into the throng up ahead. Argent ducked her head and kept shuffling steadily forward, waiting for the trouble to start. She did not have to wait long. A few seconds later the great booming bark of the guard hound started up, bouncing off the high city wall and echoing over the river. The crowd surged forward, craning their necks to see what was going on, and Argent was pushed along with them.

"Hold!" yelled one of the guards. "Stay back!"

The dog paused for breath before launching into another volley of barks. In the short silence Argent heard the sound of Lukos snarling and the rasp of a sword being drawn. Ahead of Argent the crowd gasped in unison, then the hound was barking again and both guards were yelling at once. Argent tried to see what was happening, but she was not tall enough to look over the heads of the men in front of her. Desperately she pushed her way to the western side of the bridge until she reached the stone ramparts. A little alcove was built into the wall there, where pedestrians could retreat to stand in safety when larger carriages came trundling across the bridge. Argent headed into the alcove and leaned out over the wall to see what was happening at the end of the bridge.

The crowd had turned into spectators, creating a solid barrier around the patch of ground where the action was taking place. Inside the circle, crouched in a tense, three-to-one formation, were Lukos, the two guards, and their hound. Both guards had their swords drawn with the tips pointing at Lukos's chest. The dog was dancing in place between the guards, barking so savagely there were streamers of spittle flying from its jaws. Lukos was crouched with his teeth bared, glaring from one guard to the other. Even from where she was standing, Argent could see the bright amber of his eyes and the long curve of his teeth. He was managing to stay human, but only just.

"Let me pass," she heard him snarl. "I have business in the city."

The guards looked at each other uncertainly and then back to Lukos. "What did he say?" asked one.

"Dunno," said the other, wiping the sweat from his upper lip. "Where you from?" he demanded, jerking his chin at Lukos.

"Unthank Forest," growled Lukos. "I mean you no harm."

Argent understood every word Lukos was saying, but the guards were looking at him in hostile bewilderment. It was as though they did not want to understand. They shared a sideways glance. "What's he growling about?" asked one.

"I only wish to pass into the city," said Lukos, lifting his arm to point at the gate behind the guards. The guards took the movement as a threat and jabbed their swords at Lukos. He leaped backward to avoid the sharp points and the hound lunged at him and then retreated again, its barks rising to hysterical howls. Lukos was now poised at the top of a sloping path that led down from the end of the bridge to a dirt track that followed the river along the base of the city wall. He snarled again, this time without words, and Argent could see that he was losing control.

The crowd began to mutter threateningly.

"What's he, then? He 'ent quite human, that's for sure."

"I've heard about them. It's a were-creature from the forest."

"Were-creature?"

"They can turn into animals, just like that. Rip your throat out as soon as look at you."

"Get back to the forest where you belong! We don't want your kind here!"

"Aye! Get it out of here. Vicious beast!"

The shouts of the crowd grew more hostile, and Argent felt her eyes sting with tears. Just a day ago she would have been shouting with them, but now she was not so sure. She was still suspicious of Lukos's nature, but she was no longer clear where her allegiance lay. She had seen Lukos with his family. She had seen him sprinkling herbs into a cook pot. She had seen him straining every muscle in his body to pull her from the bog.

A stone was thrown, hitting Lukos on the side of the head. He staggered, then reared upright again with blood trickling from his temple and a fierce glow in his amber eyes. The crowd grew silent, watching his lips wrinkle back in a snarl. Argent clutched her hands together at her chest. If Lukos changed now, the crowd would change too, becoming a mob intent on murder.

"Don't change!" she yelled, and her voice carried in the poised silence, as high and sharp as the call of a bird. As Lukos turned his head to look her way, one of the guards stepped forward and straight-armed him in the chest. Lukos fell backward and rolled halfway down the sloping path that led to the river before he could stop himself. The crowd roared their approval. Lukos scrambled to his feet, went into an attacking crouch, and then stopped dead. His nostrils flared. He went down on his knees and bent his head to the slope. When he stood up again, he turned his back on the crowd and gazed along the dirt track that ran beside the river. His nostrils flared again and then he began to hurry down the slope, away from the city gate.

The crowd roared, thinking they had Lukos on the run. The guard who had pushed Lukos in the chest turned to them and spread his arms in triumph. The crowd cheered their approval, and the guard strutted like a peacock, posing with his sword. Argent grimaced as she watched. She could imagine the stories he would be telling in the inn that night. With every ale he drank, the danger would grow and he would become more of a hero. By the end of the evening, he would be describing how he fought off a whole pack of were-creatures with his bare hands. She shook her head and turned from the antics of the guard to watch Lukos lope away down the riverside path. Only Argent knew what had really happened. She knew that Lukos was not running away at all. He simply had no need to go into the city anymore because he had picked up the scent of the dragon thief on the slope down to the river. For some reason the red-haired man had ridden his gray horse right up to the city gate and then turned west to follow the track around the outer wall of the city.

"What are you looking so upset about?"

Argent jumped and turned to face a plump farmwife who was scowling up at her suspiciously.

"I—thought that poor guard was going to get hurt," said Argent. "But he didn't," she continued, forcing a smile. "Hooray."

"What were you shouting just then? 'Don't change,' was it?"

"No—it was . . ." Argent thought fast. "It was 'don't charge!' I thought that were-creature was going to charge at the guard, see?"

"Aye, well . . ." The farmwife was still unsure, but just then the Bell Tower bell began to toll, and suddenly she forgot all about Argent. She grabbed up her bundle and waddled off toward the gate as fast as she could go. Argent sagged against the stonework of the bridge.

"All in! All in!" yelled the guard as a heavy grating noise came from somewhere within the wall. Argent looked at the gate and saw that an iron portcullis was descending over the entrance. She picked up her skirts, sprinted for the gate, and joined the tail end of the jostling crowd. The guards were already on the other side of the portcullis, yanking people in as fast as they could to speed up the process. For a few seconds Argent wondered whether she was going to reach the gate in time but then, finally, her way was clear. She bent double and ducked under the descending metal spikes just as the Bell Tower bell gave its final toll of the night.

Argent straightened up on the city side of the gate as the portcullis spikes thudded onto the cobbled street behind her. She pushed the hair back from her eyes and looked around.

"Are you lost, pretty lass?" The guard who had pushed Lukos grasped Argent's chin in his rough-skinned hand. "I can help you find your way," he said, leering. Argent pulled away, remembering the goodwife's words, and the guard laughed. "Come and have a drink with me," he invited, still full of his triumph over the evil were-creature.

"Can you tell me the way to the castle?" she asked, ignoring his invitation.

"No drinkies, then?"

"Up the hill," said the other guard, pushing his partner out of the way and pointing Argent in the right direction. "But you'll have to hurry. It'll be starting soon."

"What will?" asked Argent.

"Petitioners' night," said the guard.

Argent looked blank.

"It's the last Tuesday of the month," said the guard.

Argent still looked blank. The guard sighed and decided that he must be speaking to an idiot. He began to explain, talking very slowly. "On

Petitioners' night, anyone with a problem or a concern can take it to the duke. He makes a judgment, offers help or gives advice—"

"Anyone?" interrupted Argent.

"Anyone," said the guard. "If you can get near him, that is. It only lasts for two hours, and the Great Hall is usually full."

"Thank you," gasped Argent, turning and heading up the cobbled street at a run.

"He can't talk to everyone!" called the guard behind her, but Argent's heart was soaring as she sprinted over the cobbles. She had arrived in Goldstone City on the one night of the month that offered her a good chance of talking to the duke. Everything was slotting into place. The fate of the mother dragon was in her hands, and she had just been handed a golden opportunity. As she hurried up the hill toward the castle, Argent was convinced that she would speak to the duke before the night was out.

· THIRTEEN ·

THE GUT PEOPLE

Ellie skidded to a stop on the quayside cobbles and so did her pursuer. He was standing directly in front of the archway, blocking her way. They stared at each other for a shocked second before Ellie turned and raced off along the quayside with her boots slipping and sliding on the rain-wet cobbles.

"Hey!"

Ellie risked a glance over her shoulder and felt a horrified chill run through her as she saw that he was still following, loping across the cobbles with long-legged strides. Ellie tried to run faster and nearly lost her balance. She righted herself and slowed to a steady jog, heading for the harbor. It was a working harbor, and there would be people and safety there. It was not far away, but it was still out of sight around the corner, and first she had to make her way across this empty expanse of quay-side.

She ran on, not daring to look back in case she slipped again. The hood of her rain cape covered her ears so that all she could hear was the rustle of plastic, her own panting breath, and the rhythmic thud of the rucksack against her back. Her pursuer could be catching up to her right now and she would not hear him coming. Ellie gave a gasping sob and quickened her pace again.

When she finally reached the corner where the quayside followed the town wall around into the harbor, Ellie's chest was tight with panic and she was struggling to breathe. She kept pushing herself onward but it seemed to take an age for the harbor to come into view. First she saw the red and white lighthouse at the end of the pier, then a row of moored fishing boats appeared and, finally, the harbor buildings themselves. Ellie was gasping for breath by the time she stepped off the cobbles of the quayside and up onto the tarmac surface of the harbor road.

People and safety. Three fishermen stood beside the boats, wearing foul-weather gear and discussing fish quotas in disgusted tones. A car drove past her along the tarmac road, its tires hissing on the wet surface. A crocodile of bedraggled infant schoolchildren followed their teacher along to the open-sided sheds where a fish auction was underway. Ellie slowed to a walk. She was sweating under the cape, but her breathing was gradually returning to normal. She came to a stop right beside the three burly fishermen before daring to turn and look back toward the quayside.

Her pursuer was nowhere in sight. Ellie waited, staring at the spot where the quayside disappeared behind the curve of the town wall. If he were still coming after her, that was where he would emerge. She waited for a full minute, then a minute more. The quayside remained empty. Ellie gave a sigh of relief and looked about her. The three fishermen had stopped talking and were watching her curiously. Ellie realized that she was standing much closer to them than would be considered normal.

"Morning!" she said brightly, backing away to an acceptable distance. "Just—catching my breath . . ."

The fishermen glanced at one another then back to Ellie. She gave a little laugh, then turned away and walked off along the harbor road. She was beginning to feel foolish. There were plenty of perfectly innocent reasons for the dark young man to have followed her. He probably thought she had been up to no good in the old swimming pool. Or maybe he had been coming after her to explain the dangers of derelict buildings. Whatever the reason, she had not stayed to find out. Instead, she had run away like some frightened kid. Ellie shook her head as she realized that her carefully packed slices of birthday cake had probably been reduced to a congealed lump of squashed icing and crumbs after being bounced up and down across the quayside cobbles. She sighed and gazed around the harbor, wondering where to start making her inquiries.

She thought of going back to talk to the three fishermen, but then dismissed that idea. They already thought of her as a weird girl. What would they think if she started offering them pieces of squashed birthday cake?

Glint.

Ellie stopped walking as her eye was caught by a stream of glinting silver and red flowing out of one of the harbor buildings.

Glint.

The stream sparkled as it flowed over the tarmac road and into the harbor. Ellie looked at the building it was coming from. It was an old, brick-built warehouse with a big sliding metal door at the front. The door was open, and someone was standing in the doorway, swilling the silver and red stream into the harbor with a hosepipe. *Silver and red* . . . Those were the words the bag lady had kept repeating.

Glint.

Ellie hitched the rucksack onto her shoulder and

set off toward the warehouse. The person with the hosepipe stepped farther out of the building, spraying the last of the silver and red stream off the road and into the harbor. He, or she, was dressed from head to foot in protective clothing. A white cap covered the hair, rubber gloves and boots covered the hands and feet, and the body was swathed in a white overall and a full-length plastic apron. Ellie tried to get a glimpse of the face, but the person turned off the hosepipe and went back into the building.

As Ellie drew closer to the warehouse, the smell of fish grew stronger until, even in the rain, it was almost overwhelming. She walked up to the open doorway, resisting the impulse to hold her nose, and peered inside. Eight people, all dressed from head to foot in protective clothing, were working at two long stainless-steel tables. They were lifting silver-scaled fish from big white tubs, slamming them onto the tables, and then gutting and filleting them with impressive speed. Their narrow-bladed knives flashed back and forth, and a constant stream of guts, scales, fins, and fish heads flowed down the gullies in the tables, draining into black buckets on the floor beneath.

The gut people, thought Ellie. She stepped through the doorway into the warehouse. Nobody noticed her. "Excuse me?" she tried. Nobody heard. A radio was playing loudly, the rain was drumming on the roof, and the gut people were all talking and joking in a language she did not recognize. Ellie tried again, more loudly. "Excuse me!"

This time they heard her. They all stopped working at once and turned to stare at her. There were four women and four men, ranging in age from mid-twenties to early forties. Their aprons and the sleeves of their overalls were spattered with fish blood. They did not look friendly.

"Umm . . . I wonder, can I . . . I want to—to ask you some questions. . . ?"

The gut people looked even less friendly. They glanced at one another and then back to Ellie, with wary expressions on their faces. The radio played, the rain drummed, and not one of them answered her. Ellie tried again.

"I'm looking for someone."

She stepped forward, reaching into her rain cape pocket for Danny's photo. The gut people all stepped back. Two of them dropped their knives onto the table with a clatter, and another two began talking together in fierce whispers. Ellie tried to identify the language. It sounded something like Italian, something like Spanish, but it was not quite either. Ellie slowly withdrew her hand from her rain cape pocket, leaving Danny's photograph in place. She stood staring at the gut people, and they watched her with hostile eyes. She had no idea what to do next.

Then someone came up behind her and grabbed her by the elbow. Ellie gasped and looked up into the broad face of the young man who had followed her from the old pool building.

"It's okay, guys," he said, looking at her coldly but speaking to the gut people. "I'll deal with this."

He swung Ellie around by the elbow, marched her outside, and pushed her into a narrow gap between the warehouse and the building next door. Ellie turned to run but stopped when she saw a high wall blocking the other end of the gap at the back of the warehouse. She turned back. He stood in front of her, blocking the only way out. Ellie was trapped.

"Let me go!" she cried, backing away from him. Frantically she looked around for something with which to defend herself, but there was nothing except bare concrete and brick walls. Ellie yanked the rucksack from her shoulder and held it out in front of her. She felt safer with a barrier between them, even if it was only a plastic storage container full of cake.

"I'm not letting you pass until you tell me what the hell you're up to," he snapped, folding his arms.

"What *I'm* up to?" Ellie stopped backing away and stared at him. He was not trying to follow her into the narrow alley. Instead, he leaned against the warehouse wall, waiting for her to explain herself. "Excuse me?" she spluttered.

"You're the one stalking me—"

"Don't flatter yourself. I'm not stalking you."

He had an American accent. She should remember that in case she had to describe him to the police. What else? She had to remember details.

"You've been pestering Phyllis," he continued. "You shouldn't do that. She's not good with strangers." His broad face was ugly with anger. He had clusters of acne scars beneath his cheekbones. His teeth were very white.

"Phyllis. . . ?" said Ellie, checking out the make of his jacket and hat and storing the details in her memory.

"I've seen you going in there twice. You were there yesterday and now, again, this morning."

"You mean the bag lady. . . ?" asked Ellie, noting that the fringe of hair poking out under his hat was dead straight and so black it had a blue sheen to it.

"Phyllis!" he snapped. "Her name is—"

"Phyllis! All right! But why are you . . . I mean . . ."

"Bothered about some stupid bag lady?"

"Yes. No. I mean . . ." Ellie came to a confused halt.

"Are you going to turn her in?"

Ellie gaped in bewilderment. "Who to?"

"To the authorities!" he snapped. "Because I have to tell you, she's been there, done that, okay? Phyllis doesn't do well in residential care. She's much happier when she's left to do her own thing."

"I won't say anything," said Ellie. "But . . ." She hesitated.

"But what?"

"Well, what if she gets sick or something?"

"She's not on her own," he scowled. "We all look out for Phyllis."

"We? You mean the gut people?"

"Who?"

"Your weird friends back there. Why were they so scared of me?"

He countered with a question. "Who are you looking for?"

Ellie eyed him cautiously, then reached into her rain cape pocket and pulled out the photograph. Wordlessly she held it out to him. He took it and studied it, holding a protective hand over it to keep the rain off.

"Danny," he said. "This is Danny. Poor kid."

"What do you mean, 'poor kid'?" asked Ellie, staring at him suspiciously.

"I heard he was missing."

"Oh. You know him?"

"Everyone knows Danny." He stopped and glared at her. "Who's asking?" he demanded. "What are you? Some sort of cub reporter? Trying to find a scoop for your school newspaper or something?"

"I'm his sister," said Ellie quietly, and her

treacherous eyes filled up with tears yet again. Wearily she lowered her head. This day was not going well.

"Okay," he said softly. "Okay." All the anger had left his voice. He sounded shocked and sympathetic and guilty all at once. "Okay. We should start over. My name is Miguel."

"Ellie," she sniffed, glancing up at him. Now that the anger had left his face, he was still sort of ugly, but in an interesting way. "I'm trying to find Danny. The police are talking to all his school friends and neighbors, but I wanted to do something too."

"So you're going underground."

"I am?" said Ellie, looking puzzled. Then her eyes widened. "Are you saying Danny might be underground somewhere?"

"No! I didn't mean it literally. I only meant— you know—your investigations. You're going underground. It's, like, a different level, under the surface. Me and Phyllis, we're underground people. You, you're a surface person. Your brother, now, he's an unusual kid. He can move between the two levels, no problem. But mostly the layers don't mix. You surface people don't have much contact with us underground guys."

Ellie looked at Miguel in bewilderment. "What's an underground guy?"

"I dunno—someone who keeps out of sight for

one reason or another. Someone who doesn't really belong."

"So why don't you really belong? Because you're an American?" hazarded Ellie, struggling to understand.

Miguel grinned. "Mexican American. I'm a Mexican American. That means I was born in California, but my mom was Mexican. I'm studying marine biology at U.C.L.A., and I'm over here on an exchange year. I'm at college up in Edinburgh, but I'm renting a room down the coast here. It's cheaper than living in the city. And"—he gestured at the harbor behind him, sending a spray of rain-drops flying from his jacket sleeve—"I can do all my research on the doorstep. That's how I know Danny. He's always down at the harbor, checking out the fish market to see if anything unusual has come in on the boats."

"And you're an underground guy because. . . ?"

Miguel gave her an assessing look and then shrugged his shoulders. "What the hell. I'm a schol-arship student. I get my fees paid, and something toward living expenses. But not enough. I have to work to get by, but I don't have a work permit. So I do underground stuff. Cash in hand. No records."

"No tax to pay," said Ellie, before she could stop herself.

"No minimum wage, either," flashed Miguel right back at her.

There was an awkward silence, which Ellie forced herself to break. She wanted to talk to the gut people, and Miguel seemed to be a way in.

"So, you do jobs like gutting fish in the warehouse?"

"Yeah. I do a few shifts there."

"With the gut people. That's what the bag la— I mean that's what Phyllis calls them. She thought they might know Danny."

"Yeah, they know Danny. He likes to watch the gutting, and they like having him around. They spoil him. Especially the women. They miss their own kids. . . ." Miguel paused, giving her another one of his assessing looks. "Phyllis spoke to you, then? I mean properly. Not just shouting a list of pool rules at you?"

Ellie nodded.

"That's quite something for her," said Miguel. "She must like you."

"So, do you think I could go back in there and ask them? About Danny?"

Miguel hesitated. "They don't like talking to strangers."

"I noticed. But you're not a stranger. . . ."

"I get it. You want me to introduce you. You'd have to promise me something first."

"What?"

"Don't tell anyone about them working here. They're kinda underground people too. They're from Eastern Europe. Romania."

"Oh! You mean they don't have the right papers or anything?"

Miguel shook his head, "Officially they're not here at all."

"So they sneaked in."

"Don't sound so prissy. It's not as though they're planning to stay long. Just a few months. They really need to earn some money to take back to their families, okay? Things are pretty bad over there."

"But they're taking our jobs—"

"Yeah, like there are people lining up to gut fish all day in a freezing warehouse. I don't think so! They do the jobs no one else wants. The low-paid, seasonal, backbreaking stuff. And—"

"All right," interrupted Ellie, tiredly. "All right. I won't tell anyone else about them. Please. I just want to find Danny."

Miguel subsided and stepped aside to let her out of the gap. "Okay. Come with me."

Back in the warehouse, the gut people were less suspicious of Ellie with Miguel standing beside her, but still they stood in an awkward cluster, saying nothing while she stumbled through her explanation. She tried to speak slowly and simply, but they were glancing between her and Miguel, waiting for the word that would mean trouble for them, rather than really listening to what she had to say.

"Show them the photograph," murmured Miguel, seeing that she was struggling.

Ellie shot him a grateful look and pulled the snapshot of Danny from her rain cape pocket.

"Ah! Danneee!" exclaimed a tall, strong-boned woman in her forties. She dropped her knife onto the steel table, stripped off her gloves, and took the photograph to look at it more closely. "Dannee," she said softly, giving Ellie a sad smile. She turned to the others and began to talk to them in Romanian, waving the photograph. They all gathered around, stripping off gloves and passing the photograph from hand to hand. Ellie heard Danny's name a few times and then everyone looked across at her and smiled, except one younger man who still seemed to be suspicious of her.

"Sister?" said the woman who had first taken the photograph from her. "You sister?"

Ellie nodded. "Ellie," she said, pointing to herself.

"Ellee," repeated the woman.

"Can you tell me anything that might help to find Danny?" asked Ellie.

The woman turned back to the group, and they listened to her respectfully. She was the oldest of the women, and she seemed to hold a position of authority among them. While they were talking, Ellie set about retrieving the storage container from her rucksack. When she opened the plastic lid, she was relieved to see that the tightly packed slices of cake were still intact.

"Excuse me?" she said. The gut people stopped talking and looked at her again. "This is Danny's birthday cake. He wanted to share it with his friends. So, please . . ." Ellie held out the box.

There was a pause, and then the older woman stepped forward and cupped Ellie's face in her cold, rough-skinned hands. They smelled so strongly of fish that Ellie had to resist the impulse to hold her breath.

"Dannee. How old he?"

"Eleven," whispered Ellie.

"Ah! My smallest son also is eleven." She patted Ellie on the cheek, then delved into the box and pulled out a slice of cake. "Dannee is heppy boy," she said, giving an exaggerated grin and pointing to her mouth to show what she meant.

Ellie nodded in agreement. "Thank you," she said.

One by one the others stepped forward, taking a slice of cake with their scarred, reddened hands and each saying something about Danny, even if it was simply to repeat his name and smile. Only the suspicious, younger man held back, until a glare from the older woman sent him forward to take his slice with a brusque nod.

"So, guys," said Miguel, helping himself to a slice of cake. "Last time he was in here, did Danny say anything that might help Ellie find him now?"

The older woman sighed. "I heve asked. We nothing can say. No clue. Dannee is heppy. Everyone like Dannee. . . ." She shrugged and the others shrugged with her.

"Okay," continued Miguel. "Let's try another way. Have you seen anything unusual around here? Any strangers? Any strange cars?"

Again the gut people fell to talking among themselves. "They're always alert to stuff like that," Miguel explained to Ellie. "If there has been a stranger hanging around, they'll have spotted him."

But the older woman turned back to them, shaking her head. "Many strangers, always. Holiday people, yes? They walk in the harbor. They stare. They eat chips and fish. But no stranger watching Dannee. No stranger waiting without reason."

Ellie's heart sank. This was beginning to look like another dead end. Then one of the younger women stepped forward hesitantly and began to talk in a soft voice. "I not sleep good. I miss home. Last three nights I look from caravan window. There is light. Small and—" She held up one hand and set her fingers flickering back and forth.

"You mean a glinting light? Like a candle? Or a flashlight?" asked Ellie, and the young woman nodded. Ellie felt a flicker of excitement. This spiral way she had chosen to take seemed to be lit with glinting lights. Was this light another marker?

"Is not there before," said the young woman.

"Where did you see this light?" asked Ellie.

The young woman pointed out through the open warehouse doors toward Spittal Point on the other side of the harbor. There was an old factory there, with a tall, brick-built chimney, right out on the point overlooking the sea. "Is in old factory," she said. "Our vans, they are very close there. We are in—"

The young woman jumped and stopped talking as the suspicious young man suddenly let fly with a torrent of Romanian. She ducked her head and hurried back to the gutting table, pulling on her gloves as she went. One by one the others nodded or smiled at Ellie, then went to join the young woman at the tables. The moment of shared closeness was over.

Ellie stood for a few minutes longer in case the young woman found the courage to say anything else, but the young woman kept her head down and, gradually, they all got back into the rhythm of their work until their knives were moving like little lightning flashes and the filleted fish flew from the tables into the waiting tubs.

"Thank you," called Ellie. She nodded to Miguel and left the warehouse, stepping out into the rain. Miguel joined her as she crossed the harbor road to stare across the river mouth at Spittal Point.

"You planning to have a look?" he asked.

Ellie nodded grimly, staring across the gray water to the tall chimney on the other side of the river. "A glinting light that wasn't there before? That suggests there might be someone hiding out there. Maybe someone holding Danny captive. I have to look."

"Yeah, well don't go in on your own, okay?" asked Miguel. "There might be druggies in there or something. Tell you what, I have to go start my shift now, but I finish at five. I'll meet you over at the Point at six. That'll give me time to get rid of the smell of fish and grab a bite to eat first. Okay?"

"Okay," agreed Ellie.

Miguel turned and headed into the warehouse. "You never know," he called over his shoulder. "It might even have stopped raining by then!"

Ellie smiled and waved good-bye before turning away from the harbor and heading into town. She still had birthday cake to deliver.

· *FOURTEEN* ·

A MAN OF SCIENCE

Danny was lying on a cold steel table with his head resting on a wooden block. A man in a white coat was standing beside him, lining up a selection of gleaming scalpels, surgical saws, and drills on a trolley. Danny gazed at the sharp teeth of the saw the man was holding and then heard the metallic click as it was placed on the tray.

The room stank of formaldehyde. Behind the man a wall of metal shelves held rows of glass jars containing eyes, brains, hearts, and other organs. Danny gazed curiously at the jars until a high, insectlike whine brought his attention back to the man in the white coat. The whine came again as the man tested a surgical drill and then placed it on the trolley. Danny watched sleepily as the man positioned the trolley next to his head. He was not sure what was going on, but it was all very interesting. The man reached up, clicked on a microphone that was hanging above the steel table, and began to talk.

"Subject is a Caucasian male, aged eleven. His name is Danny Brody. He has bruising, swelling, and puncture wounds to the front of his right thigh and ligature marks on both wrists and ankles. He has been dead for approximately twelve hours."

Danny's eyes widened with fear as he suddenly understood what was happening. He was lying in a mortuary, and the man in the white coat was preparing to perform an autopsy on him. He tried to sit up, but however hard he struggled, he could not move anything except his eyes. He tried to tell the man that he was still alive, but no sound, not even the softest sigh, would come out of his mouth. All he could do was watch as the man selected a scalpel and poised it above his chest.

"No!" Danny's throat was aching with screams as he jumped awake, but only a muted whimper came from his dry mouth. As he lay on the cold floor, in the dark, it took him a moment to remember where he was, and then he gave a desolate groan. He had woken from one nightmare into another. He was Jabber's prisoner, and Jabber would be arriving at any moment to inject him full of drugs again. Or perhaps this time, it would be something worse. Danny had no idea why he had been taken prisoner, but he had the awful feeling that time was quickly running out.

He gasped air into his lungs and concentrated on forcing his arms and legs to move. After an age of trying, the strength began to creep back into his limbs and he managed to start rolling himself slowly across the floor. The rough concrete scraped the skin from his chin each time he rolled, but Danny ignored the pain. He had to reach the metal shelving he had seen in the flashlight beam the last time he was awake.

Danny was beginning to wonder whether he was going in the right direction when he rolled over one last time and came up against the shelving with a crack that sent a sharp pain shooting all the way from his knee into the top of his head. The shelving rocked on its metal legs, and there was a rattling, sloshing sound as the jars shivered on the shelves. Danny held his breath, but nothing fell and the shelving slowly settled back into silence.

Danny pushed himself up into a kneeling position in front of the shelving. Carefully he felt along the bottom shelf until he came into contact with one of the jars, then he shuffled around until he was kneeling to one side. He pushed his tied hands behind the jar and deliberately toppled it from the shelf. It hit the concrete floor with an explosive crash and, instantly, the eye-watering stink of formaldehyde sent him into a spasm of coughing.

Slowly the fumes became less intense, and the shards of glass on the concrete rocked and tinkled into stillness. Danny bit his lip as he stretched his hands out into the dark. He felt around as gently as he could, trying to find a shard of glass that he could pick up and hold between his hands. A sharp splinter punctured his thumb, and he hissed at the sudden sting of formaldehyde. He withdrew his hands and moved them to the left, grimacing as they came up against something cold and rubbery. He had found whatever had been preserved in the jar. Danny tried again, spreading his fingers and feeling around. This time he struck lucky. He picked up a long, curved shard of glass with one razor-sharp edge and one smooth edge that he could grip without cutting himself. He had found part of the rim of the jar.

Quickly Danny shuffled away from the broken jar and sat down on the concrete, bringing his legs up and pushing his hands down between his knees. When he was sure he could reach the plastic strip that tied his ankles together, he eased the glass shard around, holding it between his thumbs so that the sharp edge was pointing downward. Danny took a deep breath and began to saw the glass shard back and forth across the plastic strip, staring sightlessly into the darkness as he concentrated all his senses on the task of cutting through his bonds.

When he heard the sound of approaching footsteps, Danny fumbled and nearly dropped the shard. Suppressing a whimper, he turned his hands and felt along the plastic strip with his fingers. He had managed to cut it nearly halfway through! Danny wasted precious seconds bracing his ankles against the strip to see if he could break it, but the strip held firm. The footsteps were louder now, and Danny heard an exclamation as Jabber caught the pungent smell of formaldehyde. The flashlight was flicked on, and the footsteps broke into a run. With a sob, Danny closed his eyes against the blinding light and returned to trying to cut through the strip. He had nearly managed it when the footsteps reached him and the needle was jabbed into the bruised flesh of his thigh. Danny dropped the shard and slumped backward. His legs rolled over to the side and his face hit the concrete. As he began to lose consciousness, Danny felt the plastic strip around his ankles snap. His legs were no longer tied, but he could not move. He had been so close to escaping, but it had all ended in failure. Danny sobbed as he sank down into sleep again. Why had nobody come to his rescue? Where was she?

Lukos wondered where Argent was as he padded up the sloping hillside with long, loping strides, intent on following the trail of the dragon thief. It had been a good hour since he had left her in the crowd at the city gates. The blood had dried to a crust on his temple, the sun had sunk behind the western hills, and now the full moon lit his way.

Lukos frowned as he loped onward, climbing up the deserted hillside and casting glances right and left as he looked for any sign of human habitation. The path the dragon thief had taken was a puzzling one. If he had come to Goldstone looking for a buyer for the baby dragon, then he should have headed into the city itself, or turned east and ridden down to the harbor. Instead, he had turned west at the city gates, heading inland. Even more strangely, the dragon thief had only followed the river as far as the southwest corner of the city wall. When he had reached the place where the city wall curved away from the river and headed up the valley side instead, the dragon thief had turned to follow the wall.

Now the city wall and the trail of the dragon thief had parted company. The wall continued to climb, following the contour of a sheer rock bluff that rose up out of the hillside, but the trail Lukos was tracking stayed on the lower ground at the base of the rock bluff. Lukos stopped and checked the trail again. It was definitely the dragon thief. He could even catch the faintest scent of dragon, under the stronger scents of man and horse. Lukos looked up at the city wall rising out of the bluff high above him, then he shook his head and loped on, following the dragon thief's trail along the base of the bluff.

A few minutes later the trail took a sharp right and stopped directly in front of the bluff. Lukos stared up at the sheer rock face, then turned and retraced his steps in case the kink in the trail was only a diversion. He reached the spot where the trail turned and cast around in a widening circle before coming back to the cliff face. The trail definitely ended here. Lukos put out his hands to touch the moonlit rock face and one hand kept on going, disappearing into deep moon shadow. There was a cleft in the rock, hidden from the view of anyone who happened to walk past this remote spot. Lukos stepped sideways until he was looking into the cleft. The dark split in the rock was wide enough for a cart and horse to pass through, but because of the angle of the opening it appeared to be nothing more than an irregularity in the face of the cliff when looked at straight on.

Lukos took a deep breath of the cold air emerging from the cleft. He scented the dragon thief and his horse and then, as faint as a whisper, he caught the scent of the baby dragon. Quickly Lukos found a fallen tree branch and made a split in one end with his knife. He took a handful of birch-bark strips from the pouch at his belt and slotted them firmly into the split end of the stick. Crouching, he laid the stick on the ground and pulled a flint from his pouch. He held the flint over the birch strips and struck sparks from it until they kindled. Lukos picked up the stick and nodded with satisfaction as the birch strips flared up. Holding his makeshift torch high, he stepped into the dark opening in the cliff.

Argent was glad Lukos was not with her as she shuffled through the doorway of the Great Hall. He would have hated this. She was in the middle of a crush of people who were so tightly packed around her, she could have lifted her feet from the floor and still been carried onward through the doorway.

"That's it!" yelled the guard beside one of the open double doors. "We're full!"

"Doors closing!" shouted the other guard. "Try again next month! Doors closing!"

The guards each grasped a big iron handle and pulled hard. Slowly the great wooden doors began to move, each guided by an iron caster that was screwed into the wood under the outer edge of the door. The casters rolled along in two curved metal gullies that had been set into the stone floor at the entrance and, once the straining guards had managed to get the heavy doors moving, they glided smoothly and noiselessly under their own momentum.

As the gap between the doors narrowed, there was a storm of protest from the people still trying to get into the hall, and the crush around Argent grew even tighter. She stuck her elbows out to protect the parchment roll at her waist and pushed forward. She just managed to squeeze through into the hall with the huge wooden doors catching at her heels.

Behind her the protests of the unlucky petitioners were cut off as the doors grated together and slammed into place. Argent gave a sigh of relief and pushed her way through the milling crowd, moving away from the crush at the doors and into the center of the hall. There most people were standing in silence with their mouths agape, gazing around at the rich tapestries on the walls or the huge, candle-lit chandeliers that hung above their heads. Those who did dare to talk were keeping their voices to a low, reverent murmur that was easily absorbed into the echoing spaces beneath the high arched roof. On each side of the hall, two great fires were burning in fireplaces each as big as a small room and, at the far end of the hall, a raised dais supported a high-backed chair with the duke's coat of arms embroidered onto the backrest. In front of the chair, four stone steps led up to the carpeted dais. The steps were guarded by two burly soldiers, who stood with their spears crossed in front of the dais. They stared out over the heads of the crowd with stony faces, refusing to respond to any of the whispered pleading from petitioners, all desperate to talk to the duke.

A liveried servant appeared, emerging from a door that was hidden behind one of the huge tapestries. "Silence for the duke!" he roared and the murmur of the crowd instantly stopped. "No one is allowed to talk in the duke's presence, until invited to do so!" yelled the servant before turning to stand by the hidden doorway.

Argent took her chance. In the few seconds remaining before the duke emerged, she pushed as close to the dais as she could and managed to get within three rows of the front before her strength gave out. She was not as close as she would have liked, but at least she had a clear view of the duke's chair. The tapestry rustled in the silent hall and, finally, the duke himself stepped out onto the dais. Argent stared at him in fascination. This was the first time she had set eyes on her ruler, and she wanted to take in every detail.

He was a tall man but with a scholar's stoop, which took a few inches from his height. His long, narrow hands were stained with ink, and an eyeglass hung from one of the buttons on his padded jerkin. Argent thought he must be in his early forties. She could see silver streaks in his dark hair, which was thinning on top and sticking up in places. As Argent watched, the duke absentmindedly reached up and ran a hand through his hair, leaving it even messier than before.

The duke came forward and stood at the front

of the dais, looking mildly surprised to see so many people gathered in the Great Hall. Argent smiled as she watched him. She was sure she could persuade this scholarly man to leave the mother dragon alone, if only she could get to talk with him. When the duke looked right at her and returned her smile, her hopes leaped even higher. Still looking at her, the duke held out his hands with the palms facing the floor and made gentle up-and-down motions. Argent frowned, trying to catch his meaning. The duke pointed over to Argent's left and then looked back at her, his blue eyes sparkling with amusement.

Argent looked to where the duke was pointing, and her eyes widened as she saw one of the soldiers from the front of the dais bearing down on her with a furious look on his face. She took a step back and a muffled curse came from behind her as someone's hand was crushed beneath her heel. Only then did Argent realize that she was the only petitioner standing. Everyone else had sunk to their knees and bowed their heads. Hastily Argent dropped to her knees too, and the soldier sent her a sour look before turning and making his way back to the front of the dais. Argent bowed her head and waited to see what would happen next.

"All rise!" yelled the servant. There was a rustle of clothing and the creaking of many knees as the crowd clambered to its feet. The duke was now sitting in his chair, and his servant was standing next to him with a very thin, long stick at the ready. The stick was made of light, whippy wood, and there was a hook at one end. It reminded Argent of a fishing rod. As she stared at the rod, wondering what the servant was going to do with it, Argent heard a fluttering noise that grew and grew until it sounded as though a huge flock of birds had flown into the Great Hall. She looked up and saw, not wings, but hundreds of petitions flapping above the heads of the crowd.

The petitioners were not allowed to call out to the duke, but they were making their presence known in other ways. Some had attached their petitions to sticks in order to raise them higher than the others. Some had added colorful bows to make their parchments stand out from the crowd. There were even a few petitions with strange items attached to them. One had a string of sausages hanging from it; another, a pair of tiny silver bells. Argent could only guess that the sausages and the bells had some bearing on the petitions to which they were attached.

As Argent watched, the duke whispered something to his servant, who stepped forward and pushed the rod out over the heads of the crowd. He hooked up a petition with a gold watch dangling from it and pulled the rod back in toward the dais. The woman whose petition it was gave a joyful cry, quickly stifled as she hurried up onto the dais after her dangling gold watch.

"State your case," said the duke softly, and the woman launched into her story. Six years earlier she had accepted a proposal of marriage, but the man involved was still dragging his feet over setting the date. The woman desperately wanted to have children, but the years were ticking away and she felt that she was running out of time. She wanted the duke to force her future husband into naming the day.

"What does your suitor do?" asked the duke.

"He's a cheese maker, sir."

"Are they good cheeses?"

"Oh, yes, sir. The tastiest in Goldstone."

"Then tell him that if he marries you within the month, I shall give his cheeses my seal of approval."

The woman curtsied and hurried from the dais with her cheeks scarlet and her eyes sparkling. The petitions rose into the air again, and this time Argent's sheaf of parchments rose with them, but minute after minute ticked away and her scrappy roll of papers was passed over by the hooked stick again and again. By the time the duke's servant announced that only one more petition would be heard, Argent's arm was so tired, she barely had the energy to lift her parchment roll over her head. When she saw the servant walking away from her to the far side of the dais, she lowered her aching arm and stood with her head down and her shoulders slumped. She had been so sure she would talk to the duke tonight, but the two hours had passed and she had not been picked out.

Her eyelids drooped in the heavy heat of the Great Hall, and she swayed on her feet as she waited for the final petitioner to mumble through his request. Exhaustion was seeping into every part of her, and all she wanted was for the double doors to swing open again so that she could go and find a place to lie down and sleep for the night. A second later all thoughts of sleep had vanished. The petitioner up on the dais had just said "Haven's Edge" and "dragon."

Argent gasped and lifted her head. She could hardly believe what she was seeing. Standing in front of the duke, red in the face and swelling with pride, was Will the pigman. For once he had managed not to stop at every inn along the road and subsequently, he had arrived at Goldstone a whole day earlier than Argent was expecting. Will finished his story and stood with his head bowed, waiting for the duke's decision. Argent waited too, biting her lip with anxiety. The duke looked Will up and down.

"Are you sure this dragon means to harm your village?" he asked.

"Oh, yes, sir! Vicious, it is! Burned down half our crops already and nigh on killed two of our children."

Argent gasped at Will's exaggeration, but the duke was nodding sadly. "You shall have your troops," he said wearily, rising from his chair.

"Thank you, sir," said Will to the duke's retreating back.

"No, wait!" called Argent, in a much louder voice than she had intended. "You cannot kill the dragon, sir!" The whole audience of petitioners jumped and turned to stare at her. The duke had stopped too and was walking back to the front of the dais to see what the commotion was.

"No talking in front of the duke—" began the servant, but Argent ignored him.

"Will is wrong, sir!" she called to the duke. "I'm from Haven's Edge too. The dragon means no harm to us. She only looks for her stolen baby."

Will glared at her from the dais. "That girl there, sir, is the reason we have dragon trouble. She's always up at the cave, studying the vicious creatures. It was her that brought this dragon down upon us."

The duke was looking at Argent with interest. She felt hope flutter in her heart again, but the two soldiers were forging their way through the crowd toward her, and she knew she did not have much time.

"It is true that I have made a study of dragons, sir," she gabbled. "They are fascinating creatures. I have research notes and drawings here, sir, which prove that the dragons have no reason to harm us—"

The soldiers arrived, picked her up under the arms, and began to march her toward the double doors. Desperately Argent waved her sheaf of parchments above her head, pedaling her feet in midair as she gazed beseechingly at the duke. "I have them right here, sir, if you would care to see them!"

The soldiers had nearly reached the door and Will's face was a picture of smug satisfaction when the duke finally spoke. "Put her down," he said softly.

The soldiers dropped Argent to the ground and turned to face the duke, waiting for further instructions. "Follow me," said the duke, looking straight at Argent. "And you," he added, looking over at Will. "You wait here."

The duke left the dais through the hidden door. Argent stumbled up the stone steps and hurried after him with her heart beating in her throat. She stepped behind the tapestry and came out in a cozy little anteroom with two chairs and a table set out in front of a blazing fire. The servant closed the door behind her, and the shocked murmurings of the crowd in the Great Hall were cut off. The duke was already sitting in one of the chairs, and he gestured to Argent to come closer. She made a wobbly curtsy and took a few, hesitant steps toward him, holding out her drawings. Her hand was shaking so much, the parchments rustled together like autumn leaves.

"Come, child." The duke smiled. "We are all equal in this room. I am a man of science, and I can see that I am in the presence of a fellow scientist."

Encouraged, Argent stepped up to the table and spread out her notes and drawings for the duke to see. A few minutes later all her nerves had gone as she leaned over the table with the duke, explaining her theories. The duke knew exactly the right questions to ask and was particularly interested in her theory that dragons drew energy from the sun.

"So you see," said Argent as she finished her explanation, "the dragons have no reason to harm us. They don't eat us, or our cattle, because they feed from the sun. And they would much prefer to be up there in the sky than down here, where their wings are in danger of collapsing under the weight of the air."

The duke nodded, still poring over her drawings. "I see what you mean," he murmured. He tapped her parchments decisively with one of his long, thin fingers and then stepped back from the table. "I have a proposal to make," he said. "As one scientist to another."

"Sir?"

"Let us help each other. I will help you by sparing your mother dragon if you will stay at the castle to help me in my research."

Argent gaped at the duke and then remembered her manners and closed her mouth. This was the last thing she had been expecting from the night. Her mind raced as she tried to decide what an appropriate answer would be.

"Come," said the duke decisively. "While you are thinking about my offer, you can see my research facilities. I have an extensive library and an indoor garden full of rare plants. There are whole rooms full of rocks and fossils, but the centerpiece is—well, come and see!" He grinned with boyish enthusiasm, which suddenly made him look years younger. The grin was infectious, and Argent felt an answering smile spreading across her face. The duke took her smile as consent. Without another word, he hurried out of the room and, after a second's hesitation, Argent followed at his heels.

They came out in a long gallery, with windows all down one side and paintings of the duke's ancestors on the other. The duke hurried to a portrait of a rather fat duchess with a nose like a potato and pressed one of the gilt flowers on her frame. Silently the frame slid to one side, revealing a hidden doorway. The duke and Argent stepped through, and the frame silently slid shut again behind them. They were standing at the top of a spiral stone staircase that was lit by candles in wall brackets every twenty steps.

The duke started down the steps without hesitation, and Argent had no choice but to pick up her skirts and follow, listening to his glowing descriptions of a rare plant he had managed to grow in his garden, or a fossil he had found in the harbor which proved that a certain species of fish had come out of the sea to live on land. The staircase wound down and down, occasionally coming to a half landing with a door leading off.

"Library," said the duke, throwing open one door. Argent had a glimpse of a bright, warm room lined with shelves of leather-bound books before the Duke pulled the door shut again and hurried on.

"Indoor garden," he said, pausing on the next half landing to fling open the door. Argent was hit by a blast of humid heat and a perfumed smell so strong it made her slightly dizzy. She looked inside and stared in awe at the huge, glass dome high above her and the spreading jungle of vegetation all around.

"What is that one?" she asked, pointing out a plant with a flower as big as a small boat, but the duke was already sprinting down the steps again.

"Close the door behind you!" he called up the stairwell.

Hastily Argent pulled the door shut and hurried after the duke. Down and down they went, following the curving steps until Argent's legs were trembling with exhaustion. The duke, on the other hand, hardly seemed out of breath. His stooped posture was deceptive. He was full of a lean energy.

"Don't worry." He smiled as Argent tottered down the last few steps to the final door. "I have a lift operated by a pulley system for getting back up. Now here is my centerpiece. My research laboratory!"

He flung open the door, and a guard on the other side hurriedly stood to attention. The duke nodded to the guard and ushered Argent in ahead of him, leaving the guard to close the door to the stairwell. Argent stepped into a vast and echoing space, dim and shadowy after the brightly lit stairwell. Instinctively Argent looked up, seeking the only source of light. What she saw above her head made her stagger with vertigo. She was standing inside the base of one of the tallest towers she had ever seen. At the very top of the tower, she could just make out a metallic shape, glimmering in the moonlight. It was the Bell Tower bell.

Moonlight was shining in through arched openings on all four sides of the cupola that housed the bell and pouring down into the topmost section of the tower. At the farthest reach of the moonlight, a large mirror had been attached to the stonework. It had been set at exactly the right angle to bounce the moonlight down onto a lower mirror on the opposite wall. The pattern of moonlight and mirror continued all the way down the inside of the tower, and Argent's gaze followed it until she reached the point where the dressed stones of the tower were replaced by natural rock.

This change from stone to rock marked the base of the tower, but it was still way above her head. As her eyes adjusted to the pale, reflected light of the moon, Argent saw that she was standing in a chamber that had been hewn from the rock beneath the tower. Around the edge of the chamber a series of rough, low-ceilinged alcoves had been carved into the rock, and iron bars had been fitted over their entrances. The reflected moonlight did not reach into the back of the alcoves, but Argent thought she could see shapes moving in the darkness.

A sound like a muffled sigh finally brought her gaze into the center of the chamber. Argent's eyes widened and she clapped a hand over her mouth to stifle a horrified scream. There, lying in a patch of scorched earth and lit by a circle of reflected moonlight, was the baby dragon. Its jaws had been sealed shut with a hinged steel clamp. Its trembling wings were spread wide and held in place with steel bolts that had been hammered through its wing hooks and then screwed directly into the rock beneath. Argent flinched as she saw the fluid leaking from the raw holes in the dragon's wing hooks, and tears sprang to her eyes as she imagined how the little creature must be suffering, pinned down so far away from the sun and the high, wild sky.

"Impressive, isn't it?" The duke smiled proudly, misinterpreting her tears. "I knew you would be excited. I am a man of science, and I can recognize a fellow scientist when I see one. This is what I wanted to show you. My centerpiece. My grand new experiment!"

Argent turned to look at the duke. His eyes were bright with enthusiasm as he gazed at the baby dragon. "I had already deduced that dragons need sunlight," he said. "Which is why I had this system of mirrors put into place. Your theory that they feed off the sun seems very credible to me. Now we can test it out. Just think," he continued. "We can test out all your theories! We can find out how this one feeds, how he flies, and—eventually—how his internal organs work. It will be fascinating!"

As Argent looked into the duke's blue eyes, she heard the goodwife's warning in her head. *Beware the man who offers his help.* Argent realized that she had totally misread him. What she had taken for gentleness and humanity as he dealt with his petitioners had actually been a combination of boredom and a purely scientific interest in solving problems. There was no pity in his eyes now as he turned to regard his prize specimen, only pride and excitement. It dawned on Argent that the duke did not realize he was being cruel.

How could he? He did not recognize other living creatures as having feelings or emotions. The duke saw them all as objects, including her, and that made him a very dangerous man indeed.

· FIFTEEN ·

TRIANGULATION

The river was running higher than Ellie had ever seen it. The water was brown with mud, and it flowed around the long legs of the Royal Border Bridge with a thick, muscular power. Ellie was standing on the road bridge, just downriver from the Royal Border Bridge. She had been trudging across it on her way to confront Ross at his father's veterinary surgery, but she had stopped to look down at the scene below.

Parts of the riverside path were impassable, drowned by the rising water. The back gardens of the houses on the bend of the river were all underwater too. The owners had barricaded their back doors with sandbags, but the brown water was already halfway up the barrier. Ellie leaned over the parapet of the bridge to see how high the river was running. It had nearly reached the top of the road-bridge arches, and each support had collected its own ruff of debris. All sorts of stuff had been swept downriver. Bushes and small trees were tangled together with plastic bags and fishing floats. There was even a small rowing boat, upended against one of the bridge supports and half submerged in the water. And still the rain poured down from a steely gray sky.

Ellie stared intently at the debris trapped against the bridge supports, afraid of what she might see but unable to look away until she had checked everything. Her mind was seeing white, drowned arms and floating bodies, but they all turned into flapping carrier bags and half-submerged logs when she looked at them directly. Finally Ellie stood back, shook the excess water from the hood of her cape, and tramped on over the bridge. A red car swished toward her, and she turned to stare in through the window as it went by. She had been staring in at the drivers of red cars all day, wondering if she was looking at the person who had taken Danny from her.

She had spent the day working her way around the center of town talking to Danny's wide and diverse circle of friends. She had returned home twice to top up on birthday cake, but now all the cake was gone and she was no further forward. She had soon discovered that the police investigation was much more sweeping than she imagined. Police officers had already interviewed many of the people on her list, and they had done a much more professional job of it. Ellie did not even have a list of prepared questions to ask, and she soon began to feel out of her depth.

Of course, as soon as they knew who she was, everyone she spoke to was very kind and helpful. Too helpful. The police had issued a description of the red hatchback that had been seen on the bridge above Chuggie's Pool on Saturday and were asking for the driver to come forward. Everyone had a different theory about the identity of the driver, and they all wanted to share it with Ellie. She also had to listen to a surprising number of vague and groundless accusations against some of the town's more eccentric local characters, but not one of the people she spoke to could come up with an explanation for Danny's sudden disappearance. What she kept hearing over and over again was that everyone liked Danny. He was a happy boy. No one would want to harm him.

To make matters worse, Ellie kept seeing Danny's smiling face everywhere. The police had produced MISSING posters and leaflets showing Danny's school photograph, and they were plastered on shop windows, notice boards, lampposts, and telephone poles all around town.

Now Ellie's face was grim as she stomped up the road to the modern, flat-roofed building that housed the vet's surgery. Her feet were sore, her heart was sore, and she was ready to give Ross a piece of her mind about his television interview. She pushed open the front door of the surgery and strode into the little reception area, but the desk where Ross should have been standing was deserted.

Ellie faltered to a stop and stood for a few seconds, dripping rain onto the tiled floor. Her opening line was on the tip of her tongue, ready to jump out and attack him, but he wasn't there. Ellie swallowed her words and turned to look at the people sitting in the waiting area. They stared back impassively.

"Um . . . Does any one know. . . ?" asked Ellie, gesturing to the empty reception desk.

"Out back," said a woman with a parrot sitting on her shoulder.

Ellie lifted the hinged section of the reception counter and hurried through, heading for the door behind the desk. She had been to the surgery before, and she knew the door led to the storeroom where all the drugs and medical supplies were kept. As soon as she opened the door, Ellie spotted Ross at the other end of the aisle of shelving. He was standing below the high window at the far end of the room. Ellie felt anger rising inside her as she stepped into the storeroom and slammed the door.

"What were you thinking, Ross?" she demanded, stalking down the aisle toward him. "Telling them all that personal stuff?"

Ross turned to face her with a shocked look on his face. "Ellie. What—what's wrong?"

"The television interview! What was going on in your head? Or were you enjoying your three minutes of fame too much to think at all? I am so mad at you! And Mum and Dad aren't too happy with you either."

Just for an instant, Ross looked guilty. Ellie saw his eyes shift from side to side and his face began to redden with shame. But then he kicked into defensive mode. "Hey! That's not fair! I told you I would get rid of them, and I did, didn't I? They're not outside your house now, are they?" By the time he stopped talking, all the guilt had gone from his face. Instead, he was looking indignant. Hurt, even. Ellie could see that, in the space of three sentences, Ross had convinced himself that he was the injured party, innocent of everything except trying to help. This did not surprise her. Ross had never been able to put up his hands and say sorry when he was in the wrong, but now Ellie realized that if he could not be honest about something as important as this, then he was never going to change.

Ellie looked at his handsome, self-righteous face and came to a sudden decision. It was time to end this relationship, and she might as well do it before Ross beat her to it. He was obviously losing interest. He hardly ever kissed her now and, since she had returned from her summer holiday with her family, he had become noticeably more distant and distracted. Facing him in the storeroom aisle, Ellie finally faced up to her suspicion that Ross had been seeing Laura Jones while she and her family had been away.

Ellie straightened and flicked her hair back over her shoulders. This was not going to be easy. Her whole family liked Ross, and he had become something of a fixture at their house. She would not be the only one to miss him. Ellie took a deep breath and opened her mouth to tell Ross it was over. Then someone behind the shelving cleared his throat. Ellie froze in shock.

A tall figure moved into the aisle and gave her one of his grave nods. Ellie stared up at Sergeant Donaldson as though he were some mythical beast that had just wandered into the surgery. "Wh-what are you doing here?" she stammered.

"We had a break-in, last night," explained Ross. He pointed up at the window he was standing beneath and, for the first time, Ellie noticed that the frame was bent and splintered. It had been jimmied open. She gazed around the storeroom. Everything looked the same to her. The shelves were neatly stacked with all the usual supplies of worming tablets, bandages, and flea collars. "Did they take anything?" she asked.

"Only from here," said Ross, pointing into the corner where Sergeant Donaldson had been standing.

"The drugs cabinet?" asked Ellie, stepping forward to look. The metal drugs cabinet was usually kept locked, but now the doors were hanging open, one of them half off its hinges. "Wow. Someone really wanted to get into that," said Ellie, looking at the buckled metal. "What did they take?"

"Ketamine," said Ross. "Some other drugs too, painkillers and stuff. But mainly Ketamine."

"Why did they take that?" asked Ellie.

"No idea." Ross shrugged. "We use it as a cat tranquilizer."

"It's known as Special K on the street," explained Sergeant Donaldson. "It gets you high. Takes you right out of your body and gives you amazing hallucinations. You lose all sense of time or even who you are. Whoever stole it knew they could sell it on the street. Or use it on themselves."

"So it was druggies, then?" asked Ellie.

"All the evidence points to that," said Sergeant Donaldson. Ellie looked at the big police officer, suddenly remembering the flickering light in the derelict factory at Spittal Point. *Don't go in on your own*, Miguel had warned. *There could be druggies in there.* She opened her mouth to tell Sergeant

Donaldson, but he was already speaking.

"I was about to call you," he said, looking at Ellie.

Ellie felt hope flood through her tired body and all thoughts of telling him about Spittal Point went right out of her head. "Have you found Danny?"

"No. No," said Sergeant Donaldson hastily. "Not yet. None of the passengers on any of the coaches that passed through the bus station on Saturday remember seeing a boy of Danny's description. We've traced the owner of the red hatchback, though. It was all perfectly innocent. The driver was a local mum. And the boy who didn't want to get in the car was her son. They'd had an argument, and she was trying to persuade him to come home."

"Oh." Ellie slumped, not sure whether to be relieved or not. It was good to know that Danny had not climbed into a stranger's car, but it seemed that two of the leads the police had been following had come to nothing. "What about the fisherman, Mr. Lees?"

Sergeant Donaldson frowned down at Ellie. "How do you know his name? We didn't release it. As far as the press were concerned, we were questioning a local fisherman."

Ellie thought frantically. She could not admit that she had been listening to Sergeant Donaldson and Lisa outside the living room door.

"The local grapevine, I suppose," Sergeant Donaldson, answered his own question, and sighed. "There's already been some trouble at his house. People throwing bricks through his windows and writing graffiti on his walls."

"But is he still a suspect?"

"Yes and no. He doesn't have an alibi for Saturday, but we searched his house, and we didn't turn up a single scrap of incriminating evidence. He's squeaky clean. We do have another line of investigation, though," continued Sergeant Donaldson. "The techies found something on your family computer."

Ellie tensed as she waited for Sergeant Donaldson to explain. Surely there was nothing on there to make them suspect her dad? "What have you found?"

"It seems Danny was corresponding with an eleven-year-old fishing enthusiast from Canada. Did he ever mention this contact to you?"

Ellie shook her head, weak with relief. As she had known, the police had found nothing on her dad.

"It's probably nothing," said Sergeant Donaldson. "But we're checking it out, just in case there's someone out there posing as an eleven-year-old boy."

"Why were you about to call me?" said Ellie,

remembering Sergeant Donaldson's earlier statement.

"We want you to attend a press conference."

Ellie blinked with shock. "Me? But I— When?"

"In about half an hour. Then we can get it out on the early evening news. I can take you straight there, if you agree to do it."

Ellie's hand instinctively went up to her bedraggled hair before she could stop herself. Quickly she lowered her hand again, hating herself for bothering about how she would look in front of the cameras when Danny was somewhere, frightened, alone, and possibly struggling to stay alive. "Of course I'll do it," she said, more loudly than she meant to.

"Good girl. I'll tell you all about it in the car. Shall we go?"

"Want me to come with you?" offered Ross with a touch of eagerness in his tone.

"I thought you had to work on reception this evening," said Ellie frostily.

"Yeah, but I can get someone to cover for me if you like," said Ross.

"That won't be necessary," answered Sergeant Donaldson flatly, giving Ross a thinly veiled look of dislike. He had obviously seen the television interview too. Ross looked down at his feet, and Sergeant Donaldson turned his back, ushering Ellie out of the door ahead of him.

"But Ellie might need me there," said Ross,

hurrying after them. "For, you know, emotional support."

"Sorry, son. Press and family only," said Sergeant Donaldson, closing the storeroom door firmly in Ross's face.

"So where are we going?" asked Ellie, once they had reached the police car and she was settling herself into the passenger seat.

"The local primary school," said Sergeant Donaldson, starting up the engine and moving off. "We're using their main hall."

Ellie quailed in her seat. It was obviously going to be a big event if they needed a school hall to hold everyone.

"Don't worry," said Sergeant Donaldson, giving her a brief glance. "We'll be controlling the whole thing. And your mum and dad will be there too."

"Okay," whispered Ellie watching the windscreen wipers sweep back and forth.

"Ellie, we want you to do something for us. Or rather, we want you to say something. At the press conference."

Ellie turned to look at Sergeant Donaldson. "Me?"

"Yes. Your mum and your dad have jobs to do too. Your mum will be appealing directly to Danny to come home, in case he is a runaway. Your dad will be trying to make a connection with whoever might have taken him, in case he has been abducted. He'll be making the abductor see Danny as a person, with family, that sort of thing."

"And me?"

"We want you to tell Danny the police are very close to finding him, but there's one thing he needs to do to help us. Can you remember to say that?"

"Yes, but what—"

"Then we'd like you to say that you've sent Danny a text message, explaining exactly what that one thing is he has to do."

"But what does he have to do?" asked Ellie.

"Switch on his mobile phone." Sergeant Donaldson smiled.

"But . . ." Ellie faltered to a halt as she puzzled over the flawed logic of sending a text message telling Danny to switch on his phone when, in order to retrieve the message, the phone would already be switched on.

"If Danny is being held by someone," explained Sergeant Donaldson, "we're hoping your statement at the press conference will make his abductor worried enough to switch on Danny's phone in order to see how close we are to finding him. Once he does that, we've got him."

"How?"

"This is rather technical," said Sergeant Donaldson. "But, basically, it goes like this. Every phone has a unique identifier code, and every time a phone connects to the global telecommunications networks, it gives that unique code to the nearest mast. So, if we can get either Danny or the person who is holding him to switch on his phone, the network will be able to identify which mast his phone is connecting to. Once we have that information, then we can triangulate using other nearby masts to get a very accurate fix on the phone's location—"

"Which could lead us to Danny?"

"That's right."

"What if his kidnapper knows about this triangulation thing?"

"We'll just have to hope he doesn't know. You didn't, did you? It's not exactly common knowledge."

Ellie nodded. She pulled out her phone and looked at it. "Do I really send him a message?"

"Yes. There has to be a text from you waiting for him, or Danny's abductor will realize something's wrong."

"What do I say?" asked Ellie, selecting the message option from her menu.

"Just—" Sergeant Donaldson shrugged. "Something vague and encouraging, like 'don't give up hope' or 'stay calm.'"

For the rest of the short journey to the primary school, Ellie composed a text message to Danny while Sergeant Donaldson drove in silence beside her. The police radio bleeped and squawked and the windscreen wipers thudded rhythmically as she told Danny how she missed him and how much they all wanted him to come home. She told him she loved him and that the one thing he must do was keep believing that she would find him. Then, on impulse, she signed her name as Argent.

"Ready?" asked Sergeant Donaldson as he turned the car into the primary school playground. Ellie looked up from her phone screen and saw all the other cars and vans parked there. Her stomach clenched with nerves, and her courage began to drain away. Ellie ducked her head and looked at the signature she had put at the end of her text message to Danny. Argent would not shy away from doing what had to be done.

Ellie sent her text message to Danny and took a deep breath. "Ready," she said.

Her mum and dad were already in the staff room. Her mum was sitting with Lisa, staring into a coffee cup while the family liaison officer murmured words of encouragement. Her dad was pacing back and forth in front of the staff notice board, still full of the frantic energy that had possessed him since he had realized his son was missing. As Ellie stepped into the room, she realized that this was the first time they had all been together since Saturday night.

"All right?" asked her dad, holding Ellie at arm's length to look at her after they had hugged. She nodded. His breath was sour, and he looked bad. There were black smudges under his eyes, and his hands were shaking. He had shaved, but not very well. There were islands of bristles dotted about his cheeks.

Ellie bent to hug her mum and felt her trembling under her hands.

"I've been worried about you, Ellie," whispered Mrs. Brody. "Out all day."

"Only around town, Mum. Don't worry."

"You'll come home with us after this, though, won't you? If you went missing too, I don't know what I would do. . . ."

Ellie rubbed her mother's thin shoulders, trying to give her some reassurance. Mrs. Brody gave her a tremulous smile and then returned to staring into her coffee cup. She was dressed well enough in a skirt, blouse, and jacket and her face was impeccably made up, but she still looked strange. Ellie frowned at her mum, and suddenly she knew what was wrong. Her mum hated that blouse. It had been sitting untouched in the wardrobe ever since she bought it in the half-price January sales. And she never usually wore so much makeup. A touch of mascara and some lipstick was the most Mrs. Brody usually felt comfortable wearing.

Ellie straightened up and looked at Lisa. She realized that the family liaison officer must have chosen Mrs. Brody's outfit for her and then applied her makeup in order to get her looking relatively presentable for the press conference. Ellie could picture how her mum must have sat quietly on the edge of the bed, staring into space while Lisa fussed around her.

"Are you sure she's up to this?" asked Ellie quietly.

"We're doing fine!" said Lisa brightly. "Aren't we?" She tilted her head at Mrs. Brody, who gazed at her for a few seconds before nodding her head.

"We're ready to start," said Sergeant Donaldson, poking his head around the staff room door.

Mr. Brody shot out of the room after Sergeant Donaldson. Watching him go, Ellie reckoned he was running on pure adrenalin. She bent to help her mum out of the chair, but Lisa was already there with a supportive hand under Mrs. Brody's elbow. Ellie turned away and followed her dad out into the school corridor. The double doors at the end of the corridor were wedged open, and she could hear a buzz of conversation coming from the hall beyond. Sergeant Donaldson and her dad were waiting for them by the doors.

"Best if we all go in together," said Sergeant Donaldson. "There's a table set up at the front with five chairs. You take the middle three chairs. Lisa and I will sit on either side. Okay?"

Ellie nodded and looked around the corridor

walls as they waited for Lisa and her mum to catch up. The notice board opposite was headed with the words "My Family." It was covered with bright children's paintings of mums and dads, brothers and sisters. All smiling. All happy. Ellie swallowed, trying to get rid of the lump in her throat. This was the school Danny had attended until he had moved up to the secondary school at the end of the summer.

"Right," said Sergeant Donaldson, bringing Ellie back to the present. "Any time any of you want to stop, let us know and we'll call a halt."

He turned and led the way into the hall. Ellie followed him into a chaos of flashing cameras and shouted questions. She hurried to sit next to her dad, keeping her head down. Mrs. Brody stumbled into the chair on her other side, and Lisa took the end chair. Sergeant Donaldson held up his hand for silence and the voices stopped, although the cameras kept whirring and flashing. "There will be no questions," said Sergeant Donaldson in a voice that brooked no argument. "Each family member wishes to make a prepared statement, after which this conference will be over."

After that the whole conference went by in a blur for Ellie. She sat, staring down at her clenched hands while her dad talked about his son's love of fishing and movies and her mum cried as she pleaded with Danny to come home. When Ellie's turn came, she leaned toward the microphone on the table in front of her and recited her request for Danny to check his text messages in a voice that trembled so much, she could hardly form the words. Then, all of a sudden, they were being ushered out of the hall again and back into the empty staff room.

"Well done," said Sergeant Donaldson quietly as Lisa left the room to answer her radio. "As soon as Lisa's finished, we'll get you home."

But then Lisa called Sergeant Donaldson out into the corridor. They were out there, conferring with their heads together for nearly five minutes. When they came back into the room, Sergeant Donaldson did not look happy. Lisa's expression was carefully neutral, but Ellie thought she could detect a repressed excitement in her eyes.

"Mr. Brody," said Sergeant Donaldson formally. "Can you tell us where you were on Saturday morning?"

Mr. Brody stopped pacing and looked at the big police officer. "I already went through that with you," he said, casting an impatient glance out of the staff room window at the fading light. Ellie could see that he wanted to be out there again, searching for Danny.

"If you could just run through it again," insisted Sergeant Donaldson.

Mr. Brody sighed. "Saturday mornings are when

I go around doing estimates for potential jobs. Last Saturday I was fully booked from nine until twelve. That's what I was doing. Driving round in my van, going to different houses, seeing what jobs people wanted doing and working out costs."

"Can you remember the morning in more detail than that?"

"Is this really necessary?"

"Just bear with us, sir," said Sergeant Donaldson.

"All right. I started off with a central heating estimate for a semi up on North Road. Then it was over to the leisure complex. They were having trouble with one of their filter pumps. Then a shower fitting for a loft conversion in Tweedmouth, and then—"

"Just going back to the loft conversion, Mr. Brody," interrupted Sergeant Donaldson.

"What about it?"

"Would that be for a Mrs. Straughan?"

"Yes, I think it was."

Sergeant Donaldson nodded tiredly, as though he had just received an answer he was expecting but not particularly wanting.

"What's the matter?" demanded Ellie, seeing the look on his face. Sergeant Donaldson held up his hand and turned back to Mr. Brody. "Sir, Mrs. Straughan has informed us that you never turned up to give that estimate."

Ellie felt shock rip through her as she realized where this conversation was going. "Tell him, Dad!" she shouted. "Tell him he's got it wrong!"

But Mr. Brody was looking down at his feet and rubbing his nose in an embarrassed manner. "Oh, yes. I forgot. I took longer than I thought at the leisure center."

"Sir?" said Sergeant Donaldson carefully. "Dougall Moir, the duty manager at the leisure center, told us you left half an hour before your appointment with Mrs. Straughan. Is there anything else you want to tell me about your whereabouts that morning?"

Mr. Brody looked bleakly at Sergeant Donaldson.

"Dad?" asked Ellie, her voice quavering.

"I went to the promenade to have my flask of coffee."

"Sir. A witness has reported seeing you down at the river."

"Oh, yes." Mr. Brody looked even more uncomfortable. "I forgot. I went looking for Danny. It was a lovely morning, and I wanted to spend a bit of time with him on his birthday. It seemed worth missing an appointment. I tried a couple of likely fishing spots, but I couldn't find him. So then I gave up and went down to the promenade instead."

"Did you go to Chuggie's Pool?"

"No. That's how I knew to look there later on. I'd already checked out Danny's two other favorite fishing spots in the morning, see?"

"Why didn't you tell us this in your initial interview?" asked Sergeant Donaldson.

"I forgot," said Mr. Brody. "It was a spur of the moment thing. I only looked for him for about twenty minutes. When I didn't track him down, I went to the promenade instead. And then when I remembered about it later, it didn't seem important. Besides," he added, glancing at Lisa, "she was already acting as though I was the chief suspect—so I didn't say anything."

"That's right!" said Ellie. "It's no wonder he didn't say anything, the sort of questions she was asking—"

Mrs. Brody gave a horrified whimper, and Ellie broke off, suddenly realizing that this was the first inkling her mother would have had that the police were viewing Mr. Brody as a possible suspect. She looked over and felt her heart clench as she saw the anguish on her mother's face.

"Mum. They're wrong—"

"Ellie," said Sergeant Donaldson gently. "I have to ask you to be quiet." He looked at her for a moment before turning his attention back to Mr. Brody. "Sir, did anyone see you when you were parked up at the promenade?"

Mr. Brody shook his head. "I don't think so."

"Are you sure there were no witnesses to verify your location?"

"No. The car park was empty."

There was a moment of absolute stillness before Sergeant Donaldson sighed and stepped forward. "Mr. Brody, would you come down to the station with me?"

"Now just wait a minute," said Mrs. Brody, coming to her feet. "Matthew's done nothing wrong. When Danny's out fishing on a Saturday, he often goes to find him so they can spend some time together."

"And what do you do, Mr. Brody, once you find him?" asked Lisa. "Something that would make him run away rather than face another meeting with you?"

Mr. Brody gasped as though Lisa had punched him in the stomach. Everyone turned to look at Lisa with shocked expressions, even Sergeant Donaldson. Lisa seemed to realize she had overstepped the mark. She folded her arms and looked away from Mr. Brody's anguished face.

"Why are you taking him?" demanded Ellie.

"The crime squad would like to talk to you," said Sergeant Donaldson, answering Ellie's question but looking at Mr. Brody.

"Of course," said Mr. Brody quietly.

Sergeant Donaldson nodded, then turned back

to Ellie. "Lisa will take you and your mum home now," he said.

"No she won't," said Mrs. Brody, moving to stand by her husband's side. "I'm coming with Matthew."

"That won't be possible," began Lisa.

"Try and stop me!" snapped Mrs. Brody, turning to glare at the family liaison officer. "I'm coming down to the station to sort out a lawyer for Matthew and that's final. My husband would never hurt Danny, I'm telling you that now."

Lisa shrugged and looked away from the fire in Mrs. Brody's eyes. Ellie felt a surge of pride as she watched her mother. She was shaking with exhaustion and stress as she stood shoulder to shoulder with her husband, but the shattered expression of the past few days was gone, replaced with a look of fierce determination.

"Ellie, you go home with Lisa," said Mrs. Brody. "We'll be back as soon as we've sorted out this nonsense."

Ellie nodded, too choked to speak.

Mr. and Mrs. Brody left the room arm in arm, followed by Sergeant Donaldson.

"Ready?" asked Lisa.

"I'm not going anywhere with you!" yelled Ellie, turning to glare at Lisa. "You've been after my dad from the start, and now you've got what you wanted. But you're wrong!"

"We're only doing our job," began Lisa, but Ellie did not stay to listen. She grabbed her rain cape from the back of the chair and ran from the room. She kept on running, out of the school, past a few startled stragglers in the playground, onto the rainy road and down the hill. She did not stop running until the stitch in her side was so bad, she thought she might split in two. Ellie stumbled to a halt and doubled over, clutching her side and gasping for breath. Her face was wet with a mixture of rain and tears and, as she started to walk back and forth, trying to ease the stitch away, she kept shaking her head wildly. "Not my dad," she kept repeating. "Not my dad!"

Gradually, as she calmed down, Ellie realized two things. Firstly, people were looking at her, even crossing the street to avoid her. Secondly, it was all the more important now that she continued going Argent's way. She had to show the police that they were wrong about her dad, and the only way to do that was to find Danny. Ellie straightened up, suddenly remembering that she had arranged to meet Miguel at Spittal Point at six o'clock. She yanked back her sleeve and stared at her watch. It was six thirty. Ellie cursed and looked around to establish where she was. By sheer chance, she had been running in the right direction. Spittal Point was only five minutes away. She could see the narrow factory chimney ahead, silhouetted against the darkening sky. Ellie wiped the tears and rain from her face and set off for Spittal Point at a brisk walk.

There was no sign of Miguel when she walked up to the gates of the old factory. Either he had given up on her and gone home, or he was waiting for her inside, out of the rain. Ellie looked doubtfully at the dark bulk of the building beyond the gates, trying to decide whether to venture in. She cursed herself for not exchanging mobile numbers with Miguel. One phone call would have resolved her dilemma.

Ellie waited outside for a few more minutes as the light slowly faded from the sky. The rain beat a tattoo on the plastic bottles and drink cans that were scattered across the waste ground in front of the factory. Ellie grimaced as she gazed at the mess of sour earth, mud-filled craters, and chunks of broken concrete. It really was an awful place. She seemed to remember someone telling her that the ground here was contaminated with the chemicals that had been used in the factory to make agricultural fertilizer.

Ellie looked down the street one last time. There was no sign of Miguel. She did not have her flashlight with her and, if she waited for him any longer, she would lose what little light there was left to check out the building. Ellie decided to go in on her own. The gates were padlocked together, but the chain holding them was too long and it was easy to pull them apart far enough to ease through. There was already a raw, curving rut in the dirt that told Ellie the gates had been pulled apart like this very recently. Someone else had been getting into the building the same way.

She picked her way across the waste ground, heading for one of the tall, glassless factory windows. After a quick check to make sure no one was watching, she boosted herself up onto the windowsill and crouched there for a moment. She was staring into a great, empty hall that must once have been the main factory. There were four large pits in the floor that looked as though they had once housed the bases of enormous steel cylinders. Now they were filled with a mixture of rubbish and stagnant water. A section of the roof had collapsed into the building, scattering timber and slates everywhere and taking with it part of a gallery level that ran along the opposite wall. The remaining structure was obviously unsafe, with swaying metal catwalks reaching out into thin air over the pits in the floor. There was a strong smell of mildew and rot.

Ellie crouched on the sill, assessing how safe it was to go in. The main hall was dangerous, but she could see a small door in the wall over to her left. Ellie guessed that the door would lead into the factory offices and restrooms and, as she studied it, she saw that there was a track through the rubbish on the floor, running from the window where she crouched to the door in the wall. Ellie looked down at the sill. There were scuff marks in the dirt. Someone else had crouched here.

Ellie dropped into the building and waited, alert for any sound or movement. The place was still and silent, apart from the constant patter of rain.

"Danny?" she called softly.

No reply.

Ellie walked cautiously along the track that had been made through the rubbish on the floor until she reached the doorway. The main factory was full of shadows, but there was some light coming through the tall windows and the hole in the roof. Beyond the doorway it was totally dark.

"Danny?" called Ellie, louder this time.

Clap, clap, clap!

Ellie screamed and jumped backward as two pigeons exploded from the doorway, their wings flapping loudly. They flew up to one of the metal catwalks and perched there, watching her. Ellie moved back to the door and listened. The darkness beyond was completely silent. Either the place was empty, or her scream had alerted whoever might be lurking in there. Ellie bit her lip and moved on down a small passageway, her feet crunching over broken glass.

At the end of the passageway, Ellie waited for her eyes to adjust to the deeper dark. Gradually a corridor came into view, running at right angles to the passageway. There were doors leading off the corridor on both sides. Ellie dismissed the doors on her left. That side of the building overlooked a grass slope that ran down to the beach and the sea beyond. The young woman in the gutting warehouse had been in her caravan when she had seen the flickering light in the factory, and there was nowhere for a caravan to park on the side of the building that faced the sea.

That left the three doors on the right-hand side of the corridor. Ellie stepped up to the first door and pushed it open. It was a windowless hole that had once been used as a storeroom. A thick, fetid smell oozed out of the doorway, and Ellie hastily pulled it shut again before moving onto the next door. This room did have a window, set high up near the ceiling. The little bit of light filtering in showed a tiled men's bathroom with smashed urinals and a stream of water bubbling up through the floor from a broken pipe. Ellie closed the door and moved on to the final room.

The door creaked loudly as she pushed it open onto a room that had once been an office. Now there was a mattress in the corner, with an upturned cardboard box next to it.

"Danny?" breathed Ellie, sticking her head into the room.

No answer. She checked behind the door and then stepped through the doorway, making sure the door did not slam shut behind her. The room was empty, but someone had obviously been living here. There were candle stubs and matches on the box and three old coats piled on the mattress. Ellie stepped closer. A litter of beer cans, crisp packets, and doughnut wrappers were scattered on the floor by the bed, and there were two syringes, a bottle of water, and several blackened pieces of tinfoil on the box by the candles.

Ellie looked over to the window. It was large and the glass was still intact, although it was covered with a layer of grime. As she looked at the window, she noticed that there was a faint glow of light coming from outside. Ellie stepped across to the window and rubbed the grime away. There was a walled yard outside, and two motor homes were parked there, hidden from the sight of anyone who might be passing the factory. The light was coming from the windows of the motor homes, and Ellie could see the gut people sitting inside, eating their evening meal.

That was why the suspicious young man had stopped the younger woman from saying anything more about the light in the factory. The gut people were living behind the high walls of the yard. They had even rigged up a standpipe out there, tapping into the same water main as the broken pipe in the bathroom.

Clap, clap, clap!

The pigeons were flying again. Something must have disturbed them. Ellie sprinted over to the wall behind the door and flattened herself against it, holding her breath and listening for any sound. The seconds passed, and she was just beginning to think it must have been a cat when she saw a flickering light through the gap between the door and the frame. She heard the crunch of glass and the flickering light grew stronger. Someone was moving stealthily along the corridor with a flashlight.

· SIXTEEN ·

THE CAGE

"Sir," said Argent carefully. "You must let him go."

The duke tore his gaze away from the baby dragon and turned to look at her. "Him? It is a male, you think? How do you know? There are no obvious sexual characteristics."

"He just—looks like one to me. Sir—"

"Ah. I see. That is not very scientific. Be careful. Next you will be giving it a name, and that will never do."

"Sir, we have to let it go."

"We?" The duke's tones were suddenly frosty. "I paid well for this specimen. It is mine. You have no say in the matter."

"Then I shall leave, sir," said Argent. "For I do

not wish to stay and witness this cruelty."

She gave a respectful curtsy and began to walk toward the stairwell door.

"Oh, dear," said the duke. "I'm afraid that won't be possible."

Argent faltered slightly but carried on walking until the duke signaled to the guard at the door. The guard stepped smartly in front of the door and slammed the butt of his spear down on the cavern floor. Argent slowed to a stop and turned to face the duke.

"You said it was my choice whether I stayed or left."

"I lied." The duke shook his head sadly. "I am disappointed in you, Argent. I thought I had found a fellow scientist at last. Most of my subjects are superstitious yokels. Unlike you, they are afraid of dragons. So you see, I cannot let you go now. If the people of Goldstone discovered I was harboring a dragon within their city, they might just become a tiny bit rebellious."

"I won't tell anyone," promised Argent but, even as she said the words, she knew it was useless.

The duke smiled and shook his head. "Why do I not believe you? No, Argent, the only choice you have is whether you stay as my assistant, or my prisoner."

Argent looked across at the baby dragon and then lifted her chin and glared at the duke. "I refuse to assist in such a matter."

"Very well. Guard! Hold her!"

The guard dropped his spear and lunged for Argent, grabbing her by the upper arms. She struggled and kicked, but he simply held her at arm's length and waited for further instructions from the duke.

"Lock her in one of the alcoves for now," said the duke disinterestedly, turning away to gaze at the baby dragon again.

The guard grabbed Argent around the waist and carried her over to the nearest alcove. He held her in place under one massive arm while he hooked a bunch of keys from his belt with his other hand. Seconds later the gate in the metal bars at the front of the alcove was unlocked, and Argent was dumped at the entrance.

Quickly the guard checked her for weapons. He removed the knife her mother had given her from her belt and stuck it through his own belt instead, still holding on to her with his other hand. Then he turned her around, despite her struggles, and tried to remove the little round shield from her back. It was still tied to her bedroll and, after a moment of fumbling to untie the shield at the same time as trying to subdue her struggles, the guard cursed under his breath and left the shield in place.

"In you go," he growled, giving her a hard shove in the back. Argent fell forward onto a pile of sour-smelling straw, and the gate in the bars clanged shut behind her. She scrambled to her feet again and flung herself at the bars.

"Let me out!" she yelled at the top of her voice.

The duke rolled his eyes. "Don't be boring. No one will hear you way down here. Except for this guardsman. And I believe he has a very short temper. Now, if you will excuse me, I must go back to the Great Hall. Your compatriot from Haven's Edge is waiting to hear my decision."

"What will you tell him?" asked Argent.

"We can't have vicious dragons roaming the land. Of course I will send my troops to Haven's Edge. I will also ask him to take a message to your village, telling them that you have accepted a position in my employ. That should tie up everything very neatly."

Argent began to scream and rattle the bars across the front of the alcove, but the duke ignored her. He beckoned the guard to follow him as he walked over to a railed, wooden platform that rested at the bottom of the Bell Tower shaft. The duke climbed onto the platform, gripped the rail, and nodded to the guard, who saluted and stepped up to a huge winch that was bolted to the cavern floor. He unlocked the winch handle and began to turn it. The platform carrying the duke slowly rose up into the Bell Tower, pulled up by a length of thick rope while the guard strained at the winch handle, winding the slack onto the windlass.

Argent peered through the bars and saw that there was a pulley system running up one of the sides of the Bell Tower that did not have mirrors attached to it. There were also nine doors set into that side of the tower at intervals, marking each floor of the castle. Each door had a small platform at the threshold. This was the lift and pulley system the duke had been talking about. When the platform was level with a door halfway up the tower, the duke called a halt, and the guard immediately stopped turning the handle of the huge winch and slotted it back into lock position. Then all that the duke had to do was to open the door in the wall, step over onto the threshold platform, and pass through the doorway.

"Help! I'm a prisoner down here!" yelled Argent, hoping her voice would carry through the open door into the castle, but a second later the door was slammed shut behind the duke and the scowling guard turned and strode across the cavern floor toward her. Hastily Argent subsided into silence and stepped back from the bars. The guard grunted and went back to the winch. He grasped the winch handle and laboriously lowered the lift platform to the cavern floor, ready for the next time the duke would need it. Then he returned to his post at the stairwell door, from where he had a good view of both Argent and the baby dragon.

"Stupid, stupid, stupid," muttered Argent, kicking at the bars. Why had she let her shock and outrage get the better of her? She should have realized that the best tactic was to act as though she was honored to become the duke's assistant. If she had been thinking on her feet, the chances were she would still be out there now, with a fair chance of freeing the baby dragon. Instead, she was in here, stuck behind bars as though she were just another one of the duke's specimens.

Argent suddenly became very still, except for her eyes, which grew wide with apprehension. Other specimens. She remembered that when she first stepped into the cavern, she had seen dark shapes moving in the shadows at the back of some of the alcoves. What was in this cage with her, hidden in the darkness behind the pile of sour-smelling straw? Argent listened as hard as she could for any movement behind her. At the same time she slowly turned her head to see what was in the other alcoves.

The nearest alcove had much slimmer bars across the front of it, forged together in a crisscross pattern so that the spaces between them were too small for even a child's hand to fit through. As Argent stared into the shadows behind the crisscross bars, wondering what sort of creature needed such security, she saw a narrow, trowel-shaped head emerge from beneath the straw and pause for a moment, flickering its forked tongue. The head turned and headed for the back of its alcove, followed by a long, muscular, undulating body that seemed to go on and on. The body was still uncoiling from the straw at the front of the alcove when the death cry of an unlucky rat sounded briefly from the shadows before it was choked off.

Argent closed her eyes and told herself to stay calm. She could not be sharing her alcove with such a creature: the bars she was leaning against were all vertical and much more widely spaced. She turned her gaze to the next alcove, which had bars just like hers. There was something pacing back and forth, back and forth in the shadows but she could not quite make it out. Then a large moth batted against the bars at the front of the alcove, and the creature inside leaped forward with a coughing grunt. It was a huge, amber-colored beast, with a mane of wild hair around its head and neck and a mouth full of the biggest, sharpest teeth she had ever seen. An instant later the creature retreated to the shadows again, and the last she saw of it was a long, thin tail with a tuft of darker hair at the end.

Argent swallowed, trying to get some moisture into her dry mouth. Slowly she turned to see what was waiting in the shadows at the back of her alcove. Something was lying in the corner. Something large. She could see its side rising and falling with its breathing. It seemed to be striped, but she could not be sure. Slowly, carefully, Argent stepped toward the back of the alcove. The shape became clearer. It was something like a mule, but its hide was covered in black and white stripes and its muzzle looked as though it had been dipped into a bucket of tar. Its mane was short and black and stuck up like the bristles of a brush.

Argent let out a sigh of relief. This beast did not look as though it could hurt her. In fact, she thought, stepping closer, this beast looked very sick indeed. Argent stepped closer again. A bad smell was coming off the creature. Its breathing was shallow, its coat was dull, and she could count every one of its ribs. Argent let out a soft cry and knelt in the filthy straw beside the creature. It tried to get up, but barely managed to lift its large head. The poor animal was dying.

Argent jumped to her feet and looked around the alcove. There was no food and, even worse, no water anywhere in sight. Argent pulled her water bottle from the blanket roll on her back, yanked out the stopper, and knelt again. She tried to lift the beast's head onto her lap, but it was too heavy to move. Argent sobbed quietly and peeled the soft muzzle away from the square teeth. She tilted her bottle and tried to pour water between the creature's teeth, but its tongue was so swollen, the water simply dribbled out again and soaked into the straw.

Argent was horrified. It seemed the duke had become tired of this particular specimen and so it had been left to starve to death in a dark and stinking hole, far from its own land and its own kind. She moved closer to the beast and stroked its soft muzzle, giving it what comfort she could in its final hours. It was one of the longest nights she had ever spent. Some time before dawn, the creature began to shudder and fight for breath. Argent got to her knees, cradled her arms around its head, and leaned close to its ear, speaking as gently and reassuringly as she could.

"It's all right," she whispered. "It's all right. This is nearly over, my dear. You'll be out of here soon. You'll be home."

The beast arched its back, drew in one more breath, and then slowly sank down into the straw as the life left it. Argent continued to pat and stroke the cooling body for a few more minutes, and her tears darkened its scrawny neck. Finally she got up and went to sit at the front of the alcove with her back against the rock wall and her head leaning against the bars. She gazed hopelessly at the baby dragon pinioned to the ground in the center of the cavern. She had left Haven's Edge with high hopes of saving both the mother dragon and her baby, but she had failed. And now she too was trapped, with no one to help her and no hope of escape. Argent drew her legs up to her chest, wrapped her arms around her shins, and rested her head on her knees. Her eyes closed, and she fell asleep with the tears still trickling down her cheeks.

An hour later she woke with a start. Something had disturbed her. Argent clambered to her feet and peered out through the bars. Everything looked the same. The guard was still at his post, half asleep, and the dragon lay quivering in the middle of the cavern. Argent caught a movement from the corner of her eye. She looked toward the back of the cavern and thought she saw a darker shadow dart from a cleft in the rock. She blinked and looked again, but nothing moved. Argent sighed and looked up through the bars to the top of the Bell Tower. The bell was glinting with a rosy light. Dawn had arrived, and soon a bright shaft of reflected sunlight would arrow down into the cavern.

The baby dragon stirred, sensing the coming of the sun. The guard looked up too, then stretched his arms and left his post, moving toward a small brazier that stood just in front of Argent's cage. He yawned, settled a large, blackened kettle in the top of the brazier, and bent to blow some life into the embers below. That was when a dark shape flew out of the shadows at the back of the cavern, landing squarely on the guard's broad back.

With a yell, the guard straightened up and, with surprising swiftness for so big a man, he whirled and slammed his burden against the bars of Argent's cage. The bars rattled with the force of the blow, and Argent heard a grunt of pain. The guard pulled away and began using his fists to try to knock his attacker from his back. As the guard turned, a familiar face came into view, his features creased in pain.

"Lukos!" cried Argent.

The guard slammed Lukos into the bars again. Argent ran for her blanket roll and feverishly untied the little wooden shield. She ran back to the bars as the guard prepared to slam Lukos against them for a third time. If she could jab the guard in the ribs with the edge of her shield, it might deflect him slightly and take some of the pain out of the impact for Lukos. She braced her feet and took a firm grip on the shield, but the guard never reached the bars. Lukos bent over the man's thick bull neck, doing something that Argent could not see. The guard stopped, tottered, and then crashed forward onto the floor of the cavern like a felled tree.

For an awful moment, Argent thought Lukos had torn the man's throat out. She stood frozen, expecting him to turn to her with gore dripping from his jaws but, when he stood up and faced her, there was no sign of blood.

She gasped. "How did you do that?"

His teeth gleamed as he gave her a wolfish smile. "Pressure point," he said. "Just here under the jaw." He pointed to a place on his own neck, below his earlobe. "Hit it right, and they go down sweet and clean."

"The keys," said Argent. "He has a bunch of keys at his belt. Hurry!"

"I think he'll be out for quite a while," said Lukos, bending to retrieve the keys.

"It's not him I'm worried about. The duke could appear at any moment. He'll want to get started on his experiments once the sun is up."

As though to emphasize her words, the first rays of morning sun hit the mirror at the top of the Bell Tower and zigzagged down from mirror to mirror until a beam of sunlight lit up the scorched circle on the cavern floor. Lukos unhooked the keys from the guard's belt and opened the gate in the bars. Argent grabbed her blanket roll and shield, slinging them both over her back as she stepped out through the gate. She took the keys from Lukos, hurried over to the door at the bottom of the spiral staircase, and slotted key after key into the lock until she found the right one. The lock mechanism moved into place with a satisfying clunk, and Argent hurried back to Lukos, slipping the key from the ring and dropping it into the center of the brazier fire.

"That ought to stop the duke for a while," she said.

Lukos did not answer. He was grunting with effort as he tried to pull the heavy body of the guard into the alcove. Argent reached down and pulled her knife from the guard's belt before grabbing his feet and helping Lukos to maneuver him onto the pile of sour-smelling straw inside.

"See how you like it," hissed Argent, shutting the gate with a clang and slotting the key into the lock. She turned the key and then threw her arms around Lukos, hugging him fiercely. "Thank you! I am so glad to see you! How did you know I was here?"

"I didn't," said Lukos as they hurried over to the baby dragon. "I came in the back way. I was tracking the dragon thief, and I followed his trail to a bluff below the western city wall. I tracked him into a cleft in the rock—and it came out here," he finished, pointing to the back of the cavern.

"Can we get the baby dragon out that way?" asked Argent, bending to check how the bolts were secured through its wing hooks.

Lukos shook his head. "The tunnel goes on for half a mile and, right in the middle of it, there's another cavern. It has a guard post with beds and food and everything—even stabling for horses. I couldn't get across the cavern unnoticed. The dragon thief was there, gambling with three guards. I had to wait until they were all asleep, even the dragon thief's horse, before I could pass through the cavern. We'd never get back that way with the dragon."

"Could you get back that way on your own?"

said Argent, looking over at the duke's lift.

"I think so. Why?"

"See that winch over there? If I get onto that lift platform with the dragon, do you think you could winch us all the way up to the top?"

"Yes."

"Good. Once I'm up there, you can escape back through the tunnel."

"But what will you do?"

"I'm going to go through that door, head for the highest battlement, and free the dragon."

"And if it can't fly?"

"The sun is bright, and it's a clear day out there," said Argent, pointing to the top of the Bell Tower. "The dragon should rise. As long as its wings aren't too damaged." Lukos was giving her a searching stare. Argent looked away and bent to check the bolts again. "If I pull these pins out of the top of the bolts here, we should be able to lift the wing hooks off the bolts. Do you see?"

"And once you have freed the dragon, how will you escape?" persisted Lukos.

"I'll think about that later," snapped Argent, feeling the growing heat radiating from the little dragon as his wings absorbed energy from the reflected sunlight. "Right now we don't have much time. If we wait any longer, I won't be able to get near him."

Lukos nodded reluctantly. Argent handed him

the bunch of keys and then picked up a rock. She knocked the pins from the bolts with the rock and then reached out to free the dragon's wing hooks. A second later she had to pull back as the heat seared her skin. Lukos tried next but he, too, had to retreat. "What do we do now?" he asked.

"I don't know," groaned Argent. "He's too hot to touch, and he isn't strong enough to free himself. If only there was something I could wrap around my hand—oh!" Argent broke off and her eyes widened as she remembered the skin of the dragon's egg in her pouch. Quickly she pulled it out and unfolded it, holding it up for Lukos to see. "This should do!" She grinned.

Argent pushed her hand into the egg skin through the rent that the dragon had made on its way out. Fully stretched, the skin covered her from hand to shoulder. Argent adjusted her blanket roll so that the twine held the egg skin in place on her shoulder, then she stretched out her arm and gently lifted the dragon's wing hooks from the bolts. Her hand and arm remained perfectly cool within the protection of the egg skin.

The little creature writhed in pain as the bolts slipped through the holes in its wing hooks, but seemed to recover quickly once it was free. It turned toward the familiar smell of the egg skin, reached out with its wing hooks, and pulled itself onto Argent's arm. Once there, it wrapped its tail around her wrist and sat there like some strange bird of prey. It was as light as a leaf, but the heat coming off it was building with every second. Argent turned her head away as she felt the skin of her face starting to tighten in the heat. Then she remembered her wooden shield with the circle of beaten metal on the front.

"The goodwife said I would need this." She laughed, swinging the shield around and holding it up between her face and the dragon. "It seems she was right!"

The beaten metal disk on the front of the shield reflected most of the heat back toward the dragon. Now there was only one more thing left to do before they headed for the lift. They had to remove the steel clamp from around the little creature's jaws. The clamp was held in place with a metal pin in the same way as the wing hook bolts had been. While Argent held her arm steady, Lukos picked up the rock she had used to knock the pins from the wing hook bolts.

"Ready?" asked Argent.

Lukos nodded, then darted forward and hit the rock against the end of the pin with perfect accuracy. He leaped away again, grimacing with pain as his hand reddened and the hairs on his arm shriveled in the heat that radiated from the baby dragon. The pin dropped to the ground, but the clamp remained in place around the dragon's jaws.

"Why isn't it coming off?" asked Argent, trying to peer around the shield without losing her eyebrows.

"I don't know—" began Lukos from behind her. Just then the baby dragon flexed its jaws and the clamp sprang off and bounced across the floor. Argent and Lukos grinned at each other in triumph as they hurried over to the lift platform. An instant later their expressions changed to looks of horrified dismay as the little dragon threw back its head, opened its jaws, and sent a high piercing call soaring up the Bell Tower. It was something like a birdcall, something like a kettle whistle, something like the sound of air blown across the top of a bottle, only ten times louder.

"Hurry!" yelled Argent, scrambling onto the platform as the dragon sent a second cry soaring into the air, then a third. "This noise is going to bring the whole castle down on us!"

Lukos ran to the winch handle and then hesitated, looking down at the bunch of keys in his hand.

"Come on!" pleaded Argent.

Lukos growled, turned away from the winch handle, and sprinted across the cavern to the prison alcoves.

"What are you doing?" shouted Argent.

"The dragon is not the only creature imprisoned here," said Lukos, selecting a key and unlocking the first cage.

"Those animals are dangerous!" warned Argent as Lukos moved toward the next cage door.

"Maybe, but no beast deserves to be kept like this," snarled Lukos, preparing to unlock the second door. Suddenly he stopped, lifted his head, and turned to stare at the dark cleft in the back of the cavern.

"What is it?" hissed Argent, but Lukos did not answer her. He dropped the keys, ran for the winch handle, and began to crank it as fast as he could. The platform rose in a series of shuddering jerks. Argent had the dragon on one arm and was holding her shield between them with the other, so she could not grasp the railing. She staggered and nearly fell before grimly bracing her hip against the railing and spreading her feet.

The dragon called again, nearly deafening her, and then, as the echoes died away, she heard what Lukos's sharp ears had already picked up: the faint sound of shouting and running footsteps. It was coming from the cleft in the rock at the back of the cavern. Argent listened to a voice roaring out orders, and she stared down into Lukos's amber eyes. "That must be the dragon thief!" she hissed. "The dragon thief is coming!"

· SEVENTEEN ·

BETRAYAL

Ellie flattened herself against the back wall of the office as the crunching of glass grew louder and the flashlight beam grew brighter. She had been hoping that the intruder might go into one of the other rooms off the corridor, giving her a chance to escape, but the footsteps were heading straight for her. Ellie briefly thought about pushing the door shut, but it was too late for that. Her only chance was to wait behind the door until he was well into the room and then make a run for it.

The footsteps stopped, and the flashlight shone into the room, lighting up the grimy mattress and the litter of rubbish on the floor. There was a pause, and then a shadow passed across the gap between the door and the frame and stepped into the room.

Ellie held her breath. The figure moved over to the mattress and stood with his flashlight beam trained on the candle stubs and syringes on top of the cardboard box. Ellie looked at his profile and gasped with relief.

"Miguel!"

He twisted around and shone the flashlight directly into her face. Ellie stepped out from behind the door, shielding her eyes with her hand.

"Man!" growled Miguel, clutching his chest. "What are you trying to do to me?"

"Sorry—I thought you'd given up and gone home."

"I went back to my room to get a flashlight when the light started to fade. Where were you?"

"Press conference," said Ellie briefly.

"No news about Danny, then?"

Ellie shook her head. "I thought he might be here, but—" She gestured at the empty room. "Another dead end." She moved to stand beside Miguel at the window, and together they gazed down at the syringes and candle stubs on the cardboard box. Ellie frowned as she remembered the break-in at the vet's surgery. "Is that—have they been using something called Ketamine?" she murmured, peering down at the box.

"Keta-what?"

"Special K, I think they call it."

"Oh, that." Miguel shook his head as he

reached down and picked up one of the blackened pieces of foil. "No. Someone's been doing heroin."

"Are you sure?"

"Yeah." Miguel sighed. His face was bleak as he stared at the grimy mattress. "I know about this stuff."

"How?" asked Ellie, giving him a wary sideways glance.

"Just do," he said, scowling at her.

Ellie froze, suddenly struck by the thought that she did not know where Miguel was living. A suspicion began to grow in her mind. Was this his place? If so, why had he agreed to meet her here?

"This isn't—you're not staying here, are you?"

Miguel stared at her, then gave a bitter laugh and turned away to gaze out the window. "Damn," he said quietly.

"What?"

"Look."

Ellie turned to the window. The younger man who had been so suspicious of her in the gutting factory was glaring at them from the window of one of the motor homes. For a few seconds the three of them stood framed in the two windows, staring at one another. Then the young man reached up and yanked the blind down over the camper van window.

"He's not going to be happy," muttered Miguel, staring at the quivering blind.

"Why not?" asked Ellie.

"He doesn't like staying in one place for too long, and now other people know where he's holed up, he'll be jumpier than ever. It doesn't make for a happy workplace."

"Why's he so jumpy?" asked Ellie, unable to keep the suspicion out of her voice. "What's he got to hide?"

Miguel raised his eyebrows. "You mean apart from the small fact that he's here illegally?"

"What was he like around Danny?" demanded Ellie, refusing to be distracted.

"I'm not answering that." Miguel scowled.

"Why not?"

"Because I have a feeling you're going to twist everything I say."

"That's not true!"

"Oh, yeah? If I say 'he was very fond of Danny,' you'll think he's some sort of pervert. If I say 'he thought Danny was a pest,' you'll decide he had it in for him. So let's just leave it. He's not the one you're looking for. I can vouch for him."

"So you were with him for the whole day on Saturday, were you?"

"No. But they were," said Miguel, nodding toward the camper vans. "I can guarantee it. When they're not working, they're holed up in their vans. They live in one another's pockets. If he had done something to Danny, the others would know."

"Yes, but would they say anything? You lot always stick together. You said so yourself."

"Us lot?" Miguel's voice was dangerously quiet, but Ellie did not notice. She was too tied up with her growing suspicions about the young Romanian.

"Underground people. You look out for one another."

Miguel grabbed Ellie by the shoulders and yanked her toward him until her face was inches from his. "Are you saying I'd stand by and let a little kid get hurt?" he spat. "Are you?"

"N-no," gasped Ellie, staring into his eyes.

Miguel glared back at her. His fingers were digging into her arms, and he was shaking with fury. Ellie began to feel very afraid. What did she really know about Miguel? What if she had made a very bad mistake in agreeing to meet him here on her own?

"Miguel, please . . . What's going on here? Do you know where Danny is?"

"No."

"So this isn't your place?"

Miguel let go of her arms and shook his head in disbelief. "I don't do drugs."

"So, how do you know so much about. . . ?" Ellie gestured to the mess of tinfoil and syringes.

"Because my mom was an addict, okay? The last time she went missing, we found her in a place just like this. She'd been dead for three days."

"Oh! I'm so sorry!" cried Ellie, her eyes widening with shock.

"Yeah, well . . ." Miguel sighed absently, gazing down at the grimy mattress again. Ellie studied his ugly-interesting face and his sad, dark eyes and tried to imagine how it must have been for him when they found his mother. She suddenly realized that Miguel must understand exactly what she was going through now.

"I'm sorry," said Ellie again. "I—I have to go."

Miguel glared at her for a moment longer and then turned away from her. "Go, then."

Quickly Ellie moved over to the doorway of the little room and hovered there uncertainly. "Um, I'm sorry if I insulted you. I didn't mean to."

Miguel turned back to her. "Okay. And I'm sorry I got mad." He sighed. "Listen, I know how it is. You're scared, and you're worried about Danny. You're thinking anyone could've taken him. But you have to believe me when I tell you it wasn't any of the gut people. Okay?"

Ellie nodded, still staying close to the open door.

"So you won't say anything about them—to the authorities?"

Ellie hesitated and then shook her head.

"They're good guys," said Miguel tiredly, rubbing at his face. All the anger seemed to have drained out of him as quickly as it had appeared.

Ellie watched him, trying to decide what to do. She wanted to stay and talk with someone who knew what it was like to wait for news of a missing loved one, but she also wanted to get right away from him. She was afraid of what Miguel had found at the end of his search for his mother. She did not even want to think about the hunt for Danny ending that way.

"I really do have to go," she said, after an awkward pause. "I need to get home and find out what's happened to my dad."

"Okay." Miguel nodded, still staring at the mattress, lost in thought.

"See you."

Miguel raised a hand in silent acknowledgment and Ellie left him in the little room still frowning down at the old mattress and nudging at the twists of blackened tinfoil with the toe of his boot.

It was on breakfast news the next morning. "Police searching for missing schoolboy Daniel Brody have taken the boy's father in for questioning," announced the television newscaster. "Mr. Brody has been detained without charge overnight, and the police intend to continue questioning him about his son's disappearance this morning."

Ellie stood in the kitchen with her fists clenched, glaring at the television. She already knew the situation. Mrs. Brody had come home alone the previous night, long after Lisa had finished her shift and gone home. They had sat together and told each other that the police would soon realize their mistake and let Mr. Brody go, but Ellie could see that her mother was as scared as she was.

The phone rang loudly in the quiet kitchen, but Ellie ignored it and let the answer machine kick in.

"Um, yes. Message for Mr. Brody . . ." It was a woman's voice, hesitant and slightly apologetic. "About that central heating job you were going to do for us. We've decided not to go ahead with it—"

Ellie reached over and turned down the volume on the answer machine. That was the fourth cancelation of the morning. There were also two anonymous hate messages. Ellie was glad her mum had not been in the kitchen to hear them. The last time she had checked, Mrs. Brody was still curled up on Danny's bed in a deep and exhausted sleep.

"Cup of tea?" said Lisa, breezing into the kitchen as though nothing was wrong. She had let herself into the house half an hour earlier and had proceeded to make herself comfortable in the living room, which was why Ellie was hiding out in the kitchen.

"I don't want you in here," said Ellie coldly.

Lisa put the kettle down. "Now Ellie. I know this is hard for you—"

"My dad would never hurt Danny," interrupted

Ellie. "How many times do I have to tell you that?"

"I'm afraid the circumstantial evidence—"

"Go away."

"Ellie, you're safe now. Your father is at the police station, and he won't be coming back until we decide to release him. So if you want to tell me anything about your father—"

"My dad would never hurt Danny," repeated Ellie.

"So you keep saying. But unfortunately, Mr. Brody is our strongest suspect right now. The eleven-year-old Canadian boy on the Net—he turned out to be genuine."

"I don't want you in here!" yelled Ellie furiously.

"Now you're being silly," said Lisa, picking up the kettle again and moving to the sink.

"You heard her."

Ellie and Lisa both jumped and turned to face the kitchen door. Mrs. Brody was standing there with her arms crossed, staring at Lisa as though she were a large, pastel-colored blemish on her kitchen floor.

"Pardon?" said Lisa.

"We don't want you in here," said Mrs. Brody.

"Very well," said Lisa with icy politeness. "I understand. I'll be in the living room if you need me."

"No. You don't understand," said Mrs. Brody. "I mean we don't want you in the house anymore.

We can manage perfectly well on our own, can't we, Ellie?"

Mrs. Brody and Lisa both looked at Ellie. "Absolutely," said Ellie.

"Ellie, remember, if you want to talk," called Lisa over her shoulder as Mrs. Brody hustled her toward the front door.

"I won't!" yelled Ellie, and she slammed the kitchen door after Lisa's retreating back.

"That told her," said a voice. Ellie turned to see Ross standing in the kitchen behind her. He had opened the back door and walked in without knocking, as Ellie's mum always encouraged him to do. Ellie forgot all about breaking off with Ross. She flung herself at him and buried her face in his chest. His coat was soaking, but she didn't care. It felt so good to have his arms around her.

"Hey, hey," he soothed, stroking her hair. "It's okay. I'm here."

They heard the front door slam and Ross pulled back, watching apprehensively through the glass of the kitchen door as Mrs. Brody walked down the hallway toward him. "Is your mum still mad at me about the interview?" he hissed, turning to gaze down at Ellie.

"No. We've all got other things to worry about now."

Ross sighed with relief and turned to the door as Ellie's mum came into the kitchen. "Morning,

Mrs. B," he said brightly. "How are you today?"

"Oh, you know." Ellie's mum shrugged tiredly but gave him a warm smile. "It's nice to see you, Ross. We've missed you the past few days. But I wasn't expecting you here on a school morning."

Ellie pulled back and looked up at Ross. "That's a point. Why are you here? Shouldn't you be on your way to school?"

"Yes, but I wanted to make sure you were all right first."

"Come on," said Ellie, grabbing her rain cape and stuffing her feet into her boots. "I'll walk with you. We can talk on the way."

"There are television vans out front," warned Ross.

"I know," said Ellie grimly.

"I didn't talk to them," added Ross hastily.

Ellie shook her head. Ross's little slipup with the interview seemed unimportant now, after the way things had developed. "Doesn't matter. Come on. Let's go. I'm just going halfway to the school, Mum."

"Take your key," said Mrs. Brody. "You'll need to let yourself in when you get back. I'm heading for the police station this morning, and I'm staying there until they let Matthew go. Call me on my mobile if you need me for anything. And don't worry, love. We'll get your dad home, and then we'll find Danny."

Ellie hugged her mum. "Lovely to have you back," she whispered before hurrying out of the back door after Ross.

The back path was flooded. The ditch that ran alongside it could not cope with the volume of water running down from the hill, and the path was inches deep in muddy, brown overflow water. They had to edge along beside the back fences of the houses. As Ellie balanced her way past the worst of the flooding, pressing her palms against the splintery wood of the fence at her back, a familiar mantra played in her head: *I hope Danny's not out in this. I hope he's somewhere warm and dry.*

"You did really well at the press conference," said Ross as soon as they were away from her street and walking side by side toward the high school.

"Thanks," said Ellie with a sinking heart. She knew what Ross was going to ask next. He hated being on the outside rather than right in the center of things. It must be driving him mad not to know what was in the text message she had sent to Danny.

"So it sounds as though the police are following some sort of lead—apart from questioning your dad, I mean?"

"That's right," lied Ellie. "But I'm not supposed to tell anyone."

"Of course not," said Ross. There was a short silence as they both splashed down the hill past the train station, side by side but looking straight ahead.

"It's all very mysterious," said Ross lightly. "This text message you sent to Danny. This one thing he has to do—"

"Ross," interrupted Ellie, coming to a halt in the rainy street. "I can't tell you, okay? The police told me what to say in the message, and they said to keep it a secret. I haven't even told Mum and Dad!"

"Of course you can't tell me," said Ross hastily. "I wasn't expecting you to."

But Ellie could see that, actually, he had been expecting her to confide in him, and her refusal had hurt his feelings.

"I've been doing my own investigations, though," she continued, wanting to share something with him. "I've been talking to loads of people who know Danny."

"Aren't the police doing that?"

"Yes, but I've been going underground."

"Underground?"

"Yes. Talking to the people we don't usually come across. The ones on the edges of society."

"I don't get it," said Ross. "You mean you've been walking up to strangers, tramps, and weirdos—"

"I told you! They're not strangers. Well, not to Danny anyway. They're all people he knows."

Ellie turned away from Ross, trying to hide her irritation. She stared down a side street instead, watching without really seeing as a man opened his front door and stepped out into the street. He was wearing a yellow fisherman's waterproof and carrying a large bag. Ellie watched the man glance furtively up and down the street before locking his front door and scurrying away. With a shock of recognition, Ellie realized she had been staring at Mr. Lees, the fisherman the police were investigating. Remembering what Sergeant Donaldson had said about trouble, Ellie shifted her gaze to the front of Mr. Lees's house. The windows were boarded up, and the whitewashed wall of the house was smeared with angry red graffiti. Ellie turned back to watch as Mr. Lees disappeared around the corner at the bottom of his street. He was heading toward the river. Surely he was not going fishing in weather like this?

"And have you found anything?"

"What?"

"In your underground search. Have you found anything?"

"Not yet." Ellie sighed, turning back to Ross. "But I'm going to keep at it. Anything's better than sitting at home waiting for news."

"Poor you," said Ross automatically. He hesitated, giving her a sideways glance. "Ellie, are you sure it's safe?"

"What do you mean?"

"Well, I mean, what sort of people have you

been talking to? Is it, you know, wise?"

"Everyone's tried their best to help. They all like Danny. There's this group of Romanians working down at the harbor gutting fish—"

"Romanians?"

"Yes. They're trying to earn some money to take back to their families. All eight of them are living in a couple of motor homes in the old factory yard at Spittal Point. They're pretty shy of strangers because officially they shouldn't be here, but even they were happy to talk to me once they knew I was looking for Danny. Everyone likes Danny."

"Hang on. You mean they've had contact with Danny?

"Yes. He calls in to watch the gutting and they all spoil him—"

"Have you told the police about them?"

"No. I promised not to tell anyone."

Ross shook his head at her and then pulled out his phone.

"What are you doing?" demanded Ellie as he keyed in a number.

"Getting the number for the police station."

Ellie gaped at him. "What! You can't tell the police about them!"

"I thought you wanted Danny found?" demanded Ross. "These people are working illegally, hiding out from the authorities, they've had contact with Danny—and you want to keep it a secret? Sometimes I can't believe you, Ellie."

"Please, Ross. Don't," begged Ellie as he keyed in a new set of numbers. "They're good people—"

"Are you sure? How long did you spend with them, Ellie? Did you talk to all of them?"

Ellie hesitated for a second, remembering the glowering young man. Ross shook his head and lifted the phone to his ear. "This is the right thing to do, Ellie. Believe me."

Ellie tried to take the phone, but Ross turned away so that she could not reach it. "Yes, hello. I'd like to talk to an officer working on the Daniel Brody case," he said calmly. "I have some information."

Ellie stared unbelievingly at Ross's back. He had betrayed her for the second time in as many days. She was beginning to feel as though she hardly knew this person she had been sharing her life with for eight months. She left Ross standing in the street and sprinted away down the hill, heading for Spittal Point. Seeing Ross's reaction had clarified her feelings about the gut people. Suddenly she knew that not one of them would have even thought of hurting Danny. They were a close-knit group, and they all had children of their own waiting for them at home. And she had failed in her promise to keep their secret, so now the least she could do was to give them some warning of what was about to happen.

Ellie ran as hard as she could, sending up fountains of spray from her pounding boots. Her rain cape hood slipped back and the cold rain drummed down on her bare head but still she ran, with her long black hair streaming out behind her. She was on the final stretch, running along the dock road with Spittal Point chimney dead ahead, when two police cars overtook her. The second car braked, and Sergeant Donaldson turned to stare at Ellie through the back window for three long seconds. His mouth was set in a grim line, and his eyes were full of disappointment. Ellie slowed to a walk and looked down at her boots until the police car accelerated away from her with smooth power, then she bent over with her hands on her knees, trying to catch her breath.

There was a metallic taste in her mouth, her throat was burning, and her hair was hanging in cold, wet tendrils around her face. She felt terrible. Somehow, without meaning to, she had managed to let everyone down: the gut people, Sergeant Donaldson and, most of all, Danny. How could she follow Argent's way when this world was so much more complicated? In this world, nothing was black and white. People, including Ellie, did the right things for the wrong reasons, and the wrong things for the right reasons. "Sorry," whispered Ellie, staring down at the pale length of a drowning worm on the pavement. She knew just how the worm felt.

"Sorry won't help." A pair of boots stepped into view on the pavement beneath her hanging head. Ellie straightened up.

"You'll have to get in line," she said, looking wearily into Miguel's face.

"What for?"

"If you want to beat me up. I think there's a bit of a line."

"You told," said Miguel, regarding her coldly.

"Only my boyfriend. Now my ex-boyfriend. It was him who called the police. I tried to stop him, but he wouldn't listen. So I ran all the way down here to warn them, but . . ." Ellie gestured at the police cars that had pulled up outside the old factory. "I'm sorry, Miguel. I feel so awful."

"It's not as bad as you think," said Miguel, relenting slightly. "The police are looking around an empty yard right now."

"Empty? You mean the gut people have gone?"

Miguel nodded. "I've just been there. They didn't turn up for work this morning. My boss sent me over to see where they were. They must have moved out last night. I think we spooked them, looking at them through the window like that."

"But—where have they gone?"

Miguel shrugged. "Fruit picking down south. Or potato picking. Or mushroom picking. Take your pick."

Ellie began to sob.

"Okay, so it was a feeble joke," said Miguel.

She tried to laugh, but instead the sobs turned into loud, embarrassing howls. Miguel shuffled his feet and rubbed his nose. He was obviously waiting for Ellie to come to a stop, but she couldn't. The more she tried to stop, the louder the howls became.

"Come on," said Miguel quietly. "Walk with me."

He led her away from the road and the passing cars and onto a footpath that wound its way through a quiet residential part of town. He walked beside her until she had howled and hiccoughed her way into silence. After that they talked. Or, rather, Miguel listened as Ellie poured out the whole story about the police and her dad.

"My dad wouldn't hurt Danny," she finished. "The police are wasting their time trying to get him to confess to something he didn't do! So it's more important than ever that I keep looking for Danny. If I find him, I get my dad back too. The trouble is, I don't know where to look next."

"We're here," said Miguel, coming to a halt.

Ellie had been walking without paying any attention to where they were going. When she looked up and realized that they were standing on the stone bridge overlooking Chuggie's Pool, she felt her heart clench with shock. The last time she had been here, there had been lines of candy-striped police tape and white-suited searchers combing the riverbank. Now the police tape had been removed, and the river was so swollen with rainwater, it had swallowed up both Chuggie's Pool and the bank beyond.

"Why've you brought me here?" asked Ellie, staring down into the brown torrent that foamed and roared beneath her, skimming the very top of the bridge arches. Once again she felt a prickle of fear as she turned to look into Miguel's dark eyes. Had she let him walk her into a trap?

"To pick up my wages," said Miguel.

"But I thought you worked down at the harbor?"

"I do," said Miguel. "But I work up there, too." He pointed to a large, stone-built detached house on the hillside overlooking Chuggie's Pool.

"That's the residential home, isn't it?" asked Ellie, gazing up at the house.

Miguel nodded. "I put in ten hours a week there as a cleaner. Just as well, really. My boss down at the harbor will be putting everything on ice until he finds some new gutters, so this job is all I have right now. Maybe I could get some extra hours. I like working at the home. The kids are great. They're a real mixture. Down's syndrome, autistic kids, brain-damaged kids . . ."

Glint.

Ellie looked up. Someone had just opened a window at the front of the big house. Miguel talked on, telling Ellie all about the residential home, but his voice had faded into the background. She was staring up at the house, trying to grasp a thread of an idea that was forming at the back of her mind.

Glint.

Another window was opened. Ellie frowned up at the glittering glass, then her eyes widened and she whirled on Miguel.

"The residential home overlooks Chuggie's Pool!"

"Yeah . . . ?"

"So someone might have seen something the morning Danny went missing!"

"Ellie, the police have already been in, asking if anyone saw anything."

"Oh." Ellie frowned, then her face brightened again. "But did they talk to any of the kids?"

"Not directly. Some of the kids are a bit scared of strangers, so the police asked the staff to check it out and report anything back to them."

"And did they check it out?"

"The staff? Yeah. They made an announcement at the morning meeting, but nobody came forward with anything."

Ellie turned to gaze up at the residential home again. "But did they go along and talk to every kid who has a room overlooking the river?"

"They would've tried, but some of those guys are hard work to communicate with—" Miguel stopped as he realized what Ellie was getting at. "You think they might have missed something, don't you?"

Ellie nodded. "What if one of those kids saw something? Maybe one of the quieter ones. Someone who wouldn't come forward. Someone who would have to be coaxed."

"You have a point," mused Miguel, rubbing his chin as he stared up at the residential home.

Ellie straightened up, patted back her wet hair, and blew her nose. "Can you take me to meet them?"

Miguel hesitated, looking from the residential home to Ellie's face, which was shining with a new supply of hope. "Sure," he said. "Why not?"

After Miguel had collected his wages from the little office behind the reception desk, he led Ellie up the stairs. She was half expecting a member of staff to call them back, but nobody batted an eye.

"Don't they mind people just wandering about, then?" she asked once they rounded the corner and were out of sight of the entrance hall.

"You're with me," said Miguel. "And I often hang out here after work. There's a kid called Alice who plays a mean game of chess. Then there's Taylor, he's into body building, and I sometimes work out with him in the gym. Then there's—but I tell you what. Why don't I just introduce you?" said Miguel, pushing open the fire door at the top of the stairs and holding it for Ellie to pass through into the corridor beyond. "They'll still be in their rooms. They don't go down for lessons until ten."

Miguel and Ellie worked their way along the corridor, calling in on all the rooms that had windows overlooking Chuggie's Pool. Everyone was pleased to see Miguel. He was hugged and kissed and sung to, and his shoulders relaxed and his smile widened until it was so broad, his eyes were creased into narrow slits. Ellie stayed in the background mostly, except for showing her photograph of Danny when Miguel got around to asking questions. He was not having much luck. No one remembered seeing anything unusual on Saturday morning, and Ellie could see why. The home was a noisy, lively place with loud music playing and a constant traffic up and down the corridor as people went in and out of rooms, borrowing CDs or sharing makeup. Not many of these young people would have spent their Saturday morning gazing out of the window. Ellie felt her new hope fading with every room they left.

Miguel hesitated outside the door of the third from last room. It was the only door in the whole corridor that was shut. Miguel looked at the door and then moved on. "Let's try Alice next," he said, heading toward the second from last door. They spoke to Alice, and then the boy in the final room, but neither of them had seen Danny.

"Sorry," said Miguel, turning to trudge back along the corridor.

Ellie followed him but then stopped outside the closed door that Miguel had bypassed earlier. "What about this one?"

· EIGHTEEN ·

FIRE AND SWORD

Danny could hear the splash and splatter of water. He licked his cracked lips, but he did not wake up. Instead, his dreams became full of sand and sea and breaking waves. When a wave of icy water flowed across the cold, hard floor of his prison and lapped at his ankles, Danny thought he was paddling down at the local beach. When it spread along the length of his legs, seeped beneath his back, and pooled under his head, Danny's brain responded by imagining that he had fallen into the sea. In his dream Danny scrambled to his feet and walked up the beach, cursing and laughing, but in the darkness of his prison, Danny's unresponsive body did not move. He lay on his back on the floor as the water level slowly rose around him. The jars on the shelves behind him began to rattle as the water crept higher, but even when it lapped against his ears, Danny barely moved. The water flooded his ear canals and beat against his eardrums, but Danny slept on, listening to the roaring in his head. . . .

The roaring voice came again, echoing down the tunnel into the cavern. It was louder this time, and Argent could pick out one or two words in it. The dragon thief was shouting at the other guards to wake up and follow him. As the pounding feet drew nearer, Argent looked down from the lift platform into Lukos's upturned face.

"Did you hear that?" she cried. "He's yelling at the other guards to get a move on. That means he's on his own for now. Let me down again, Lukos. We can fight him together."

Lukos stopped turning the winch handle briefly and gazed up at Argent as she leaned over the platform railing. His amber eyes were unreadable.

"Lukos?"

Lukos's reply was drowned out as the baby dragon on Argent's arm sent another cry winging up to the top of the Bell Tower, but his intent soon became clear as he bent to the winch handle and once again set his shoulder to the task of turning it as quickly as he could. The lift platform began to move again, rising up the side of the Bell Tower in a series of violent jerks.

"Stop!" screamed Argent, leaning out over the railing. "We have to stay together! You can't fight him on your own!"

Lukos ignored her and went on grimly turning the winch handle. The lift platform jerked and lurched as it moved on up the Bell Tower shaft at a much faster pace than was safe, and Argent nearly tumbled out over the railing. She stumbled backward and then braced her feet and wedged her hip against the railing. It was too late to jump. The platform was already past the second door.

Argent concentrated on keeping the shield between her and the baby dragon. The sunlight was streaming down into the Bell Tower now, bouncing from mirror to mirror with increasing intensity, and the dragon was absorbing energy and heating up at an alarming rate. The beaten metal disk set into the front of the shield was reflecting most of the heat back toward the dragon, but the wooden rim around the disk was beginning to smoke. Argent was grateful for the soft skin of the dragon's egg that was still protecting her arm from fingertip to shoulder. She could feel no heat at all through the leathery skin, but she prayed that the dragon's wing hooks would not tear a hole in the protective layer.

Argent looked up, judging how far the lift had left to go. It had already passed six of the nine doors and had nearly reached the seventh when it came to a sudden halt with the threshold step of the door just above the platform railing. Argent looked at the threshold step, which was on a level with her chest, and then peered over the railing on the outer side of the platform, trying to work out why it had stopped. Seven floors below her, Lukos was locking the winch handle into place as he glared over to the cleft in the rock at the back of the cavern. Argent bent and peered down and bit her lip at what she saw. The red-haired hunter had reached the chamber.

He was standing in the tunnel entrance, calmly assessing the scene in the cavern. By the look of him, he must have been asleep when the calls of the dragon had come echoing down the tunnel. He was barefoot and dressed only in a shirt and leggings, and his red hair was still sticking up from sleep, but his green eyes were sharp and alert. As he turned to look up at Argent and the dragon, she had to resist the impulse to shrink away. She was looking into the cold eyes of a hunter.

The dragon thief dismissed Argent. He could see that she was no threat and, furthermore, she was going nowhere. He turned his attention back to Lukos, who was still crouched beside the winch handle, waiting to see what the dragon thief would do. The dragon thief reached over his shoulder, feeling for a crossbow that was not there. His face showed a trace of irritation as he glanced back into the tunnel behind him. The guards would have weapons with them, but they were still nowhere in sight.

Lukos nodded with satisfaction as the dragon thief reached for the knife at his belt instead. The man was tall and powerfully built, but Lukos had a good chance against him as long as he only had a hand knife as a weapon. Lukos stepped forward at the same time as the dragon thief moved toward him. They did not stop until they were on opposite sides of the scorched circle of ground directly beneath the Bell Tower bell.

Argent saw Lukos go into a crouch, and she saw the knife flash in the dragon thief's hand as he flicked it from side to side. Then the two of them rushed together, meeting in the dancing shaft of sunlight under the blazing mirrors, and Argent could see nothing clearly anymore. Desperately she screwed up her eyes, trying to see into the blinding shaft of sunlight. She could hear grunts of effort and the scuffling of feet as the two fighters struggled with each other, but she could only catch glimpses of the action. She thought she saw Lukos for an instant, and then she thought she saw the long snout of a wolf. She caught the flash of the dragon thief's knife, and then there was a growl and a gray, clawed blur shot through the shaft of light. One hoarse cry of pain and the metallic clatter of a knife falling to the floor was followed by silence.

"Lukos?" cried Argent, and the baby dragon echoed her cry with a high, whistling call.

Argent stared at the bright shaft of sunlight until a stumbling figure emerged. It was the dragon thief. He was clutching at the shoulder of his knife arm, and bright blood was seeping out between his fingers. The dragon thief backed toward the tunnel, watching the shaft of sunlight warily. A second later Lukos stepped out, and Argent gave a short cry of relief. Lukos's shoulders were hunched, and his face had more than a hint of wolf about it, but he seemed to be unharmed. The dragon thief continued to back away toward the tunnel, and Lukos began to follow him with a long, loping stride.

"Let him go, Lukos!" called Argent. "We're running out of time!"

Lukos turned and, for an instant, the golden eyes that looked up at her had no recognition in them, but then he straightened up and gave her a brief nod. The dragon thief was still backing toward the tunnel, leaving a dotted line of blood on the floor of the cavern. Lukos plunged back into the circle of sunlight and reemerged carrying the dragon thief's knife. He slotted the knife into his belt and then dismissed the wounded man and headed back toward the winch.

At that moment the first of the guards arrived in the tunnel mouth, panting loudly. As the man stood openmouthed, taking in the scene in the cavern, the dragon thief reached out with his good arm and snatched the crossbow from his back. It was already loaded.

"Look out!" shrieked Argent as the dragon thief turned and, holding the guard's crossbow one-handed, leveled it at Lukos.

Lukos took one look at the deadly metal bolt pointing at his heart, and then he leaped right over the winch and caught hold of one of the thick ropes that formed the pulley system for the lift. Up on the platform, Argent gave a shocked cry as the whole structure lurched sideways and slammed into the wall beneath the threshold of the seventh door. The platform continued to jerk violently as Lukos climbed up the rope toward her. Argent staggered and began to slide down the slope of the platform. She thought she was going to fall from the edge to her death but, to her surprise, the baby dragon slowed her slide, buoying her up until she found her footing again. The creature was still clinging to her arm, but the energy it had absorbed from the sun was causing its whole body to rise into the air. Only the wing hooks and the curled tail were keeping it anchored in place. Argent knew that the dragon was simply responding to the call of the sun rather than consciously saving her life. As far as the dragon was concerned, she was nothing more than a handy perch wrapped in the familiar skin of the egg from which it had so recently emerged, but still she was grateful to the little creature as she found her feet and got a purchase on the sloping floor of the platform.

Below Argent, Lukos was swarming up the pulley rope at such a speed, the dragon thief kept having to adjust the aim of the crossbow. Argent remembered how Lukos had climbed down a nearly vertical gully wall in the Goodie Patchie, and she began to hope that he could reach the platform without being hit by a crossbow bolt. At that moment the dragon thief decided that Lukos was too difficult a target to bring down one-handed. He adjusted his stance and brought the nose of the crossbow up until it was pointing directly at Argent.

Argent gasped and moved away from the front of the railing until her back was pressed against the wall of the Bell Tower, but the dragon thief stepped back too, keeping her in his sights. She was trapped. A sitting target.

"Come down, wolf boy," called the dragon thief. "And I shall spare her life."

Lukos had reached the threshold of the fifth door, but he stopped climbing as soon as he saw where the crossbow was pointing.

"Keep climbing, Lukos!" yelled Argent.

"Come down here," countered the dragon thief calmly, keeping the crossbow aimed at Argent. Lukos hesitated, turning slowly as he hung from the rope, trying to decide what to do. "Now!" ordered the dragon thief. "Or I shoot."

"You might miss me and hit the dragon," said Argent. "That would make the duke very unhappy."

"I think not." The dragon thief smiled coldly. "I never miss."

With a growl of anger, Lukos began to descend to the cavern floor.

"Lukos, no!" yelled Argent, but Lukos kept on going.

The dragon thief's smile widened. "You have a sword?" he asked, talking to the guard beside him, but keeping his gaze fixed on Argent and Lukos.

"Yes, but—" The guard paused uneasily, watching Lukos climb down the rope with animal ease.

"Then get over there!" snapped the dragon thief.

As the guard drew his sword and hurried over to wait for Lukos at the base of the pulley rope, the dragon thief glanced away from Argent for an instant to watch him go. In that instant Argent made a split-second decision. Counting on the increasing upward pull of the dragon to help her, she leaped onto the handrail of the platform, found her balance, then took two light steps along the top of the rail and jumped up onto the threshold step of the seventh door. The whole maneuver only lasted two seconds, but it seemed to take an age before she felt the solid stone of the threshold step under her feet. Argent took a deep, trembling breath of relief.

"Stop, or I fire!" yelled the dragon thief, realizing that his prey was about to get away. Hastily Argent pushed open the door with her hip and almost fell through it in her haste to get out of the way of the crossbow. Still holding the shield between herself and the dragon, she lifted her foot and slammed the door shut just as the crossbow bolt thudded into the wood on the Bell Tower side. The door jumped open again. Splinters flew, and Argent winced as one of them embedded itself in her neck. She looked up and saw an inch of gleaming metal protruding through the door.

Argent stuck her knee into the gap between the door and the frame, levering it farther open. "I'm safe, Lukos!" she yelled into the cavern. "Climb!"

Lukos needed no second telling. As the guard hurried over to the dragon thief, pulling another crossbow bolt from the bandolier across his chest, Lukos was hauling himself up the rope as fast as he could go. He reached the second floor door, transferred his hands to the rough stone of the threshold step, and unwound his legs from the rope. As he hung there, gathering the strength to boost himself up onto the step, the guard reached the dragon thief and grabbed the crossbow. He fumbled the bolt into the loading slot, held the weapon between his knees, and began to turn the ratcheted handles that would build up the pressure within the cross-bow and give the weapon its deadly firing power.

"Come on, Lukos!" yelled Argent. Lukos surged up onto the step, but he did not push through the door that led to the second floor of the castle. Instead, he turned to face the pulley rope, going into a crouch to make himself a smaller target. He pulled the dragon thief's knife from his belt, grabbed the pulley rope, and began to saw through it.

"Lukos!" yelled Argent again as the dragon thief grabbed the loaded crossbow and took aim. Lukos only sawed harder. The rope was thick and tough, but he kept cutting through it until the very last second, only stopping when he heard the creak of the crossbow trigger being pulled back. Argent closed her eyes, unable to watch. She knew Lukos had left it too late. He could move like lightning when he wanted to, but even he was not fast enough to get out of the path of a speeding cross-bow bolt. There was no way he could fling himself through the doorway to safety in time.

Then everything happened at once. There was a coughing roar, the crossbow bolt exploded from the weapon and whistled through the air, followed by a splintering impact and a scream of agony, quickly choked off. A pause, and then Argent heard the clink and clatter of Lukos's knife falling to the floor of the cavern.

Argent gave a terrified sob and stuck her head through the doorway into the cavern, heedless of her own safety. She had got Lukos into this and now he was dead, brought down like a hunted animal as he tried to save her and the dragon. She gazed down at the threshold step of the second-floor door, but the step was empty. His body must have fallen to the floor of the cavern. Argent transferred her gaze to the base of the pulley system, but the only thing lying there was a crossbow bolt.

Argent blinked, and then her eyes widened with hope. The crossbow bolt must have been what she had heard clattering to the floor of the cavern, not Lukos's knife. She looked back to the second-floor doorway, and this time she spotted the raw gouge in the sandstone wall where the bolt had hit. As she watched, the door swung shut, clicking into place as the latch caught. The dragon thief, the hunter who never missed, had sent his shot wide of his target, and Lukos had escaped. Argent slumped against the doorframe, weak with relief.

The coughing roar came again from the cavern below. Argent turned to look and, for a few seconds, she struggled to make sense of what she was seeing. Then, suddenly, she understood why the dragon thief had missed his aim. There was a spreading pool of gore on the floor of the cavern. The dragon thief was lying in the center of the pool, and the great, honey-colored beast was standing over his lifeless body with blood dripping from its jaws. Behind the beast, the door of the cage that Lukos had unlocked was standing open.

The beast must have scented the blood from the dragon thief's arm wound, come to the front of its cage, and found the door ajar. It had launched itself onto the dragon thief at the instant he had pulled the crossbow trigger, knocking the bolt off course. The scream Argent had heard was from the dragon thief as the beast had taken his neck in its jaws and crushed the life out of him. Argent felt nausea rise in her throat as she stared at the mess that had once been the dragon thief, but there was a sort of natural justice there, she thought. The dragon thief had probably captured this beast and imprisoned it here in the cavern below the Bell Tower. Now the beast had taken its revenge.

Argent jumped as a clatter came from the back of the cavern. She saw that the terrified guard had been slowly backing away toward the cleft in the rock and had knocked up against the brazier. The beast looked up from its meal, fixing its golden eyes on the guard and shaking its thick, honey-colored mane. The man froze in place, whimpering with fear, but the beast did not attack. Instead, it bent and, taking the dragon thief's arm in its jaws, began to drag the body back into the alcove behind it.

The guard could not believe his luck. He waited until the beast was well inside the alcove, and then he scurried forward and slammed the door shut. The guard turned to look up at Argent, and she pulled back into the doorway. A second later the last fibers of the rope parted, and the whole pulley system came apart. The lift platform plunged down the side of the Bell Tower and crashed to the cavern floor. There was now no way for the guard to follow her or Lukos. The lift lay shattered on the floor of the cavern, the door to the spiral staircase was locked, and the key was hidden in the center of the brazier fire.

Suddenly Argent became aware of the smell of burning and remembered the baby dragon on her outstretched arm. She had wasted precious seconds checking to see what had happened to Lukos. Now she pulled back and closed the door to the Bell Tower with her foot. As soon as it was shut, the door merged into the wood paneling that sur-rounded it. The join was so cleverly disguised, it would have been impossible to spot the door were it not for the crossbow bolt sticking through it. A wreath of smoke coiled around Argent's head, and she turned to look for its source. She was standing in a long gallery, similar to the one that had been behind the Great Hall, except that this gallery was hung with tapestries, not paintings.

Argent gasped and stepped away from the wall as she realized that the nearest tapestry was in flames. The heat coming from the dragon had caused it to catch fire. Argent looked up and down the long gallery. It was deserted at this early hour, but the smoke was growing thicker, and she thought that soon it would bring people running. Quickly she looked for an escape route. The leaded, arched windows in the far wall of the gallery looked out on a large, paved courtyard with orange trees in pots and stone benches around an ornamental fountain.

Farther down the gallery, Argent spotted an open door. She headed toward it as fast as she could. The rim of the shield was smoking even more and, although her face and arm were protected from the heat, the rest of her body was becoming uncomfortably hot under her clothes, and her best skirt was beginning to scorch. She burst out of the gallery into the courtyard and hurried out of the shadow of the castle, heading for the sunny part of the courtyard near the battlement wall.

The dragon had been silent while they were in the gallery but, as soon as the sun touched its wings, it began to call again, sending a series of high, whistling cries up into the blue sky. Argent flinched. It was astounding how much noise the dragon could make. She looked back at the castle. There were two more stories rising above the courtyard, and Argent expected to see windows opening and people sticking their heads out to discover what was making such a noise, but nothing stirred. Argent decided that only servants must be up at such an early hour, and they would all be down in the lower levels of the castle, where the kitchens and the stables were situated.

The dragon called again, and Argent looked for somewhere to hide. Over to one side of the castle, the Bell Tower rose into the sky. The courtyard curved around behind the Bell Tower, out of sight of the castle windows. Argent hurried around the curved side of the Bell Tower and came to a quiet flagstone circle, ringed by a turreted wall. The circle was a dead end, but there were no windows in the side of the Bell Tower wall, and she would not be overlooked here as she waited for the dragon to fly.

Argent came to a halt and lifted her arm skyward. "Fly!" she hissed, shaking her arm in an attempt to dislodge the dragon. It simply dug its wing hooks farther into the leathery egg skin, seeking a firmer grip. Hastily Argent stopped trying to dislodge the dragon. If its sharp wing hooks punctured the skin of the egg and dug into her flesh, her arm would burn through to the bone in seconds while she howled in helpless agony.

Argent headed for the turreted wall and peered over the edge of the parapet. There was no escape that way. The flagstone circle was set high above the city, and the lower buildings of the castle, the houses of Goldstone, the harbor, and the sea were spread out beneath the parapet like a huge, colorful skirt. The only place higher than the courtyard was the Bell Tower itself. Argent briefly considered trying to reach the top of the Bell Tower, but then dismissed the idea. If the dragon would not fly from this high battlement, there was no guarantee that it would fly from the top of the Bell Tower.

Argent stuck her arm out over the parapet, hoping the high, windy spaces beyond the wall would encourage the little dragon to catch an updraft and lift off. She pressed herself against the turret and wedged her shield into the gap in the wall to block off the worst of the heat. Her arm stopped aching as she rested it on the top of the parapet, and her legs and hips began to cool off as she leaned against the wall. The splinter of wood embedded in her neck was sending out throbbing flares of pain in time with the beat of her heart, but she had no hands free to tug it out, so she tried to ignore it. Argent pressed her burning face against the cool stone of the turret and prayed for the dragon to fly, but still it stayed anchored to her arm, crying its wild, piercing call. What was it waiting for?

Suddenly Argent's head came up and she listened intently. She could hear the sharp click of boot heels on stone. Her heart sank as she realized that the footsteps were coming closer. Someone was striding across the courtyard toward the hidden circle. Whatever the dragon was waiting for, it had just run out of time. Argent stared at the curve of the Bell Tower wall, waiting to see who would emerge. She hoped it would be Lukos, but she feared it would be the duke.

Her fear was realized when the tall, slightly stooped figure of the duke appeared around the curved wall of the Bell Tower. His hair was sticking up more than ever, and his shirt was unbuttoned and hanging loose, but there was nothing of the bumbling scientist about the look on his face or the wickedly sharp sword he carried in his hand. Argent stared into the duke's cold blue eyes and wondered how she had ever thought him a sane, reasonable man.

"Bring the dragon in from the wall," said the duke, walking toward her with the sword pointed at her throat.

"How did you know I was here?" asked Argent, desperately playing for time.

"You left a trail," said the duke. "The crossbow bolt in the door, the burning tapestry, the open door to the courtyard. You were not hard to find. Now, bring the dragon in from the wall and walk it back into the gallery."

The dragon called again, but still it would not fly. Argent willed the little creature to lift off. "Aren't you afraid someone will see you with the dragon?" she asked.

The duke considered for a moment but then shook his head. "No one stirs in the higher part of the castle—and we do not have far to go before we are out of sight. There is a hidden door in the gallery, leading to the spiral staircase. Now, you will walk the dragon back down to the cavern, or I shall kill you and drag your body inside with the dragon still clinging to your arm."

He stepped closer and brought the point of the sword to the hollow at the base of her throat. "But the fire will bring them running!" Argent gasped, feeling the sharp steel pierce her skin.

"The fire is out," snapped the duke. "I hooked the tapestry from the wall with my sword and doused it in the fountain. Now, move!"

"No."

The duke shrugged and drew back his arm, preparing to run her through. Argent pulled away from the parapet and swung her arm around so that the dragon was only inches away from the duke. He staggered backward with a yell of pain, but not before the wall of heat coming from the dragon had singed his shirt and blistered his chest.

Cowering behind her shield, Argent heard the duke give a muffled curse, and then there was silence, apart from her frightened breathing. Argent could see nothing beyond the shield, and she dared not lower it to see what the duke was doing; the heat from the dragon was too intense. Was the duke lying unconscious on the flagstones, or had he gone to summon reinforcements from his trusted inner circle of guards?

Argent waited until she could stand it no more, then she twisted around to see what was happening. Steel flashed, and she jerked backward from the waist just in time to avoid being skewered on the duke's sword. He had been standing silently, waiting for her to swing the dragon away from him and, stupidly, she had done just what he wanted. Only her fast reactions had saved her.

Time seemed to slow as Argent watched the duke's sword lunge harmlessly into the space between her chest and her shield instead of embedding itself between her ribs. The duke hissed his annoyance and pulled his sword arm back, preparing to thrust again. With a wordless yell, Argent jumped out of the way and stumbled backward out of the hidden circle and into the main courtyard, holding the dragon out in front of her.

Out of the enclosed space of the hidden circle, Argent was much more vulnerable. All the duke had to do was to keep out of range of the scorching dragon heat and wait for Argent's concentration to falter so that he could dart in and finish her. Argent turned on the spot, trying to keep the dragon between her and the duke, but the sweat was dripping into her eyes, and she was beginning to feel dizzy with the growing heat. The protection of the goodwife's shield was starting to fail. The beaten metal disk was red hot now, and the wood behind it was becoming too hot to touch. Argent could feel the skin of her arm scorching where it passed through the leather strip on the back of the shield, and there were concentrated points of pain from the metal studs that held the strap in place.

Suddenly the duke was there, darting in on her exposed right-hand side with his sword ready to strike. Argent screamed and took a giant step sideways. Her anklebone cracked against one of the orange-tree pots that were scattered around the courtyard, and Argent was thrown off balance. She tried to save herself and nearly managed to stay upright, but then the orange tree toppled over behind her and became tangled in her skirts, tripping her up.

Argent fell backward onto the flagstones with one arm held stiffly out in front of her and the other still holding the shield between the dragon and her face. There was no way she could break her fall, and so she slammed full length onto the hard flagstones. Her head cracked against the orange-tree pot and all the breath was knocked out of her. A wave of pain and dizziness flooded over her, and black spots began to dance in front of her eyes. Argent lay still, pulling whooping breaths into her lungs and trying not to pass out.

She heard the duke's footsteps approaching, but

she could not move. It was all she could do to keep the shield in place over her face. Argent whimpered and closed her eyes, waiting for the sword to push up under her ribs and stop her heart. Then the baby dragon gave one last cry and uncurled its tail from her arm. Argent felt the egg skin tear from top to bottom as the dragon's wing hooks ripped away from it.

"No!" roared the duke as the little dragon rose into the air. He lifted his sword two-handed, preparing to hack the dragon out of the sky. The dragon called again and, finally, it was answered. A great, breathy roar, like the rush of wind in a chimney, sounded above the Bell Tower. The roar was so loud, it rattled the glass in the castle windows. The duke stood, transfixed, with his sword poised over his shoulder as the mother dragon curved around the Bell Tower and hovered above the courtyard, blotting out the sun. It had been barely twenty minutes since the baby dragon had sent its first, high call soaring to the top of the Bell Tower but, in that short time, the mother dragon had traveled from Unthank Forest to Goldstone, flying as straight as an arrow on her great ribbed wings.

Argent heard the creak and flap of those wings now as the mother dragon began to descend. Dizzy and winded as she was, Argent had just enough presence of mind left to roll behind one of the stone benches. There she curled up into a ball with her spine pressed against the curved back of the bench. She covered her head with the shield, pulled the torn dragon's egg skin from her arm, and shook it out to its full size. The baby dragon's wing hooks had sliced open the whole length of the egg, and now the leathery skin covered the front of her from forehead to feet like a protective blanket. In the space of a few seconds, Argent had created a tiny, fireproof cocoon.

Behind her the duke was spurred into action as a scorching wind began to whirl around the courtyard. Inside her protective shell, Argent heard his heels striking the flagstones as he ran for the gallery door, but he was too late. The mother dragon roared again as she swooped down to meet her baby, and the courtyard turned into a furnace. The duke's footsteps faltered, and he began to scream. Argent wanted to cover her ears with her hands, but she had to hold her protective shell in place. She heard the soft *whump* of flame as the duke's clothes and hair caught alight. She heard his screams rise higher as the fire took hold, and she heard the staccato dance of his heels on the flagstones as he ran from place to place in a hopeless attempt to escape the burning pain. His screams turned to a high, parched sigh as he breathed in fire and scorched his vocal cords. Then there was a thud as his body hit the flagstones. His heels drummed for a few more seconds and, finally, there was silence, apart from the hiss and crackle of flames.

Argent stayed curled up behind the bench, gasping for air in the intense heat. She was crying, but the tears were evaporating as soon as they squeezed out between her closed eyelids. She heard the creak of the mother dragon's wings as it rose into the air again and, gradually, the intense heat began to subside. Argent felt a breath of cooler air find its way inside her protective shell, and she began to lower the leathery blanket of skin, but hastily raised it again as she heard running footsteps.

The footsteps burst out of the gallery onto the courtyard, and Argent heard a gasp of indrawn breath. She became completely still beneath her protective shell, but the footsteps were not fooled. They headed straight for her, and an instant later someone wrenched her smoking shield away and threw it into the bowl of the ornamental fountain. Argent heard the hiss as the hot metal connected with what was left of the water in the bowl. She cowered behind her upraised arm, waiting for a sword to slash down, but nothing happened so she lowered her arm and squinted up at the silhouetted figure above her.

"It's me," said Lukos, crouching beside Argent so that she could see his face.

Argent felt a huge wave of relief flood through her. She let her arms drop into her lap and leaned against the hot stone of the bench. "You took your time," she said, wincing as Lukos reached out and pulled the splinter from her neck. "What did you do, stop for breakfast?"

"Your skirt is on fire," retorted Lukos. He said it so calmly that Argent did not react straightaway. Then the meaning of the words sank in, and she sat up and stared down at her skirt. Lukos was right. A piece of the hem that had been sticking out from under the dragon's egg skin was on fire, and the flames were slowly creeping along the skirt toward her leg.

"Oh! Oh!" Argent jumped up, yanked her skirt off, and tossed it away from her. Then she pushed her hair out of her eyes and looked around the devastated courtyard. The orange trees were shriveled stumps on the scorched flagstones, the fountain was almost dry, and the ornamental bowl was cracked. A pool of black water lay in the bottom of the bowl, along with the ruined tapestry and her blackened shield. Argent spotted a charred and smoking lump over to one side and hastily turned away. She did not want to see what remained of the duke after his encounter with the mother dragon.

"The dragons . . ." Argent raised her head and scanned the sky. The mother and baby were nowhere in sight.

"Over there," said Lukos, pointing southeast. Argent followed his pointing finger and saw two dark shapes, one large, one small, flying across the sea and rising higher with every second that passed. They were leaving, belatedly heading south and following the sun to warmer lands to join the rest of their kind for the winter. Argent watched the shapes shrink into specks in the sky before she finally shook herself into action. They had saved the dragons. Now it was time to save themselves.

"Come on," she said, pulling her dripping shield from the fountain and slinging it across her back. "We have to get out of here before anyone sees us."

"Like that?" asked Lukos, nodding down at her bare legs.

Argent blushed, then pulled her blanket roll from her back and extricated her father's work trousers and hat. Quickly she pulled on the trousers and tied the belt, then she tucked her hair up out of sight under the hat. Finally she slung the blanket roll and shield over her shoulder and, together, they headed back into the gallery.

A few minutes later the alarm went up. Someone had gone to investigate the window-rattling roar and had found the charred body of the duke in the courtyard. A growing stream of servants and sleepy officials hurried up the main staircase, heading for the seventh floor.

"Why have you woken me?" panted a portly man who was climbing the sweeping stone steps dressed in nothing but a nightshirt and a chain of office.

"It's the duke, sir!" gasped his servant, pushing two young men to one side of the stairs to clear a path for his master. "There's been some sort of an explosion on the courtyard level. One of his experiments gone wrong, they reckon."

The servant hurried on up the stairs, followed by his panting master. The two young men who had been pushed to one side shared a glance before continuing on their way to the bottom of the staircase. Nobody paid them any attention as they pulled their hats low over their eyes and slipped out through the main doors of the castle, followed only by the frantic barking of a dog.

· NINETEEN ·

"MISTY BOAT"

"That's Richard's room," said Miguel, retracing his steps along the corridor of the residential home to join Ellie outside the closed door. "He won't have anything to say."

"Can we at least try?" asked Ellie, looking from Miguel to the door.

Miguel sighed, then knocked gently, turned the handle and opened the door.

"Richard?" he asked quietly. "Can we come in?"

No answer.

Ellie craned her neck to peer over Miguel's shoulder. She was vaguely aware of a bright, yellow room, but her attention was focused on a large desk positioned in front of the window. A figure was sitting at the desk, with his back to the door.

"Richard?" said Miguel, stepping into the room.

No answer.

"Richard, this is Ellie," said Miguel.

"Hello," said Ellie, stepping through the doorway behind Miguel.

No answer.

Ellie moved farther into the room and studied Richard. She guessed him to be about twelve years old, but his face had a strangely ageless quality about it, so she could not be sure. He was a thin, bleached boy. His hair was so fair it was almost white, and his skin was as pale as a mushroom. He was wearing a bright yellow T-shirt, which did nothing for his pale complexion, and his arms stuck out from the sleeves like two sticks. He was gripping the arms of his desk chair so hard that his knuckles and wrist bones showed white through the skin.

"Hey, Richard," said Miguel, crouching beside his chair and looking up at him. "We wanted to ask you a few questions."

Richard refused to look at Miguel. He sat up very straight in his chair and began to rearrange the objects that were lined up on his desktop. He made sure a pile of meticulous drawings was aligned with the edge of the tray they were sitting in, then he pushed a pencil sharpener a millimeter closer to an eraser and checked that a row of pencils were exactly the same distance apart.

"Richard? Can you remember seeing a boy fishing down at the river on Saturday morning?"

"This is him," said Ellie, placing Danny's photograph on the desk in front of Richard. "His name's Danny." Richard did not look down at the photograph. Instead, he sat up even straighter, gazing from the window into the middle distance. His hands returned to gripping the chair arms and he began to hum a familiar tune in a voice that was high and breathy with tension. Ellie hastily removed the photograph from the desktop, and Richard relaxed slightly but continued to hum under his breath.

Miguel tried again. "Richard. Did you see the boy fishing? Did you see anyone else? Did anyone take the boy away with them?"

No answer. He might as well have been talking to a slab of white marble. "Sorry." Miguel sighed, straightening up and looking at Ellie. "This isn't going to work. Richard is kinda locked away in his head. Sometimes he'll talk for a little while, if someone finds the key that'll open him up and get him going, but mostly he's locked away."

The key. Ellie's eyes widened as she recognized the tune Richard was humming. It was the theme tune to *The Simpsons*. She looked more closely at his yellow T-shirt and then at the yellow room. The duvet cover had the Simpsons emblazoned across it; the yellow walls were covered in Simpsons posters.

"Oh!" said Ellie softly, reaching into her rain cape pocket and pulling out the little figure the bag lady had given her. "The key," she murmured, gazing down at Bart Simpson, lying in her hand. "She said I would need a key."

"Excuse me?" said Miguel.

"The key," said Ellie, placing her closed fist on the desk in front of Richard. "To unlock him."

Ellie opened her fist, and Richard stopped humming. He looked down at the little figure, and a smile lit up his face. "Bart!" he cried in a thin, reedy voice.

Ellie closed her fist around the giveaway toy. "You can have him, Richard. But first, can you tell us, did you see anything down at Chuggie's Pool on Saturday morning?"

Richard drummed his fingers on the desk and stared out of the window. After ten long seconds, Ellie sighed and turned to leave, but Miguel held up his hand to tell her to stay. Ten more seconds passed, then Richard opened his mouth and said two words: "Misty boat."

"Misty boat?" Miguel looked over to Ellie, who shrugged.

"Maybe he means a boat came early in the morning," she guessed. "When the mist was still on the water."

"No!" Richard shook his head fiercely. "Misty boat! Misty boat!" He pulled the tray of drawings toward him and went through them until he found the one he wanted. He pushed the drawing at Miguel and then turned to stare greedily at Ellie's closed fist.

"What is it?" asked Ellie.

Miguel turned the paper so that she could see the drawing. It was a pencil sketch of a little rowing boat nosing into the near bank at Chuggie's Pool. A figure stood in the boat, legs braced and holding out a hand to help a smaller figure step aboard. Ellie grabbed the drawing and stared down at the smaller figure.

"That's Danny," she breathed, her voice thick with tears.

"Are you sure?" asked Miguel, peering over her shoulder. "It's a back view."

"I'm sure," she said, gazing at the familiar shape of his head and the tufts of thick fair hair. "That's his jacket, see? And look! His new fishing tackle laid out on the bank just as Dad and I found it!"

Miguel nodded. "What about the guy in the boat? Recognize him? Or her?"

Ellie transferred her attention to the other figure but, in contrast to the careful detail of the rest of the drawing, the face of the figure in the boat was a black smudge, scribbled in with angry pencil strokes. It appeared to have been done deliberately. "Why is there no face?" asked Ellie.

"That's Richard's way," said Miguel. "Have you

noticed he won't look you in the eye? He doesn't like faces, so he never draws them. He prefers objects."

"Oh, that's just great," muttered Ellie, peering at the figure in the boat, as though staring at it might bring the face into view. "Well, I can tell you one thing for sure," she said, giving up on the face and looking at the whole drawing again. "Danny's not being forced into the boat. He's getting in of his own accord. Look at the way he's reaching for the person's hand. He either knows this person, or he's been told something to persuade him into the boat."

"What about the boat?" asked Miguel. "Recognize that?"

Ellie shook her head. "It's just a standard little rowing boat. There are so many of them around. I can't even tell what color it is because the drawing is in pencil. What about you?" she asked, looking at Miguel. "You're around boats more than I am."

"Nope," said Miguel, shaking his head. "Every fisherman on the river has a boat like that."

Fisherman . . . Ellie tensed and stared at Miguel with wide eyes. "Mr. Lees, the police suspect! They already searched his house, but he might have a boat. He might even have a boathouse. Have they looked there?"

"Ellie, I'm pretty sure the police will have that covered."

"I saw him leaving his house earlier today. He looked really, I don't know, sneaky. He was carrying a big bag. What if he's got Danny—"

"Stop it, Ellie. You're jumping to conclusions. The guy's probably moving in with a friend or something."

"Why? Why would he do that?"

"I've heard what's been happening to him. Would you stay in your house with people shouting and throwing stones outside?"

"No," said Ellie reluctantly.

Miguel shook his head and then looked back to Richard's drawing. "Let's stick to the facts. Look. We have a name," he said, pointing to the prow of the boat in the drawing.

"'Mysti,'" read Ellie. "Misty boat! That's what Richard was telling us—the name of the boat. That is a strange spelling, though, isn't it? 'Mysti'? Do you think he's got it wrong?"

Miguel shook his head. "Richard always draws exactly what he sees. But an unusual name like that should make it easier to find the boat," he added. "Hey, Richard."

Richard did not answer. He was still gazing patiently at Ellie's hand, waiting for Bart.

"Show him," said Miguel. Ellie opened her hand, and Richard smiled. "Bart," he said softly, holding out his hand.

"Richard," said Miguel. "Which way did the

boat go once Danny was aboard?"

Without taking his eyes off Bart, Richard lifted his arm and pointed upriver.

"Thank you, Richard," said Ellie, holding out the little promotional toy. Richard took it reverently and immediately set about rearranging his desk, placing Bart exactly midway between his Simpsons ruler and his Homer pencil case. Ellie and Miguel looked at each other over his head.

"What now?" asked Miguel.

"I'm going to head upriver, checking out the names of all the rowing boats I can find," said Ellie determinedly.

"How?" asked Miguel, nodding at the swollen river racing past below Richard's window. The footpaths on both banks were totally submerged.

"I'll have to cross the bridge and follow the road that runs parallel to the river," said Ellie. "There are driveways or paths down to every boathouse and jetty along the way."

"That's going to take forever," muttered Miguel, frowning as he gazed from the window.

"I don't have a choice," said Ellie, heading for the door.

"Hang on," said Miguel, catching up with Ellie in the corridor. "I think I can get us some transportation. There's a guy who works in the kitchen here. He owes me a favor. Wait here," he said as they reached the bottom of the stairs. "I'll only be a second."

Miguel disappeared through a swing door into the kitchen at the back of the house before Ellie could object. She sighed and paced impatiently back and forth in the little reception area. She had a boat, a name, and a direction. This was the first real clue she had found, and she was anxious to get to work. While she waited for Miguel, Ellie pulled her phone from her pocket to check for messages. There was nothing, but as she began to slip the phone back into her pocket, Ellie came to a halt and stared down at the little screen. It had suddenly occurred to her that she should let the police know about the boat called Misty. They might know who owned it.

Ellie went into her phone menu and selected the contact number that Sergeant Donaldson had given her. She hesitated, with her thumb poised over the OK button. The last time she had seen Sergeant Donaldson was on the Spittal Point road, and he had not looked at all pleased with her. She bit her lip and pressed the BACK button on her phone. She could not face talking to the big police officer just yet.

"We have wheels." Miguel grinned, sticking his head around the door and holding up two crash helmets. "Let's go find ourselves a boat."

A few minutes later Richard was staring at the little skateboarding figure of Bart on his desk when he heard an engine whine outside. He raised his head and looked out the window. A bright yellow moped emerged from around the back of the home and headed off down the curving driveway at the front of the building. The moped was carrying two riders. They were both wearing crash helmets, and Richard could not see their faces. Richard watched the moped indicate right and then head off across the bridge. He studied the moped until it had disappeared along the road on the other side of the river, then he picked up a pencil and pulled his drawing pad toward him. Richard smiled as he bent his head over the paper. A bright yellow moped and no faces. This would be a good drawing.

"Had enough yet?" asked Miguel two hours later. He had stopped the moped at the top of a graveled track, and they were both standing beside the little machine, stamping their feet for warmth.

"Not yet," said Ellie, wiping the rain from her face. She could not remember ever being so wet while still fully dressed. Her jeans from the knee down were so heavy with water, she was creating her own puddles whenever she stood still. Her sleeves were soaking from sitting astride the moped with her arms wrapped around Miguel's waist, and a constant stream of rainwater was flowing from the base of her crash helmet and down the inside of her rain cape. Ellie shivered and tucked a strand of dripping hair under her helmet. "Can we go on a bit farther?"

Miguel looked as wet and cold as Ellie, but he simply nodded at her request and climbed back onto the moped. They had just returned from checking out a wooden jetty at the bottom end of the track. The jetty had been underwater, and the three rowing boats moored there had been tugging at the very end of their tether ropes, bobbing in the fast-flowing current like kites in a strong wind. Their bows were dipping farther and farther down into the river as the floodwater rose higher. As Ellie had read out the names painted on the sides of the boats, she could see that it would only be a matter of time before the tether ropes snapped, the boats sank, or the whole jetty was swept away.

It had been the same story all along the river. At the end of every track or lane they had ventured down, they had found boathouses underwater up to the roof timbers and boats submerged at their moorings or smashed against bridges. In some places whole stretches of bank had collapsed, sending bushes, trees, and fences swirling away down the rain-swollen river. In every flooded boathouse or submerged boat, Ellie dreaded finding Danny's floating, lifeless body. Her neck muscles had grown tight with tension as the search wore on, but they had found no sign of Danny, no trace of a boat named Misty, and no glimpse of Mr. Lees's yellow fisherman's jacket.

Wearily Ellie climbed onto the moped behind Miguel, leaned into his back, and took a firm grip on his belt. Miguel turned the ignition key, started the engine, and switched on the headlight. "Ready?" he yelled.

"Yes!" shouted Ellie, tapping him on the back.

Miguel turned the moped onto the river road and set off, swerving to avoid the worst of the puddles. Ellie hid her face below his shoulders and closed her eyes, trying to keep out of the stinging rain. She stayed like that until she felt the moped slowing down. When she opened her eyes again, she saw the orange flash of the right-hand indicator reflecting back at her from the wet, black road. Miguel had found another track. He turned the moped and brought it to a halt.

"I think we'll walk down this time," he said, turning off the engine. "We barely made it back up to the road at the last lane."

Ellie nodded, remembering how the little engine had strained as the wheels of the moped sank into the wet gravel. Miguel waited with his feet braced in the gravel on either side of the moped until she had climbed down, then he walked the machine behind a bush so that it was hidden from the road. He kicked the stand into place, eased his helmet off, and hung it from the handlebars. Ellie took her helmet off too and handed it to Miguel before lifting the hood of her rain cape over her hair and turning to see what lay at the bottom end of the track.

"Oh," said Ellie softly as she finally realized where they had stopped.

Miguel came up beside her. They were standing at the top of a driveway that led down to a square of raked gravel at the side of a large, detached house. The house was solid and elegant, built with local sandstone and slate. The garden below the house had mature trees and sloping lawns, most of which were now submerged beneath muddy flood-water.

"Rich folk," said Miguel, starting off down the driveway. "What's the betting they'll have a boat?"

"They do," said Ellie quietly.

Miguel stopped. "They do what?"

"Have a boat. A rowing boat. I've been out in it once."

"You know these people?"

Ellie nodded. "This is where Ross lives. My boyfriend. I mean ex. My ex-boyfriend. He just doesn't know it yet."

"Want to take a look?" asked Miguel.

Ellie shook her head. "No point. Their boat's not called 'Misty.' I can't remember what it is called, but I know it's not 'Misty.' "

Miguel nodded and went to retrieve the moped. *Glint.*

Ellie had been about to follow Miguel, but she

turned back to see what had caught her eye.

Glint.

A warm yellow light was shining from the kitchen window at the lower corner of the house and glinting on the water below the sill. Ellie frowned. There should not be any water below the kitchen windowsill. As far as she could remember, there was a little sunken patio there, with stone steps leading down into the cellars under the house. It was usually a pleasant place to sit out for a coffee in the sun, but not today.

Glint.

Ellie's eyes widened as she realized what was reflecting the light from the kitchen window. A flood of brown river water was pouring onto the sunken patio below the window and cascading down the stone steps into the cellar.

"Their cellar is flooding!" cried Ellie, breaking into a run. "I'd better let them know! Wait here. I won't be long."

She raced off down the driveway. Miguel shivered as he watched her go. His wet clothes were chilling him to the bone. He stamped a short distance down the driveway, trying to bring some warmth back into his feet. When he stopped, he could see the little rowing boat that belonged to the family. It was in the lower garden. It had been hauled up onto the grass well above the river, but now it was floating on floodwater and bumping against the partly submerged tree trunk it was chained to. Miguel thought he might as well check it out while he waited for Ellie. He swerved off the driveway and cut down through the trees, heading toward the boat.

Ellie reached the graveled square at the bottom of the driveway and hurried over to the kitchen window at the lower end of the house. The sunken patio below the window was completely submerged. There were steps descending from the edge of the patio to the river, and this was where the rising water had found a way through. It was flowing in between the higher grass banks on either side of the steps. Ellie bent to peer into the dark cellar. The water was already waist high down there, and more was gushing in all the time.

Ellie stepped away from the sunken patio and backed up the graveled slope until she was high enough to peer through the kitchen window. She was expecting to see Ross's mother inside, and she gave a little gasp of surprise when she saw Ross standing there instead. He was alone in the big kitchen, leaning back against the oversized table and glumly eating a solitary lunch of Cheerios straight from the packet. Ellie pulled back the sleeve of her rain cape and glanced at her watch, even though she already knew it was only midday. Ross must have come straight back home after calling the police, instead of going into school.

Ellie hesitated. The last thing she wanted to do right now was speak to Ross, but she knew he must be on his own in the house. His parents would never let him stay home from school unless he was actually throwing up or running a temperature. Ellie glanced up to the detached double garage at the top end of the house. There were no cars parked outside, which meant that both his parents were definitely out. Ellie bent and picked up a small piece of gravel. However angry she was with Ross, she had to let him know that the cellars were flooding. The fuse boxes were down there, and she did not know what would happen when the floodwater reached them.

She pulled back her arm and threw the piece of gravel at the window. It plinked against the glass, and Ross glanced up. Their eyes met, and his widened in shock. He straightened up, dropping the Cheerios packet to the floor, and turning to look for something on the table behind him. Ellie frowned as she watched him. He looked—guilty. Yes, that was it. Ross looked as though she had caught him out doing something wrong.

Ellie looked at the kitchen table through the rain-streaked glass, trying to see what it was Ross was feeling so guilty about. She spotted the mobile phone a split second before Ross's hand closed over it, hiding it from view. It was a very distinctive phone. It had a lime green cover, customized with a hand-painted tree frog. Ellie stiffened with shock as she watched Ross stuff the phone deep into his trouser pocket. She knew only one person who owned a phone customized with a hand-painted tree frog—and that person was Danny.

TWENTY

THE BRANDING

Ellie gazed openmouthed at Ross through the kitchen window as he pushed Danny's phone into his trouser pocket. Her mind was still struggling to cope with this astonishing piece of information. Ross had Danny's phone. It was like seeing a clown at a funeral. The two things did not go together. Clown and funeral. Ross and Danny's phone. Ellie shook her head. Why did Ross have Danny's phone?

Ross turned and walked up to his side of the window. He tried a surprised smile and a wave, but Ellie was looking at his eyes, and they were not smiling at all. His eyes were full of fear. Ellie stared into his frightened eyes, and Ross stared back. The smile disappeared, and he watched her warily. Then his gaze dropped and glanced toward the cellar door below the window. It was no more than a downward flicker before he hastily brought his gaze back up to Ellie, but that was all she needed. Her eyes widened, and her hand came up to cover her mouth. Suddenly she knew where Danny was. He was down there, in the flooded cellar below the house.

Ross saw that she knew. He slammed a hand against the glass, and then he turned and ran from the kitchen. Ellie knew he would be heading for the back door. With a sob of fright, she jumped from the graveled drive into the flooded sunken patio. The brown water curled around her legs with muscular power, nearly taking her feet out from under her. Ellie caught herself and then shuffled stiff-legged toward the cellar, feeling for the start of the stone steps.

Her boot tipped over the edge of the top step, and again she nearly went down. She grabbed the decorative, curled end of the metal handrail that was sticking up out of the floodwater. Holding on tight, she eased down into the cellar, step by step, grabbing a large flashlight that was hanging on a nail as she went. She turned on the flashlight, but the beam could not penetrate the thick, brown water and so she had to move on down the steps blindly, feeling her way with her feet.

Ellie was in freezing river water up to her waist

by the time her boots hit level ground. She was shivering convulsively from a combination of cold and shock and fear, and the flashlight beam wavered madly as she tried to hold it steady.

"Danny?" she cried. "I'm here, Danny! I'm here!"

There was no reply. Ellie waded farther into the cellar, swinging the flashlight beam. She saw tools hanging from nails on the whitewashed walls, bikes on racks, a shelving unit full of spare bulbs and batteries.

"Danny?"

A large wine rack. Garden furniture. A row of fuse boxes. Garden tools. Stacks of boxes, the cardboard dark and soft with water. No sign of Danny. Ellie waded around, feeling into every corner with her feet. She found a submerged work bench, more boxes, but no Danny. The cellar was just a normal, family storage room. Ellie turned back to the steps, and that was when she saw the large chest freezer in the corner beside the stairs.

Dread flooded through her as she stared at the white chest. It was more than big enough to hide the body of an eleven-year-old boy. Ellie waded over to the freezer, gripped the handle, and lifted the lid. The freezer was packed to the rim with cuts of meat and bags of vegetables. Ellie dug her hands in and heaved out armfuls of frozen food. She did not stop until she could see the ice-caked floor of the chest. Only then did she step back and let the lid of the freezer slam shut. As she did so, Ellie saw blue sparks rise from the side of the chest freezer. The floodwater was lapping at the panel that held the electrical workings.

Hastily, Ellie backed away from the freezer. "Danny. . . ?" she faltered, her voice hitching with tears as she gazed wildly around the cellar once more.

The doorway darkened behind her. Ellie whirled, shining the flashlight up into Ross's face. He had reinvented himself during his run from the kitchen to the cellar door. His face was now a picture of wounded innocence.

"Ellie," he said gently, "I know you've been under a lot of strain—"

"Where is he?" shrieked Ellie. "Where's Danny?"

"I don't know, Ellie. I can't tell you where he is. But I can tell you he isn't in our cellars. Now, why don't you come out of there, hmm?"

Cellars. Ellie gasped and then turned and waded toward the far end of the room as fast as she could. Ross had said "cellars." She had forgotten there was more than one room down here. There was another door in the back wall, nearly hidden by the tools and gardening clothes that were hanging from it.

"Ellie," called Ross, his voice suddenly sharp with fear. "Come back! It could be dangerous!"

Ellie ignored him and continued to wade toward the far wall. Her flashlight beam found the little door and she headed toward it. It had been pushed slightly ajar by the flowing water. Ellie forced the door farther open, ducked under the low doorway, and waded into the inky blackness of the next room. It smelled bad. A mixture of sewage, river water, and some sort of a chemical underlay, sweet and cloying.

Swallowing down nausea, Ellie straightened up and shone the flashlight around the cellar. There was a tangled pile of industrial metal shelving against the far wall. The flooding had caused it to topple sideways, spilling the contents of its shelves into the brown water. Ellie flicked the flashlight back and forth across the surface of the water. At least a dozen large glass jars were bobbing around. She stepped forward to see what was in the jars, and glass crunched under her boot. There must be more broken jars on the cellar floor beneath the water.

The flashlight beam lit up one of the bobbing jars, and Ellie gave a muffled scream as she saw what was inside. It was a small, curled snake, milky pale and with a white film over its eyes. Ellie realized it was floating in formaldehyde. Formaldehyde! That was the chemical smell that was coating the back of her throat. There were other things bobbing in the brown water all around her, and Ellie realized they must have come from the broken jars that crunched under her feet. A large, pale ox tongue bumped up against her arm and then the head of a cat floated into the flashlight beam, its blind eyes winking in the light.

Ellie turned to one side and threw up into the water. As she straightened up again, wiping her mouth on her sleeve, she saw a dark shape floating in the corner of the room. Ellie stared at the shape for a second before she realized she was staring at Danny's green fishing jacket.

"Danny!"

She surged through the water toward him. He was floating facedown. His hair was plastered to his head, and she could see the pale curve of his neck above the jacket collar. She grabbed his jacket and flipped him over onto his back.

"Oh, Danny . . ."

His eyes were closed. His face was purple, and his lips were swollen. Ellie slipped one arm under his shoulders to support him in the water. She pulled his body close to her and pushed the flashlight into her hand as her supporting arm emerged from the water on the other side of his thin shoulders. With her free hand, she checked for a pulse, pressing her fingers against Danny's cold neck, but her own heart was beating so fast and hard, Ellie could not be sure what she was feeling.

She stared down into Danny's face, frantically trying to remember the details of the first-aid course she had completed as part of her Duke of Edinburgh Award. She pulled his mouth open, checking for obstructions. There was a fine froth in his mouth and nostrils. Ellie cleared the froth away, then she let Danny's head fall back over her arm and pinched his nose shut with her free hand. Placing her mouth over his, Ellie breathed out, willing her life into his. She watched his chest as she breathed into him, to see whether it was rising, but she couldn't tell. The flashlight beam was wavering about in her other hand, and his body was rising and falling with the movement of the water.

Ellie let out a small, panicked cry. It had all seemed so easy in the classes, in a warm, dry hall, with good lighting and a tutor telling her what to do. Now she had no idea whether she was doing the right thing at all. She bent and sent six more breaths into Danny's mouth in quick succession, and then she began to wade back toward the cellar door, easing Danny's body along beside her. She ducked through the door, pulling Danny through after her, and then bent again and gave him two more breaths. There was slightly more daylight in the outer cellar, so she discarded the flashlight, letting it float away on the water.

"Ellie?" called Ross, from the steps. "I didn't know the cellars were flooding."

Ellie ignored Ross. She stared at Danny's chest in the flashlight beam but she could see no rise and fall, and his face was still livid. She had to get him onto solid ground and start chest compressions. Ellie grabbed Danny under the arms and began backing toward the steps, pulling him along on the surface of the water.

"Oh, no," moaned Ross as Danny's purpled face came into view. "I didn't know about the water. I didn't know!"

"Help me get him out, Ross!" shouted Ellie, but Ross stayed where he was at the top of the stairs, his face full of a guilty terror.

"I only meant to keep him for a couple of days," whined Ross. "I was going to let him go, once you'd all realized how much you needed me. But then, after the television interview, I thought you were going to finish with me. So you see, I had to keep him for longer. And then things just kept getting more out of my control." He looked at Ellie with a bewildered expression on his face. "Why do things do that? Go out of control?"

Ellie was hardly listening. She was concentrating on towing Danny toward the steps.

"Is he dead?" asked Ross. "Because if he is, it's not my fault. I didn't know about the water until now. I didn't know the cellars were flooding. Anyway, if you hadn't been so nasty to me after my television interview, I would've let him go much sooner. In fact, when I look at it that way, it's obvious whose fault this is. Yours! This is all your fault!"

Ellie stopped halfway across the cellar to give Danny more air and then set off again.

"Stop ignoring me," snapped Ross, his voice tightening with anger. "I don't like it when you ignore me."

Ellie reached the steps and pushed Danny's head and shoulders up onto the step that was lying just under the surface of the water.

"Get his arms," she ordered, looking up at Ross.

Ross squatted down on the top step and tried an awful parody of a smile. "We can still sort this out," he coaxed. "If we carry the body down to the river now, the police will find it downstream, and everyone'll think he fell in and drowned. Yes, that would work." Ross's eyes grew distant as he thought through his new idea. "Then I won't have to tell them I took him, and nobody would know this is all your fault. We could carry on as a family. We could carry on as normal."

As *normal*? Ellie shuddered as she stared up into Ross's mild blue eyes. What he was saying was utterly, dangerously insane, but he actually thought he was being reasonable.

"Ross, please . . ."

"Oh, I see," snapped Ross, suddenly shaking with anger. "When you need my help, it's all 'Ross please,' but none of you thought twice about going off on holiday without me. How do you think I felt, being left behind? And then you all come back and try to carry on as though nothing had happened."

Ellie stared at Ross in horrified bewilderment for a second, but then she gave up trying to understand and turned back to Danny. She struggled to lift him from the water on her own, but her arms were not strong enough.

"Help me, Ross," she pleaded.

Ross ignored her. He squatted on the top step and continued to complain, talking as though they were sitting in his kitchen rather than facing each other in a flooded cellar with a drowned boy floating between them. "And then what do you all do next? You go ahead and arrange Danny's birthday party—and you leave me out again!"

"Ross! Get his arms!"

"I'm as much part of this family as Danny, you know!" yelled Ross, clenching his fists and rising to his feet so that he towered over her threateningly.

Ellie glared up at him. "What are you talking about? You're not part of our family, Ross! Danny's my brother, not you!"

Ross reeled back as though she had punched him and then sadly shook his head. Suddenly he looked like a little, lost boy. "See what I mean? Always Danny first." He looked down at Danny's body with an expression of bitter jealousy on his face. "That's why I had to take him. This really is all your fault."

Ellie stopped listening. She flipped Danny over,

then ducked into the water and came up under him. She settled him across her shoulders and pushed herself into a standing position with a deep groan of effort. With Danny over her shoulder and one arm gripping him behind the knees, Ellie grasped the metal handrail and began to drag herself up the cellar steps.

Ross stood up and watched her struggle. She had nearly reached the top step when he leaned down and straight-armed her in the chest. Ellie lost her grip on the handrail and fell back into the cellar. Brown water closed over her head and poured into her mouth and nose. She fought to reach the surface, but Danny's body was floating above her. Ellie turned and swam out from under Danny, surfacing halfway across the cellar. Coughing and spluttering, she surged back to Danny, ducked under him and settled him across her shoulders again.

"If you won't listen to reason, you can't come out," said Ross. "Just—stay there! I have to think about what to do."

Grimly Ellie waded to the steps, grabbed the handrail, and began to climb again. She was halfway up the steps when the floodwater reached the top of the panel in the side of the chest freezer. A loud crackling came from the side of the freezer, and the cellar was lit up with flashes of white fire. A sudden explosion of sparks arced across the water toward her, and Ellie realized that she was standing in

water, one of the most efficient conductors of elec-
tricity there was. Ellie opened her mouth and
screamed in terror.

Miguel stood at the edge of the floodwater staring
at the little rowing boat as it bumped and scraped
against the tree it was chained to. He could not read
the name on the side because the boat was covered
with a smart, blue fitted tarpaulin. Miguel stretched
out over the water and tried to grab the stern of the
boat as it swung his way, but it was just out of reach.
He stepped back and looked around for something
he could use to hook the boat over to him, but
there were no fallen branches left lying around in
this well-tended garden. Miguel looked at the boat,
then down at his soaking boots, then back to the
boat. He sighed. What the hell. He couldn't get
much wetter.

Stepping into the floodwater, Miguel waded
toward the boat, drawing in his breath with a curse
at the shock of the cold water. He grabbed the bow
of the boat and hung on to it with one hand while
he untied the cord holding the tarpaulin in place
with the other. Miguel flipped the tarpaulin back
and stared at the name that was painted in gold let-
tering on the bow.

Mystique.

Still hanging on to the boat, he reached inside
his jacket, pulled Richard's drawing out of his shirt

pocket, and fumbled it open one-handed. In Richard's drawing there was a coil of rope looped over the bow just beyond the last letter of the boat name. Miguel nodded, remembering how Richard always drew exactly what he saw. He stuffed the drawing back into his pocket and then grabbed a corner of the tarpaulin and draped it over the bow of the boat, in the same position as the coil of rope in Richard's drawing. The tarpaulin covered the last three letters of the name. Miguel stared grimly at the remaining letters.

Mysti.

He pulled the tarpaulin back to the stern and then looked down into the well of the boat. His jaw was clenched as he scanned the boat. He was half expecting to find a body curled up beneath the tarpaulin, but apart from a large Hessian sack under one of the seats, the boat was empty. Miguel let his breath out in an explosive gasp of relief. He was pulling the tarpaulin back into place when Ellie screamed. It was a high, raw scream, full of terror, and it sent a current of shock running through his body. Miguel abandoned the boat, splashed out of the floodwater, and powered his way through the trees toward the house.

More sparks crackled in the flooded cellar. Hastily Ross stepped out of the water-filled sunken patio and up onto the higher level of the graveled slope at the side of the house.

"Ross!" screamed Ellie. "Help me get Danny out of here!"

"But what are you going to say to people when you get out?" asked Ross, tilting his head to one side to peer in at her.

Ellie screamed again as the freezer crackled, sending another explosion of sparks arcing toward her. She dragged herself up the steps, desperate to get out of the water. Danny was a dead weight on her shoulders, and her legs were beginning to tremble uncontrollably.

"Please, Ross . . ." she gasped.

Ross shook his head and was straightening up to kick her back into the cellar when Miguel suddenly cannoned into him from the side. Ross was sent flying, landing on the gravel slope with a grunt of pain and surprise. Ellie grabbed the handrail again and heaved herself to the top of the cellar steps. She stood on the sunken patio and tipped Danny off her shoulder so that he was lying on his back on the gravel slope, and then she crawled out of the floodwater and kneeled on the gravel beside him.

Out in the daylight, he looked worse than ever. His face was a mottled, purplish gray and his eyelids did not flinch when the raindrops hit them. His wrists and ankles were tied with plastic strips. The flesh around the strips was cut and swollen, and thin trails of blood trickled from the cuts, merging with the river water that was running from his clothes.

Ross and Miguel were wrestling on the gravel slope, swinging punches at each other as they rolled back and forth, each trying to get the upper hand. Ellie hardly noticed them. All her attention was on Danny.

"Okay," she gasped, positioning the heel of her hand over his breastbone and placing her other hand over the top. "Here we go, Danny. Come on. You can do it." Ellie straightened her arms, rocked forward, and pressed down on Danny's chest half a dozen times. Then she squeezed his nose shut, put her mouth over his, and breathed into him once, twice.

"Come on, Danny," she whispered, repositioning her hands on his chest. "One, two, three . . ." She counted the number of compressions and then gave him two more breaths. There was no response. Tears began to stream down her face as she returned to the chest compressions and her mouth twisted in horrified grief.

"Please . . . please . . ." she gasped, pressing down on his chest. "Don't die. . . ."

Beside her, Miguel and Ross were on their feet now. Ross landed a punch that sent Miguel staggering backward. Miguel recovered and suddenly ran at Ross, ramming into his chest. Ross stepped back and fell into the water at the top of the cellar steps. He put out his hand and grabbed at the ornamental curl at the top end of the stair rail. As soon as his hand made contact, there was a flash of light, and Ross was thrown several feet through the air. The chest freezer in the cellar had not been earthed, and now the water and the metal handrail had become electrical conductors.

Ross landed on the gravel with a thud and lay there, dazed. His hand fell open and there, burned into the palm like a brand, was the spiral imprint of the end of the handrail. Ellie twisted to stare at Ross, but then turned back to Danny when she heard a noise. Danny coughed, coughed again, and then convulsed as brown water erupted from his mouth and nose. Quickly Ellie turned him onto his side, rubbing at his back as more water and thick strings of mucus vomited from his mouth.

"Thank God," she whispered, looking up at Miguel with tears in her eyes. A blue flashing light made them both look up to the top of the driveway. Sergeant Donaldson's police car appeared between the stone gateposts like a mirage. He was followed by two more police cars and then, miraculously, an ambulance turned into the driveway and crunched slowly down the gravel slope toward her.

"Go, Miguel," hissed Ellie. "Quickly!" She turned her back on him as a car door slammed. "It was Ross!" she shouted to Sergeant Donaldson as he sprinted toward her. "He had Danny tied up in the cellar!"

Miguel backed away, leaving Ross sprawled on the gravel, groaning and shaking his head. Sergeant Donaldson hauled Ross to his feet, marched him up the slope to the police cars, and handed him over to two other officers. Then he hurried back down the slope, speaking into his radio as he jogged toward Ellie and Danny.

Ellie tried to stand but then sat down heavily on the gravel, clasping Danny's cold hand in hers while first Sergeant Donaldson and then the two paramedics checked him over. It was not until Danny had been loaded into the ambulance, with Ellie sitting alongside him wrapped in a foil blanket, that Sergeant Donaldson thought to look for the dark-haired young man who had been backing away from the scene when he first arrived. By that time Miguel had disappeared.

Ellie watched from the ambulance as Sergeant Donaldson scouted around the grounds of the big house, looking for Miguel. When the ambulance reached the top of the driveway, Ellie peered into the bushes at the side of the road. The bright yellow moped had gone too. Ellie turned back to her brother, staring at his pale face. His eyes flickered and then tried to open. Ellie felt her throat thicken with tears.

"It's all right, Danny," she whispered, laughing and crying at the same time. "Everything's all right now."

· TWENTY-ONE ·

GLINT

Argent frowned in concentration as she rubbed at the little round shield in her lap. The tip of her tongue was sticking from the corner of her mouth, and there were beads of sweat on her forehead. She was sitting by the pool in the glade at the edge of Unthank Forest. She had been there all morning, working on the shield. First she had used her knife to scrape away the charred surface layer of wood, then she had used a stone to sand the good wood underneath until it was smooth to the touch. She had cleaned the beaten metal disk with water from the pool and polished it using a corner of her woolen sleeping blanket. Now she was clutching a chunk of beeswax that Lukos had found for her, painstakingly rubbing a coating of wax onto the wooden rim of the shield.

Argent sat back to take a rest and admire her work. The metal disk was a bright, shining silver once again, and the wooden rim glowed with a rich sheen. Argent gave a grunt of satisfaction and leaned back against the roots of the tree behind her. The autumn sun was at its height now, warming her upturned face as it filtered through the trees. Argent pushed her dark hair behind her ears and closed her eyes.

"Good as new," said Lukos, right beside her.

Argent jumped and sat up straight with a scowl on her face. Lukos was squatting next to her, looking down at the shield. He had moved so silently through the wood, she had not heard his approach. "I wish you wouldn't do that!" she snapped.

"What?"

"Sneak up on me like that!"

Lukos grinned and held out a little glass jar with a cork stopper. "The goodwife sent this."

"What is it?" asked Argent, sulkily.

"Salve, for your burns," said Lukos, sitting alongside her and trying to keep the amusement out of his voice. He pulled the stopper from the jar and scooped out a dollop of the yellow ointment inside. "Let's see."

Argent pulled up her trouser legs and allowed Lukos to smear the ointment onto the red bands of skin across the front of her shins. They had caught a blast of heat when the swirling air in the courtyard had lifted the protective curtain of dragon's egg skin.

"I gave the goodwife your message. She promised to make sure it was delivered safely to your mother."

Argent nodded gratefully. She had scribbled a note on the back of one of her dragon parchments to let her mother know she was safe and well. "Did the goodwife say anything else?" she asked, wincing as the ointment touched her raw skin.

"She said you can keep the shield," murmured Lukos, scooping out another dollop of ointment and moving on to the line of blisters across Argent's shield arm, where the dragon-heated metal studs on the back of the shield had left their mark.

"I meant, is there any news?" snapped Argent impatiently.

"Yes. The goodwife gets to hear everything, in time."

"News from Goldstone?" asked Argent, wincing as Lukos smeared the cooling ointment over her blisters.

"Yes."

Argent bit her lip as she looked up at Lukos. They had been hiding out in the forest for three days now, with no idea whether the duke's men were out combing the countryside for them or not. "So, tell me," she said. "Are we to be outlaws?"

"It seems not." Lukos smiled. "The city is full of rumors. People are claiming they saw a dragon in the sky, hovering over the Bell Tower at the time the duke died, but the castle is denying it. The official story is that the duke died when an experiment with fireworks went wrong. They say the exploding fireworks are what people saw in the sky, not a dragon. So nobody is looking for us. We are safe."

Argent leaned back against the tree roots with a sigh of relief. "Who rules us now?" she asked, looking into Lukos's amber eyes.

"Apparently the duke had a daughter. She has been brought back from some remote convent where she was being schooled, and now she rules, with the help of an inner circle of advisers."

"Poor girl," said Argent, imagining how hard and strange the life of the duke's daughter must suddenly have become.

"The goodwife says she has spirit," said Lukos. "Already she is showing signs of good leadership. Remember the creatures we had to leave caged in the cavern?" His face twisted with regret as he said the words.

Argent nodded, and her face grew sad for a moment as she remembered the death of the striped horse creature in the alcove.

"The goodwife's source told her that the castle advisers were all for killing the creatures quietly and covering up the evidence, but the duke's daughter has ordered a ship to take them across the sea and set them free in their own land," said Lukos. "It sails on the tide later today, under the guise of an ordinary merchant ship."

Argent nodded her approval. "She will do well as our new ruler," she said.

"And you," said Lukos, turning his golden-eyed gaze on Argent. "What will you do, now that you know you are not doomed to an outlaw life? Will you stay here with us, or return to your village?"

Argent frowned and looked down at her hands. She loved the freedom of living with Lukos and his family in the forest, and she was slowly becoming used to their were-creature natures, but she missed her mother and her father. If she returned to Haven's Edge, she would be married within the month and expected to start a family within the year. Could she stand to be so constrained after her brief taste of freedom? On the other hand, if she stayed in the forest with Lukos, there would be no marriage and no children. *At least not yet*, she thought, glancing sideways at Lukos.

"You know you would be very welcome here," said Lukos, studying his own hands intently. "I, that is, we all—Mother, Father, Reya, Tawn, and myself—we all want you to stay. But we would understand if you chose to return to your own family."

There was a moment of silence. Argent could

not decide. Neither choice seemed quite right. She picked up the little shield and turned it so that she could stare at her face in the metal disk. A lot had happened to her over the past few days and she felt changed in some irrevocable way. She frowned as she studied her dark eyes and thin, white face, trying to find an answer there. Argent turned the shield slightly and it caught the sun.

Glint.

Ellie frowned into the little mirror on the wall of Danny's hospital room, studying her dark eyes and her thin, pale face. A strong glint of light had reflected from the glass into her eyes and, just for an instant, her face had seemed to blur and double in the mirror. She could not understand where the light had come from. The shade was down in Danny's room, and only a small lamp glowed on the cupboard beside his bed.

"Ellie?"

Ellie turned away from the mirror. Her mum and dad were standing by Danny's bed, and Ellie could not help smiling as she looked at them. They were holding hands again. It had been a dreadful time for all of them when the police had taken Mr. Brody in for questioning, but Ellie and her mother had never doubted him for an instant, and it seemed the experience had only served to make their family stronger. Since the moment they had all been reunited in Danny's hospital room, her mum and dad had hardly been apart.

"Will you be okay on your own for half an hour?" asked Mrs. Brody. "Me and your dad want to nip down to the hospital cafeteria for a bite to eat."

"I won't be on my own." Ellie smiled. "Danny's here. You go, we'll be fine. Bring me back a sandwich."

The door clicked shut behind Mr. and Mrs. Brody, and Ellie settled down in the chair beside Danny's bed. A few seconds later she looked up as the door clicked open again and a nurse bustled into the room. She watched the nurse check the intravenous drip attached to Danny's arm and then study the monitor screens, making a few notes on Danny's chart.

"How's he doing?" asked Ellie anxiously. It had been three days since she had dragged Danny from the cellar below Ross's house, and for most of those three days, he had lain pale and still in the narrow hospital bed with his bandaged arms resting neatly above the covers, and his nose and mouth hidden behind an oxygen mask. When he did wake up, he would be fully conscious and lucid one second and hallucinating the next. The doctors had explained that this was caused partly by the aftereffects of the Ketamine tranquilizer Ross had been injecting him with and partly by the infection in his body, but still Ellie found it frightening to watch Danny slip away into a place where she could not reach him.

"He's a little fighter." The nurse smiled. "We'll be able to take him off the drip today."

Ellie nodded, staring at the bag of clear fluid suspended from a metal stand beside Danny's bed. He had been severely dehydrated when he arrived at the hospital, which Ellie had found somewhat ironic, given that he had also nearly drowned. The nurse pulled back the covers and gently lifted the cage from Danny's right thigh. Ellie winced when she saw the swollen mess of ulcerated flesh there. Ross had been injecting him with Ketamine two or three times a day, ramming the unsterilized needles through Danny's jeans and into his thigh. The flesh had become swollen and infected, and the skin had sloughed away to leave an open wound that needed cleaning regularly. The nurse bent to her task, and Danny whimpered in his sleep. His eyelids began to flutter.

"Nearly done," soothed Ellie, moving up to the bed and taking hold of the hand that did not have the intravenous needle stuck into the back of it. She gazed down at the oxygen mask over Danny's face, watching as it misted and cleared, misted and cleared with his shallow breathing. This fight for air was the biggest battle Danny was facing. The Ketamine had depressed his respiratory function and that, combined with the dirty river water that had entered his lungs, meant that he was struggling to get enough oxygen into his system.

"His breathing is much easier today," said the nurse, replacing the cage over Danny's leg and straightening the covers. "And the oxygen levels in his blood are much higher. See?" The nurse pointed to one of the monitor screens. "The antibiotics are starting to work."

"Thank you," whispered Ellie.

The nurse nodded and quietly left the room. When the door clicked open again a few minutes later, Ellie looked up in surprise. She wasn't expecting anyone. Her mum and dad had only just left, and the doctors weren't due to come around again before tea.

"Can I come in?" asked Sergeant Donaldson, sticking his head round the door.

"My mum and dad are in the cafeteria," said Ellie.

"I know," rumbled Sergeant Donaldson. "I've just had a word with them. I wanted to see Danny. Is that okay?"

"Is Lisa with you?"

"No."

Ellie nodded her consent, and the big police officer stepped into the room and moved up to the other side of the bed. This was the first time she had seen Sergeant Donaldson since the afternoon of

Danny's rescue. When the line of police cars had appeared at the top of the driveway, she had thought it was nothing short of miraculous, but later Sergeant Donaldson had explained that Ross had finally switched on Danny's phone to see what was in the mysterious text message she had talked about at the press conference. As soon as the position of Danny's phone had been triangulated, he had rounded up some backup and headed off along the river road to Ross's house.

"The rain's stopped at last," said Sergeant Donaldson, trying to make conversation. "The river's still high, but they've stopped issuing flood warnings."

"Where is he now?" asked Ellie. She was in no mood for small talk.

"You mean Ross?"

Ellie nodded, unable to say his name.

"He's still being assessed over in the psychiatric wing."

Ellie shuddered. She didn't like to think of Ross being in the same hospital as Danny, even if he was over on the other side of the complex.

"I've just come from interviewing him," said Sergeant Donaldson. "He's in a bit of a state."

"Good."

"He keeps saying he didn't mean to hurt Danny—"

"Don't!" Ellie glared at Sergeant Donaldson. "I

don't want to hear about how sorry he is. He actually invited me over to his house! Can you believe that? He suggested we go back to his place for a coffee when he knew he had my brother tied up and drugged in the cellar!"

"Ellie, Ross Avery is a very sick young man. He was probably deluding himself as much as he was deluding you when he invited you back to his house. That's how he managed to carry on as normal and fool everyone. When he needed to, he could completely block out the knowledge of what he had done. At least, that's what the doctors tell me."

Ellie was not interested in Sergeant Donaldson's explanations. "I don't care what the doctors say. He's a monster. To give himself an alibi, that monster spent Saturday afternoon in the cellar, rehearsing with his band, when he knew my brother was trapped and helpless on the other side of the door. And speaking of alibis, how come his parents said he was at home with them on Saturday morning, when he was out on the river in their rowing boat? Were they covering up for him?"

Sergeant Donaldson shook his head. "No. They always have a lie-in on Saturday mornings. They just presumed he was doing the same. They didn't check up on him. I get the impression they're not exactly a close family. And Ross is an only child. He was probably a very lonely boy at home."

Ellie scowled. She had been doing a lot of thinking over the past few days as she sat by Danny's hospital bed watching him fight the infection that was raging through his body. She blamed herself for not spotting the real reason for Ross's lack of passion toward her. She had thought he was growing bored. Instead, he had been harboring a growing delusion that he belonged with her family. His distant behavior after they returned from holiday was not because he had been seeing Laura Jones. He was hurt because, in his eyes, her family, his real family, had gone off without him.

"So the whole thing is his parents' fault? He was neglected at home so he latched onto my family instead? That's rubbish."

Sergeant Donaldson thought for a moment. "It's not as black and white as that, Ellie. It's not just cause and effect. There are other factors involved."

"Such as?"

"The doctors say Ross would've become ill whatever his family life was like. There are a number of mental illnesses—schizophrenia, for example—that tend to be triggered in the teenage years. The doctors are still in the process of diagnosing Ross's illness but, whatever it is, it was not brought on directly by a lack of love or attention from his parents."

"So are you saying it was our fault? That's what

he kept saying, in the cellar."

"Nobody is to blame for Ross becoming ill. But, when you all welcomed him into your family, it gave him a focus for his mania. He had something to be obsessive about, do you see?"

Ellie nodded reluctantly.

"He's a very mixed-up young man," continued Sergeant Donaldson. "We're still piecing everything together, but it seems he thought Danny was taking his own rightful place in the family. For some reason he believed that if he took Danny for a while, you would all turn to him instead. I think he was planning to let him go again, eventually."

"It doesn't matter what he was planning," said Ellie coldly. "Danny nearly died. He nearly killed my brother." She glared at Sergeant Donaldson defiantly. If he was expecting her to show any understanding toward Ross, he was going to have to wait for a very long time. Sergeant Donaldson gazed at her mildly for a few seconds and then seemed to accept the fact that he was not going to change her feelings.

"Now," he said, changing the subject, "do you mind if I ask you a few questions?"

Ellie looked at Sergeant Donaldson warily. She had a feeling he was going to question her about Miguel. Quickly she thought of a question of her own. "So, did you find out why all those formaldehyde bottles were down in the cellar?" she asked, suppressing a shudder as she thought of the pale, bloodless organs floating in the brown floodwater. They had featured in her dreams every night since the afternoon in the cellar.

"Gruesome, weren't they?" said Sergeant Donaldson. "Nothing sinister about them, though. As you know, the father's a vet. They were his specimens. He's been collecting them since his veterinary school days."

"I always thought he was a bit odd," muttered Ellie, shuddering again. "Like father like son."

Sergeant Donaldson looked as though he was going to try to explain about Ross all over again, but he only gazed at her briefly before turning to stare down into Danny's pale face. "Well, it looks like you saved him," he said, watching the rise and fall of Danny's chest with his usual serious expression.

"You were there only a short while after me," said Ellie.

Sergeant Donaldson shook his head. "Danny would have been dead by the time we found him. We would have knocked on the front door first and interviewed your boyfriend and—"

"Ex-boyfriend," spat Ellie, glowering at Sergeant Donaldson.

The big police officer held up his hands, acknowledging his mistake.

"It seems Ross knew Danny would be fishing at

the river last Saturday."

Ellie nodded. "Ross knew what we were getting Danny for his birthday. He was in the kitchen with us when we were choosing the fishing tackle from the catalogue." She sat up, remembering another question that had been troubling her. "How did he tempt Danny into the boat?"

"He pretended he had an injured swan under a sack in the bottom of the boat. Danny jumped in immediately. He was bending over to lift up the sacking when Ross rammed the needle into his thigh and held him down until he was unconscious."

Sergeant Donaldson lifted the bedcovers to check the site of the injections in Danny's thigh. He looked down at the swollen leg under the protective cage and winced. "Nasty."

"But Danny would've recognized him right away," said Ellie. "How did Ross think he was going to get away with it? Surely he knew Danny would've remembered all about him once the drugs were out of his system? I don't think he was planning to let him go again."

Sergeant Donaldson shook his head. "Ross said he had his cap pulled low, and he deliberately made his voice rougher and deeper when he called to Danny from the boat. He was pretty sure he hadn't been recognized."

"That's crazy," sneered Ellie.

"Exactly," replied Sergeant Donaldson.

"What about the break-in at the surgery?" asked Ellie, after a pause "Was that connected somehow?"

"Yes, it was."

"But Ross took Danny on Saturday. The break-in wasn't until a few days later."

"Yes, that was very clever of him," said Sergeant Donaldson. "Ross had already stolen the Ketamine a few days earlier, but he faked the break-in because he knew his father would be checking the drugs cupboard. He had to provide an explanation for the missing Ketamine."

Ellie nodded and then racked her brains for another question but came up with a blank. Sergeant Donaldson watched her shrewdly for a moment before he spoke. "Speaking of slippery customers, we still haven't been able to identify your mystery helper."

"No?" Ellie shrugged. "I can't really help you there. I didn't get a very good look at him."

"I see. And he was on the scene because. . . ?"

"He must have heard me screaming," said Ellie.

"Aha. So, he just happened to be walking along the river road, in the pouring rain."

"Apparently," said Ellie.

"And he heard you screaming in the cellar, all the way from the top of the driveway? He must have had very good hearing."

"Yes," said Ellie.

Sergeant Donaldson nodded. "Can you describe him to me?"

"Young guy. Wet. That's about it," said Ellie. "As I said, I didn't get a good look at him. I was too busy with Danny."

"Young. And wet," said Sergeant Donaldson.

"Very," said Ellie. She looked blandly into the police officer's face. She had already been back to the old swimming pool to leave an extra-large order of burgers, fries, and milkshakes outside the bag lady's house, but she had not seen Miguel since that afternoon. She was planning to meet up with him again once all the fuss had died down. In the meantime, she saw no reason to get him involved in this. She had already betrayed the gut people, and she was not about to betray Miguel, too.

"And you were at the house because. . . ?"

"To visit Ross."

"He wasn't expecting you."

"No. I wanted to surprise him."

"So you walked all the way out there, in the rain, on your own?"

Ellie shrugged. Sergeant Donaldson looked at her for a moment, then straightened up and brushed down his uniform. "Thank you, Ellie. And thank you for letting me see Danny. I must get back to the station now, but I'll be seeing you again soon."

"Okay," said Ellie.

Sergeant Donaldson nodded gravely. "I'm glad everything worked out," he said, and then he left the room, closing the door quietly behind him.

"Has he gone?" asked Danny in a muffled voice.

"Danny!" Ellie rushed back to the bed. Danny's eyes were open, and they looked clear and focused. He lifted his arm and fumbled weakly with the oxygen mask on his face, trying to dislodge it.

"Just for a minute," said Ellie, easing the mask down and tucking it under Danny's chin.

"That man said you saved me," croaked Danny.

"Yeah," said Ellie in a disgusted tone. "What was I thinking of?"

Danny gave her a shadow of a smile. "How?"

Ellie hesitated and then lifted the bedclothes at the foot of Danny's bed and gently touched her finger to his ankle, tracing the path of the spiral tattoo. "I went Argent's way."

"Thought so," said Danny, settling back into the pillows with a satisfied look on his face.

"Danny, you have no idea where I've been, looking for you," Ellie began.

"Yes I do," interrupted Danny.

"Go on, then," challenged Ellie. "Tell me."

"You started off at the dragon's cave," said Danny. "Then you went to see an old witch, and she gave you something that would help you in your search. Then you discovered a family of outcasts, and one of them helped you too. Then you went into a great hall and finally, down into a cavern. And then you rescued me."

"No, that's all wrong," began Ellie, but then she stopped and stared down at Danny with a growing look of wonderment on her face. He had just described her visits to the dragon cave, the bag lady, the gut people, the old factory, and finally, the cellars under Ross's house. "How did you know?" she asked softly.

"Because that's what Argent did," croaked Danny. "I saw her do it. And you were following Argent's way."

Ellie smiled gently at Danny. "You didn't see Argent, sweetie, not really. It was the Ketamine. You were hallucinating."

Danny shrugged and then coughed. "Whatever," he whispered tiredly. His eyes grew vague, and he smiled. "She's in the forest now," he said, his voice slurring slightly.

"What is she doing?" asked Ellie, trying to keep Danny with her for a while longer before he drifted off again.

"She's choosing," said Danny. "She's deciding which adventure to go on next." He opened his mouth and gave a high, breathy laugh. It sounded something like a birdcall, something like a kettle whistle, something like the rush of wind in a chimney.

———

Argent tilted the shield back and forth, watching the metal disk catch the sun. She laid down the shield and looked up at the sky. "I've decided," she said.

"Which is it to be?" asked Lukos. "The village or the forest?"

Argent got to her feet, still staring up at the sky. "Neither. I'm going to follow them."

"Who?"

"The dragons. I'm going to journey across the sea and find out where they go for the winter." She bent and swung the shield up onto her shoulder, then pulled her father's cap down and tucked her hair up into it. "If I'm quick, I can catch that ship before it sails. I'll offer my services as a creature handler. I reckon they'll be grateful to have someone on board who isn't afraid of the strange beasts they carry."

Argent picked up her tattered blanket roll and slung it across her back. The water bottle was already filled. She had her knife at her belt, and her belly was still full from the breakfast of rabbit stew she had shared with Lukos and his family. She turned to look up at Lukos, who was regarding her with his head tilted to one side.

"Another adventure, then?" said Lukos.

Argent nodded. She reached up and rested the

back of her hand gently against his cheek for a moment, staring up into his amber eyes.

"I'll miss you," growled Lukos.

Argent stepped back and grinned up at him. "You don't have to."

"I don't?"

"No, you don't," said Argent. "I'm going on another adventure. What about you?"

Lukos smiled.

Glint.

"What about you?" asked Danny sleepily.

"Me?" asked Ellie.

"Are you going on another adventure too?" murmured Danny.

"Oh, no," said Ellie firmly. "I've had enough of Argent's way. I'm not like her at all. I'm staying where it's warm and safe from now on. No more adventures for me."

"You have one thing in common." Danny sighed.

"What's that?" asked Ellie, leaning in close to hear what he had to say.

"Both brave," he murmured. "Very, very brave."

Danny unfolded his wide smile for Ellie, and her eyes filled with tears. Her throat closed up, stopping her from speaking, but she squeezed his hand as he drifted off to sleep again.

"There you go," she whispered, gently putting the oxygen mask back in place. She brushed her brother's thick, fair hair from his forehead, then bent and kissed him on the cheek. "I've got you, Danny," said Ellie, pulling her chair up to the side of the bed and taking his hand. "I've got you. You're safe now. You're safe."